Too Much, Too Soon

✿ ✿ ✿

C E Andrews

Dedication

I would like to dedicate this final book of the trilogy to all of those families who struggled through the Great Depression; those generations who brought this country back from one of the hardest times anyone could image. While my dad left home early, so did many others whose stories haven't been told. Thank you for hanging in there and making this country what it is today. If you would like to share your story with me, please email me at dr68chuck@aol.com. I'd love to hear it!

This era included the second group, those military men, women, and their families who fought, worked, and sacrificed so valiantly for our freedoms in World War II and other conflicts around the globe. Then to those who continue to fight for the freedoms we have in this country: You and your families have given and continue to give so much for this country.

As I researched my family tree, I found that a family member had fought during the Civil War. He was wounded and returned to battle, only to be wounded again. The greatness of this country does not merely lie in Washington D.C., but directly on the backs of both those who have fought and given the ultimate sacrifice, their lives, for our freedoms.

So I dedicate this book to all the above. If you had or have a family member in the military, please use this page to honor them. Then email me at dr68chuck@aol.com and I will acknowledge them on the facebook page for this book.

This book is dedicated to:

NAME _____

BRANCH OF SERVICE _____

RANK and WHEN/WHERE SERVED _____

Acknowledgement

This is an acknowledgment to those who have touched my life, some for the good and some for, well, you know. From my early years growing up in Redwood City, California, on Jefferson Street through my teenage years in Grover City, California, to the present time; many have touched my life.

To my friends during the time in Redwood City: Rodney, Ronnie, Janice, and Chris. While years distance us, you still come to mind at times. To my third grade teacher who never gave up on me. Then to my friends in Jr. High: Don Carnate, David Griffith, and many others. Thanks for your friendship. Then through the high school years at Arroyo Grande High: To the teacher who said I wouldn't amount to much, thanks for your inspiration. To my classmates, not only those who graduated the same year as I, but those I knew through the years. A special acknowledgment to those who knew me better than the others: my close friends, Daryl, Kenny, Joe, and Ray, thanks for being there and encouraging me. There is one person during those years who was as close as a brother. If I can use this term, he was a brother from a different mother. His family adopted me as ours adopted him. Ron Bone was and continues to be a dear brother. When I needed help, he was always there for me. He never let me down, even when I failed him; he stood by me through thick and thin. Thanks, my brother, for being so faithful.

These next few people I want to say thanks to impacted my life when I needed them most. My deepest gratitude goes out to; Bob Baldwin (who has passed on), his wonderful wife, Sally, and their family Susan, Bruce, and Randy. To Geri Burington, whom I love dearly, as a second Mom. I don't know if you realize the impact you had on my life. Thanks to each for being you.

I never thought I would ever write a book, let alone three, so for those in my life now who have encouraged me through these times, I say thank you. I will not attempt to name everyone, as I would likely leave someone out, thus making both them and me feel bad. You know who you are; those who love me and care for me. You have come alongside when I've been down and lifted me up. I am forever indebted to you. Thank you so much for loving me.

Dr. Chuck Andrews

Contents

Chapter 1
IN A CLOUD OF DUST

It's been a long time since the family's been together for the holidays and everyone scurries around the house to get ready to leave.

My bride of so many years scrubs and rinses the morning dishes before handing them to me to dry. Sure, we have a dishwasher, but where is the fun in that? I steady myself at the kitchen counter and reflect back over the past few days. My mind, as it does so many times, drifts off into another world. I must have slowed down my labor, as a voice brings me back. "Honey, are you okay? Do you need to sit down?"

"Nah, I'm fine," I reply as I put down the towel. "Just thinking about the past few days, that's all." I tilt my head down and place both hands on the counter. "You know, it's hard to believe that our family has grown up so fast. It seems like only yesterday we were going to their school activities and watching them play sports."

Mom notices the tears well up in my eyes. She picks up a towel, dries her hands, and steps over and embraces me. She always seems to know the right thing to do at times like this. We've been together all these years and, while it hasn't been perfect, the Lord has graciously shown His love to our family.

"God has been so good to us," she says, "and yes, it has passed a lot faster than we would have liked, but look at what He's done for our kids. He's blessed them with wonderful spouses and we have these precious grandkids. What a special blessing!"

Nodding my head in agreement, I recall them lying on the floor in front of me with their beautiful eyes gazing up in anticipation of the next part of my story. I look at my bride and give her a peck on the cheek as our oldest son walks in.

"Hey you two, enough of that." We turn with red faces as he announces, "We've packed the van and are going to drop the others by the airport on our way out of town, if that's alright with you."

"Thanks, that means a lot," I acknowledge. "It's getting a little tougher for me to get around these days."

"You take it easy, Pop," he says and glances over at Mom. "Make him slow down a bit."

"That's like trying to corner a bull," she proposes, which brings a chuckle from each of us. We walk arm in arm to the front door, then on out to the driveway where everyone is waiting. Hellos are a lot easier than goodbyes, especially this set of goodbyes. Each of the grandchildren stops to give Grandma and Grandpa their honorary hugs and kisses before piling into the van.

Once the grandkids are buckled up, the really hard goodbyes begin. Even though they have their own lives now, a piece of me goes with them each time I say it. With three boys and a girl, the hugs seem never ending. In reality, we don't want them to end, either. As everyone tries to hold back his or her emotions, the hugs are longer and the goodbyes seem more final.

I finally break the ice. "If you don't get a move on, that plane will fly without you."

My daughter, the last one to hug, can't hold back any longer. With tears running down her cheeks, she's grabs hold of my collar, gives a big sniff, and inhales the comforting smell of my aftershave. She buries her head in the cradle of my neck, as if she wants to remember this time forever. As she lifts her head and slowly presses her soft cheek against my whiskers, she thinks *I wish this would never end. Now I know how Grandpa Clyde must've felt giving his dad that last hug, only he didn't know it would be his last.* Then she whispers, "Thank you, Pop, for being you. I want to always remember this moment. I love you and always will."

"I love you, too," I whisper back. "You take good care of that wonderful family God has blessed you with."

"I will," she assures me as she quickly turns and jumps into the van.

After everyone is in, I give the door a tug and step back as they slowly back down the drive. As Mom and I stand waving, I sigh, "Thank you for giving me such a wonderful family."

Sniffling, she says, "It was God who did that, we just did our job. It wasn't always perfect, but with God's help we did the best we could." I gently place my arm on her shoulder and continue to wave until they are out of sight.

As the gravel dust settles, we head back into the house. She steadies my arm and helps me in. Then we move to the couch and take a seat. Once she makes me comfortable, which always seems to be her goal, she sits down next to me and asks, "How did your mom and dad meet each other? I've heard the stories you told the grandkids before, but I don't think I've ever heard about your mom's side of the family. Do you think now would be a good time to fill me in?"

Wiping the tears from my eyes, I reach for a tissue to blow my nose. "There's no better time than the present."

My bride readjusts herself on the couch, places my hand on her knee, and puts her hand over it. "I'm ready. Sorry, but I'm not going to lie at your feet on my belly," she says with that wonderful smile I have gotten so accustomed to seeing.

We both let out a laugh as I begin. "Let's see, where did I stop? Oh yeah, Clyde had just left the graveyard and headed out of town when he decided to go by the old Livingston place. If you don't mind, Honey, I'll fit my mom's story in as I go."

"Sounds good to me!"

✲ ✲ ✲

Clyde turns the truck around and heads toward the old homestead in a cloud of dust. As he drives down the road that he walked hundreds of times before, he thinks, *Things sure look different. I don't remember these tall fences.*

As he pulls up, a guard steps out to block him from entering. "May I help you, sir?"

"I sure hope so. Ya see, I grew up here and wanted to take a look around, see the old place again. I won't hurt anything or disturb anyone."

"Sorry, sir," he quickly responds, "can't let you do that. We have orders not to let anyone on the place without clearance."

"Oh, okay. How do I get clearance?" Clyde inquires.

The guard leans over and places his forearm on the top of the truck. "That only comes from the big guy, and he's not here. He's at some wedding in town."

"That would be my sister's wedding," Clyde snickers.

The guard takes a step back. "Yeah, sure, kid! If it's your sister's wedding, what're you doing here?"

"The wedding's over and . . . oh, it's a long story."

"Sorry sir; rules are rules." The guard takes a closer look and asks, "You the Lewis boy?"

"Yep, that's me."

"I heard your pop died or was killed somewhere around here. That right?"

"Yeah, ya could say that. Can I ask one more thing?"

"Alright, go ahead, but make it quick; I got my rounds to make."

"Like I said, my family lived on this property in that old house down the road there," Clyde points out. "There was a lucky old horseshoe my pop put up above the doorway. If it's still there, it would sure mean a lot if I could grab it. Ya see, Pop used to lick his fingers and slap that thing every time he'd walk through. Do ya know if it's still there?"

"Yep, just saw it the other day and was wondering if there was a story behind it." He glances around to make sure no one else can hear. "I'll tell ya what," he whispers, "I'll let ya grab it, but ya gotta be fast, 'cause I don't wanna get fired."

"I'll be as fast as a jack rabbit," Clyde assures him.

"You'll have to leave your truck here. Just park it outside the gate."

"Will do! Thanks a bunch, mister, this really means a lot."

"Yeah, yeah, just hurry!"

Clyde hastily pulls the truck out of the way and takes off like he was shot from a cannon. The house isn't too far from the gate, so it's not long before he's standing on the creaky front porch. The place is in pretty bad shape; the windows are boarded up and the sagging front porch is missing a few boards. Clyde stands there for a moment gathering his thoughts before looking above the door. Sure enough, the old horseshoe is still there. For old times' sake, he licks his fingers and gives it a slap. "That's fer you, Pop. I'm not too short in the britches anymore," he says with a chuckle.

Curiosity gets the best of him, so he decides to take a peek inside. As he pushes on the door, it opens with a squawk. Stepping inside, he reflects back to the last time he was here. *I remember watching Mom walk to the back room after she asked me to leave. Wow, that was one bad day!* He turns to the fireplace and envisions the family sitting on the floor on a Friday evening, singing and playing games. *How'd we all fit in here? It's so small.* Realizing he's been here longer than he promised, he walks back outside. *Got to get back to the business at hand,* he thinks.

He pulls out his pocket knife and pries the bottom of the horseshoe from the header. Once the bottom's free, he takes hold of it and gives a yank. It starts to fall, but he catches it in midair as the nails drop to the ground. Taking one last look around, he turns and heads back to the gate. A few yards past the broken-down picket fence, he stops dead in his tracks. *Wait a minute,* he thinks, *Dad's old steamer chest is in the barn.* He glances toward the gate and realizes the guard's watching him, so he can't turn back. He slowly walks back thinking *there's got to be another way I can retrieve Dad's steamer.*

As he approaches, the guard asks, "Ya get it okay? I noticed ya stopped a short piece back. Forget something?"

"Nah, I got it. Thanks a bunch! That old lucky horseshoe was something special to my pops. I stopped just a moment to think back on my childhood. I remember the place being a lot bigger than it is."

The guard nods his head. "Yeah, that happens to all of us. Well, Cowboy, you better be on your way before I get myself in all sorts of trouble."

"Thanks again for the walk down memory lane," Clyde replies, before jumping in the truck and heading back down the road. *I have to get that chest before I leave. It's just under that board in the barn.*

✣ ✣ ✣

The wedding reception is breaking up and the loving couple has already left for their honeymoon. Sara, Rachel, and a few others stay behind to help Mom clean up the Western Drake. Sara cautiously asks Mom, "Did ya find 'im?"

"Who?" Mom asks.

Sara gives her one of those looks she is famous for. "Clyde!" she answers impatiently.

"Nope, I got there too late."

Sara decides to push it a little further. "I don't understand, Mom. Why would ya even want to see him after what he's done to us?"

Wincing, Mom answers, "Sara, until you have your own children, you won't understand. He's still my son."

Wow, that is surely not the response she thought she was going to get. "Yeah, you're right, I guess. I just know I never want to talk to him again."

"Sara!" Mom warns, "You always jump to conclusions that fog up your judgment. Please don't be so judgmental of your brother! We may not know the whole story."

"Like what?" Sara inquires.

"Let's finish up here. We can talk later," Mom concludes as she finishes clearing the tables.

"Okay, I guess!" Sara snaps back.

✣ ✣ ✣

It's Saturday and Harold just finished his ride. He somehow managed to hold on for the full eight seconds before being tossed to the ground a split second after the horn sounded. He won day money but will have to do a lot better tomorrow if he wants to earn any more.

He lingers around the back of the chutes as the crowd thins out, hoping to get a lift back to the motel, when a cute young lady spots him.

"Looking for something or someone, Cowboy?" she inquires.

"Nope, just lookin' to grab some dinner and head back to my room to wait for my partner."

"Oh. Ya hitched?"

"No," Harold laughs, "my travelin' partner. He had to take care of some personal business out of town."

"I can tell ya where a great place to eat is," she grins, "and it don't cost no arm and a leg."

"That would be great. Ya from around these parts?"

"Not really, I just help out with the rodeo. I ride in the opening and closing ceremonies and my daddy organizes different events."

"Thought ya looked familiar, just couldn't place ya," Harold acknowledges.

As she talks, Harold takes inventory: *cute, wavy shoulder length strawberry-blond hair, light green eyes, medium build with long slender arms, stands around 5' 6" or so. Oh, and that voice; a little southern accent that will lull you into another place. She's finely dressed in a blue patterned western blouse and tight jeans, with a classy looking Stetson.*

Breaking the silence, Harold asks, "And just where is this place?"

"It's just around the corner from the motel. The best place in town, Lilly's."

"Great! Thanks, I'll try it out." Harold turns to go, when a thought comes to mind. Spinning back around, he asks, "Hey, ya hungry? I'm buyin'."

"Sure!" she answers, "But only if we go Dutch."

"That sounds good to me!" Harold agrees.

✲ ✲ ✲

It's dusk as Clyde slowly drives away and looks for a place to hide the truck that's not too far from the ranch so he can sneak back to retrieve the steamer. He spots a small dirt road off to the west and drives a short distance until he locates a huge boulder. *Perfect for hiding the truck behind* he thinks as he pulls over and turns off his lights. By the debris, he can tell others have parked here before.

It's a short hike back to the ranch's fence line where he can see the silhouette of the old barn in the distance. He approaches the barbed wire fence, lies on his back, and carefully scoots under it. He hears muffled voices off in the distance that become clearer the closer they get. Thankful for the tall grass and a large tree shadows to hide him, he carefully lifts his head to locate the guards. *Please don't look this way,* he thinks. *Oh my, they're closer than I thought. I could spit on the closest guy.* He quickly takes inventory; they both have side arms, and one has what looks like a Winchester, too. They're so involved in their conversation that they don't even notice Clyde lying in the grass about ten feet away from them. *I could probably crawl right past them and they wouldn't even notice,* he thinks, *but I better not try. Let's see, what's the best way to get to the barn and back?*

It seems like hours before they resume their patrol and walk out of sight. Clyde slowly makes his way around the tree stumps and old tractor parts to reach the back of the barn. Then it dawns on him: *I hope no one's inside.* Knowing he can't enter through the doors, he looks for another way to enter.

Maneuvering to the far corner, he feels around for loose boards. It doesn't take long to locate a couple and quietly move them aside just far enough to slowly poke his head through. It's so dark that when he glances around to see if anyone's inside, he realizes he probably couldn't see them anyway. He sure is grateful for being as small as he is as he squeezes the rest of his body through the small opening.

Once inside, he finds himself behind a short stack of hay. Waiting for his eyes to adjust, he peeks over the hay, only to realize he's on the wrong side. Again, he scans the area for guards and begins his slow trek to the other side. He tries to stay as close to the walls as he can by squatting and moving from one haystack to another. When he finally runs out of haystacks, he makes a beeline for the other side. He drops to the dirt floor behind an old tractor as the barn door swings open and the beam of a flashlight circles around and passes above him a couple of times. As with most of us when we are in tight situations, we always seem to pray for help and Clyde is no different. The guard walks toward the back corner where Clyde moved the boards to get inside. Clyde thinks, *If he notices those, I'm history.*

Chapter 2

THE STEAMER

They park the car at the motel, take the short hike around the corner to Lilly's, and find a booth. Always the gentleman, Harold stands until his newfound friend slides in. He then removes his hat and places it on the seat as he slides in across from her. It doesn't take them long to begin a conversation. She formally introduces herself as Audra and Harold can tell she loves to talk. They order dinner and chat through the meal, dessert, and endless cups of coffee. She loves to ask questions and find out every detail of his life.

Time seems to stand still until Harold finally looks at his watch. "Whoa, I can't believe that it's almost 2 o'clock!" The diner had closed some hours before, but the owner knows Audra and allows them to sit there while they clean the place up.

"I hate to end this," Harold says, "but I have to ride tomorrow, and I need my beauty sleep. Are ya movin' on to the next rodeo?"

"Sure am! How about you?" Audra inquires.

Blushing, Harold stutters a little and asks, "Well . . . think we could get together again? Maybe lunch or somethin'?"

"I'd like that," she confirms. "By the way, when's your partner comin' back?"

"He's probably already back, waiting at the hotel. But if not, sometime tomorrow for sure. Can I escort ya back to your room?"

"Sure can! It's just down from yours."

How does she know what room I'm in? Harold wonders. *Oh well, no matter.*

After dividing the ticket, paying the bill and bidding Lilly a good morning, he walks Audra to her room, says good night and walks away grinning from ear to ear. *It don't get no better than this* he thinks.

✵ ✵ ✵

The guard with the flashlight is almost to the back of the barn when his partner peeks in and hollers, "Hey, I think I just saw something go around the back of the house! Hurry!" He retreats and sprints out the side door, closing it behind him.

Clyde thinks, *I've only got a couple of minutes. If I don't move now, I'm going to get caught.* He scurries to the corner and, on his hands and knees, brushes away enough dirt to feel the false floor. Pawing away at debris, he finds a loose board, lifts it, and feels the blanket he'd wrapped the chest in so long ago. He quickly unfolds it, revealing the chest just where he'd left it. Reaching down, he grabs both handles and pulls, but it doesn't budge. Having been down there so long, it's stuck to the dirt, but one swift tug frees it, leaving the blanket. It's so dirty that it's hard to feel the fancy carvings on top. He starts to brush it off but figures he'd better hightail it out of there before the guards return. Placing it under his arm like a football, he swiftly retraces his steps to the back of the barn. *Now to get out of here,* he thinks. *Always thought this was heavier. Oh well, I can move a lot faster with it being so light.*

Under the cover of darkness, he retreats faster and more deliberately than before, now that he has what he came for. When he reaches the back corner, there's little hesitation as he slips between the parted opening; first the chest, then himself, all in one motion.

In his excitement to get out, he's not as careful to be quiet as he was going in. Once through the hole, he spots two guards about twenty yards away. They stop talking and start looking around, listening. As their flashlights canvas the area, Clyde freezes behind a huge tree stump just as a beam lights it up. Down on one knee, he knows that any movement is going to alert them and who knows what will happen then? After all, they're both packing side arms.

✻ ✻ ✻

The WD is clean and, though the night's still young, Al's given the staff the rest of the night off. He's saying goodnight to the last of the guests when Dorris and the girls pick up their shawls. "May I walk you ladies home?" he asks.

Always quick to respond, Sara quips, "No, thank you, we can find our own way."

Dorris glares at her. "Thank you, Al, but I'm sure you're anxious to get out to your place. We'll be fine."

"I wouldn't mind doing it," Al assures her. "In fact, it would be my pleasure. I'm walking Maggie home, anyway."

Stepping up behind him, Maggie asks, "Did someone mention my name?"

"I was just telling the ladies that I was going to walk you home and would consider it a privilege to be their escort, too."

Maggie places her arm in Dorris's. "Come on, why don't you walk with us? We pass right by your place. Besides, it's dark and it's good to have the protection of a man."

Not wanting to disappoint Maggie, Dorris reluctantly agrees. The group makes its way down Main Street with Rachel holding Sara's hand, leading the way, and Al, Maggie and Dorris right behind. Ever the gentleman, Al walks on the outside closest to the street. Rachel keeps glancing over her shoulder at Al, then finally slows down and wedges herself between Al and Maggie. She reaches over and grabs Al's hand and looks up at him with a smile as they continue their walk. Dorris keeps her eye on Rachel and thinks, *I hope she's not becoming too attached to him. Elmer, what should I do? I missed Clyde today, and now Rachel's clinging to Al. Oh my gosh, what in the world could be next?*

✻ ✻ ✻

As Clyde kneels behind the stump, one guard, now only a few feet away, pauses and turns to his partner. "Did ya hear something?" he asks.

"Yeah, I think so, but I don't hear anything now," he whispers.

"Shhh, listen a minute." Hearing someone approach from behind, they turn around and raise their weapons. In the distance they hear, "Put those things down! What are you two so jumpy about?"

"We heard a noise and . . ."

"Probably an animal," the third guard says. "The boss just got back and you two are needed at the house. Better hurry, it looks like he's not too happy." When they hear that, they take off on a dead run.

What a lucky break! Clyde quietly exhales. *See there, that old horseshoe is already paying off.*

With the last guard out of sight, Clyde makes a beeline for the fence and slides the chest under it. As he follows, he gets hung up on a barb. In a hurry to free himself, he tears the cuff of his shirt. Not wanting to take the time to untangle it, he leaves it hanging on the fence.

Once on the other side, the thrill of almost getting caught has his heart racing and his adrenalin pumping. He scoops up the chest and sprints back to the truck. He can't wait to open it.

With the truck windows down, he sets the chest on the passenger seat, runs around to the driver's side and slides in. Winded, he places his hands on the steering wheel and inhales as deeply as he can as he leans his head back against the back of the seat and closes his eyes for a moment. He reaches over to the steamer and notices his hands shaking. As he begins to open it, he thinks he sees a beam of light off in the distance moving his way. *I tore my shirt on the fence,* he thinks, *and part of it's still there. If they find it, they'll come looking for me. Better put some distance between me and this place, just in case.* He starts the engine and, as quietly as possible, pulls away with his headlights off.

✲ ✲ ✲

With his fellow guards back at the ranch house, the third guard decides to go back and check the area where they heard the noise. As he passes the barn, he shines his flashlight toward the back corner and notices some boards moved aside. He moves the light around the area and observes tracks leading off across the field. On closer observation, he finds the grass matted down where Clyde had been lying, and cautiously traces Clyde's steps across the field, looking around to make sure he doesn't get jumped. Deep down inside, he hopes he doesn't find anyone! When he shines his light in the direction of the fence, it exposes something hanging from it. His curiosity piqued, he nervously approaches and discovers a piece of fabric. As he untangles it from the barbs, he thinks, *Well I'll be. Looks like a piece of cloth off a shirt or something. Where have I seen this before?*

In the still of the night, he hears a vehicle start and drive away. He hurriedly shines his light in the direction of the sound, but it's too far away to see anything. Then it dawns on him. *I know where I've seen this shirt before! It was on that Lewis boy. I wonder what he wanted and why he came back. Looks like he got into the barn. Better go check and see if anything's missing.*

☆ ☆ ☆

Not far down the road, curiosity gets the best of him and Clyde looks for a place to pull over. As he comes around a bend in the road, he spots a turnout and hastily steers to the shoulder while he slams on the brakes. Dust and gravel fly everywhere as all four tires lock up in a slide. The truck comes to a stop just a few feet from the edge of a small gully, but that doesn't matter to him. All he can think of is opening the chest.

He turns off the engine and turns the chest so that the latch faces him. A beam of moonlight shines through the back window and illuminates the cab. It's as if God is turning on the light to reveal what's in the chest. Not sure whether his hands are shaking from fear of being caught or in anticipation of opening the chest, he flips the latch and slowly lifts the lid, stopping midway to flash back to the day

Mom gave it to him. *I remember walking into her room when she took it out of the closet and opened it. As she placed Dad's things in it, I asked her if I could have it.* A smile crosses his face. He remembers her asking, "Why would you want the steamer?" *and I said, "It's something I can remember Dad by." The next thing I recall is bursting into tears and running to the barn with it. I grabbed a small blanket as I ran in the barn, wrapped the chest in it, and set it in the hole. It's hard to believe that so many years have passed and here I have it again.*

As the moon shines even brighter, Clyde turns his attention back to the chest and opens it the rest of the way. He takes a deep breath and tries to focus on the contents. He pulls the item on top partway out and thinks, *It's his old slicker.* As he holds it up, a vignette pops into his head. *It's raining as Dad steps onto the front porch, takes off his slicker, and shakes out the rain. Then he steps in the house and hangs it on the coat rack just before I run up and jump into his arms. He sure loved this old coat.*

Clyde sniffs a couple times, trying to hold back his tears and notices that something's wrapped in the bottom of the coat. As he holds it up and places it on the passenger's seat, Dad's Stetson falls out onto his lap. He picks it up and holds it to his face, deeply inhaling the aroma of the leather and felt fabric. This again sends his mind reeling and the years fall away. As he rubs his face with it, he can still feel Pop's whiskers against his cheek and his strong arms around him. When he thinks about the last hug he got from his dad, it's so painful that he props up his elbows on the steering wheel, buries his face in the Stetson, and weeps like a baby.

✲ ✲ ✲

The guard makes his way back to the barn where he meets the other two. He fills them in on what he found and shows them the corner where the Lewis boy must have crawled in. Then all three guards head inside to see if they notice anything missing.

They walk to the middle post in the barn and light a couple of lanterns, before they split up to search the inside. It's not long before one of the guards hollers, "Hey, over here! I think I found something!"

The others make their way to the corner where their partner is bent over, pulling a blanket out of a hole.

"What's that?" one asks.

"An old blanket; it was down in this hole. Something must've been wrapped in it."

"Like what?"

"I don't know, but we better get the boss."

"Do we have to? He's going to be upset."

"Yeah, I know, but it may have been something real important. You two stay here and I'll go get him."

✧ ✧ ✧

It takes a while for Clyde to regain his composure. When he does, he puts the hat on and says, "I left mine with you, Dad, and now I have yours."

As he wipes his nose with his sleeve, he peeks back in the chest and notices that there's something lying in the bottom. *What's this?* Reaching inside, he pulls out a big oval belt buckle with something stamped on it. Now the moon is blocked by some slow moving clouds and the moonlight is quickly fading. That, along with his puffy eyes, makes it hard to read what it says. He moves it around in an attempt to grab just one ray of light. Finally catching a good angle, he's able to make out a bucking horse in the middle. As he moves it closer, he reads, "Bronco Riding" just above the horse and "Champion" below it. ELMER LEWIS is engraved on the back. He stares at the buckle in shock: he never knew his dad had ridden in the rodeos. Resting his head back on the seat, he looks up and cries out, "Pop, I miss ya!"

He puts the buckle and coat back in the chest. *What a day!* Then he thinks, *I'd better take a nap. I don't think I can drive in this condition.* He pulls Pop's hat down over his eyes and drifts into a shallow sleep.

✧ ✧ ✧

The guard returns with Al and explains the whole story, including the part about when Clyde came to the front gate, but leaving out the part about allowing him inside to get the horseshoe. Al can't understand why Clyde didn't just come to him and ask for whatever it was. He thinks, *This must have been pretty important to risk getting caught.* On his way back to the house, he decides to give Dorris a call. It hasn't been that long since he escorted her and Maggie home, so he's sure she'll still be awake.

✯ ✯ ✯

When the ladies walk in, Mom tells Rachel to get ready for bed and then she'll read her a Bible story. Excited, Rachel scampers off to her room. She always looks forward to these times with Mom.

Sara takes a seat in the main room. Mom can tell from her squirming that she's waiting for an opportunity to start a conversation.

With Mom off in the kitchen putting things away, Sara finally quips, "This has sure been a wild day, don't ya think?" trying to bait Mom into a response.

"It's been a long one," Mom replies. "I'm dog tired and I bet you are, too."

"Yeah, I guess so. It sure was weird seeing Clyde all grown-up and all."

"I'll bet it was," Mom adds, "and Ruthie sure did look pretty in that dress, didn't she?"

"Yeah, I guess; but how did Clyde know about Ruthie getting married?" Sara persists.

Mom's about to answer when Rachel hollers, "Mom, I'm ready!"

"Okay," Mom hollers back. As she passes Sara on the way to the bedroom, she says, "Got to take care of your sister. We can talk about this later. You need to get yourself ready for bed, too."

Sara thinks, *Yeah, yeah, that's what you always say when it comes to Clyde.*

✯ ✯ ✯

Al walks into the parlor, picks up the phone, and asks the operator to ring Dorris's place. After a couple of minutes, the phone rings and he hears a voice answer, "Hello?"

"Dorris, is that you? This is Al."

"No, sir, this is Sara. Mom is reading Rachel a story. Hold on, I'll get her."

"Thank you, Sara."

It doesn't take long for her to come to the phone. "Hello, Al?"

"Yes Dorris, it's me."

"Is everything alright? Why are you calling so late?"

"Dorris, I'll get right to the point. I think Clyde came by the ranch today. Did you know he was in town?"

"Yeah, Sara saw him. I tried to find him, but missed him. What was he doing out at the ranch?"

"That's what we're trying to figure out and the reason for my call. He came to the gate and my guard sent him away, but it looks like he snuck back on and broke into the barn."

"What? Broke into your barn? That doesn't make any sense! What in the world would he want in your barn?"

"That's where I thought you might be able to help. We found a hole in the corner that had a blanket sticking out of it. Looks like there was something wrapped in it. I thought maybe you might have some clue as to what it could be."

"I can't imagine what he would be looking for in your barn . . . wait a minute!" Dorris stops midsentence. "No, it can't be!"

"What is it, Dorris?" Al asks, his curiosity piqued.

"No, I mean it has to be," Dorris concludes as she steps back and drops the receiver. "It has to be the steamer. I can't believe it!"

"Hello? Dorris, are you still there?" Al asks. "Hello? Hello? Claire, are you there?"

"Yes Al, I'm here," Claire answers, having listened to every word of their conversation.

"Please get her back on the phone," Al begs.

"The line is still open; she's there. It sounds like she dropped the earpiece."

After getting ready for bed, Sara walks out in time to see Mom drop the phone and step back. "Mom, you okay?" she inquires as Mom mutters under her breath. Hearing Al hollering from the earpiece, she picks it up. "Hello Al, this is Sara. I'll have Mom call you back. Something's wrong."

"Wait Sara, don't hang up!" Al implores. "Sara!"

But it's too late.

Chapter 3
DOWN BUT NOT OUT

The honking horn on a passing car wakens Clyde out of his sleep. Taking hold of the steering wheel, he pulls himself up and rubs his eyes. *I feel worse now than when I went to sleep.* He thinks, *I don't know how much good that did, but I have to get a move on. Harold's waiting and so are the bulls.* Riding has become intoxicating for Clyde. That next ride for him is craved as much as that next drink for a drunk.

Not very far down the road, he drives through a small town and looks for a filling station. There's only one, and it's about to close, so he pulls in front of the pumps. "Can I still get some fuel?" he asks.

"If that's all you want," the young attendant answers. "I'm not going to check anything on your car. I'm closed."

"All I need is fuel," Clyde assures him. As the attendant fills the tank, Clyde calculates that this should be enough to get him back to Harold. At least that's what he hopes, as his funds are running out. He took just enough with him for the trip.

He pays the attendant, and then pulls out of the driveway and back onto the two-lane interstate heading east. The drive back seems longer than the one going out. The moon's rays fade in and out of the clouds moving through the area, and it's not long before the gentle patter of rain on the top of the truck and the steady rhythm of the wiper blades make for a dangerous combination. Clyde's having a hard time staying awake and he realizes he needs to stop or he may fall asleep at the wheel. Soon he spots a big weeping willow tree just off the road and pulls over and parks. He closes his eyes and within seconds falls into a deep sleep.

✽ ✽ ✽

Al stands in the hallway, shouts into the receiver, and then slams it down contemplating what to do next.

Sara walks toward Mom as she sits at the kitchen table. "What did Al say?"

"He said your brother snuck onto the ranch," Dorris replies, "and broke into the barn."

Sara shakes her head in bewilderment. "Why in the world would he do a dumb thing like that?"

"He was after the steamer."

"What steamer? You mean Clyde stole Al's steamer? Why would he do that?" asks Sara.

"No, no, no!" Mom says, shaking her head. "It wasn't Al's steamer! It was the steamer chest I gave him when your dad died. He must've buried it in the barn. I had forgotten all about it. Today, he went back after it and the guards wouldn't let him on the property, so he snuck on to get it."

Mom suddenly remembers that she dropped the earpiece. "Oh, my gosh! Al's on the phone!" She jumps up and notices that the phone is hung up.

"I told Al you'd call him back," Sara assures her.

Dorris snatches the earpiece from the wall and asks Claire to connect her to Al.

The phone rings at Al's and he grabs it off the base. "Hello!" he answers.

"Al, I am so sorry, I just . . .," Dorris begins.

"Are you okay?" he interrupts. "I was just getting ready to head over and check on you."

"I'm fine. I think I know why Clyde came to the ranch."

"Really? I'm all ears."

She starts at the beginning and probably shares more than what's needed.

"Dorris, all he had to do was ask," Al finally interrupts.

"I know, I know," Dorris answers, "but things probably hadn't gone the way he expected them to. He probably thought you'd tell him no. Anyway, I apologize for his behavior."

"No need for that. I most likely would have done the same thing. Mind if I ask what was in it?"

"The best I can recall," Dorris strains to remember, "I put Elmer's raincoat and hat in it after he passed. Don't really know what else was in it. It was his and I didn't want to put my nose in where it didn't belong."

"I understand that perfectly," Al chuckles. "Thanks for calling back. I sure am sorry you missed your boy. Have a pleasant evening, at least what's left of it."

"Thank you, Al, and you, too." She hangs up and turns to Sara, but before she can say anything, Sara blurts out, "I can't believe you!"

"What did you say, young lady?"

Sara repeats herself, and then adds, "Apologizing for Clyde and what he did. That's been the case ever since he left. You act like it's not his fault; won't even talk about it, and now this."

Mom's face turns a bright red and Sara realizes she's crossed the line.

"Sara! I will not tolerate your rebellious attitude!" Mom screams. "What I do and what I talk about is none of your . . ." Mom hesitates before she continues, "business, do you understand me?"

Sara's never heard Mom scream this way and realizes she's lucky she didn't get a slap across the mouth, although she's pretty sure it wasn't that far off. "Yes, ma'am," she quietly answers.

"What did you say? I didn't hear you!" Mom sternly demands.

"I said, 'Yes ma'am'." Sara turns and walks toward the bedroom and is met by Rachel. Sara spins her around and pushes her back toward the door into their room. "You don't want to come out here," she whispers.

Mom walks out on the front porch and slams the door behind her. She sits in the swing and starts talking to herself. *What are you doing? Are you crazy? Screaming at Sara like that! What's wrong with you?!*

She then does what we all do, rationalizes her behavior. *If she hadn't said what she did, I wouldn't have responded the way I did. She had that coming for a long time. She'll get over it. After all, I am the parent. That's right, just take a couple of deep breaths and go back in and act as if nothing happened. It'll all blow over.*

✳ ✳ ✳

The light of dawn breaks through the early morning darkness. As the dim rays of a new day light up the inside of the truck, Clyde awakens to find that he's slept longer than he'd planned. Still drowsy, he starts the truck and heads on down the road. Before long, his stomach starts to growl. Knowing he doesn't have much cash left, he decides to stop in the next town and grab whatever he can with the little money he has.

After a while, he comes upon a quaint little town and parks on the outskirts, figuring he needs to walk a bit. As he swings the truck door open, he reaches back and grabs Dad's old hat, puts it on, and squares it up with his index finger, just like Dad used to. He walks around to the passenger side, places the steamer on the floor board, and covers it up. Finally he picks up his lucky horseshoe from the seat and stuffs it in his back pocket before securing the truck.

Stepping upon the sidewalk, he thinks, *It sure does feel nice to stretch my legs. Sleeping in the truck ain't nothin' like sleepin' in that big ol' car we used to have. That sure would've been nice.* He strolls down the main street taking in the sights, and about half a block away spots a small diner across the street as the waitress turns the "Closed" sign in the window over to read "Open." It's a cute place with two picture windows in the front and a brown canvas awning above the door.

He reaches into his pants pocket and pulls out two bits. "Well, it can't get much, but it'll have to get me by," he mumbles to himself.

A bell rings as he opens the door. "Good morning, sir," the waitress greets him. "Sit anywhere you like."

"Thanks," Clyde says, making his way to the counter. He starts to sit down, but when his fanny hits the seat he jumps up, having forgotten about the horseshoe in his back pocket. He reaches back and pulls it out, glancing around to see if anyone had seen him. Thankfully, no one's around and he places it on the counter in front of him and his hat on the seat next to him.

The waitress saunters up and asks, "What can I get for you, Cowboy?"

Hanging his head in embarrassment, Clyde whispers, "Whatever two bits'll get me."

"Well, we'll see what we can come up with," she says with a grin.

As she walks away, he can't help but notice how young and pretty she is. *If I was spending more time in this town, I'd like to get to know her better,* he chuckles to himself. *That's the same old line I tell myself in every town. Maybe someday I'll be able to settle down like Ruthie.*

His mind wanders back to the wedding, and daydreaming, he picks up the horseshoe and softly taps it on the counter, just enough to draw the attention of the waitress. She walks up with coffee, biscuits, and gravy, which just happens to be his favorite meal.

"What's with the horseshoe?" she asks as she sets the food down in front of him,

Clyde looks into her beautiful blue eyes and says, "Oh, it's a long story."

"I've got some time on my hands," she smiles.

Since it's early and he's the only one there, she leans over, places her elbows on the counter and rests her chin in her hands as he tells the story about his dad and the horseshoe. Her long auburn hair drapes down over her hands as she hangs on his every word.

About the time he wraps up his story, other customers start to mosey in and she excuses herself to get back to work. Clyde stands up and puts on his hat, picks up the horseshoe, leaves all his money on the counter, and walks toward the door. On his way, out he passes the waitress and apologizes for not having a tip, then tips his hat and bids her "good day."

As the door closes, he turns right and leisurely heads toward his truck. He glances around and stops a few times to peer into the windows of various storefronts as different items grab his attention. As he approaches one of the businesses, he hears movement inside and pauses to look in. The name on the window reads, "The First Bank of Colorado" and on second glance, he observes two guys running toward the front door. He manages to step aside just in time to avoid being knocked over by the first one as he bursts through.

As the second guy clears the doors, however, Clyde bends over like a linebacker making a tackle to brace for the collision. His shoulder catches him in the thigh and they tumble out into the street as a loud explosion goes off in the bank, sending wood and glass shards everywhere.

Hearing the explosion, townsfolk rush out to see what all the commotion is. Lying there on his back, covered with debris, Clyde can't believe what just happened. He thinks, *What if this guy has a gun? No, thanks. What do I do now?* While it happens so fast, it seems to Clyde like it's in slow motion. They hop up as the first robber runs to their car. The second one grabs Clyde by the collar. Standing toe-to-toe, they look into each other's eyes. As he winds up to hit Clyde with the money bag, his eyes widen, his mouth drops open and he lets go of the bag. He shoves Clyde to the ground as his partner yells, "Pick up the bag, pick up the bag! Never mind, leave it! Hurry!"

By this time, people are gathering in the street and someone hollers, "It's a bank robbery! They blew up the bank!"

The second robber sprints to the car and jumps in. He looks over at Pete, his partner, and says "Let's get out of here!" As they drive away, he looks back and shakes his head. "We're in trouble, Pete!" he warns. "No, let me change that. We're in big trouble!"

✵ ✵ ✵

Harold completes his ride and once again finishes in the money. He and Clyde make a great team; both love to ride and they share their winnings. He starts his two-mile jaunt back to the motel, excited about finishing in the money and eager to share his success with Clyde. As he walks along at a good pace, he thinks, *I sure hope he's waiting for me at the motel.* Harold gets into a rhythm when a car pulls up alongside and a lady's voice hollers, "Hey Cowboy, want a ride?" He turns to see a beautiful smile, one that he's come to appreciate.

"You betcha!" he replies.

When they get back to the motel, Audra pulls up to his room. He looks around for his truck, but doesn't see it. "That's funny," he says, "the truck's not here! I wonder what's happened to him? Hope everything's okay!"

"Oh, I'm sure it is. He probably got together with his family and decided to stay a few extra days, that's all."

"Yeah, you're right. I don't quite know what to do now, though."

"What cha mean?" Audra inquires.

"Well, do I sit around here and wait, or move on?"

"That's a tough one, but if it's a ride ya need, I'm sure my dad won't mind if ya tag along with us. You can leave Clyde a note at the front desk."

"That sounds great. Thanks a bunch!"

Harold jumps from the car and heads to his room to pack his bag and leave Clyde a note. Audra pulls over to her room to pick up her dad.

Once he finishes the note, he throws his clothes in his suitcase and, as he closes it, someone knocks. He steps over to open it and there stands an older gentleman wearing a ten-gallon hat. He sticks out his hand and says, "Howdy there, I'm Myron, Audra's daddy. Ya ready?"

Harold grabs his hand and gives it a firm grip. "Hello, Myron, I'm Harold. I'm almost ready, just gotta run to the office and leave a note fer my buddy."

"Make it quick, daylight's a burnin'," Myron says and turns to head back to the waiting car.

"Yes, sir," Harold replies as he reaches back and grabs his bag, closes the door and double-steps it to the office. He swings open the office door and greets a middle-aged lady behind the counter.

She looks up, smiles, and asks, "Ya checkin' out?"

"Yes ma'am, I am, but I got a favor to ask."

"Oh, yeah? What's that?"

"Well, my partner's comin' through in the next day or so and he'll be lookin' fer me. If ya could give him this here envelope, I'd appreciate it. I put his name on the outside."

"I guess I could, but what's in it fer me?"

Harold reaches into his pocket, pulls out a few bills and hands them to her. "Here's a little somethin' to help ya remember."

"I'd consider it a privilege to help."

Harold rolls his eyes and says, "Thanks," as he walks out. Myron and Audra are parked outside the office, so he jumps in the back seat and off they go.

* * *

Clyde picks himself up and is dusting himself off when three or four townsfolk come running. One of them gives him a shove and he falls back to the ground.

"Hey, watch it!" Clyde hollers. "What do you think you're doing?"

"Someone get the sheriff!" the guy shouts. "They left one behind!"

"Wait!" Clyde yells. "I didn't do anything! The guy ran into me!"

"Sure, that's why the money bag's sitting next to ya."

"That's not mine!"

"You can say that again! It's ours. Now you just stay right there and wait for the sheriff." As Clyde lies on his back, a big guy steps forward and plants his foot in the middle of his chest, pinning him to the ground.

* * *

When the explosion goes off, several guys quickly exit the diner to see what's going on as the rest of the crowd remains inside, clustered around the glass door and windows. The waitress tries to peer out, but she is unable to get a good look. She asks a customer to explain what he sees and, like a typical male, he's brief and not very descriptive in his reply. She quickly loses interest and heads back behind the counter. *There's nothing I can do about the situation, anyway,* she thinks, *so I may as well get back to work.*

* * *

As Clyde lies on the ground waiting for the sheriff, he thinks, *What just happened? I'm minding my own business when this guy runs into me! He sure did look familiar, though. I know him from somewhere . . . just can't put a name to the face.* The big guy's foot has crept up toward Clyde's neck and is beginning to choke him.

Clyde glances over at his hat about three feet away. The big guy notices and asks, "That your hat, boy?"

Clyde gasps, "Yes, sir."

The big guy maneuvers around and lifts his leg off of Clyde long enough to stomp on it before he says, "That's what we think of crooks like you. But I can say, you're a polite one."

If looks could kill, this big tub of lard would have dropped dead right there on the street, but Clyde is in no position to do anything. The sheriff meanders up and says, "You can let 'im up now. He isn't goin' anywhere." As the guy backs away, the sheriff offers Clyde his hand and pulls him to his feet.

Clyde brushes himself off and thanks the sheriff, who says, "Didn't get far enough away before you blew it up, huh?"

Still trying to catch his breath from the boot on his chest, he wheezes, "What? What're you talkin' about, Sheriff?"

"I've heard about your little group. It finally caught up with you, didn't it?"

"My little group? Sheriff, I ain't got no little group, and I ain't a bank robber either!"

The sheriff chuckles as he looks around at the crowd. "Sure, that's what they all say when they get caught."

"Sheriff, that may be what others have told ya, but this ain't what it looks like!" Clyde pleads.

"Listen up, young man. Do you and me a big favor."

"What's that?" Clyde asks.

"Come quietly. Don't make it any harder on yourself than it already is. We caught you red-handed, with the money bag right next to you."

"But Sheriff, you don't understand!"

"I'm sure I don't, but you can tell your story to the judge."

Clyde can hardly believe it. The sheriff picks up the money bag and grabs him by the arm as the big guy with the big shoe picks up

Clyde's hat and slaps it back on his head. Clyde turns to him and says, "Thanks!" As they walk away, Clyde tells his story and the sheriff nods his head in agreement.

Finally he says, "Don't try to fool me, son. I've heard 'em all. You think I was born yesterday?"

Inside the jailhouse, the sheriff tells Clyde to empty his pockets onto the desk. Clyde reaches in and pulls out the old horseshoe, along with his car keys.

✲ ✲ ✲

The two robbers move down the road as fast as they can without drawing too much attention to themselves. Pete looks over at his partner and asks, "What'd ya mean, 'We're in big trouble'?"

"You know that guy I ran into?"

"Yeah. So?"

"I recognized him from somewhere. He's older now, but I know it was him!"

"You think he recognized you?"

"Not sure. He didn't act like he did, but if he thinks about it, it may dawn on him who I am."

"Let's hope not, or we may have to hunt 'im down and take care of 'im."

"Yeah, I hope it don't come to that."

✲ ✲ ✲

Once Clyde empties his pockets and hands over his belt, the sheriff escorts him to his cell. All the while Clyde continues to plead his innocence, but the sheriff isn't listening. As the cell door opens, Clyde slowly walks in and sits on the bed.

"Toss me that hat," the sheriff says, "You won't be needing it in here."

"But Sheriff, this hat means a lot to me. Please let me keep it."

"Nope, I don't care. It's my policy: no hats in the cell. That old thing has seen better days, anyway."

Clyde takes it off and tosses it to him. "Please take care of it; I know you don't care, but I do."

Laughing, the sheriff says, "I'll put it in a safe spot."

Looking down, Clyde hears the noise he never wanted to hear again; the slamming of a cell door. It brings back memories of being locked up with Sara, and the whole situation with Whiskey. He thinks back to that night and how Whiskey looked after Sara hit him with the rock. Then it dawns on him. *Wait a minute! That's who that guy looked like! And he was missing his front teeth, too. That was Jonathan, I know it was! I knew he looked familiar.*

With Clyde secure in his cell, the sheriff goes back out to interview witnesses. The stories line up; they all say they saw Clyde with the other robber that got away.

One gentleman even testifies, "I was looking down the street when that guy you arrested came running out of the bank, tripped over his partner, and fell right on top of him. After the explosion, they both got up, and the other guy panicked. He pushed this guy down so he could get away. Ain't no honor among thieves."

"Did anyone get a good look at the car?" the sheriff asks.

They all shake their heads. One states, "We were too busy with this guy to notice."

The sheriff thanks them for their time and heads back to the jail.

Chapter 4
A SHOT OF WHISKEY

By midmorning, the fugitives have moved on to the next town where they stop for fuel. They run over a small rubber hose that makes a bell ring inside the office as they pull in the driveway, signaling the attendants who jump into action. As the last attendant leaves the office, he reaches over and turns up the volume on the small Philco radio on the counter just inside the door. While they wash the windshield and check the tires, a special report comes over the radio.

"There's been another early morning bank robbery. Two robbers got away, leaving a third behind. Part of the money was recovered. As soon as we have more details, we'll pass them along."

Pete steps from the car to stretch his legs as the attendant who is checking the tires looks up. "Boy, there sure have been a lot of those lately!" he comments to his customer.

"A lot of what?" Pete asks.

"Those bank robberies," he responds, surprised. "Haven't you heard?"

"Can't say that we have," Whiskey pipes in.

"Ya'll must not be from around these parts. Towns all around here have been getting hit, and their trademark is blowin' up the bank."

"No kidding! They've probably hurt a bunch of people, maybe even killed a few, too, huh?" Pete asks.

"Nah, I can't recall anyone gettin' hurt. They usually break in long before the bank's open and blow it up as they leave."

Whiskey glances at Pete. "Wow! Glad we're just passing through. They must know what they're doing."

"Yeah, they must. But it sounds like they caught one. Betcha it ain't long before he turns the others in."

"Ya think so?" Pete asks.

"Oh, sure. You know the old saying. 'There's no respect among thieves,' or something like that."

"Yep, guess you're right," they agree.

The attendant stands up and removes the gas nozzle. "Where're you two headed?"

"We're catching up with the rodeo circuit," Whiskey answers.

"That sounds excitin'! Is that how ya lost those front teeth?"

"Sure is. We better a get a move on. Does everything look okay?"

"Yep. This here thing's a beaut'. Hard to believe you have this thing around all those cowpokes."

"Yeah, that's what most people say. What do we owe ya?"

"Eighty-five cents."

"Here's a buck. Keep the change."

The attendant takes the bill and crinkles and snaps it like an accordion, "Wow, this thing looks brand spankin' new."

"You're right about that! It was our last winnings and they always pay off with new bills."

"That's good to know. Thanks, and you two be safe."

They climb back into the car and return the attendant's wave as they pull away from the station.

"Why'd you give him that?" Whiskey asks. "If that kid remembers you, every cop from here to the state line will be lookin' for us."

"That never entered my mind. You're right; we better put some distance between us and this place. Things are getting too hot around here," Pete suggests.

"Let's drive through the night." Whiskey adds, "We can probably make the state line by morning,"

✲ ✲ ✲

Clyde fluffs up the pillow, sits back on the small cot and leans against the cool wall as he mulls over his predicament. *I can't believe this! Doing good for someone ain't what it's cracked up to be. All I wanted to do was attend my sister's wedding and what do I get for that? I get chewed out by my other sister and hafta steal the steamer chest without getting shot in the process. Now I'm sitting here in a jail cell for something I didn't do. I'm done; I've had it. The only good thing that came out of this was getting the horseshoe and Pop's hat. Thanks, God, you've really done a number on me this time.*

A short time later Clyde hears the jail's front door swing open and slam shut. He hollers, "Hey, Sheriff, that you? If it is, I got somethin' ta tell ya."

There's silence, then the sheriff shouts, "Listen here, young man, I have numerous eye witnesses that place you at the scene of the robbery. That's all I need."

"But Sheriff, you don't understand!" Clyde protests.

"I don't?" he asks as he walks to the back room. "Oh, you want to give up your buddies? Yeah, that's right, you know them by name, don't you?" he says. "Well, son? Want to tell me who your partners are?"

Now Clyde's really stuck between a rock and a hard place. He quickly contemplates, *If I tell the sheriff I know one of 'em, he'll think I'm one of 'em. But if I don't say anything, I'm helping 'em get away. What a mess!*

"Sorry, Sheriff, can't help ya. Just wanted ya to know I'm innocent."

"If that's all you can say for yourself, then I feel sorry for you and we have nothing to discuss. You know, I don't understand people like you. Here you sit while your buddies go free. But if that's the way you want it, sit back and enjoy the next few days. It'll take that long to get the judge down here."

Great! Just what I need, to miss another rodeo! Some way, Whiskey, I'm going to get even, Clyde thinks.

✣ ✣ ✣

By daybreak, and after several stops off the main roads to rest, Whiskey and Pete are almost to the other side of the state. As they pull into this small Oklahoma town, they look for a motel where they can rent a room for the week. While they have the money to stay at nicer places, they pick these because they're used mostly by transients. The last thing they want to do is draw attention to themselves.

There's also a method to their madness. They'll befriend someone who's not staying long. Then, in the middle of the night, while everyone else is asleep, they'll switch license plates, just in case someone from their last job jotted down their license plate number while they were making their getaway.

This is the closest they've come to getting caught, so they pull out all precautions.

✫ ✫ ✫

The trio travels to the next stop on the rodeo circuit.

While Harold settles into his room, he wonders what's happened to Clyde. *What should I do if he doesn't show up soon? I could call his mom, but I'm not sure if she even has a phone. I could get ahold of the sheriff, but he'd probably not know anything. I know, I'll call Mr. Goldberg: he gave me his number. I'll wait until morning, and then I'll start my search. Hopefully he'll show up tonight.*

As he reclines on the bed, there's a knock on his door. He jumps up hoping it's Clyde, but when he jerks open the door, Myron's standing there.

"You hungry?" Myron asks. "We're headed out to grab some grub and thought you might like to tag along."

"Sure, sounds good to me. Just let me grab my hat."

On their way to dinner, Myron gives Harold the third degree. He asks him how he and Clyde got on the rodeo circuit and where they're from. Harold explains how he and Clyde teamed up and fills them in on what happened to Clyde's dad. They're amazed at the story.

"I can't wait to meet this young fella," Audra says. "Sounds like a good kid."

"He's had it pretty rough. That's why I'm concerned for him. Bad things just seem to follow him," Harold shares.

Turnabout's fair play, so over dinner Harold asks Myron to share their story. As Myron shares, Audra fills in the gaps when she can.

Harold has a hard time believing that anyone could out talk Audra, but he's doing a good job.

"We came from a big horse ranch in Oklahoma," Myron explains. "Audra's mom and I were truly in love. She was the lady of my dreams. When we got married, we wanted a quiver full of kids," he says with a smirk on his face. "Yep, we had it all planned out. I was going to run a small store in town and she was going to help me. You know, a family business."

"Yeah, sounds nice," Harold agrees as he listens intently. "Well, what happened?"

He chokes up as he starts to explain, and has to stop. That's when Audra interjects, "I happened."

"What? I don't understand," Harold says as Myron puts his head in his hands.

"You see," Audra continues, "Mom got pregnant and they were both thrilled."

"That's right, we were going to have our first of many," Myron adds before blowing his nose.

"But that was the plan from the beginning, right?" Harold says.

"Yep, but The Man upstairs had other plans," Audra quickly replies.

"Now I'm really confused," Harold states.

"Ya see, Mom carried me for the full nine months and when the time came for me to enter this world, it was her time to leave."

Harold leans over the table and now understands why Myron's having such a hard time.

"She had complications in the delivery," Audra continues. "I came out okay, but she didn't. The doctor did all he could, but she passed away while giving me life."

Harold sits back in his seat and thinks, *Wow, what do I say now?* He looks at Myron, who has regained his composure, and says, "I'm so sorry. That was quite a while ago. How long have you two been with the rodeo?"

"Ain't nothin' to be sorry about. We've done pretty well for only doing it for the past few years."

"If ya don't mind me asking, how'd ya get involved?" Harold inquires.

"The longer I stayed in the store, the more the memories would pop up. I just couldn't bring myself to run the store anymore, but I had a little girl to take care of. So I moved back to our hometown to be with my family and went to work on a ranch. My family saved us: they were so supportive. Then came the depression."

"Yeah, I know all about that," Harold recalls.

"Audra learned about horses and loved ridin', so when this guy who handles the rodeos asked if I'd help him with it, since I had business sense, I said 'sure' and the rest is history."

"I think one thing I've found out is that everyone has a story to tell yours, ours, and probably a million others to boot," Harold says. "Thanks for sharin'."

Audra gives Harold a little wink. "Thanks for listenin'."

They talk their way through dinner and on their way back to the hotel Audra asks, "Any plans to check up on Clyde if ya don't hear from him?"

"Yeah, I was thinking that if he's not here by mornin', I'm goin' to make some calls."

"Sounds wise," Myron says. "Let us know if there's any way we can help."

"Will do. Thanks for the offer," Harold replies as he walks toward his room.

✳ ✳ ✳

The happy couple returns home with stories to share, so everyone gathers for dinner at Buck's to hear about their honeymoon. After dessert is served, Buck excuses himself, heads off to his room, and returns with an envelope.

"Son, I got somethin' here for ya. It came on your weddin' day. Herman, from the telegraph office, was 'bout to walk into the church when I stopped him and asked what he needed. He pulled out this telegram and, said he needed to give it to you. I told him I'd take it. He refused at first, said it was somethin' he needed to give you directly. I snatched it from his hand and read it, then decided you didn't need to read it 'til ya got back. So here it is."

Bewildered, Martin stands as Buck hands it to him. He slowly opens it and begins to read.

"Honey, read it out loud," Ruthie suggests. "I want to know what it says."

Buck looks at Ruthie. "Sweetie, I think it's somethin' he needs to read to himself first."

Everyone's eyes are fixed on Martin. When he finishes, he steps back and flops down in his chair. With shoulders slouched and his chin to his chest, he mutters to himself. Confused, Ruthie scoots closer and puts her arm around his shoulder.

"What's wrong?" she asks. "What does it say?"

He slowly hands her the telegram. She begins to read it to herself, and then realizes she needs to read it aloud for the others. She clears her throat and begins:

> *To: Mr. Martin Miller*
> *Stop... The wedding invitation for Captain Janice Moore was forwarded to Pearl Harbor...stop...We have been informed... stop...that Captain Moore was killed during the bombing of Pearl Harbor... stop...Please confirm that you received this information.*
>
> > *Signed,*
> > *Informational officer*

* * *

Harold wakes up early the next morning and has to decide whether or not to register Clyde for the next rodeo. Following through with what he told Audra and Myron the night before, he elects to call the last motel first to see if Clyde's picked up the envelope yet; if not, he'll call Mr. Goldberg.

With no change for the payphone outside the motel lobby, he asks the clerk inside and she politely obliges. With change in hand, he opens the folding glass doors, steps into the phone booth, and closes them behind him. Placing the change on the small metal shelf below the phone, he picks up the receiver and dials O for the operator.

When she answers, he asks her to connect him to the Western Wheel Motel. She asks him to deposit thirty-five cents for five minutes. He reads her the number from his receipt, then drops a quarter into the quarter slot and a dime in the dime slot. As each coin is deposited, he hears four clinks for the quarter and two for the dime.

"Thank you, sir," the operator says, once she's confirmed the proper amount. "I will connect you now."

The phone rings and a lady answers, "Hello, this is the Western Wheel Motel."

"Yes, my name is Harold and my partner and I stayed there last week. I left an envelope with his name, Clyde Lewis, on it. I'd like to know if he's picked it up yet."

"Just a minute, sir. I'll check."

It seems to take forever. In fact, the operator comes on and says, "If you want to continue your call, please deposit ten cents."

Harold picks up a dime and drops it in the coin slot, followed by two clinks. "Thank you," says the operator.

The next voice he hears is the motel receptionist. "Sir? The envelope's still here. Is there anything else I can do for you?"

"No ma'am, thank you very much." He pushes down the lever for the earpiece and lets it up again to hear the dial tone, then once again dials O.

The operator answers, "What number may I connect you to?"

"Oh, I forgot. Hold on, please," Harold requests as he fumbles for his wallet. He pulls out a small piece of paper with the Goldbergs' number on it.

"Okay, here it is; the number is Emerson 4-6760, in Colorado."

"Thank you, sir. That will be fifty-five cents, please."

Harold drops two quarters in the quarter slot, then a nickel in the nickel slot. When the operator hears the coins drop, she puts him through.

It rings a few times before someone picks it up. "Hello, this is the Goldbergs'."

"Mister G, is that you? This is Harold."

"Harold, yes it's me. That was fast! Have you already decided to come work for me?"

"No, not yet,' Harold chuckles, "but I was wondering if you could help me?"

"Sure, what cha need?"

"You see, Clyde left a number of days ago to go to his sister's wedding."

"Yeah, I remember him going."

"Well, he hasn't gotten back yet, and I was wondering if you've seen him."

"You know, now that you mention it, I don't remember seeing him at the wedding, but that doesn't mean anything. I couldn't stay long myself. Tell you what I'll do, I'll check around town and see what I can find out. Why don't you call me later tonight, but make sure to reverse the charges."

"Thanks, Mr. G, I really appreciate it. I hope nothing's happened to him."

"Yeah, me too. We'll talk later and don't forget about that offer."

"No, I won't. Thanks again! Goodbye, Mr. G; we'll talk later tonight."

"Goodbye for now, Harold."

☆ ☆ ☆

Three days into Clyde's incarceration, a young boy and his dad walk into the sheriff's office. The dad explains that a few days back his son left early to do some fishing and almost got run over just outside of town by a speeding car.

"Last night we figured out that it was the same morning as the robbery," he continues. "My son's really good with numbers and he remembers the license plate number, so we thought we'd come to town and see if that'll help ya at all."

The sheriff rocks forward, grabs a pencil, and peers over his glasses at the young boy. "You remember the numbers on that car, young fella?" Too timid to say anything, he nods his head. "Don't be scared, now. Go ahead and give me those numbers, son."

He smiles. "Yes, sir. It was *D*, just like my name, *David*, and then 4343. That was pretty easy to remember."

The sheriff reaches over his desk and tousles the young man's hair. "Thank you, young fella. You might have helped us catch ourselves some bank robbers."

Not wanting to waste any time, he gets on the radio and puts out an APB (All Points Bulletin) on the vehicle with the license plate number. Shaking the dad's hand, the sheriff tells him to take his son to the diner for a meal, on him. As they leave the office, he gets on the landline and calls the state patrol with the number.

Clyde hears the commotion and yells, "Hey Sheriff, what's going on out there?"

"Just got a bead on your partners. It shouldn't be long now."

"Good!" Clyde shouts. "Then they can tell you I'm innocent."

The sheriff lets out a hoot.

"Go ahead and laugh, you'll see. Hey, by the way, do I get lunch anytime soon? Since ya didn't give me any breakfast?" he hollers as his stomach growls.

"It's a comin'; hang on to your britches. We're getting special delivery today and if you're not quiet, I'll eat yours and mine."

✵ ✵ ✵

Sam Goldberg heads to town to see if he can find out anything about Clyde. He decides to stop by Dorris's first. He pulls up in front and doesn't notice any movement inside, so he steps up on the porch and knocks. When no one answers, he decides to head over to Pastor Red's.

As he drives past the WD, he spots Al and Red walking down the sidewalk. He quickly pulls over and they walk over to greet him.

"Afternoon, you two. Where are you headed?" Mr. Goldberg asks.

"Going to the church," Red says. "I need to grab a couple of things. What are you doing in town in the middle of the week?"

"Well, I got a phone call from Harold this morning."

"Harold?" Al questions.

"Yeah, you remember him, don't you? He used to work for the Livingstons."

"Oh yeah, I think I do," Al responds.

"Why was he calling you?" Red asks.

"Well, I saw him and Clyde at a rodeo awhile back and told them about Ruthie's wedding."

"Clyde Lewis?" Al asks.

"Yeah. Ya see, they've teamed up and are riding in rodeos. Anyway, he said Clyde left to come to the wedding, but he hasn't seen him since. He sounds pretty worried."

"I saw him standing in the back," Red recalls. "But I didn't see him at the reception. Not sure what happened to him."

Al clears his throat. "I haven't seen him, but I can confirm that he was here and then left town."

"How's that?" Red asks.

"He came out to the ranch and broke into my barn to get his old man's, I mean his pop's, steamer chest."

"Do you know where he went from there?" Ben inquires.

"Don't have a clue. I imagine he got out of town pretty quickly, though. You know, just in case we found out," Al reasons.

"I can't believe he'd do that! That steamer must have been pretty important to him. Thanks for the info. I'll pass it on to Harold when he calls tonight," Sam says.

They all say their goodbyes and head off in separate directions.

Chapter 5
FREE AT LAST

The front door of the jail opens and the cute young lady from the diner walks in carrying a tray of food.

"Good afternoon, Sheriff! Here's some lunch for you and your prisoner. Where would you like me to set it?"

"Thanks, Elizabeth," he replies. "You can just set it on my desk."

"Please, Sheriff, just call me Beth. So your prisoner is one of the bank robbers?"

"Yep, caught him red-handed, but he claims to be innocent."

"Don't they all?" she remarks.

"Yeah, they do. But you know, the more I think about it, things just don't add up," he confesses.

"How's that?" she asks.

"All the other reports about these 'blow-up bandits' say there are only two. You'd think that if he was part of it, he'd have money in his pockets, but he was broke. Only thing he had was a . . ."

Arthur from the auto repair shop steps in. "Afternoon, Sheriff. I hate to barge in like this, but I got something to ask ya. Afternoon, Ms. Beth," he says, removing his cap.

She nods a greeting.

"That's okay, Arthur. We were just talking about the prisoner. Why, what cha need?" he asks.

"Well, you know Ethel; lives in that house just as ya come into town?"

"You mean Ethel McCoy?" the sheriff inquires.

"Yeah, that's the one. I got a call from her about an hour ago. She says there's been a truck parked by her house for the past few days and no one's been back to get it; wants me to take it away. Is that legal?"

"Whose is it?" the sheriff asks.

"She don't rightly know. That's the problem. She says she's never seen it before."

"Sheriff," Beth jumps in, "did your prisoner have anything on him?"

He glances over at her and asks, "What's that got to do with anything?"

"You said things didn't add up, right?

"Yeah, that's right. All he had on him was a set of keys and this silly old horseshoe," he answers as he takes the horseshoe from his desk drawer.

"A HORSESHOE?" she squeals.

"Yeah, why?"

"Sheriff, you got the wrong man. I betcha those keys fit that truck Arthur's talking about. You see, the morning of the robbery this stranger came in real early; only had a few pennies to his name, but he had this old horseshoe and he told me all about it.

"Oh, my gosh," the sheriff groans, "it makes sense now. Can you ID him for me, Beth?"

"Sure can!"

✲ ✲ ✲

Harold can't wait to call Mr. G back. As soon as the sun starts to fade, he walks to the pay phone and places his call, but to no avail. There's no answer. Not giving up, he reinserts the change; again no answer. Time and again, there's no answer and the change drops into the return slot.

Just before the three leave for dinner, he decides to try one more time. As he drums his fingers on the metal shelf under the phone, his mind races through the 'what if' questions.

Finally, Mr. G picks up. "Hello, this is the Goldbergs."

"Mr. G?" Harold asks. "This is Harold again." Getting right to the point, he asks, "Did ya find out anything?"

"Hello, Harold. You didn't call me collect like I told you to."

"I forgot, I'm sorry. I've been anxious to hear if you found out anything. Did ya?"

"As they say, Harold, I have some good news and I have some bad news," Sam offers with a chuckle.

Clinching his teeth, Harold says, "I don't like the sound of that, but go ahead and let me have it."

Going into more detail than Harold cares for, Sam says, "First, I went by the family's home, but no one was there. Then I decided to go see Pastor Red. When I found him, he was with Al."

"Pastor Red and Al were together?" Harold asks.

"Yeah, that's another story I can fill you in on later," Sam continues.

"Okay, go on."

"Like I said, I went to see Pastor Red to ask him if he had seen Clyde. He said he saw him at the wedding."

"Good, at least he made it to the wedding," Harold confirms.

"That's the good news. Even though he made it to the wedding, he didn't go to the reception for some reason. But he did go out to the old Livingston place."

"Why would he do something like that?" Harold inquires.

"Not rightly sure, except when they wouldn't let him on the property, he snuck on; broke into the barn and took an old steamer chest. I guess it was his pop's."

"If it was his pop's, then he didn't really steal it, did he?"

"Technically you're right, but he did break into the barn."

"Did they arrest him?"

"No. No, he must have left town right after that because no one's seen him since. I know that doesn't help much, but he's probably on his way back."

"And you say that was the same day as the wedding?" Harold asks.

"Yep. Sorry that's all I could find out for ya," Sam apologizes.

The operator chimes in and asks Harold to deposit another dime for an additional three minutes. Sam tells her to charge his home phone and gives her the number.

With that taken care of, they continue to discuss some possibilities of what could've happened to Clyde. Then they exchange their goodbyes, and hang up. Harold's at a loss about what to do next. He climbs into the backseat and heads to dinner with Audra and Myron.

✲ ✲ ✲

Pete and Whiskey lay low for a few days and settle into their room. Pete, the social one, meets a family that's heading west and looking for work. The dad is doing repairs around the motel to help pay for their room. They have three young children and they're all crammed into one small room, but they're grateful for the roof over their heads.

The family's been there about a week, and Pete has gotten to know each of them by name. He can be a bit of a softy at times. When he finds out they've been on the road for months, moving from place to place looking for work, he slips them some much needed cash without Whiskey knowing it.

While Pete's been befriending the family, Whiskey's been in the next town, about 10 miles east, casing the bank. He always parks on the outskirts of town and walks in, trying to blend in with the crowd. Having done this numerous times before, it doesn't take him long to scope out the bank and its surroundings. He quickly finds the easiest way in and out of the bank.

When he gets back to the motel, Pete informs him that the family is leaving the next morning, so they decide to step up their pace on the next job. Later that evening, right after midnight, they get to work. With Pete as lookout, Whiskey swaps the license plates from their car with the family's out-of-state plates.

✲ ✲ ✲

Sitting quietly on his bed, Clyde hears the door to the backroom swing open and looks up to see Beth with the sheriff. Embarrassed about being there, he buries his face in his hands.

They walk up to the cell and the sheriff says, "Young man, look up here, please."

Surprised by the sheriff's polite demeanor, Clyde takes a deep breath and looks directly at Beth. She looks at him, turns to the sheriff, and softly declares, "That's him, he's the one."

"What?" Clyde retorts, "I'm the one for what?"

"Relax, young man," the sheriff assures him as he unlocks the cell door. "I think we have this all straightened out. You're free to go."

Clyde jumps up. "I'm free to go?" he exclaims.

"Yep, this little lady told us about you and that horseshoe," the sheriff says as all three walk into the outer office. He picks up the horseshoe and hands it to Clyde. "That must be a lucky one, son; don't ever let 'er go. It saved you," the sheriff advises as he hands it to Clyde along with his keys.

"I won't, Sheriff, but what about my lunch?"

"Ms. Beth, you can leave the tray here and this young fella can escort you back to the diner for his, if you don't mind," he proposes.

"That's fine with me," Beth smiles, thinking *I don't mind being escorted by a cutie like him.*

"Thanks, Sheriff, but where's my truck?" Clyde inquires.

"It's still where you parked it. That's what started all this! I'll tell you what; give Arthur there your keys. He'll fill 'er up on us and make sure everything's fine."

"Thanks, that sounds good to me," Clyde acknowledges as he tosses him the keys, "but there is one more thing."

The sheriff thinks, *Yeah, kid? Best be quiet and move on,* but asks, "Yeah, what's that?"

"I did recognize one of the robbers."

"What?!" the sheriff hollers. "Why didn't you tell me?"

Clyde puts his lips together and cocks his head to the side. "If I had, ya would've thought I was one of 'em. Right?"

"Yeah, you're probably right. What's his name?"

"His nickname's Whiskey, but I know him as Jonathan. Don't rightly know his last name, though. He's the one who ran over me."

"Thanks, I'll let the others know. By the way, how'd you know him?"

"He worked in my hometown 'til he crossed the wrong guy. Then he had to run for his life."

The sheriff shakes his head. "Some guys just don't learn."

"Yep, you're right about that, Sheriff," Clyde agrees.

"I know you're innocent, but why don't you just hang around town for the next couple days?" the sheriff suggests. "I may need some more information. After all, you are an eye witness."

"I don't know. I'm trying to join up with my partner on the rodeo circuit, but I guess if ya really need me to, I'll stay."

"Well, I can't force you to, but . . ."

The phone rings and the sheriff excuses himself to answer it. "Hello?"

"Sheriff, we found a car with the license plate number of the robbers, but it belongs to a family, not two guys. They must have made a switch. We asked the family about it and they explained that they stayed in a place east of here where they made friends with two guys fitting the robbers' descriptions. We've informed the local police."

"Thanks! Please keep me informed."

"10-4, Sheriff."

Clyde and Beth turn to walk out just as the sheriff hangs up, but stop as he reports, "It looks like we're closing in on those boys; we'll probably have them in custody by tomorrow. I'll make arrangements at the hotel for you. It shouldn't be long now."

Clyde waves and then points to his head. "Oh Sheriff, by the way, I need my hat."

"Oh yeah, your hat. I'll have to try to find it," he replies.

"What do you mean 'try to find it'? I asked ya to take care of it! It's the one my dad left me," Clyde angrily retorts.

"Sorry, son, I thought where you were going you wouldn't be needing it, but I'll see what I can do."

"I really need that hat," Clyde laments as they walk out the door.

They don't even make it to the diner before the sheriff beelines it over to the general store. He walks in and the clerk, the big guy who had Clyde pinned to the ground, is behind the counter.

"Hey, Bobby, where is that young man's hat?"

"Got it up there on the wall. Wanted everyone to see what a bank robber's hat looks like."

"Well, I got some news for you," he says before explaining the whole story.

After hearing it, Bobby says, "Now I feel downright awful about treating the kid that way. I even stomped on his hat, and you say that there hat was his pop's? I'll take care of it and get it back to ya by tomorrow."

"Thanks," says the sheriff. "I'd appreciate it."

Bobby takes the hat down from the wall and heads over to the local hatter to have it worked on.

✳ ✳ ✳

The early morning sky becomes lighter by the minute as the police surround the motel where Whiskey and Pete were last spotted. A couple of them go to the office and the owner greets them, "Can I help you gentlemen?

"Yeah, we're looking for two guys who have been staying here. One's kind of tall with damaged front teeth, while the other one's shorter and a little pudgy. They've probably been here a few days."

"I've only got one room rented to two guys, so it must be them."

"Yeah? Which room is it?"

"Oh, they left real early this morning and headed east."

"How do you know they headed east?"

"I let my dog out and watched them drive off."

"Where's the closest bank?" one deputy asks.

"In the next town, about ten miles east of here," the owner replies.

"Thanks," the deputy responds.

He walks out and hollers, "They're not here, they've headed to the next town. Let's go, but stop on the outskirts so we can sketch out a plan. I'll radio ahead, so the local police will know what's going on."

They all jump in their cars and head out. It doesn't take long to get there and the local police are waiting for them outside of town. The deputy explains the town's layout and the location of the bank. Some officers position themselves at the far side of the bank, while others cover the back. The rest slowly pull up within shouting distance.

✲ ✲ ✲

It's still dark as the two make their way from their room to the car. All the other rooms are dark with the only light coming from the sign flashing the name of the motel at the corner of the driveway. As they back out of their spot, the light outside the office comes on, and the owner steps outside with his dog. They wave as they drive by.

The dark sky is beginning to turn light just enough so Pete can see to jimmy the lock on the side door of the bank. They cautiously enter and head straight to the safe. The reason they pick these small town banks is that the vault systems are less sophisticated. In fact, for Pete, they're a breeze to peel. It doesn't take but a couple of minutes for him to open the safe and for them to fill up the money bags.

While Pete cracks the safe, Whiskey positions the sticks of TNT so as not to hurt anyone, but to let people know they were there. He learned the skill while working for the railroad, when they would have to blast their way through granite and all sorts of rock. Then he went to work on the Livingston ranch, helping clear parts of their property and finally to the Goldberg's. To him, this is like serving ice cream; he can do it in his sleep. Not wanting to run into another situation like the last one, he makes the fuses longer this time.

Once he's done, he moves to the safe to help Pete fill the final few bags before scurrying to the back room to light the fuse. Once it's lit, he hurries to the front to pick up his bags before dashing to the side door to leave. That's when he hears someone outside.

He falls to his knees, peeks out the front window, and whispers to Pete, "Get down! There's someone out there." He squats and takes another glance, and sits back with his knees bent. "Pete, it looks like we're surrounded; there must be thirty or more cops out there!"

From flat on his belly, Pete peeks out the glass front door and whispers back to Whiskey, "Now we know what Custer must've felt like. What are we going to do?"

"Die, I guess!" Whiskey hisses.

"Why do you say that?" Pete demands.

"I've already lit the fuse and they're not going to let us just walk out of here."

"You did what?! You lit the fuse?! Go back there and stop it."

"Can't, I'd have to go to the other side of the room, and if I do that, they'll see me and start shooting."

A voice from outside says, "You two come out with your hands up and all will be fine. Come on now, we know you're in there."

"Whiskey, I'm giving up!" Pete says. "I may have to go to prison, but at least I'll be alive."

"Yeah, that's what you think!" Whiskey says with a laugh. "What do you think they do to guys like you in prison? You're going to spend the rest of your life in there."

"Yeah, yeah," Pete answers, "you're right." Without thinking, he says, "Here goes nothing!"

"No wai. . ." Whiskey responds, jumping behind one of the bank's support columns. Trying to grab Pete, he falls to the ground. It's too late.

Pete kicks open the front door and bursts out with his gun blazing. The officers hold their fire for a second, but once that first shot is fired, the sound is deafening. It doesn't take long with around thirty weapons of all kinds; rifles, shotguns, pistols and Thompson machine guns, to cut him down. Before long, the place looks like Swiss cheese. Some of the stray bullets find their way to the oil heaters on the back wall and oil begins to spill all over the floor.

When the firing stops, Whiskey's still inside and realizes he only has a few seconds before the explosion. He knows his time is up. As he jumps to his feet to head out the door, the TNT goes off, sending him flying through the air and slamming him into the front door jam. Almost simultaneously, the oil from the heater ignites and sends a flash of fire throughout the building. Flattened against the door jam, Whiskey feels the concussion of the explosion and the heat from the flames. The explosion breaks the teller's cage loose and sends it hurling toward him. Within seconds, it penetrates his upper body and sticks him to the door jamb like a dart hitting a dart board. It's over.

Chapter 6
CATCHING UP

Clyde sits at the counter enjoying his freedom and breakfast. He pulls Pop's old horseshoe from his pocket and sets it down next to his biscuits and gravy. The diner's busy as Beth scrambles around taking orders, but she still has time to acknowledge Clyde. "That sure is one lucky charm!" she remarks.

"Sure is! It's been faithful to me," Clyde boasts.

These past few days he and Beth have spent a lot of time together. He's helped out around the diner and is beginning to take a liking to her. *She sure is easy to talk to,* he thinks, *and always has a smile and makes me feel special. Besides that, she's as cute as a bug's ear. It might be nice to find some work around here and get to know this girl a little better.* Then reality sets in; he's got to get back to the rodeo and Harold. While this girl is sweet, there's nothing like the excitement of riding a bull.

Beth stops to take a breather, and, as they chat, the sheriff and Bobby walk in and grab some coffee. They invite Clyde to join them on their way to a table.

"Got some good news for you," the sheriff says, taking a sip of his coffee.

"For me?" Clyde asks, pointing to himself as he sets his cup on the table.

"You can leave anytime you want," the sheriff says as he leans back in his chair. "I do appreciate you hanging your hat here these past few days."

Clyde readjusts himself in his chair. "You don't need me anymore? I thought you said I was an eye-witness!"

"You are, but we don't need one anymore. You're free to go!" the sheriff repeats.

Puzzled, Clyde says, "Sounds like there's more to the story."

"I just got a call from the state troopers. They found Jonathan and his partner in a small town by the state line east of here. They were in the process of robbing the bank when they were both killed."

"WHAT? Jonathan's dead?" Clyde shouts.

"Yep, blew himself right up. So you're free to go."

Clyde leans back far enough to lift the chair's front legs off the floor. "That's hard to believe. Just don't ever know when your time is up, do ya, Sheriff."

"You're right there, young man, especially when you're in the line of work they were."

"I guess that makes it easy for me, doesn't it? But I do need one more thing my hat."

Bobby leans forward. "That's why I'm here," he sheepishly says. "Sorry I took your hat, Clyde. Thought ya wouldn't be needing it. Now that I know the truth, I feel really bad about the way I treated ya, so I had it cleaned and fixed up a bit. Not much they could do with it, being so old and all, but they did what they could." Bobby brings it out from under the table and hands it to Clyde.

"Thank you!" Clyde says. "It was my dad's before he passed on."

"That's what I told the hatter. He said it may have been your dad's, but this thing is older than that. It was probably your grandpa's."

"My grandpa's? Holy cow, he must have passed it on to my dad!" As he holds it up to his nose, Clyde can see his dad walk through the door of the house and toss it on top of the old coat rack. To think it was his grandpa's brings a smile to his face. "Thanks again! It sure looks better than when I got it," he acknowledges.

"You're welcome," Bobby says, extending his hand.

As they shake hands, the sheriff announces, "Son, your truck's parked out front with a tank of gas, and your bags are in the back. Drop in and see us when you're close by. Not too soon, though. You see, some folks don't change their minds very easily. Remember, that was their money." The sheriff stands up, gives Clyde a pat on the back, and sets his keys on the table. "Here's a little cash for the road. Have a nice life, son."

"Thanks, Sheriff," Clyde answers as he stands up and watches the sheriff and Bobby walk out. Then it hits him; now he has to say goodbye to Beth.

He grabs his keys off the table and says "It's been nice getting to know ya."

"Where're you going?" she asks, disappointed.

"Have to catch up with the rodeo, but I hope to see ya again."

"Okay, Cowboy. I won't say goodbye, then. I'll just say 'see you later'." She turns to walk away, but Clyde gently grabs her arm and turns her toward him.

He looks into her eyes, then bends over and gives her a peck on the cheek and whispers, "Thank you for everything!"

He picks up his hat, squares it on his head, and walks to his truck with his head down, wondering what's happened to Harold.

As he heads out of town on the main highway, he can't seem to take his mind off of Beth. *She sure is a sweet young thing, with them pretty eyes and that soft voice; enough to make one stand up and take notice.*

Just as quickly, his thoughts wander to Whiskey. *I can't believe he turned to robbing banks and blew himself up. What would make someone go that far? He wasn't really that bad of a guy. Well, maybe he was. He never was one to make good choices. I hope I never get that far down. I remember Harold saying that our choices make us who we are. Boy, is that ever true! I'm sure thankful for Harold.*

Oh yeah, poor Harold! He's probably wondering what happened to me; sitting in his room all by himself with no transportation. Do I have a story to tell him! I can't wait to ride that next bull. It's so exciting being on the back of those beasts! Look out, world, 'cause here I come, he chuckles to himself.

✵ ✵ ✵

Uncle Conrad looks out the serving window from the kitchen stove as Elizabeth stands at the counter watching Clyde walk to his truck. She thinks, *I sure wish things had worked out differently. That's a guy I would like to get to know better.* As Clyde drives slowly past the diner, she notices him looking in and glances around to see if anyone is watching. Then he gives a short little wave with one hand and touches her cheek with the other, knowing he probably can't see her.

As she finishes waving, Uncle hollers, "Two eggs over easy. Come on, Beth, let's get the food out before it gets cold."

She walks to the window, gives half a grin, and delivers her order to the first booth. Uncle Conrad thinks, *That poor girl is so far away from home and doesn't know many people her age here. This past week is the happiest I've seen her since her parents sent her out. Sure wish that young man could've stayed around longer. I'll have Anna talk with her tonight when we get home.*

✵ ✵ ✵

The drive back is long. When he gets tired of driving and has a hard time staying awake, he just runs his last bull ride through his mind again, and that gets his adrenalin pumping. He replays it over and over, feeling each buck and hearing each crack of his back as the bull tosses him like a rag doll. Before he knows it, he's pulling under the overhang of the motel where he left Harold over a week ago. Just as the outside lights flicker on, he stops in front and peers in the glass doors of the lobby. An older man behind the counter glances up when he hears the bell chime, indicating someone was entering.

"What can I do for you, Sonny?" the clerk asks as Clyde approaches the desk.

"I dropped my partner off here a while back and was wondering what room he's in."

"I don't rightly recognize you, young fella, so I can't give out that information."

"No, it wasn't me," Clyde sighs. "It was my partner."

"Heard ya the first time," the clerk responds without looking up, "but still don't recognize ya."

Clyde takes a deep breath. "Can ya please just tell me which room he's in?"

"Would love to. What's his last name?"

Clyde freezes in place. "I don't know his last name."

"What? How long you known him?"

"A few years now, but never had a reason to ask. You have to know who I mean, though. He's a cowboy, rides in the rodeo, and stands about this tall," Clyde gestures with his hand up above his head.

"Oh, that guy! He checked out a few days back."

"Where'd he go?" Clyde asks.

"Don't know, just checked out and left."

"With who? He didn't have a ride!"

"Can't tell ya . . . wasn't here," the Old-Timer replies.

"Who was?" Clyde presses.

Just then a lady walks in from the room behind the office. "Having a problem?"

Clyde greets her with a "Howdy," and explains the situation.

"What's your name, Sonny?" she inquires.

Visibly annoyed, Clyde asks, "What difference does that make?"

"Can't tell ya. Just answer the question!" she demands.

"Okay! Clyde! My name's Clyde."

"Just what I thought," she says.

He's more confused now than ever. He watches as she reaches under the counter and pulls out a weathered envelope.

"Your buddy left this for ya," she says as Clyde reaches for it.

Just before he grabs it, she pulls it back. "What's it worth to ya?" she asks with a smirk.

With his hand in midair, Clyde gives her a funny look, reaches in his pocket, and pulls out some change.

"That all ya got?" she smirks.

"Yep. Ran into some trouble along the way and barely made it back," he explains.

"Well, just keep it; you'll probably need it. Sorry for askin' those questions. Could tell ya was gettin' all upset. Just wanted to make sure you were the right guy."

Putting the change back in his pocket, Clyde apologizes, "I'm sorry if I got a little short with ya. I've had a tough few days."

"Think nothin' of it, Sweetie, but ya better get goin'. Your buddy has a couple of days start on ya."

"Did you see who he left with?"

"Yup, some cute little thing."

"Really?" Clyde asks, surprised.

"Yup, and an older guy, too," she recalls.

"Okay, gotta go. Thanks for the help!" After he gets in the truck, Clyde opens the envelope under the glow of the flashing hotel sign and pulls out two papers; a map and a note:

> *Clyde,*
>
> *Waited for ya to return, but didn't want to miss the next ride so I hitched a ride with Myron and Audra. Hurry, so we can get moving. This last weekend I placed in the money, so I left ya a little till ya catch up. Also a map to where we'll be. Follow the arrows. See ya soon.*
>
> *Harold*

Clyde thinks, *What a great guy, always looking out for me. I don't know what I'd do without him! He's like the older brother I never had, but I reckon I do need to know his last name!* Clyde starts the truck and takes a gander at the map. He turns it in all different directions as he attempts to get his bearings to finally figure out which way is north. As he puts the truck in gear and lets out the clutch, he thinks, *on the road again. Don't know where I'm going, but at least I got a map. I wonder who Audra and Myron are.*

✳ ✳ ✳

Uncle Conrad locks the front door of the diner and Beth takes a seat. She rests her arms on the counter as Conrad walks by and hits the keys of the cash register, making the chime go off. Beth sits upright on the stool and spins the seat around a few times, bringing a grunt from her uncle. She grabs the counter to stop herself. "I sure am tired tonight, Uncle."

"You had a busy day, young lady. How did you do in tips?" he inquires.

"Haven't added them up yet, but I think I did okay."

"I'm tired, too. Let's head home," Conrad suggests. "You have the place looking pretty good. We need to fill some of the salt shakers, but we can do that early in the morning. I got myself a mess in the kitchen; maybe I can talk your aunt into coming in to help." They both snicker, knowing there's little chance of that happening.

Beth nods, "I hope she will. Another day like today and I'll need a week to recuperate. Uncle Conrad, can I ask you something?"

"Sure, fire away. There isn't anything you can't ask your favorite uncle," he says with a smirk.

"You know how your name means 'Wise Man'? If that's true, then you can answer this question for me."

"Okay, I guess. We'll see if it's true, won't we?"

"Oh, I think it's true, so here goes. Do you think I'm a bad girl?" Beth somberly asks.

Taken aback by the question, Conrad takes a moment to gather his thoughts. "Sweetie, I don't think you're a bad girl; you've just made some poor choices. We all do. The key is realizing when we do and learning from it so we don't do it again."

"Mom and Dad must think I am or they wouldn't have sent me all the way out here. I mean, I love spending time with you and Auntie, but there isn't much for me to do here, if you know what I mean."

Conrad was hoping she would have this conversation with Anna, but since she started it, he may as well finish it. "I know things are hard for you right now and you don't want to be here, but make the most of the situation and learn what you can to make your life different. Can I say one more thing?"

"Sure, go ahead. I'm all ears."

"The last few days I've seen a different Beth. Smiling, joking with the customers like you really want to be here, and now this. How come?"

"You probably didn't notice, but you remember that young man they arrested and later found out he wasn't one of the robbers?"

"Yeah, I remember," Conrad replies as he thinks, *Give me a little credit for being observant.*

"He was so nice. I enjoyed being around him; he was easy to talk to. And boy, the story of his life! He's had a rough time of it. Do you know that his mom asked him to leave when he was eleven? Now if that doesn't make you think!"

"Beth, remember that everyone has a story. You have a story. When you start looking outside your own life and at others, that's when you can have an impact on them; just like that young man had on you. But when you're stuck in your own little world, you aren't much good to yourself or others. I think you're starting to get it."

"I think so, too. Thank you, Uncle. It is true."

"What's that?"

"You really are a wise man." Reaching over, she gives him a peck on the check, and then wraps her arms around his neck. He puts his head back and enjoys the moment.

✲ ✲ ✲

Clyde pulls into the parking lot of the arena just as the bull-riding event starts. As he makes his way around to the back of the chutes, he hears the announcer say, "Coming out of chute number two, Harold Ritter on top of Full of It."

He stops in his tracks. *That's right, I've heard that before. Why couldn't I remember it back at the motel? It's sure great to be back.* He jumps on the back of the chute and hollers, "Go get 'im, big guy!"

As he settles on the back of the bull, Harold looks up and smiles. "Good to see ya, Half-Pint! Be right back!"

"Don't hurry," Clyde shouts back.

Harold settles in, gives the nod and the chute springs open. It doesn't take long for him to realize he's in trouble, and, sure enough, with one mighty buck, he flies over the back of the bull's right hindquarters. As he sails through the air, he flails like he's trying to swim.

From Clyde's angle, it looks hilarious, and he's busting up inside until he realizes Harold may be in trouble. As those thoughts flash through his mind, Harold lands hard on his back. The clowns jump into action as he lies motionless for what seems to be minutes, but it is actually only seconds. The crowd goes silent as the clowns get the bull from the arena and sprints to Harold's side. In a split second, Clyde jumps the chute and rushes over to help, but by the time he gets there Harold's already being helped up. Clyde's befriended the main clown, Homer, who says, "He's okay; just got the wind knocked out of him."

Harold looks at Clyde and whispers, "Guess we'll have to wait 'til next week to eat."

Clyde laughs. "Needed to lose some weight, anyway, and there's always tomorrow." He puts his arm around Harold and helps him to the back of the chutes.

They watch one rider after another before Harold finally can't wait any longer. "Where in the world have ya been?" he demands.

As another rider hits the dirt, Clyde answers, "You're not going to believe me when I tell you."

"Try me! I'm all ears."

Clyde and Harold walk over to watch the last set of bulls being loaded into the chutes. Clyde begins his story with standing in the back of the church at the wedding and wraps up the summary of his adventure just as the last rider finishes, and they head to the exit.

Harold is flabbergasted. "You mean to tell me that all that happened since you've been gone? And Jonathan's dead?"

They reach the truck and Clyde tosses the keys to Harold. "Yep, happened just as I said. You drive; I'm tired of sitting behind that wheel."

Harold unlocks his door, and reaches over to unlock Clyde's. As he leans over the seat, he notices the steamer on the floorboard.

Clyde slides in and moves it to the side. "Can't wait to show you what's in here!"

Harold smiles as he starts the truck, and they make their way back to the motel.

Chapter 7

A NEW TWIST

Al stands in the doorway talking to Maggie while she works in the kitchen. He's pretty much a regular visitor since she moved in. In the middle of their conversation, Sara knocks on the door.

"I'll get it," Al tells Maggie.

"Thanks, my hands are all wet, and I don't want to get the new apron you got me dirty."

"Good evening, young lady," Al greets Sara. "Come on in. Maggie's in the kitchen, and I was just about to leave."

"Good evening, Mr. Al. Don't leave on my account."

"Oh no, I just dropped by to see how she was doing."

Al turns and hollers, "Maggie, it's Sara. I'm going to run, see you later. Got to stop by and see Pastor Red before I head back to the ranch."

"Tell him 'hi' for me!" Maggie hollers back. "I'll be right there, Sara. Have a seat."

"Okay, take your time. I'm in no hurry."

Maggie unties her apron and walks to the front room. She goes over to Sara and gives her a hug. "It's wonderful to see you," Maggie says. "Rachel didn't come with you?"

"No, I didn't tell anyone I was coming." Sara pauses.

With her brow wrinkled, Maggie asks, "Oh? How come?"

"Well, I have a couple of questions to ask you, and I didn't want anyone to know. If they did, they might ask what I wanted."

Now Maggie's really puzzled. "What kind of questions?"

Without hesitation, Sara blurts out, "Okay! Here's the first one; you know what happened at Ruthie's wedding between Clyde and me, right?"

"Yeah, I heard some things. Why do you ask?" Maggie inquires.

"When Mom found out Clyde had been there, she acted strange. She took off on a run to try to find him, and then when we found out he broke into Al's barn, she apologized for him! I don't get it. After what he did, this is how she responds! I'd just as soon never see him again, and I told him so."

"So is there a question in there, or did I miss it?"

"The question is: Do you know why Mom would act this way? You two are real close, and she must have told you something."

Maggie sits back and contemplates her answer. *I can't tell her what I know; Dorris would never forgive me. So what do I say? I can't lie!* Sara waits and silently observes.

Maggie leans forward with a serious expression. "You know, Sara, I never had children. You kids are the closest thing to family that I have. I imagine, though, that if you had a child you hadn't seen for a while, you would be anxious, too. Remember the story of the Prodigal Son in the Bible?"

"Yeah, I think so. Didn't he run off with some money?"

"Yes, his dad gave him his inheritance early. Do you remember what happened after he lost all his money and was working by feeding the pigs?"

"He decided to go back home, didn't he?" Sara recalls.

"Yes, and when his dad saw him coming, he ran and embraced him. I imagine that's what your mom was feeling. It's something we just don't understand until it happens to us. So the reason for Clyde's leaving isn't important. What matters is that he came home."

Sara looks down at her feet and then raises her head to look directly at Maggie. "Do you think what I did was wrong?"

"Sweetie, it doesn't matter. What's done is done. What matters is that we learn from it and move forward."

"Thanks, Maggie. That helps a lot. I better get back before someone misses me." Sara gets up, gives Maggie a hug, and heads out the door.

✵ ✵ ✵

Once they get in their room, Clyde flops down on the bed as Harold fills him in on how well he's done while Clyde's been gone.

"Wow," Clyde jokes, "you sure couldn't tell that watching you ride tonight."

Having finished washing his face, Harold throws his damp towel at Clyde, who catches it. Then he runs over and snaps it at Harold's fanny. Harold grabs another towel and the war is on. They're both laughing so hard that they barely have the strength to snap their towels. With one final snap, Harold hears a metal sound. "What was that?" he asks.

Bent over from laughing so hard, Clyde whimpers, "You hit the horseshoe."

"What? You have a horseshoe in your pocket?" Harold giggles.

"Yeah, it's my good-luck charm! Oh, wait a minute. The steamer! I have to show you what else I got." Clyde makes a beeline out to the truck. He quickly returns with the steamer and sets it on the bed.

"Did you really break into Al's barn?" Harold asks.

"Yep, I had to! I knew they wouldn't let me back on."

"What do you mean 'back on'? When I talked to Mr. G, it sounded like you couldn't go on the property at all."

"Remember, I told you the guard let me on to get the horseshoe?"

"Oh, that's right; you did. Anyway, what ya got there?"

Clyde lays the raincoat on the bed, and hands the buckle to Harold.

"You mean this was in the barn the whole time?" Harold inquires as he examines it closely.

"Yep, it sure was. I hid it pretty well, didn't I?"

"You sure did, Half-Pint. Got a question for ya."

"What's that?" Clyde asks.

"Where'd you get that old hat?"

"Oh, that was in the steamer, too. I can tell you another story about that, but I sure am hungry. How about grabbing something to eat?" Clyde suggests.

The words are barely out of his mouth when there's a soft knock on the door. Harold leaps from the bed to answer it. With his head at the foot of the bed, Clyde leans over and sees a good-looking "doll" standing at the door.

"Good evening! Would you like to come in?" Harold asks.

As she enters, Clyde leaps to his feet. "Good evening, my name's Clyde."

"Why, good evening, Clyde. I'm Audra."

"I'm glad to make your acquaintance," Clyde replies, not knowing what else to say.

He's surprised when Harold says, "She's joining us for dinner, if ya don't mind."

He looks at Audra and asks, "Is your dad coming?"

Clyde thinks, *Now Dad's going, too? How about inviting Mom and Uncle Joey? I just want to get caught up. This isn't what I was expecting at all.*

"Nah," Audra explains, "he's tired and already ate a little earlier."

"You okay?" Harold asks Clyde.

"Yeah! I just thought . . ."

"Thought what?" Harold asks.

Feeling the tension, Audra says, "Ya know, maybe you guys should just go. I'll grab something later."

"No, no," Clyde assures her, "let's just get going. I could eat a horse."

After a short walk to the diner, they enter and slide into a booth. With it being so late, there is little selection left. They all order the same: a big plate of spaghetti. Their other option is meat loaf, but they aren't exactly sure what it's made of.

As the evening passes, Clyde becomes more comfortable around Audra. He can see the chemistry between the two as they talk, and wonders *How long will it be before our partnership splits up?*

✳ ✳ ✳

68

It's early morning and the summer is winding down. Beth is busy in the diner as Uncle Conrad puts the bread in the oven. She stops just outside the swinging kitchen doors with two things on her mind; the smell of the bread baking and wondering if she'll ever see Clyde again. She's having a hard time understanding how in just those few days he left such an impression on her.

Conrad notices her staring off into space and slowly walks up behind her. "Hey there, little lady; what cha thinking?"

Startled, she replies, "Oh, the smell of the bread baking just brought back some memories."

"Like what?" Conrad inquires.

"When I was younger and we lived above the bakery."

"Out on Long Island?" Uncle asks.

"Yeah," she sighs. Then with a puzzled look, she asks, "We have always lived on the island, haven't we?"

"You have, but has anyone ever told you the story of the family?"

"Not that I remember."

"It's funny that you should say the smell of baking bread brings back memories. You see, when I was a small boy, we lived above our bakery, too, in Yorktown of the Upper East Side."

"I remember Dad saying something about that," Beth recalls.

"Oh yeah, it was quite the family affair. You see, our family immigrated to New York in the mid 1800s. From the time they arrived on Ellis Island, they knew what they would do, bake."

"So this food business goes back a ways?" Beth asks.

"It sure does, generations! We lived in the Upper East Side in a neighborhood made up of mostly German immigrants. They called it 'Little Germany.' I was just a kid then, but I remember hearing about it."

As he finishes, the front door opens and a middle-aged man pokes his head in and asks, "You open?"

"We sure are," Beth responds. "Come on in." She glances over at Conrad and adds, "I'd love to hear more later, Uncle."

"Will do; just remind me."

Beth smiles as she pours a cup of coffee and sets it down on the counter in front of the customer.

☆ ☆ ☆

The guys say goodnight to Audra and head to their room, with Clyde talking nonstop in his excitement of being back.

"After tomorrow's ride, what are we doing?" he finally asks.

"Well, I figure it this way," Harold says, happy to get a word in. "Since Myron (that's Audra's dad) and Audra have been doing this for a number of years, we'll just follow them and register as we go. There's a lot more ridin' to do!"

Now he's really got Clyde excited. "I like the way that sounds! You going back to the saddle broncs?"

"That's what we did before you left, and it was workin'; and I've been told that if it ain't broke, don't fix it. By the way, how're ya feelin'?"

"Right now, I feel great. I think I'm almost totally healed. Ya know, it's funny; when I was cooped up in that cell I was stiff, but since I've been here, I haven't felt a thing."

"Well, I better get some shut-eye," Harold chuckles, "or I may not make any money tomorrow, either." It doesn't take Harold long to start sawing logs.

Clyde lies awake daydreaming about tomorrow, wishing he could be riding and eagerly anticipating next week. Then his thoughts return to Beth. *I sure hope one day I'll be able to see her again. Probably not, though. This is a big country for two people to cross paths again. Well, at least I get to ride,* he thinks as he drifts off to sleep.

☆ ☆ ☆

Over the next few days, Conrad tells his wife about the conversation he and Beth had and encourages Anna to discuss it with her.

After church on Sunday, Anna asks Beth to help her in the kitchen. As they prepare lunch, Anna probes, "You doing okay? Uncle told me a little about the talk you two had."

"Yeah, I'm okay, I guess. I just miss home," she confides before backing up a little. "I don't mean any disrespect, Auntie. I'm enjoying my time with you guys, but it just isn't home. Does that make sense?"

Anna stops chopping the vegetables. "It makes perfect sense. It looked like you were beginning to like being here those few days that young man was in town."

Blushing and stumbling for words, Beth explains, "I did enjoy talking with him. Did Uncle tell you about his life?"

"Yes, he did. That poor boy! But you know, there are a lot of young people out there with similar stories."

"I know, but for some reason hearing his really helped me to reevaluate my place in life. Boy, am I a lucky girl! You know, Mom and Dad could have just put me out."

Anna nods her head. "They sure could have, but they love you and we love you. Maybe it's time you got on with your life."

Beth stops stirring the pot of soup. "What do you mean by that?"

"Sweetie, I have seen a big change in you. I called your mom last night and told her I thought you were ready to come home."

"What? Really? What did she say?"

"She's excited about having you back in New York with them, so we'll go down tomorrow and get you a train ticket back home. You can leave sometime this week."

Beth drops the spoon in the sink and gives Anna a bear hug. "Thank you so much for all you've done! I am a new woman with goals and desires."

"You're welcome! Now grab that spoon and stir; we don't want to burn the soup."

✲ ✲ ✲

As the sun pours into the motel room early, Clyde can't believe it's already morning. He didn't sleep well with his mind racing about his next ride. They quickly dress and walk down the street to the local diner before heading to the arena. While Harold has little chance of finishing at the top, he can still win enough to help them with their expenses.

They grab a booth, and, as they're about to order, Audra and Myron walk in. Harold waves them over and then moves across to Clyde's side of the table. Myron slides in across from Clyde and Audra across from Harold.

The conversation begins with all the normal greetings, and then Clyde changes the subject. "Okay, I have to know. Where's the next rodeo? I want to ride!"

Myron smiles. "That's what I like, enthusiasm! I haven't heard someone talk like that in a long time. We've got a couple of little ones over the next few weeks, then a little bigger one before one of the majors."

"A major?" Clyde inquires.

"Yeah, that's one of a few where they have bigger prize money."

"That's good! Those are the ones we want. Right, Harold?"

Harold's too busy looking at and talking to Audra to hear what Clyde just said, so Clyde repeats a little louder, "Right, Harold?"

He doesn't even turn his head. "Sure, Half-Pint, whatever you say."

"You're not even listening to me, are you?" Clyde asks.

"Clyde," Myron interjects, "I'm getting the same responses from that little girl of mine. Don't worry, it'll pass."

Clyde shakes his head as the waitress brings their breakfast and takes Myron's and Audra's orders. By the time their order arrives, the guys have already finished. Not wanting to be rude, they stay and visit until everyone finishes.

As Harold pays their bill, Clyde asks, "What towns are the next few rodeos in?"

Myron, the last one out, says, "Just a few little towns down the road. In fact, in a couple of weeks, we'll be in that there town you were arrested in. They got a nice little rodeo there and have it each year."

That brings a smile to Clyde's face as he thinks, *That small town where Beth is? Alright! I'll get to see her again, and she'll get to see me ride. I can't wait!*

They drive to the arena and Audra and Myron head toward the announcers' booth. Clyde decides to hang around behind the chutes with some of the other riders as Harold goes to prepare himself for his ride.

✳ ✳ ✳

Beth's so excited about going back to Long Island that she awakens early and gets ready while it's still dark. She'll finally get to see her friends again, even though some of them will be off-limits. As she and Anna walk over to the train station to get her ticket home, Beth says, "Thank you so much for taking me in. I don't know what I would have done without you."

Anna puts her arm around her. "Sweetie, you're our blood relative, and that means we all stick together. Your parents didn't know what to do with you, so we volunteered to put you up for a while."

"And I'm thankful you did. Do you think that boy, Clyde, will ever come back through?"

"Oh, he may, and if he does, he'll probably come through the diner, and we can tell him what happened to you."

"You'd do that?" Beth asks.

"Sure would! I saw how you looked at him, and how he looked at you. It was only a couple of days, but you could see it," Anna notes.

When they arrive at the train station, Anna inquires about the next train to Chicago, and then to New York.

"Well," the clerk states, "our Super Chief comes through once a week going to Chicago from Los Angeles. It's due in early Friday morning."

"What's the price of a ticket to Chicago," Anna asks, "then on to New York?"

"Hold on, I'll check my chart. Is this for the two of you?"

"No sir, just one."

"Let me see here. It says $10.75 to Chicago and another $14.50 to New York. That's if we have room."

Puzzled, Anna asks, "If you have room?"

73

"Yes, ma'am. These days, with all the soldiers . . . they get first priority."

"Oh, that's right. Well, I think you'll have enough room for a small girl, won't you?"

"I'm sure we can arrange something," the clerk assures her as he smiles at Beth.

"In that case, I'll take a ticket for this coming Friday." Anna opens her purse and hands the clerk the money.

He fills out the paperwork and finally hands her a stub for Friday. "See you bright and early! Make sure you're here on time; they don't wait for nobody. That Super Chief has to be on time, or else the boss man gets upset."

"Oh, I'll be here with bells on," Beth promises. "You just make sure the train is on time."

Anna and the clerk laugh.

"See you Friday," the clerk chuckles.

"Okie dokie," Beth answers. They head to the diner walking faster than when they came.

✲ ✲ ✲

The last event is coming up and Harold is the third rider out of the chute. He's drawn a pretty tough bull, which Clyde heard the guys out behind the chutes talking about. He listened intently to what they said and shared it with Harold. To finish in the money he's got to have a pretty good ride.

Harold climbs the chute and straddles the bull. "This time next week, you'll be you doing this. This is my last bull for a while."

Clyde smiles. "Then ride like there's no tomorrow, partner!"

Harold grins, takes his rope, and tightly wraps his hand. As he scoots himself up to the bulls hump, he pulls his hat down over his brow, nods, then says, "Let 'im out!"

The gate swings open and the bull takes a mighty leap. His hind legs come up almost as high as the top of the chute. Then, with his snout almost touching the ground, he takes an enormous jump to the right and lands on his rear legs. Harold is doing a great job of staying on. The bull stumbles a little before taking his final twist to the left. Harold squeezes his legs together as hard as he can and finally hears the buzzer sound. What a ride! He lets go of the rope, timing it perfectly with the next buck of the bull, and lands safely away. The clowns quickly maneuver the bull from the arena and the scores are announced. Harold finishes in the top ten, earning some much needed cash.

Chapter 8
PEACH PIE

Beth can't wait until morning to board the train for home. She remembers how long the ride out was and thinks, *It's probably because I wasn't excited about coming.* The best she can recall it took around 27 hours, but she had a long layover in Chicago waiting for the next train to arrive.

While she packs her bags she thinks, *I enjoyed Chicago. I remember reading a poster there that explained how it took twelve years to build Union Station! It sure is a busy place. I almost got lost! At least I didn't have to go outside the station. Thank goodness they had that tunnel between the two buildings. When I first walked in, I couldn't believe the high ceilings and marble floors and walls; can't wait to see it again!* Placing her bag by the door, she lies down to try to get some sleep.

When the sun peeks through her bedroom window, she jumps to her feet to get ready. Before long, she's waiting at the front door for Anna and Conrad to escort her to the train.

They arrive about a half-hour before the train is scheduled to arrive. The clerk greets her, and then warns them that they have a pretty full train. An elderly lady is also waiting and they strike up a conversation.

"Where are you headed, young lady?" she asks.

"Oh, I'm going home to Long Island," Beth says with a grin. "How about you?"

"I'm headed to Chicago to see my son," she sadly replies.

"Your son is in Chicago? That sounds like a good time."

"Thanks, Sweetie, but it won't be fun. You see, that's where they're going to bury him."

"I'm so sorry," Beth murmurs as she sits down on the bench next to the lady. "Do you mind if I ask what happened?"

"Not at all; it makes it easier if I talk about it," the lady assures her as she sets her purse down between them.

"He was in the Army, you see, and was killed in Europe. We're from Chicago. I was out here visiting some friends when I got the telegram from his wife, so I'm headed home for the funeral. Maybe we can keep each other company on the train?"

"I'd like that," Beth responds.

"I am so sorry for your loss," Aunt Anna says. "You stay close to her and help her all you can," she directs Beth.

"Yes ma'am, I will."

The train whistles its arrival from a distance. Beth stares down the tracks and asks, "What's that hanging out the windows? It looks like . . . it is! It's people!"

The clerk walks up and gives them the bad news. "They telegraphed me that they're full, because of a big movement of troops. We can only allow on as many as get off."

The train slowly pulls to a stop and the two wait patiently for people to exit. The elderly lady laments, "I have to make it to Chicago; I can't miss my son's funeral!" Just then, a gentleman exits the train with his bag.

"There's room for one of you," the clerk says, "but you have to hurry. They're not staying long."

Beth tells the elderly lady, "You go ahead. I'll take the train next week."

She gives her a hug. "Thank you, dear sweet one. May God repay you a hundredfold. You do believe in God, don't you?"

Beth returns her hug and nods her head. "Now you better hurry or neither one of us is going anywhere."

She picks up the lady's valise and accompanies her to the train. As the train pulls out, with tears in her eyes, Beth waves goodbye.

Anna walks up and puts her arm around her. "You make us proud, and we get to have you for one more week." She gives her a kiss on the top of her head as the clerk walks up.

"Sorry, young lady, but I couldn't do anything else. That was downright big of you to do that. Tell you what, we got a freight train coming through on Wednesday that is pulling a passenger car. Won't be very fancy, but it'll get you there. It's a lot slower, too, but I'll reimburse you and get you a free ticket if you want to go."

Beth looks at Uncle Conrad. "What do you think?"

"That's usually how I travel. We just wanted you to have something nicer."

Beth turns to the clerk. "That'll be wonderful. I'll leave on Wednesday."

"What about her connections?" Conrad asks.

"Oh, that's no problem. They always have trains going to the city."

"Okay then, let's get the paperwork done."

✳ ✳ ✳

It's Wednesday morning, travel day, and Clyde's up early. This rodeo is one he's been itching to ride in. He thinks, *What could be better? Back on the circuit and seeing Elizabeth again. Without her, I'd probably still be sitting in that cell.*

Harold's taken some nasty falls in the last few rodeos, which has left him stiff and sore, so it takes him a little longer to get moving. With Clyde's encouragement and help, Harold finally gets all his parts moving in the same direction.

Clyde packs up, throws his bag in the truck, and knocks on Myron and Audra's door. "You two ready? I'm all loaded up and ready to get a move on." He grins at Myron, "Daylight's a burnin'," he says, echoing Myron's favorite saying.

Myron cackles, "Yes it is, my boy, yes it is. Why ya in such a dad gum hurry?" he asks.

A soft voice from inside the room says, "He's met some little filly, Pop, and can't wait to see her again."

79

"Thought it must be something like that," Myron snorts and turns back to Clyde. "Ain't seen ya this worked-up since the last time ya rode. Be careful, young man. Women will do that to ya; they'll make ya do things you never dreamed of doing."

"Now, Dad," Audra shouts, "don't you go ruining it for him, just because you haven't got anyone you can drool over."

"Now how do you know that?" he demands. "You're not always around, you know, with you drooling all over that there man of yours."

"Dad! Stop that right now," Audra pleads. Wanting to change the focus, she asks, "Dad, you got your eye on someone?

"I ain't tellin' ya. If I do, you'll find out soon enough," he says, giving Clyde a wink and smile.

Audra comes to the door and slaps him on the shoulder. "Dad!"

Clyde excuses himself. "I'll go see if Harold has pulled himself together yet."

"How's he doing?" Audra asks.

"Really sore," Clyde responds with concern. "I don't know how he's going to ride in the next one. I think he should just relax and wait for the last one. By the way, where is the last one?"

Myron starts to answer, but Audra interrupts, "Let's finish getting ready. We can talk later. I know you want to get a move on."

As she finishes, Harold walks up with bag in hand. "Everyone ready? Let's get moving."

✲ ✲ ✲

The sun has barely popped up over the horizon when Beth leaps from her bed, excited to be headed home. After getting herself presentable, she grabs her bag and stops in the doorway, panning the room for one last time, trying to remember all she can. *This has been great,* she thinks. *Didn't think so at first, but all's well that ends well, and this is ending up just fine.*

Conrad walks up behind her and places his hand on her shoulder. "You ready to go?" he asks.

"Just trying to absorb all I can. Thank you, Uncle Connie, for all you guys have done."

"The pleasure was all ours," he says as he picks up her bag. "Now go home and make us proud."

She puts her arms around his neck and says, "I love you."

"And we love you, too," he replies. "You're like our own daughter."

They make their way to the train station where Beth notices that the train has already arrived. As she steps onto the platform, the clerk hands her the ticket to Chicago and asks, "You still have the one to New York, right?"

"Yes sir, right here in my purse," she assures him, patting the side of her purse.

"Good. Have a safe ride!" he says, then walks back to his office.

She takes a deep breath, fighting her emotions as she then turns to say her goodbyes. Conrad reaches into his pocket and pulls out some money. "Your aunt and I want you to have this. It's going to be a long ride, and we want you to enjoy it."

The conductor hollers, "All aboard!" as Connie hands her the money. She opens her purse and places it in her coin pouch, grabs her bag, and takes a couple steps toward the train. Having second thoughts, she drops her bag and purse and runs back to her aunt. They embrace, then with one arm still around Anna, Beth pulls Connie in close and whispers, "Thank you, I love you two very much."

With tears in their eyes, they both say, "We love you, too." She lets go, picks up her things, and scampers to the steps of the train.

As she boards, they holler, "Come back and see us," as they wave.

Beth is having a hard time getting everything on the train when it starts to move. She grabs the handrail; then out of nowhere comes a soldier who grabs her bag and asks, "May I help?"

She quickly looks up. "Thank you so much," she replies as she hands him her bag and offers her arm.

"It sure doesn't take her long to get noticed," Conrad chuckles. Anna slaps him on the shoulder as they continue to wave.

Finally on board, Beth quickly takes a window seat and leans out and hollers, "I'll miss you guys."

Observing the soldier standing next to her, Anna says, "I hope she'll be all right."

"Are you kidding me?" Conrad replies. "She has the Army looking out after her."

"I know," Anna confides, "that's what I'm afraid of." As they walk from the platform toward the diner, she laments, "This is going to be one long day."

Conrad thinks, *She's barely gone and I miss her already. Yep, it sure will be.*

✵ ✵ ✵

They finally pull into town after a long day of travel. The drive made Harold stiffer, so it takes him a while to get checked in at the motel. Clyde's biting at the bit to get to the diner.

"What's wrong with you?" Harold asks. "You got ants in your pants, Half-Pint?" That's one of Harold's favorite terms. When Clyde hears it, he knows he's being too squirmy. "If you want to go to the diner, go ahead," Harold encourages him. "I'll catch up with you later. Besides, Audra and Myron will want something to eat, too. Just take the truck and go."

"I don't need the truck; it's just down the street." He realizes how selfish he's being and says, "That's okay, I'll wait for ya. Anything I can do to help?"

"Just help me with my gear."

"I've been thinking," Clyde ventures.

"We could all be in trouble if you start doing that," Harold jokes.

"No, really," Clyde continues, "I had some time off to heal, and I think you should take this one off. Then you can be somewhat refreshed for the major one we have left."

"Thanks for suggesting it, but we really need the cash," Harold reminds him.

"Oh, we'll be fine. In fact, I plan on being in the money every day this weekend. So you relax. I know with you coaching me, I can win."

"We'll talk about it over dinner," Harold suggests. "Let's get Audra and Myron and head to that diner you've been telling us so much about."

"Sounds good to me," Clyde agrees as he opens the door.

They gather outside their room and take a stroll down Main Street. The town looks so different with banners hanging across the street and the store windows painted with rodeo scenes; it gives the whole town a new look. Clyde's enjoying the walk when he comes across a familiar store front, the bank. He slows to a stop as his mind races back to that dreadful morning.

Harold notices and asks, "You okay?" The words are no more out of his mouth when he notices the boards on the windows and the bank's name on the new doors. "Is this the place?"

"Yep! I was standing right about where you are when it happened."

Workers are busy inside trying to get it ready to reopen as Myron walks up to the door. "Sure is a mess in there. I thought you were stretching it a little, but by golly, you didn't tell us it was this bad."

"You guys ready?" Clyde asks. "I need to get away from here. It gives me the willies. Besides, I'm hungry."

"Hungry? For what, a little lovin'?" Myron asks, letting out a hoot.

"Dad, that's enough!" Audra protests. Harold chuckles and pats Myron on the back.

On the move again, it's only a short walk to the diner. Before Clyde opens the door he adjusts his collar and hat. Harold rolls his eyes at Audra and shakes his head. Clyde pulls the door open and motions with his arm for Audra to go ahead, but instead she pushes him through and follows closely behind with Myron and Harold. They scan the room looking for an open booth. Harold notices one in the far corner, grabs Audra's hand, and leads her to it. He steps aside for her to slide in before taking a seat next to her. Always wanting to be on the outside, Myron lets Clyde slide over before taking his seat.

Clyde cranes his neck trying to find Beth. *She must be in the back,* he thinks.

Anna walks up with four waters. "Afternoon, folks, or maybe I should say evening. I haven't seen you around these parts before; must be here for the rodeo."

"Yes ma'am, we are," Harold politely responds, "and we're as hungry as a bear. Got any suggestions?"

"We do have our specials for the day," Anna suggests. "Country fried steak, potato soup, or liver and onions. If none of those tickles your insides, the rest of the menu is there above the counter."

"Can you give us a minute?" Myron asks.

"Sure can; you take all the time you need. I'll be right back." She makes a quick turn and heads to the kitchen where Conrad's at the grill. "I think that young man that Beth liked is here," she whispers.

"What? The one who was arrested? What makes you think that?"

"I'm sure it's him." She stands on her tip-toes and peeks out through the pass-through window. "Come here and look! He's in that booth over there the one with three guys and a gal. They said they were with the rodeo!"

"Did you ask him?" Conrad inquires as he prepares a plate of liver and onions.

"No, I didn't know how to. What do I say, 'You that boy that my niece has a crush on?' You know I can't do that."

Conrad rolls his eyes. "No, you say. . . Oh, never mind. When I get done with their order I'll go over and ask him."

Anna smirks as she walks out front to take their order. *It worked again. When I don't want to do something, all I have to do is say something ridiculous, and then wait for Connie to jump in and do it. Do I know my man, or what?*

Harold asks Clyde, "Where's the cute little doll you were telling us about?"

"I don't see her," Clyde says as his face turns red. "She must be helping out in the back, or it could be her day off."

Harold winks at Audra. "You sure it wasn't your imagination?"

Audra shakes her head and mouths, "Stop it".

Naturally, Harold ignores her. "You know they say when people get stressed, they can make things look better than what they really are. Maybe it's our waitress."

Clyde shakes his head and lowers his chin to his chest. "Come on, she's old enough to be my mom." Clyde no more gets that out of his mouth when Anna walks up. *I hope she didn't hear that,* he thinks.

"Are you ready to order?" she asks.

"I think so," Harold responds. "Audra, why don't you go first?"

Anna takes their orders and walks away. When she's out of range, Harold asks, "Why don't you ask her?"

"Nah, that's okay. She's around here somewhere," Clyde assures himself.

It's not long before Anna brings their food, with Conrad following close behind. As she places the plates on the table, Conrad asks Clyde, "Aren't you that young man who ran into some trouble here a while back?"

"Yes, sir, that's me," Clyde tentatively responds. "Guess you could say I'm a little bit famous for all the wrong reasons." This brings a chuckle from the group. "But I'm looking to change that this weekend."

"Oh yeah? How's that?" Conrad asks.

"By the way I ride," Clyde says as he looks up from his food. He introduces the others at the table, and then says, "Now I have a question for you."

"Go ahead, shoot," Conrad answers. "That may not have been the best choice of words."

Clyde smirks. "I'm wondering . . .is this Beth's day off?"

"Oh no, she left on the train this morning, going home," Conrad answers.

Clyde's countenance changes immediately. "Oh, thanks," he stammers before he takes another bite.

Seeing his disappointment, and not knowing what else to say, Conrad excuses himself. "Well, I'd better get back to the kitchen. Nice meeting you folks. We'll be there to watch."

"Okay, it was nice seeing you again," Clyde says while the others nod.

He hurries to the kitchen where Anna's slicing pies. "Did you see the look on that young man's face when I told him that Beth had left this morning?"

"Yes, I feel so sorry for him. I wish there was something we could do," Anna remarks.

"That would be nice, but I can't think of anything."

Anna snaps her fingers. "I have an idea."

"Yeah, what's that?" Conrad asks.

"Before Beth left, she baked these peach pies, right?"

"Yeah, so?"

"What if we give them a free dessert?" Anna suggests. "We can tell him that Beth made it, and we're sure she would want him to have one."

"That sounds pretty corny to me," Conrad snickers, "but if you think they'd like it, why not?"

Anna picks up a pie and carries it to their table as Conrad watches from the pass-through window. She sets it down in the middle of the table and says, "We want to do something special for you guys." Smiling at Clyde, she adds, "Beth baked some pies before she left, and I'm sure if she were here she'd want you to have one, so this is on the house."

Before Clyde can say anything, Harold jumps in, "Thank you so much; it's very kind of you. I love pie, so I'm sure we'll enjoy it." Myron and Audra nod in agreement.

Clyde puts his fork down and asks, "Is it peach?"

"Yes, it is! How did you know?"

Grinning, he says, "I told her peach was my favorite."

"Well then, you should really enjoy it," Anna adds with a grin.

They each take a hearty piece; well, all except Audra, and it's not long before the pie is devoured. They pay their tab and head back toward the motel, walking slower on the way back than on their way there. Clyde's pretty quiet, looking into the store windows as they go. The others discuss how good the dessert was and the upcoming rodeo.

A block away from the motel, Harold allows Myron and Audra to walk ahead and lingers back with Clyde. He puts his arm on Clyde's shoulder and inquires, "Hey, Half-Pint, you doin' okay?"

"I really don't want to talk about it. I need to just focus on my rides. I told you I was going to ride like you've never seen before, and I mean it. Nothin' is getting in my way."

Audra overhears Clyde, and, when they reach her room, she winks and mouths to Harold, "See you later."

He mouths back, "Okay."

Without saying goodnight or anything, Clyde goes straight to his room. He flings the door open, takes his hat off, and slings it to the other side of the room where it just happens to land on the dresser drawers in the corner.

Harold laughs, "Hey, nice shot there, Half-Pint."

Clyde looks up and snickers, "Yeah, I guess." He flops down on the bed, fluffs up his pillow, and leans back against the wall.

Harold walks between the beds and sits on the edge of his. "Hey, I know you're disappointed. I would be too, but ya hardly knew her. There's goin' to be a time when someone comes along that will make ya feel special. So don't take it so hard." As he waits for Clyde to respond, he thinks. *Just like Audra does for me. There have been others, but this girl makes my ticker tick.*

"I thought she was the one," Clyde sighs as he sits up. "We could talk so easily. I thought she was that special someone."

"Partner, you're still a young whipper-snapper with a lot of days in front of ya. She won't be the last one to grab hold of your insides and turn them every which way but loose."

"But . . ."

"No buts," Harold interrupts. "You need to listen up. This is the first time a little filly has gotten to ya. Now you can either focus on what could be or on what will be. I suggest you get your head together and forget about her for now. You're going to get on the back of a big angry beast tomorrow, and you better have your full concentration or you may not come out alive. Understand?"

"Yeah, I guess you're right," Clyde reluctantly agrees.

"Besides," Harold continues, "I'm taking the weekend off. We need for you to pull your weight around here and make some money. You've been loafing."

"You're not going to ride?" Clyde shrieks as he jumps to his feet. "Harold, I think that's smart, the way you're walking, or should I say limping around. That's a wise decision. Okay, let's get some sleep; I want to get an early start."

Laughing, Harold says, "You hit the sack; Audra and I are going on a walk. See you in the morning!"

"Okay, partner, see ya in the morning," Clyde says, thinking, *This is the first time Harold has trusted me to make some money. I can't let him down.*

✵ ✵ ✵

Mr. Goldberg heads to the bullpens early Sunday morning. He doesn't usually stay on the circuit this long, but since they're short on help, he needs to. He looks forward to being home in a couple of weeks.

On his way, he passes a small tent. He knows what goes on in there. They have it each Sunday a religious service for those in the rodeo. Anyone's invited, but he never takes the time. Besides, he's Jewish.

As he passes, the preacher catches his attention with something he says, so he stops just outside the entrance to listen. Mr. G recognizes the scripture he's preaching on; it's out of Isaiah. *That's different,* he thinks. *I wonder why he's preaching from there.* Mr. G knows the Old Testament pretty well, so he's intrigued about what this old pastor has to say. He slowly moves the flap of the tent back and slips into the back row.

"There are more than 300 Messianic prophecies in the Old Testament that reveal the identity of the Messiah," the preacher shares. "For example; where He'd be born, when He'd live; how He'd die, and *why* He'd die. In fact, it says He would be rejected by His own people."

Then he begins to preach from Isaiah 53. Sam thinks, *This guy is doing a great job teaching this passage. It's my favorite one because it describes our coming Messiah and some of the things He will go through. I've heard this taught before, and he's pretty good for a non-Jew. I'm impressed!*

Then the message takes a turn that Sam doesn't see coming. The pastor jumps to the New Testament and begins to show how the prophecies from Isaiah are fulfilled in the New Testament.

Then he does the unthinkable, "Yeshua fulfills these prophecies, written hundreds of years before He was ever born, in such detail. There are objective proofs of His Messiahship and the supernatural nature of Scripture."

Most Jews have a hard time with that name, *Jesus*, but by this time, Sam is so enamored with the pastor that he hangs on to his every word. He's heard about this Jesus before but never really allowed himself to listen. The pastor turns to Jeremiah 31:31-33 for further confirmation and puts it together so clearly. He makes it easy to understand and accept. As he closes his teaching, he asks if anyone would like to ask Christ into their life. Without even thinking, Sam walks down the short aisle and stands before the pastor with tears in his eyes. "I'm a Jew and I have never had Jesus presented to me like that before. I believe in the prophecy, so how can I not accept Him?"

The pastor smiles and places his hand on Sam's shoulder. "I'm Pastor Richter and I'm also Jewish. Greetings, my Jewish brother and soon-to-be brother in the Lord!" He leads Sam in a short prayer asking God to forgive him of his sins. Then they shake hands and Pastor Richter hands Sam a Bible. He accepts it, and heads on over to the bullpens.

Chapter 9
MAKING DEALS

The girls have gone for a walk, and Dorris is pacing. She knows the rodeo is coming soon and, if she's right, Clyde will be in town to ride. *How could I be so foolish in keeping this from the girls? What was I thinking? That he'd never come back? What am I going to do? I guess I'll get everyone together and have a talk. That sounds good, but when? Let's see, there's no sense in doing it too early; then the girls will have time to think about it. I know, I'll do it the night before he gets here. That will work out best for all.* She takes a deep breath and forces a smile. *I still have another week or so.*

Her thoughts are interrupted when she hears someone step up on the porch. She can tell it's Jim by his heavy walk. Before he knocks, she swings the door open. He takes a step back and laughs, "Guess I'm not one who can sneak up on people, huh?"

"Not with those heavy cowboy boots on," she explains. "It's early in the day for you to drop by; have something special on your mind?"

"You could say that," Jim hesitates.

She waits a second before she asks, "Well? You have something to say?"

"Sorry, I was just admiring your beauty," he says, looking off into space.

She's not sure if he's telling the truth or what, but decides not to pursue it.

"I was wondering," he continues, "if you'd like to take a walk in the park. We haven't done that for a while."

"Jim, I can't recall ever going for a walk in the park with you."

Jim chuckles, "Guess you're right. Then let me rephrase that; how about our first walk in the park?"

Dorris vacillates, then grabs a shawl and wraps it around her shoulders. "I thought you'd never ask."

✲ ✲ ✲

It's the middle of the night when Al's awakened by sharp pains shooting between his shoulder blades. He moves around trying to get comfortable, but nothing is working. He finally gets up and soaks in a hot tub. As he lies there, he thinks, *I must have pulled a muscle today when I was helping Red in his garden. It'll go away in a couple days. I'll just have to be more careful when I'm doing things like that; after all, I'm not getting any younger.*

A couple days go by, and, while the pain has subsided some, it's still there and the cough he thought he had gotten rid of has returned. He has dinner planned with Red but decides he'll have to cancel. He grabs the phone, calls the WD, and tells his manager to relay the message on to Red.

✲ ✲ ✲

Pastor Red wanders over to the WD for his weekly dinner meeting with Al. As he enters the big double doors, he notices that Al's not in his normal spot. One of the workers walks up and says, "Evening, Pastor. You looking for the boss?"

"Yeah, it's our night to have dinner," Red replies.

"I haven't seen him not for a couple of days now. Heard he wasn't feeling well and decided to stay out at the ranch."

"Not feeling well?" Red inquires. "Do you know what's wrong with him?"

The manager spots Red and hollers, "Evening, Pastor! Sorry I didn't see you come in."

"That's okay," Red acknowledges. "Your worker here was saying something about Al not feeling well?"

"Yeah, he called a few minutes ago and told me to apologize for him, but he's not feeling up to coming in tonight."

"Did he say what was wrong?" Red asks.

"No, not really; you know how he hates to go see Doc. It ain't like him to stay away this long."

"What do you mean 'this long'?" Red inquires.

"He hasn't been in for quite a few days now, but I figure he's a big boy; he can take care of himself. I have enough worries keeping this place afloat."

"I think I'll run out to the ranch and see how he's doing. You think the guards will let me on?"

"From what I've heard, they have strict instructions that anytime you come out, whether he's there or not, they're supposed to. I can guarantee you there won't be any problems." The manager turns to go, and adds, "Oh, one more thing. Tell him that Benny called looking for him today and he didn't sound too happy, either."

"Will do," Red says with a smile, "Thanks for the info. See you later."

"Okay, let me know how the big man's doing," he hollers as Red walks out the door.

☆ ☆ ☆

Clyde talks to the bulls, as he always does before he rides. When a shove comes from behind, he glances over his shoulder and all he sees is a horse standing there. He ignores it until it happens again. Then he turns and grabs it by the bit, looks into its eyes, and stops. "Warrior? Is that you?" he asks. Once again the horse brushes up against him with his nose, and Clyde puts his arms around his neck.

"Hey sonny! What cha doin' with my horse?" a cowboy yells as he walks up.

Clyde rubs his hand between Warrior's eyes as he explains, "Well, Warrior here was mine before he was yours. Where'd ya get 'im from?"

"From some guy who had a ranch west of here. How'd ya know his name?"

"I told ya; he was mine before he was yours. He's the offspring of my dad's horse. When my dad died, he left me Warrior. It's a long story, but it's good to see someone's takin' good care of 'im." As they talk, Clyde hears someone call his name.

"Clyde, is that you?" He turns to see Sam Goldberg standing right behind him. "What's going on? How have you been?"

"Oh, I'm fine, Mr. G. I was just talking here with . . . sorry, I didn't catch your name."

"It's Ernie," he replies, extending his hand.

"Well Ernie, I'm Clyde and this is Mr. G. He raises bulls for the rodeo."

"Glad to meet you two," Ernie acknowledges.

"And who is this?" Sam asks, stroking Warrior's mane.

"Don't know if you remember," Clyde says, "but this is Warrior, the horse Pop left me."

"Oh yeah, I remember." Sam recalls the conversation he and Al had about one of Al's regrets being getting rid of Clyde's horse.

"I gotta go check out the bulls," Clyde says, "so if you don't mind, I'll excuse myself."

"Go right ahead," Sam responds.

Clyde clears his throat and says, "Hey, Cowboy, it was great meeting ya. Take good care of Warrior."

"Sure will. Hope to see ya later."

Sam hollers, "I'll catch up with you in a minute." Clyde waves in acknowledgment and Sam notices Clyde take his handkerchief from his back pocket and blow his nose. Once he's out of earshot, Sam asks the cowboy, "How much for the horse?"

"What? Sorry, sir, but he's not for sale."

"Listen, I'll make you a great deal."

"Mister, I need a good horse. This is my livelihood and together we've won a lot of money."

"I want to explain something; this young man lost his dad when he was eight, and this horse was going to be his birthday present from his him. On the day of his dad's funeral, the former owner of the ranch gave him this horse. At eleven, he had to leave home and leave the horse behind. He broke this horse and worked with him for almost two years. I want to buy him as a present. Now, how much for the horse?" Sam demands, staring at the cowboy.

Uncomfortable, the cowboy doesn't know what to say. "I don't know Mister," he finally mumbles.

Being the good business man that he is, Sam knows he has him on the ropes. He remembers the old adage, "The first one who speaks loses." *If that's true, Cowboy,* he thinks, *you just lost.*

"Tell ya what," Sam proposes, "the next stop on the circuit is my hometown. You ride in that rodeo and when it's over, you meet me at my ranch east of town. I'll pay you whatever you want and let you pick any horse you want from my herd. Deal?"

"Mister, you must really want this horse. I can take you to the cleaners if I want to."

"You sure could, young fella, but that's something you'll have to live with the rest of your life. We got a deal?"

"You got yourself a deal, Mister. You're a good businessman, but a better human being, doing this and not getting anything out of it."

"Oh, I'm getting plenty out of it. Let's take a walk and I'll explain." As they walk away, Sam shares his experience in Cowboy Church, how doing something like this for Clyde is nothing compared to the price Jesus paid for us.

Over at the pens, Clyde looks over the bulls he's drawn. "Checking out your rides?" Sam asks as he catches up with him.

"Yes, sir," Clyde answers. "Thought I'd take a look at some of the new ones I haven't seen before."

"You always were on top of things," Sam smirks.

"I try to be. I believe that to be the best at anything, you have to learn all you can about your opponent and study hard what cha doin'."

"And I don't mind saying you're living proof of that," Sam acknowledges. "You've been very successful in a short period of time. Congratulations!"

"Thanks, Mister—uh, I mean Sam," Clyde awkwardly acknowledges.

As they talk, Clyde bends over to get a closer look at the bull's eyes. "I bet you're excited," Sam observes.

"Yeah, you could say that. It's been a few weeks since I've ridden." Clyde responds enthusiastically. "I can't wait to get back on top of one of these!"

"I bet, but that's not what I meant," Sam says, puzzled. "I was talking about having the opportunity to ride in front of your friends and family next week."

"What? Ya mean riding at home?" Clyde asks as he stands upright.

"You didn't know? Next week is the county rodeo. It sure will be nice to be back home. I'm inviting you and Harold to stay out at my place, okay?"

Clyde can't believe it. *Why didn't Harold tell me?* he wonders.

Sam notices Clyde's expression change. "You okay?" he asks.

"Oh, yeah," he assures him, "I'm fine, but I gotta run." He takes off at a quick pace, then hollers back, "It was nice seeing you, Mister G—I mean Sam. I'll tell Harold about staying at your place."

Sam waves as he wonders what just happened.

Clyde heads straight to their room to speak to Harold. When he doesn't find him there, he knocks on Myron's door. Still unable to stir anyone, he figures there is only one more place they can be; the diner. He double times it there, and slows his pace before opening the front door. Quickly scanning the room, he sees them sitting in the back corner talking to Anna.

Taking a deep breath, he saunters up and interrupts, "Excuse me! Why didn't you tell me next week's rodeo is back home?"

Taken back by Clyde's rudeness, Harold answers, "Didn't want ya to think about it until next week. I thought knowing about it would be a distraction, and I wanted this rodeo to be behind ya."

Anna steps back and excuses herself. Visibly upset, Clyde continues, "That's fine! You don't have enough faith in me to handle that? I'll tell you what; it's not goin' to distract me because I ain't goin'."

"What cha mean, you ain't goin'?" Harold asks as he scoots his chair back.

"Just what I said; I ain't goin' home. I'm stayin' right here. What makes you think I'd go someplace where no one wants me?"

Harold stands up and puts his hand on Clyde's shoulder. "I'm sorry for not having more faith in you. Pull up a chair and let's talk about it." Clyde grabs a chair, slides it between his legs, and sits cowboy style. "All I ask is for you to think about it," Harold tries to reason. "How are you going to stay here? You know what happened last time you stopped here."

"Harold, I can't go back there!" Clyde insists. "My family doesn't want anything to do with me! It's too hard." He puts his chin on the back of the chair and stares at his boots. "I'll make you a deal. I'll ride like a wild man this weekend. If I earn enough for you to go and for me to stay here, then I'm staying here. If not, I'll go, too."

Anna overhears the conversation as she wipes the counter and sets down her bar towel. "If you'd like, you could stay with Conrad and me. We have the spare room, now that Beth's gone."

Clyde looks over his shoulder. "Ma'am, I couldn't impose on you that way."

"It wouldn't be a problem," Anna rebuts, "but if you'd like, you can help out around here. I remember how much help you were the last time."

"You'd really let me do that?" Clyde asks, "In that case, you got yourself a deal." He extends his hand and Anna smiles as she shakes it.

"I don't know, Clyde," Harold says, "I think you're making a big mistake. In times like this you have to face your skeletons. I think you're making way too much of this."

Clyde extends his hand to Harold. "Is it a deal or not?"

"Alright, if that's the way you want it, but you have to ride like a madman."

"Deal!" Clyde grabs Harold's hand. "Goodnight to all of you. I have to get my rest for this weekend. You're going to see something you've never seen before."

✫ ✫ ✫

Not getting any better, Al summons one of his guards to pull the car around front. As he does, another escorts him slowly down the steps to the car. Al hates to be chauffeured, but realizes he doesn't have the strength to drive himself; just getting to the car saps his energy.

While Al lies in the backseat, the driver pulls away from the house. As he exits the gate, they see a car coming up the road and Al instructs the driver to pull over and wait for it to pass. As the car pulls up alongside, Al recognizes it and rolls down his window.

"Where are you headed?" Red asks.

"To town, to see Doc," Al whispers.

Red gets out and walks over to the car. "Al, you look like . . . Sam notices Clyde's expression change. Well, let me say, not so good; and you sound even worse. Why don't you go on back inside and I'll go fetch Doc?" Red suggests.

"I thought it would be good to get out, but getting to the car exhausted me."

"Take him back inside," Red tells the driver. "I'm going to get the doctor." As Red's taillights disappear in the distance, Al asks his guard to help him upstairs.

The drive is short. He parks out front and runs into Doc's office. "Could you tell Doc I'm here, please?"

The receptionist glances up from her magazine. "Afternoon, Pastor. I hate to be the one to tell you, but the doctor's not in; he just left for the Carpenter's place. You know, she's ready to deliver at anytime!"

"Oh, that's right." He thanks her for the information and decides to follow him. As he drives north out of town, he checks his fuel gauge and realizes he needs some. Thank goodness, Buck's fuel stop is just down the road.

He pulls in over the bell hose and hears it go off in the office. Martin looks up and waves. It doesn't take him long to stop what he's doing and make a beeline to the car. "What can I do for you, Pastor?"

"Why don't you fill it up, Martin," Red requests.

"Sure enough, I'll check the oil and tires, too."

"You can if you do it quickly, but I'm in a hurry. I have to go to the Carpenter's; heard Doc was headed that way."

"You looking for Doc?" Martin asks as he checks the tires. "He was just here, oh, 'bout an hour ago and he did say he was headed to the Carpenter's."

"You said about an hour ago?"

Martin looks up. "Yep, about that, give or take ten minutes."

Knowing where the Carpenters live, Red calculates about how soon Doc could be back. "Did he say anything about how long he'd be there?" he asks.

"By the way he was talkin', I think he pretty much thought he was going to be there a while," Martin responds.

"Can you put that on my tab?" Red requests.

"Will do, Pastor," Martin replies. "Take it easy; that road goin' out there ain't the best," he warns as Red starts his car.

"Thanks! Have a good evening and say 'hi' to Ruthie for me."

"Will do. See ya later!" Martin calls out as Red drives away.

He drives for about ten minutes, and then takes a left off the main highway onto a gravel road. It's not long before the road narrows and begins a steady climb. When the car begins to lug, Red downshifts to a lower gear, and, with the engine at a high pitch, prays he doesn't meet another car. The road is so narrow that if he does, one or the other will have to back up to allow the other to pass. He's only traveled this road once before and doesn't care for it at all; too many sharp turns for his liking. As he approaches each curve he slows down and honks. When he finally reaches the top, he begins his descent into a small valley where the Carpenters live. Now, with the more normal hum of the engine, Red hears another vehicle's engine roar from the climb, and then a honk. He pulls over as far as he can and stops about 20 yards before the turn.

The car carefully maneuvers around the corner, and, sure enough, it's Doc. Red rolls down his window and waves him down.

He slows to a stop and pokes his head out the window. "Red, what are you doing all the way out here?"

"Looking for you," Red hollers back. "I need you to come to Al's with me."

"Is he okay?" Doc asks. "I haven't seen him in a while."

"I hope so. I went out to see him and he was on his way to see you," Red explains.

"Al was coming to see me?" Doc exclaims. "That's not like him; he avoids me like the plague."

"Then you'll go?"

"By all means. Whenever someone like Al wants to see me, I don't waste any time getting there."

Go ahead and back up to that turnout and I'll get by and head to the office. There's a larger turnout just down the hill; you can turn around there. Pick me up at the office."

"Will do. See you there." Red backs up, and heads down the hill to turn around.

Doc hurries back to his office and grabs a few things he may need.

Red walks in just a few minutes behind him. "Need any help?"

"I think I have everything," Doc replies. "Let's go." He locks the office door and they climb into Red's car and head out. Doc can't believe it; he was there when Elmer breathed his last; then again when Walter died, and now he's going to see someone else there who's not feeling well. He thinks, *It seems like every time I go out to this place, something bad happens. I sure am glad I'm with a man of God.*

✧ ✧ ✧

Still upset with Harold, Clyde keeps his promise; he rides like a man possessed. Harold can't believe what he's seeing. Over the next few days Clyde spends much of his downtime alone; each night he's in bed early while Audra, and Harold spend the evenings with friends in the local taverns.

It pays off; Clyde wins the overall competition hands down and takes top honors all three days. The Beckers are there each night and can see why Beth was so enamored with this young man.

After closing ceremonies, Clyde's behind the chutes putting his gear away when someone taps him on the shoulder and he turns. "Mr. G— I mean Sam— it's good to see you again."

"Congratulations, Clyde," he says. "I can't ever recall seeing a performance like that. You make all of us homefolk proud. I wanted to remind you about staying out at my place next week."

"Thanks Sam, but I won't be coming. I don't want to be where I'm not wanted."

"What? After, what you just did? Son, I think you're making a big mistake. Come on back and mend those fences," Sam pleads.

"Mend the fences?" Clyde asks, unfamiliar with the expression.

Laughing, Sam answers, "Sorry. What I mean is, patch things up with the family. You can't ignore it forever."

"Oh, I see what you mean," Clyde says, chuckling. "I don't think they're too interested in mending any fences. They pretty much closed the door the last time I was there."

"You have to make up your own mind, but if you want some advice, I think you're making a big mistake. Stand up and be a man. Well, I have to run. Hope to see you next week."

"Thanks, Sam. I'll see you later," Clyde replies as he waves goodbye.

He finishes packing and catches up with Audra and Harold as they're leaving the chute area. They walk along together to the outside gate where Anna and Conrad are waiting.

"You can really ride those bulls, young man," Conrad acknowledges.

"I agree," Anna says in her tiny shrill voice, "I didn't think you had a chance, but you stuck on them like glue on a stick."

"Thanks," Clyde responds, embarrassed. "It's something I've always been able to do."

"You haven't changed your mind about staying with us, have you?" Conrad inquires.

"Nope, not all," Clyde answers as he looks at Harold. "You did say I can work for my room and board, right?"

"You don't have to," Conrad suggests, "but if you'd like to, you may."

"You take this," Clyde says to Harold as he pulls out his winnings from his pocket. "I'm going to keep a few bucks for myself."

"Clyde, you need to come with us," Harold commands. "You're on a roll. Don't worry about what others say. They probably don't have the story right, anyway."

Clyde's eyes fill with tears. "Harold, I just can't. You didn't see the hate for me that my sister had in her eyes just a few weeks back. I just can't."

Seeing how hurt he is, Harold backs off. "Okay, suit yourself. We're leaving first thing in the morning. I want to get back and take a look around."

"Good luck with that. I told you they wouldn't let me on the property.

"I just want to make sure the Livingstons are okay," Harold reassures Clyde.

"We'll drop him by the diner in the morning, if that's okay," Harold tells the Beckers. "We're going to celebrate tonight. This young man is going to be one of the best."

"That's fine; that will give us time to get the room ready," Anna says.

"See you in the morning!" Clyde calls out.

Chapter 10
STAYING BEHIND

The early morning sun peeks through the clouds as the rain slows to a drizzle, accompanied by the smell of fresh air. The group pulls up to the diner to drop off Clyde just as Anna's unlocking the front door. She calls out, "My Connie's fixing up some breakfast; you can't travel on an empty stomach. Now get out of those vehicles and get inside. It's on the house."

She doesn't have to say it twice. Clyde grabs his bag, Harold and Myron shut off their motors, and they all head into the Corner Café.

They make their way to the corner table that Anna is setting up and take a seat as Conrad exits the kitchen with a feast fit for a king. He places a platter stacked with hot cakes in the middle of the table, and then another one heaped with scrambled eggs. Anna brings out a big bowl of grits, along with a plate filled with bacon and sausage.

As they pass the food, Harold shares his excitement about going back to the place he calls *home*. Clyde doesn't say much, just listens, taking it all in and enjoying this wonderful meal.

They eat until they can't eat any more, and, with the final cup of coffee Harold announces, "I hate to break up a great party, but we best be hitting the road. We want to get there before the sun goes down."

Clyde looks at Audra and chimes in as Myron says, "Daylight's a burnin'," mimicking him perfectly. Audra shakes her head and laughs while elbowing Harold in the ribs. Myron, not knowing what's going on, looks at Clyde and catches the last word. He pushes Clyde so hard that he almost falls off his chair. Clyde catches himself, and stands up and begins to clear the table.

Hearing the commotion, Anna walks up and takes the plates from him. "You let that go. Your shift hasn't started yet."

"I might as well get used to it," Clyde teases.

Harold walks up behind him and puts him in a headlock, then rubs his head with his knuckles. "Take care of yourself, Half-Pint. See you in a week."

"You make sure you win us some money," Clyde threatens, "or I may just stay right here."

Everyone laughs because they know how much Clyde loves to ride. They say their goodbyes and Clyde watches out the window as they drive away, thinking, *I should have gone. That darn Sara; it's all her fault. Oh well, maybe someday I can move forward with my family. Better clear off the table.*

✲ ✲ ✲

With that rodeo over, Sam packs up and heads out of town. To get home, he drives through the night and is relieved to finally be heading down his long driveway. He pulls in next to the bull corrals as the cowhands are stirring and instructs them on what needs to be done before heading in to get a few hours of shut-eye.

The town is buzzing with excitement; the rodeo is helping everyone forget about world events for a while. Through the years they've had a small local rodeo, but this year it's going to be a county wide event with hundreds coming from throughout Rio Grande County. Sam is one of the main organizers, and his wife is leading the committee for the town celebration.

It's late afternoon before Sam wakes up and decides to run to town to pick up a few things. He makes his way to the store where Jim and Dorris are standing outside talking. He tips his hat as he passes by and greets them with "Afternoon."

"Afternoon, Sam," Jim says. "It's good to have you home. How was last week's rodeo?"

"It was fine, but it's sure nice to be home." He takes a few steps into the store before it dawns on him to tell Dorris about Clyde. "Oh, Dorris, I watched Clyde ride last week and boy is he good! You should be very proud."

Anxious to hear more, Dorris steps a bit closer. "Sounds like his dad. Did he happen to say when he's coming into town?"

Sam stops. "I hate to be the one to tell you, but I don't think he's coming. He told me he doesn't want to be where he's not wanted."

"Did he say what he meant by that?" Dorris asks.

Now in a conversation he doesn't want to be in, Sam confesses, "Said something about the way he was treated last time he was here."

While disappointed, Dorris is relieved at the same time. She thinks, *I'm glad Sam told me that. I was about to ask Jim to help me tell the girls the truth. Whew, what a relief! Okay, back to life. Sure would have been nice to see him, though. Oh well, I can't focus on what's not going to happen. We'll have a fun time at the rodeo this weekend.*

"He's right; he didn't get a very warm welcome the last time he was here," Dorris quickly adds. "Thanks for the info, Sam. Got to run. See you at the rodeo." She says goodbye to Jim and scurries down the street toward home.

Sam makes his way into the hardware store thinking, *That sure was an odd response. I thought she would have been upset about not seeing a son she hasn't seen for a few years. Sometimes I can't figure people out. Oh well, that's her problem; I don't need to spend any more time thinking about it.*

☆ ☆ ☆

Once Clyde gets in the swing of the diner business, it becomes pretty routine. The first day drags on, but the Beckers make him feel right at home. The day winds down, they close up, and within the hour, they're relaxing at home. Anna shows Clyde his room. When he goes back to the main room, Conrad is sitting next to their RCA floor model console radio, trying to adjust the station. He motions for Clyde to pull up a chair. "It's almost time for the 'Abbott and Costello Show'," Conrad informs him as Clyde sits down.

The reception isn't the best and the station fades in and out. Clyde closely examines this beautiful piece of furniture; a gorgeous cabinet about three and one half-feet tall with a walnut veneer finish. He can see the outline of the speaker behind the woven light brown, wavy fabric covers, just below the radio's control knobs. When the broadcast begins Conrad leans back in his chair while Anna relaxes on the couch.

Clyde wants to ask about Beth, but doesn't want to interrupt the show. At the same time, Anna pays little attention to the radio, being more curious about Clyde's thoughts about Beth. She wants to broach the subject, but doesn't quite know how.

Conrad turns off the radio when the program's over and one look at Anna tells him she's up to something, so he decides to head it off at the pass. "Can I see you for a second in the other room, please, Anna?" he requests.

They get up at the same time and go into the kitchen. "What are you thinking?" he asks.

"What do you mean?" Anna coyly responds.

"Don't give me that. You have that look on your face," Conrad warns.

"Oh, I was just going to ask him if he enjoyed his time with Beth," she says with a smirk.

"Now Anna, if he wants to know about her, let him do the asking. Don't butt in; you might make him uncomfortable." She knows he's right, but she thinks, *I'll get Clyde by himself sometime this week and find out.*

He returns to the living room and flicks the radio back on just as the phone rings. Only a few steps away, Anna picks it up. "Hello, this is Anna."

"Anna!" a cheery voice says. "You have a long-distance call from New York. Go ahead, caller."

"Auntie, this is Beth. Can you hear me?"

"Oh, Elizabeth, it's great to hear your voice!" Anna exclaims. "We've been praying you got home all right."

"I'm sorry for not calling sooner," Beth apologizes, "but I got stuck in Chicago for a while and was late getting home."

"Well, we're just happy you made it home safely," Anna assures her, waving to get Conrad's attention.

"Auntie, I was pretty much protected," she giggles. "There were soldiers all over the place."

Conrad notices Anna motioning with her arms and turns down the radio. When he hears that it's Beth, he walks over and stands next to her. Hearing the dialog, Clyde decides to give them some privacy and goes off to his room. Like most ladies, Anna's getting every detail of the trip while Conrad waits patiently.

"That's enough," he finally says, "let me say 'hi'." Anna tries to hand him the receiver, but the cord's not long enough, so he steps in front of her to talk into the mouthpiece.

He bends over and hollers, "Beth, can you hear me?"

"Yes, Uncle," she replies, "but you don't have to holler; we have a real good connection this time."

Lowering his voice, he asks about the family.

Anna glances around and notices that Clyde's gone. *I wish he was here*, she thinks. *I'd give him the phone so he could talk to her. Wait, that's right, I didn't tell her he's here.* Without thinking, she grabs the phone from Conrad and just about pulls it from the wall.

"Hey, what ya doing?" he hollers, "Are you crazy?"

"Forgot to tell her something," Anna replies. "Sounded like you were about done, anyway."

Conrad shakes his head as he walks back into the living room.

"Beth, you'll never guess who's here!" Anna exclaims.

"What?" Beth asks. "You already have another boarder? You sure didn't waste much time," she chuckles.

"He's only here for about a week, though," she adds.

"Did you say, 'he'?" Beth inquires.

"Yes, I did," Anna giggles.

"Let me think. Hmm . . . can't think of anyone out there that would need a room, especially a *he*," she contemplates. "The only he I met that didn't live there was . . . Auntie, it's not Clyde, is it?"

Anna begins to laugh. "Boy, do you have the Becker's instincts, or what? Yes, it's Clyde!"

"WHAT? He's really there with you guys? For how long? Oh darn, when did he show up?"

"Yep, he's staying in your room, but he'll be leaving in a week. He's even helping out in the diner. He rode in the rodeo here last week and didn't want to go to the next one. Oh, it's a long story. I'll write you a letter to fill you in. He showed up the afternoon you left."

"You mean I missed him by just a few hours?"

"Seems to be that way," Anna remarks.

"That's just my luck," Beth complains. "Those things always seem to happen to me. If it wasn't for bad luck, I wouldn't have any luck at all."

"Now you listen to me," Anna scolds. "It doesn't have anything to do with luck. People make their own luck. It just wasn't meant to be and you should be thankful for that, so keep your mind thinking right. You hear me?"

"I'm sorry, I hear you. Thank you, Auntie. I better get off. I love you guys, and please say 'hi' to Clyde for me."

Anna smiles. "Oh, I will be glad to. Write me soon! We love you. Goodbye."

✲ ✲ ✲

The road is lonely when you travel by yourself, and Harold is exhausted by the time they finally pull into town. All along the way, God seems to give His approval as the sky turns into another Colorado masterpiece. As he drives down Broadway, with Myron and Audra close behind, he slows down to enjoy the evening sky. The place looks pretty much the same. The only changes he recognizes have taken place at the Western Drake; a few new swirl designs around the balcony and a fresh coat of paint.

They'll be staying at a place a few blocks from the WD, one he's pretty familiar with. The owners always say hi when they see him and even tried to get him to take their daughter out.

They greet him and give him the best two rooms they have. Once they settle in their rooms, they meet in the lobby. "Let's get some grub," Myron suggests. "I'm so hungry; I could eat a bear."

"Would the place a couple blocks back work?" Harold asks.

"You mean the Western Drake? I think that was the name," Audra recalls.

"Yeah, the locals call it the WD. They've got great food and we can walk. I really need to stretch my legs."

"That sounds wonderful," Audra says. "If we hurry, we can enjoy what's left of that sunset on our way. It doesn't get much prettier than that. Is that okay with you, Pop?"

"Don't much care how we get there," Myron comments, "let's just get going. You two can enjoy the sunset or whatever along the way."

Harold grabs Audra's hand. "Better get a move on before your pop passes out or something." They both snicker as they head toward the WD.

While the couple's admiring the sunset, they fail to notice a truck pull across traffic and stop right next to them. The driver cranks down the window. "That's who I thought it was," he says. "Harold, when did you get into town?"

"Mr. G!" Harold exclaims as he approaches the truck. "We just got here and checked into the motel."

"Did Clyde come with ya?"

"Nope, I tried talking him into it, but he decided against it."

"That boy: I told him he had to bury the hatchet. He's still got some growing up to do."

Thinking this could be a while, Myron butts in, "Excuse me, Harold, Audra and I are heading in. Want us to order something for you?"

"Sure, get me the special; it's always good."

"Okay, see you inside."

Audra let's go of Harold's hand. "See you in minute," she says with a wink and grabs hold of her dad's arm.

"Okay, I'll be right there," he says as he turns his attention back to Sam. "Now where were we?"

"I said Clyde needed to do some growing up."

"Yeah, he does, but we have to remember he's still a youngster. He got too old, too fast, and getting over that is going take some time."

"I guess you're right; that there boy has experienced too much, too soon. I hope and pray that you can teach him how to make good decisions," Sam implores.

"I think that's something each one of us has to do on our own. All we can do is be good examples to those around us and hope they recognize it. He's a good kid, you know."

"Oh yeah, he is, and he has a great future in front of him if he'll stay on the right path. You know the influences out there; they can surely sneak up and bite you when you're not looking," Sam warns.

"Yeah, ya can say that again! It happened to me," Harold confesses.

"Well, I don't want to keep you from your dinner. Did Clyde tell you that I had a place for you to stay?"

"Yeah, he mentioned it, but I thought with Myron and Audra it was best for us to stay in town. We thank ya for the offer, though!" Harold says.

"We could have accommodated all of you, you know. There's always next year, and I won't take no for an answer."

"Will do," Harold says, laughing. "I'd better be getting inside or I'll be eating a cold dinner."

"Just one last question before I let you go."

"What's that?"

"You going to ride bulls or saddle broncs this weekend?"

"Whenever Clyde's not around," Harold grins, "I ride the bulls."

As Harold walks away, Sam hollers, "See you later," then rolls up his window and drives away.

✵ ✵ ✵

Clyde walks out of his room as Anna hangs up. Trying to bait him into a conversation, she asks, "Everything okay?"

"Yes ma'am, just wanted to give you guys some privacy," he sheepishly replies.

"You didn't have to do that; it was only Beth," she offers, still trying to get him to ask about her.

Conrad walks into the room as Anna tells Clyde, "Beth wanted me to say 'hi' for her."

Surprised, Clyde asks, "She remembered me and wanted to say 'hi'?"

"Oh yeah, she said she was sorry she missed you."

Smiling, Clyde asks Anna, "Are you guys related?"

She starts to answer as Conrad walks up behind her and puts his hands on her shoulders. "She's Conrad's brother's daughter; grew up on Long Island, in New York."

"Is that close to New York City?" Clyde inquires.

"About 60 miles east of it. Have you been there?" Conrad jumps in.

"No, but I've heard about it. That's where I want to go," Clyde answers.

"Why would a country boy like you want to go to a place like that?" Conrad asks.

"I got a couple reasons; I want to ride at a place called 'The Garden,' and Harold told me about some really tall building. Is that true?"

"What, the tall building?" Anna giggles. "You must be talking about the Empire State Building! Yeah, it's true, and it's really tall."

"Then you've seen it?" Clyde asks.

"Sure have. In fact, we've been to the top of it," Conrad states.

Amazed, Clyde asks, "You mean you can climb clear to the top?"

"Yes, you can, but there are elevators that take you there, too."

"An elevator? Wow, it must go pretty fast."

"Clyde, there's not just one elevator; there's sixty-four," Conrad explains.

"Sixty-four, all in one building?"

"Hard to believe, isn't it? You know, when you go there, I bet Beth would be glad to show it to you," Anna suggests. Conrad squeezes her shoulders as if to say, "Don't go any further."

"You really think she would?" Clyde asks.

"Oh, I'm sure she would. You made quite the impression on her, you know," Anna replies as Conrad squeezes a little tighter.

"Do you mind me asking you something, Mr. Becker?"

"What's that, Clyde? And please, call me Connie."

"Where did you grow up? Was it in New York? How did you get all the way out here? Sorry if that's being nosey."

Conrad leans his head back. "Now that's a long story. I'll tell you what; I'll start tonight, but finish later, if that's okay."

Anna rolls her eyes and thinks, *Clyde, you shouldn't have ever gotten him started on his family. He loves to tell their story. Oh well, I'll just sit back and correct him when he tells it wrong.*

"That's fine with me," Clyde agrees and scoots up on the couch, "I'm all ears."

Conrad clears his throat and begins, "Our family immigrated from Germany and landed on Ellis Island in the harbor of New York in the 1800s."

"Ellis Island? What's that?" Clyde asks.

"That's where people from other countries come if they want to settle in New York—mostly Europeans that flee for different reasons."

"It was originally named Castle Garden," Anna injects. "It's a small island in New York Harbor."

"New York is by the water?" Clyde asks, surprised.

"Yes," Conrad replies, "It's right on the water."

"So when I go to New York," Clyde continues, "I can see the ocean, too?"

"That's right, you'll see the Atlantic Ocean," Anna says, smiling.

"Holy cow, I can't wait. Sorry for interrupting. How did they get off the island?" Clyde inquires.

"You mean the Beckers?" Conrad asks.

"Yeah, they were stuck on that island."

"If didn't take long to be cleared to enter the United States," Conrad chuckles. "They settled in a place called Brooklyn; it's a borough of New York City. In the 1820s, a German neighborhood took shape and reached a peak population of around 750,000 by the turn of the century."

Clyde wanted to ask what a borough was, but thought *they'll think I'm a real dummy if I keep asking questions, so I'll just sit here and nod my head.*

"So were you born in Brooklyn?" he asks.

"Yep, our whole family was. Our parents came from the old country, though."

"Clyde," Anna jumps in, "that means Germany. That's what we call 'the old country'."

"Oh, okay. So Elizabeth was born in Brooklyn, too?" Clyde asks.

"Oh no. Crime started going up in the city, so our family, along with a lot of others, moved out to a place called Long Island. That's where little Beth was born."

"So you went from one island to another?"

"Yes, but this island was different. They had cities you could live in."

"How did your family make money?" Clyde inquires.

"From the time we arrived on Ellis Island, the family knew what we wanted to do," Conrad assures Clyde. "We would carry on the family tradition, taught to us by our parents, the art of baking. I remember waking up in the morning to the sweet aroma of baking breads."

"So that's how you started the diner," Clyde concludes.

"That's another story, for another time," Conrad explains.

"I have to stop you there," Anna says. "It's getting late and we can pick this up later. I'm tired."

Conrad agrees. "You're right. Goodnight, Clyde. See you in the morning."

Clyde stands up and heads to his room. "Goodnight," he answers, glancing over his shoulder.

✳ ✳ ✳

The guard sees Red coming and waves him through the ranch's front gate. As they pull in front of the house, Doc reaches into the backseat and grabs his bag. They make their way to the porch when the door swings open and the maid takes them to Al's room.

When she opens the door, there sits Al, leaning against the cherry wood headboard. "Yeah, Doc," Al wheezes as he coughs and hacks for a few seconds before he can catch his breath, "I guess it's good to see you," he says with a raspy voice.

"Evening, Al," Doc replies. "I just wish it was under better conditions."

Al nods. "Me too, Doc, me too," he acknowledges before he starts to cough again. When he regains his composure, he looks at Red and says, "Thanks for getting Doc."

"Think nothing of it. After all, that's what friends do," Red whispers, not wanting to speak out of turn. "Now just be quiet and do what he tells you."

"Why don't you tell me what's been going on?" Doc probes.

"Had this cough for a while now," Al begins, "can't seem to shake it. Just when I think it's gone, it comes back again."

Doc takes out his stethoscope, places it on Al's back, and tells him to take a deep breath. Al inhales as deeply as he can before coughing. When he's catches his breath, he whispers, "See what I mean?"

"Yep, I do," Doc answers. "When you can talk, what else?"

Al takes a moment to think. "Over the past few months, I don't seem to have the energy I used to. I know I'm not getting any younger, but when I try to do things around here or the WD, it doesn't take me long to get winded."

Doc raps his fingers along Al's rib cage, and then moves toward his back and taps just under his left arm. Al grunts and twitches.

"Did that hurt?" Doc asks.

"It's a little touchy. Must have pulled something the other day when I was helping Red."

Doc gently lifts Al's left arm, "Does that hurt?"

"Not really a hurt, more like discomfort."

"How high can you lift your arm?" Doc inquires.

"All the way," Al answers as he lifts his right arm.

Doc shakes his head. "Not that one, your left one."

"Not as high as my right one," Al laughs, "it's been a while since I've been able to."

"How long?" Doc asks.

"Oh, I'd say about six months or so. I pulled a muscle lifting some things at Maggie's. It's taken a while to heal."

"Looks like you've dropped some weight, too."

"Yeah, just haven't felt much like eating." Doc pulls some medication from his bag, along with a syringe. Al eyes the needle and asks, "What're you going to do with that thing?"

"Make you better!" Doc smiles. Then with a devilish look he says, "This is the part of my job I love the most."

Al rolls up his sleeve. "Oh no, that's not the area I need," Doc chuckles. "For quicker results, we need the other end."

"Ah Doc, just give it to me here," Al pleads as he points to his arm.

"Don't think so, Mister. You need to get over this as soon as possible. Red needs to be fed and he hasn't gone to the WD for dinner for a while now. Look how skinny he's getting! Just roll over on your side and take it like a man. It'll only take a second."

Al reluctantly rolls to his side and Doc quickly administers the medication. Then he reaches into his bag and pulls out a small bottle of pills and instructs Al how to take them. When Doc is through, Red steps in and places his hand on Al's head and begins to pray. Doc stops what he's doing, bows his head, and says "amen" when Red's done.

"I'll come back and check on you in a couple of days," Doc assures Al.

"Thanks, Doc, I think I'm feeling better already."

Doc grins. "Meet you down at the car, Red. I need to give the maid some instructions."

"Be right there," Red replies. "I'll come back tomorrow," he promises Al. "You do everything Doc told you to, okay?"

"Sure thing, my friend," he says as he yawns. "See you tomorrow. I'm getting a little tired, think I'll take a nap."

On their way back to town, neither one is very talkative. Red finally breaks the silence. "Everything okay? You seem a little quiet."

"I think so. I'm just running things through my head."

"Anything I can help with?" Red asks.

"Nope, don't think so, but I'll call you if I need you."

"Okay, sounds good to me," Red concludes as he drops Doc off at his office.

Chapter 11
FEELING RIGHT AT HOME

Harold wakes up early and takes a stroll downtown, stopping to admire the auditorium. He wonders how they got such a beautiful building built in such a small town. During the daytime, he notices more changes than he did last night. A few of the old buildings have new facelifts, and there are some concrete sidewalks and freshly paved roads. *It's amazing how you can be gone for a while* he thinks, *and when you come back it all seems the same, yet different at the same time.* Before he knows it, he's all the way on the other side of town, standing in front of Buck's station, right where the paved road turns to gravel.

The sign out front reads "Buck's Repair Shop and Service Station." Harold contemplates all the times he's stopped here to fill-up. Then he recalls the last time, when he and Clyde were headed out of town and talked with Martin, the kid who worked with his dad. Now he's Clyde's brother-in-law. Who would have ever thought that? The place looks pretty nice; Harold notices the new window and the door leading into the office. The iron double doors to the service bay look the same though, and the old truck used as a tow truck is still there.

The sun peeks over the top of the building. A truck pulls to the side of the station and a young man steps out. "Can I help you find something, sir?" he asks.

Harold smiles. "You're Martin, Buck's son, aren't you?"

"Yes sir, I am, but I don't recognize you."

Harold pushes his hat back with his fingers, exposing his face.

"Oh, you're Harold!" Martin exclaims. "You used to work out at the Livingston's place."

"That's me," he confirms as he extends his hand in greeting.

Martin grasps his hand and asks, "You in town for the rodeo? I heard you were ridin'. Also heard Ruthie's kid brother was ridin', too. That so?"

"Yep, we're ridin' and travelin' partners," Harold confirms.

"So, where's Clyde?" Martin asks. "He didn't take a walk with ya?"

"Nope, he decided not to ride; takin' some time off."

"Aw, now that's a shame. Ruthie was lookin' forward to watchin' 'im."

"Really? Well, he doesn't think that. He thought no one wanted him around."

"Well, I could see how he'd think that," Martin acknowledges. "Knowing what he did to the family and all."

"Don't rightly know what cha mean by that," Harold comments.

"You know, with Clyde leaving and all," Martin concludes as a car pulls in.

The driver cranks his window down. "You guys open yet? Sure could use some fuel."

"Sure are; just give me a second," Martin says. He excuses himself and hurries in to open up.

Harold tips his hat and walks away thinking, *What was that all about? I didn't understand any of it. Now I understand why Clyde didn't want to come here.*

✲ ✲ ✲

Up early the next morning, Clyde can't wait to hear more of the family story. It doesn't take much to get Conrad going, so during their drive to the diner Clyde asks, "How many brothers and sisters did you have?"

"Of the four kids, I'm the oldest; then there's George, Fred Jr., and Ida. We all worked in the bakery. In fact, Dad had the first bakery delivery truck in New York."

"The first one; that must've been great," Clyde acknowledges.

"It's always great to be first at something. No one can ever take it away from you. Everybody else is just following," Conrad says.

"You're right about that," Clyde agrees as they pull up to the diner.

With business being so slow Clyde decides to get Conrad talking again. "Okay, now that you guys are in the city, how'd you get to the island?" Clyde inquires.

"Let me think. It was after George was born that the neighborhood started to change. What was once a friendly area was becoming one you didn't want your kids to be in. The streets were becoming violent and the business community corrupt; no place to raise a family, if you didn't have to. So they began exploring other avenues."

"When we moved out to Long Island, we opened a bakery; it was a whole family affair. Fred, Beth's dad, along with our other brother, Carl, and I ran it. Then, when the kids got old enough, they would take turns getting up in the wee hours of the morning and going downstairs to help prepare the breads and pastries for each day's sales. They each had a job to do and they started at an early age. It took a total family effort to make enough to pay the bills for all the families."

"Wow, it sure sounds like a lot of fun. What a great family! But I still want to know how you got out here," Clyde persists.

"How about if we get to work?" Anna demands. "If you worked as much as you talked, you'd be rich by now."

Clyde shrugs his shoulders. "Yes, ma'am," he calls back as he picks up another pot to scrub.

✡ ✡ ✡

Harold makes his way to the motel, still confused about what Martin said. When he walks under the canopy of the office, Audra exits her room. "I've been looking for you. Where have you been?"

Harold places his arm around her shoulder. "Just went for a walk to look over the old place."

"I sure wish you had asked me. I would've loved to go with you," Audra pouts.

"Gee, I never thought of that," Harold says. "I didn't think you'd be that interested in seeing the town. I'm sorry."

"It's okay. Just remember it for next time," she says.

Trying to make her feel better, he asks, "Want to grab some breakfast, and then run out to the ranch I used to work at?"

"I don't know; let me check in with Dad," Audra replies. "He didn't have a very good night, fighting a head cold. I'll be right back."

"Okay, I'm going to my room. Just let me know when you're ready."

Harold no more gets settled than Audra knocks on the door. "Dad wants to rest today, but told me to go ahead and enjoy myself, so I'm all yours for today."

Harold grins. "Well let's get going. Day's . . .

"Don't you dare say it. I hear that all the time," Audra interrupts.

Harold laughs, "You mean you're tired of hearing your dad's favorite saying?"

"Yes, I am. 'Daylight's burnin'' is getting really old."

Harold chuckles, "Do you realize what you just did?"

"What? What did I do?" Audra demands.

Harold grabs her hand. "Let's walk to breakfast. You said what you didn't want me to say."

"No, I didn't!" she counters.

"Oh, yes you did, but it doesn't matter. I just want to walk with you and enjoy our time."

Audra leans her head against his shoulder as they walk toward the diner.

After breakfast they climb into Harold's truck and head to the ranch. As they drive, they talk about their plans once the rodeo season is over. They're laughing and enjoying themselves as they pull up to the front gate where they're greeted by a guard. "Good morning, sir, may I help you?"

Harold rolls down the window. "Morning! My name's Harold and I used to be foreman here when the Livingstons owned the place. I'd like to take my girl and have a look around, if I could."

Audra leans back in the seat, a little shocked. *He's never called me his girl before,* she thinks. *It sounded nice, so nice I could get used to hearing it.*

She smiles as the guard squats down and looks inside. Harold glances over just in time to see the smile on her face. *I was hoping that didn't offend her* he thinks. *Oh good, must not have; that's a pretty big smile. Must have hit a good nerve. Sounds great to me, too!*

"Sir, can't let you on unless the boss approves it," the guard answers.

"Can you see if he will? I've known Al for a number of years."

"I'll see what I can do. Please wait here." Standing up, he instructs Harold to pull to the side as another car pulls up.

As the second car pulls up to the gate, the driver glances over and asks the guard, "Is that Harold?"

"Yes, Pastor, it is. Do you know him?"

Red waves and Harold waves back. "Sure do. What's he doing out here?"

"He wants to walk around the place to show his girl where he used to work, I guess."

"What did you tell him?"

"That I'd have to clear it through the boss."

"Don't disturb Al; I'll vouch for him. Go ahead and let'em walk around. Just tell them to stay away from the main house. I'm going to see your boss."

With hesitation, the guard says, "Oh, okay I guess, if you say so." Red takes off to the house and the guard relays to Harold what Red said, "It's okay for you guys to walk around, but please stay away from the main house. The boss isn't feeling too well."

"Will do. Can I park over there?"

"Yes sir, just make sure it's out of the way."

✵ ✵ ✵

Another busy day at the diner is wrapping up. While Clyde's in the back cleaning his last batch of dishes, Anna finishes filling the salt and pepper shakers on the counter and tables and starts sweeping the front. Only a few feet from Clyde, Conrad diligently scrubs the grill. The clanging of the dishes and the screeching of the metal scraping the grill are the only sounds you can hear.

Clyde breaks the silence. "I can think of one thing that would make this go a lot faster."

"What's that, young man?" Conrad bellows.

"If you'd tell me more about Beth's family. I guess it's your family too, huh?"

"Yeah, I guess it is. I can do that," Conrad agrees. "Where did I leave off?"

"Something about exploring other avenues," Clyde recalls.

"That's when the family decided to move out to Long Island."

"Did you have to take a boat to get there?"

"No Clyde, the island's connected to land; you can drive or take a train. It's located east of New York City and sticks out northeast into the Atlantic. There's a body of water to the north called the Long Island Sound, while the Atlantic Ocean borders the south. The island's about 100 miles long and roughly 20 miles wide."

"Does it have any mountains?" Clyde asks.

"Not like out here. It's pretty much flat as a board. It has a wonderful train system called the Long Island Railroad. It was built sometime during the 1830s and purchased around the turn of the century by the Pennsylvania Railroad. A few years back the rail system was finally completed into Manhattan. The island is larger than the entire state of Rhode Island.

"Really? Always thought you had to take a boat to islands," Clyde confesses, embarrassed.

Before he can ask, Anna hollers, "Hey, you two, I'm tired and want to head home. How about less talk and more elbow grease?"

"Yes, ma'am!" Clyde hollers back.

"Am I getting too detailed for you? I know I have a habit of doing that," Conrad admits.

"Oh no, not at all. I'm enjoying the story, but maybe we should continue it later. You know, so she doesn't get upset."

"That's sounds like some good advice. You're wise beyond your years, young man."

They go back to finishing their jobs and soon they're all on the way home. The house is pretty close to the diner, but each night Anna falls asleep on the drive home. Clyde sits in the back and laughs to himself.

✳ ✳ ✳

After spending a couple of hours wandering around the ranch, they make their way back to the truck and begin a slow drive to town. Harold's been talking almost nonstop and Audra's soaking it all in. She enjoys hearing every detail about his life.

They drive down Main Street and pass the movie theatre. "Would you like to see a movie?" Harold asks.

"That sounds like fun," Audra replies, "but can we stop by the motel to see if Dad would like to go, too?"

They pull up by her room and she runs in to see how he's doing. When she returns she informs Harold that he's still not feeling well, so he declined.

With the rodeo in town, the theater tries to take advantage of it by offering a double feature. Not only that, it's half-price for the matinee showing, so they get their tickets and enjoy the afternoon together.

When they leave the theater, the sun is sinking in the western sky and Harold's stomach is growling. The popcorn didn't do much to curb his appetite, so they head for the WD. When they walk in, there sits Myron, talking with a lady standing by his table.

Not waiting for Harold, Audra strides up to the table. "Hi, Dad, what are you up to?" she asks as she glares at the lady. "Evening, ma'am. I'm Audra, his daughter." Harold watches, holding back a smirk; he can't believe how protective she is.

The lady introduces herself, "I'm Edna and I'm on the welcoming committee for the rodeo. I was welcoming your dad to town." Leaning against the back of the chair, she turns slightly. "And welcome to both of you, too! I best be getting along; hubby's expecting dinner. You folks have a great evening and enjoy our little town."

She turns to go and Audra feels really silly. Harold, sensing her discomfort, walks up and pulls out a chair for her. She slowly sits down, puts her elbows on the table, and places her head in her hands.

Harold takes a seat next to her. "What was that all about?"

"I'm so embarrassed," she mumbles.

Myron starts to laugh, and then tries to control it, but it gets the best of him. When he's finally able to talk, he says, "Can I order you some humble pie?" and lets out another big belly laugh. By this time, others are staring, but he doesn't care. It's the first time he's seen Audra try to protect him and he thinks it's funny. He takes a couple of deep breaths to compose himself and asks, "What movie did you see?"

Not laughing, Audra refuses to answer, but Harold smiles and replies, "It was a double-feature; 'Yankee Doodle Dandy' and 'Road to Morocco.' I can't remember the two guys' names in the Road to Morocco, but they were funny."

"I think one was Bing somebody and Bob Hope," Audra pipes in, "and they were funny."

"That's right. I'm famished; I need to order. It's been a long day," Harold concludes.

Audra stands up and goes over to give her dad a hug. "Sorry, Dad, I got carried away."

"No worries, I thought it was pretty cute."

They order and enjoy their dinner together before they head back to the hotel.

✳ ✳ ✳

It's only been a few days, but Red's seen improvement in Al's condition. Still uncertain about his diagnosis, he decides to go by Doc's office to see if he has any new information. As he opens the door, Doc steps out. "Hey Doc, looks like you're in a hurry."

"Just got off the phone with Don Carpenter; the misses' water broke and they don't think they can make it to the hospital, so I'm heading out there."

"Okay, I'll let you go. I was just dropping by to see if you have any more info on Al."

"I need to talk to you about that. When you see him, tell him I need to run some blood tests."

"Blood tests?"

Doc reaches his car and hollers back, "They may be able to clear up a few things. He's doing better, right?"

"Oh yeah, much better," Red shouts to Doc as he pulls away.

✳ ✳ ✳

When they pull in the driveway, Anna makes her way inside and then off to bed. Conrad finished a cup of coffee at the diner and is wide awake. Clyde's not in any hurry to hit the sack either, so he asks Conrad if he'd continue the story.

"The family would go out on the island on Sundays," he begins. "With the bakery closed, everyone could go. One Sunday afternoon, they drove through a township named Blue Point. It was the perfect little community for them and only fifty miles east of the city, to boot."

"So is that where they settled?" Clyde asks.

"Yep, they figured they had found the right town; all they needed to do was find a home. They drove around for quite some time. Finally, they saw the home of their dreams, right on a corner, a little small, but placed perfectly on a large lot. Best of all, there was a 'For Sale' sign in the window. Before they got too excited, they had a few more things to check on, like where the closest school was and how far it was from downtown."

"Why would they have a check list?" Clyde inquires.

"There were certain things they thought the family needed," Conrad answers before continuing. "It didn't take long; about three blocks away was a small school."

"Three blocks, is that all?" Clyde protests. "I had to walk almost a mile to get to school."

Conrad laughs, "I guess we had it pretty easy." Clyde nods in agreement and Conrad continues, "We drove a little further and at the end of the road was a large pond. I remember saying, 'Look! During the winter that will freeze over and we'll be able to skate on it and play hockey'."

"You played sports?" Clyde asks.

"Oh yeah, that's how I kept busy, but Mom didn't care for it . . . thought it was a waste of time. I remember her saying, 'Oh no, you don't, not without your dad or me with you,' which was really disappointing because I knew they wouldn't have the time to go."

"Did they ever go with you?" Clyde asks.

"A couple of times, but me and my friends would sneak off and do it without them knowing."

Clyde chuckles, "Seems like everyone has those types of stories. Harold told me a few of his."

"What about you, Clyde? Do you have any?" He no more gets it out of his mouth when he realizes what he said.

Clyde hesitates for a moment. "Well, can't really recall doing anything except when my sister got us arrested."

"Got you arrested? How old were you?" Conrad probes.

"I think I was around ten."

"Ten! Was that when she hit the guy with the rock from the sling shot?" Conrad asks.

"That's it. Boy, was I one scared kid! You know, come to think of it, the only two times I've been in jail were because of that Whiskey fella," Clyde concludes.

Conrad sighs. "You don't have to worry about that anymore."

"Sure don't. Now back to the story. You guys must have moved, right?"

"Oh yeah, but it wasn't that simple." Conrad explains.

"Why not?" Clyde asks, thinking about how easy it is for him to just up and leave.

"You would have had to know my mom. She was a fabulous lady, but she wore the pants in the family. Dad wanted people to think he did, but when push came to shove, it was Mama who did the deciding."

"The best I can remember, my daddy was the one who did the decidin'." Clyde injects. "Mama had a say, but Pop's word was final."

"When it came down to deciding on the move, I recall Mom said something like 'We ain't moving until we've prayed about it. If this is where God wants us, He'll have to work out the details.' After that, everyone knew that it was the end of any further discussion. As soon as Mom said there was going to be prayer about any topic, even Dad knew the conversation was over. It was time to wait and see what the Lord would do."

Clyde yawns while he stretches. "Sorry, guess I'm a little more tired than I thought."

"Why don't we call it an evening," Conrad suggests as he stands up and walks toward his room. "Morning is just around the corner. G'night, Clyde."

"Goodnight, Conrad."

✵ ✵ ✵

Standing in the parlor, sipping on a small glass of wine, Al welcomes Red as he walks in. He looks better than he has for quite some time. "Now I know why you're feeling better," Red smiles.

"First one I've had in a number of days," Al chuckles. "You just came at the wrong time. I know the answer already, but can I get you a glass?"

"No, thanks; I had mine at the WD." They both laugh at the thought of Red bellying up to the bar.

"That'll be the day," Al cackles. "So, what cha doing back out here?"

"I had to check up on my dinner buddy. Haven't eaten since you've been sick," Red teases.

"Yeah, I'm sure. You don't look any thinner, but I'm glad you came out. I have some things I need to talk over. Why don't we take a seat? Sure I can't get you something to drink?" Al offers.

"Do you have sarsaparilla or ginger ale?"

"Sure do, coming right up." Al walks behind the small bar, pulls out a glass, chips off a little ice from the block and pours Red some ginger ale.

"So, what is it that you want to talk about?" Red asks.

"These past few weeks have got me thinking about eternity more than ever," he says as he hands Red his drink and sits down. "It also made me reflect on some of the things I've done while I've been here. I can tell you some that aren't too pretty, if you know what I mean." Not wanting to interrupt, Red simply nods as Al continues, "I have a couple of regrets I wish I could make right."

"Al," Red says. "You know doing that won't get you in a better light with God. You have already taken care of that."

"Yeah, I know, but I just can't seem to get past these two things. But before I get to those, I was wondering if you'd be the executor of my will."

"What?" Red says as he sits up straight in his chair. "Why would you want me to do that?"

"To be totally honest," Al states, "there're some things in it that may get some people upset. My thinking is, with you being a man of the cloth and all, they may listen to you better than anyone one else. Besides, you're the closest friend I've ever had."

Embarrassed, Red hangs his head. "Thank you, Al. I appreciate you saying that, but about people listening to me; I'm not so sure I agree. But if that's what you want, then it's okay by me. Now, what are those two things you regret?"

Al leans back, looks up at the ceiling, and takes a deep breath. "The first one happened a while back. It's about the Lewis girl, Ruthie."

With his brow furrowed, Red asks, "What about her?"

"Well, it's what I did to the family by hiring her. I'm the reason Clyde left that house. If I hadn't hired her, none of that would have ever happened."

"You don't know that," Red insists, shaking his head. "Remember, God has a purpose for everything. He works out even the worst of things for the good to those people who love Him and want to walk with Him."

"I know, you've told me that before, but it don't make me feel any better."

"And I know I've told you this a lot too; doesn't really matter what you feel, it's a matter of believing the truth found in the Bible. So that's the first, what's the second?" Red asks, trying to change the subject.

"The second is getting rid of that horse, Warrior. Poor little Rachel. Red, if you could've seen her face when I told her the horse was gone, it would have broken your heart. It did mine. Sure wish I could get it back for her."

Red stands up and places his hand on Al's shoulder. "I don't quite know what to say, but I do know what we can do."

"What's that?"

"Let's pray and ask God to help you deal with these two things."

"Okay, I'm with you."

Red begins to pray, asking the Lord to take care of these matters and to fill Al with peace and comfort in dealing with them. As Red closes, he's surprised when Al joins in. This is the first time he's heard Al pray out loud. It's a short one and as Red looks up, he sees Al take out his handkerchief and wipe the tears from his eyes as they both conclude with a hearty, "Amen!"

Chapter 12
SAM'S SPECIAL GIFT

As they sit around the house on Saturday evening, Clyde can't help but wonder how Harold's doing. When a commercial comes over the radio, Conrad asks, "Would you like to come to church with us in the morning?"

Not wanting to disappoint, he politely says, "Thanks for asking, but I really don't have proper clothes to wear. Besides, I need to get packed so when Harold comes, we can head out."

He sits back and finishes listening to the last minutes of the broadcast. Then Conrad reaches over and turns off the radio.

"How about wrapping up that story about the family?" Clyde asks.

"Sure, but it'll be the condensed version," Conrad chuckles. "I need my beauty sleep."

"Yeah," Anna chimes in, "and I don't need to hear the whole story again."

Turning his chair around to face Clyde, he asks, "Do you remember where I left off?"

"Let me see," Clyde replies. "I think it was right after the family moved to that island."

"That's right," Conrad nods, "I was telling you about how Mom wore the pants in the family."

"Connie!" Anna says in disbelief. "You didn't tell him that, did you?"

"Sure did; you know it's the truth," he says with a chuckle and winks at Clyde. Anna shakes her head and retreats to the kitchen.

"Anyway, where was I before I was interrupted?" he asks, raising his voice so Anna can hear.

"I heard that," she shouts.

"Oh yeah, that's right. We moved the entire family, started a bakery in the township, and got us kids enrolled in a new school," Conrad remembers, ignoring Anna's comments.

"What about the bakery they already had in the city?" Clyde asks.

"That's a good question. When all three families decided to move from Brooklyn, after a lot of prayer. they put it up for sale. There was quite a bit of interest because we had our own delivery trucks, the only bakery in New York to have them. It seemed like the more we prayed, the quicker things moved. Even before the sale of the bakery, they totally believed God was behind it and negotiated for a building close to downtown Patchogue to begin the new one. Everything fell into place; they set the date for the grand opening, and it was full-steam ahead."

Sitting back in his chair, Conrad starts editing the story, but by the time he's finished, he's sitting on the edge of it. He takes a deep breath and a sip of his coffee before continuing, "One of the main things I recall was how hard it was leaving my friends, but I really liked our new home. It had so much grass that I could run around until I dropped if I wanted to."

He's on a roll and each time he starts to get too detailed, Anna hollers from the kitchen, "Remember, it's the condensed version." This quickly gets him back on track.

Close to eleven o'clock Anna walks by and announces she's going to bed. Conrad wraps up the story and follows Anna to their room. Clyde also heads off to bed, eagerly anticipating tomorrow.

✲ ✲ ✲

It's Sunday morning and Harold's up early. Realizing that everything would be closed in the morning, he had grabbed a few things at the store the night before for breakfast. He's excited about today. Being in the top ten means he'll probably make some good money.

Audra and Myron have to leave early for the arena, so Harold stays behind to finish breakfast. Knowing his event is last, he lies back on the bed to relax. He closes his eyes and lays out his plans. *By the time the rodeo's over and I've collected my money, it'll probably be past suppertime. I don't want to start the long drive to pick up Clyde that late, so I'll just spend another night here.* They'd normally stay for a couple days after the rodeo, but with the next one being in the opposite direction from Clyde, he'll have to hightail it back to get him, then get a move on to make it there in time.

He hears a truck pull up out front; then a door slam, and a knock. He leaps from the bed and gives the door a yank.

"Morning, Harold!" Sam says. "I was hoping to catch you before you left. Do you have a minute to talk?"

"Sure," Harold says, stepping aside, "come on in. Excuse the place; haven't picked up since I got here."

"No need to worry about that," Sam laughs. He pulls out the chair by the desk and takes a seat, while Harold plops down Indian-style on the bed.

Sam clears his throat. "Harold, are you happy with what you're doing?"

"You mean am I happy with my life right now?" Harold asks.

"Yeah, that's another way of putting it," Sam counters. "Before you answer, I want you to really think about it for a few minutes."

Puzzled by the question, Harold says, "I don't know what you mean, Sam. If you're asking if I like what I'm doing, then I'd have to say yes. Clyde and I make a pretty good team. He needs someone to watch after him or he could head down the wrong road. Why do you ask?"

Sam nods his head in agreement. "Do you think he'd want to come back here and work for me?"

You're kidding, right?" Harold chuckles. "He wouldn't even come back to ride in the rodeo, let alone move back here."

"I guess you're right," Sam agrees. "Harold, I really need someone like you at my place. The business is growing so fast that I can't keep up. I want you to stay and run the place while I follow the rodeo. Next weekend is the last one for the year, and then what are you going to do? You could work for me until next season."

"I was just thinking about that. Right now our plans are to follow Myron and Audra home. They have a place they go to and said there is work there for guys like us."

"So there's no way I can talk you into staying and helping me?" Sam pleads.

"Sam, think about it," Harold chuckles. "Would you stay here and let that cute little dame get away or would you follow her?"

Sam smirks. "I guess you're right. Hey, you better get a move on or you may miss your ride."

"Oh my God, I gotta hurry. Let yourself out," Harold says as he grabs his gear. "See you at the arena."

✲ ✲ ✲

Conrad and Anna are up early Sunday morning and head off to church. It's been a ritual for both of them since they were little. They grew up in religious homes where church was an important part of their lives. Since they moved west, they've had to make adjustments in their beliefs. The closest church of the denomination they grew up in is about fifteen miles away, so they've decided to stay local. They had a hard time adjusting at first, but they've grown accustomed to the church's music and messages now. At times, Conrad thinks, *The pastor sure preaches a lot about hell and it not being a place anyone would want to go.*

Clyde's lying in bed when he hears them leave. Once they're gone, he makes his way to the kitchen to cook up some breakfast. After preparing scrambled eggs and grits, he sits down at the small kitchen table and admires the hand-carved edges. He outlines one of the small figures with his finger as he recalls the stories Conrad shared the night before about moving to the island, opening the family bakery, and how one by one, the siblings moved out on their own.

One story that stood out from the others was the one about the lake down the street from the house. In the wintertime, they used to play hockey on the ice, but their mom always warned them not to go without having an adult along. Being kids, they never saw the danger in it until one cold winter afternoon.

Clyde can still see Conrad's face as he recalled that day like it was yesterday, and how he remembered every detail. "The sky was gray, with a storm blowing in, but we wanted to play hockey. We talked each other into going to the lake, even as we watched the sky. The sun peeked through an opening in the clouds on our way down the street. It was like a spotlight, lighting up the evening sky, and it made the ice glisten in an inviting way. As we talked, we saw it as a sign from heaven and hurriedly donned our skates. Off we went across the ice."

Clyde readjusts himself in his seat, and then recalls seeing tears form in Conrad's eyes. "We had skated for about an hour when the storm hit. I didn't want to stop, but the others had already started to skate toward the embankment. I decided to take one last shot. It missed the branches we had laid out for the goal and slid further across the ice. My younger brother took off after it. We hollered for him to stop, to let it go, but he either didn't hear us or ignored us. We'll never know. He got to the puck and slapped it back toward us, but as his stick hit the ice it began to crack. He knew he was in trouble and hollered for help. Most of the other boys had already removed their skates except me, so I took off across the ice. When I was almost there, the ice gave way under my little brother, and he fell through. While ice is smooth on the top, water is flowing quite rapidly underneath. He was hanging there by his armpits when I grabbed his hands. With our hands clasped together, I pulled as hard as I could, but the current was too strong. Finally, our hands slipped from each other, and my brother tried to hold on to the lip of the ice as the water tried to take him under."

With his emotions boiling up in him, Clyde can still hear Conrad say, "I worked my way around the back of him and once again grabbed his arms. I can still hear him screaming, 'Help me! Connie, help me!' I can feel the ice giving way under me and I know I have to do something quickly. That's when my brother looked up to me with those beautiful blue eyes of his and said, 'I'm so cold and tired. I can't hold on anymore.' I hollered for him to hold on, that I was going to get him out, so I reached for the collar of his jacket. About the same time, my brother's arms gave out and now all of the weight was on my arms. I gave a mighty tug and then realized that the jacket wasn't zipped. As I tugged, my brother's wet body began to slowly slip from the jacket."

Sitting at the table and staring out into space, Clyde can still see the painful expression on Conrad's face. He hears him clear his throat, trying not to show his emotions, even after all these years. Clyde puts his head back and closes his eyes as he remembers Conrad's voice describing what came next. "Trying with all my might, I attempted to readjust my grip. That's when the combination of the weight of his body and the flow of the water took him under the ice. In a panic, I quickly jumped up and ran along the ice with the other boys, trying to break it to make another hole, but it was too late. I can still see his face looking up at me. Then his eyes closed as the current took him away. I fell to the ice as the other boys raced up to me, flinging the jacket over my head. Then I lay prone, pounding the ice with my fists and screaming. A couple of adults arrived and tried to comfort me. It wasn't long before my parents got there and found out what happened."

The next thing Clyde recalls Conrad saying really hit home. "From that day on, things never seemed right at home between my parents and me. Whether it was my guilt or their blame, I'm not sure. When I finally had the opportunity to leave, I did. That's how Anna and I got here. Never had much more contact with my parents. My siblings stay in contact when they need something. Anna and I are alright with that. That's how Beth got here." Clyde puts his elbows on the table, puts his head in his hands, and thinks, *It's the same for me. Things just don't seem right at home now; I have no contact with anyone there. It's funny how life can just creep up on ya and bite ya in the butt. Oh, well. Like Harold says, we all have a story.*

✻ ✻ ✻

The announcer signals the beginning of the bull-riding event as Harold makes his way to the back of the chutes. He jumps on the back railing and scans the packed bleachers. People have come from miles around. This is the highlight of the year, and it looks as if the whole town has shown up. He spots a few people he knows and his stomach begins to knot up.

As the first rider slides down on his bull, Harold spots Clyde's family in the stands; Ruthie with Martin, Buck next to them, then Sara, Rachel, Dorris, and finally Jim. Harold thinks, *There must be something going on between Dorris and Jim. I've seen them together a lot this week. Glad to see they're here. I just wish Clyde would have come. They'd be so proud to see him ride the way he does. Okay, wishful thinking don't get ya nowhere. It's time to focus on the matter at hand.*

Still peering into the stands, Harold hears, "Now, out of gate number one, our own Harold Ritter on the back of homegrown bull 'Upside Down'." It's the first time someone with local ties has come through on the circuit, and now he's on the back of a bull that was raised just outside of town. The crowd stands in anticipation and watches Harold settle in. He slowly wraps his hand as Upside Down turns his head. Harold pauses for a second and looks right into his eyes. It looks like Upside Down is staring back. *Did he just wink at me? I know what you're thinking; come on, cowboy. Let's give 'em a show they'll never forget.*

Harold finishes wrapping his hand and scoots himself up, just to the base of the bull's big hump. Before nodding at the gatekeeper, he pushes his hat down over his forehead with his left hand. With a mighty yank, the gate swings open and frees Upside Down. He takes a step to his left before taking an enormous leap out of the gate. Harold is thrown back and their backs touch as the bull's hind legs kick up in the air. After another tremendous jump, they are almost halfway across this small arena. The leap helps Harold get into a rhythm with the bull, and it's not long before the buzzer sounds, signaling the end of the ride. As Upside Down turns to the left, Harold exits to the right and almost lands on his feet before tumbling and rolling to the ground. He jumps up, takes off his hat, and throws it into the air. The crowd stands up, applauds, and shouts their approval as he scans the crowd for Maggie. Once he locates her, he makes his way over toward the stands, blows her a kiss, and hollers, "Thank you! That was for Walter."

With the combination of the din of the crowd and her loss of hearing, she can hardly hear him. She leans over to Sara and asks, "What did he say?"

"He said, 'Thank you. That was for Walter'."

Maggie chokes up for a moment at the mention of Walter, then blows a kiss back and mouths, "Thank you".

Exiting the arena, he waits behind the chutes for the final riders watches Audra ride in the closing ceremonies. While he's standing there, Sam comes by to congratulate him and invite him, Audra, and Myron out to his place for an evening barbeque, which he gladly accepts.

☆ ☆ ☆

After the rodeo's over, Sam heads back to the ranch to wait for the cowboy to bring Warrior. He doesn't have to wait long; a truck towing a horse trailer pulls up the long drive and Sam walks over to the corrals to great him. They shake hands and walk out to the back of the barn where he keeps his purebreds.

"That's one beautiful collection of horses you got there," the cowboy says. "And I can choose any one I want?"

"Yep, take your choice," Sam reassures him.

"Are you sure? These horses are worth double what Warrior is."

"I'm sure they are, but this isn't a matter of money."

"I don't understand!" the cowboy exclaims. "Why would you do something like this?"

"I wouldn't have a while back," Sam admits, "but, like I explained, that day at the cowboys' Sunday service, I learned that life is more than possessions, and I'm trying to live that out."

The cowboy shakes his head. "I sure don't understand that and don't know if I ever will, but if you say so, I'll take that Paint over there."

"He's all yours." Sam hollers for one of the hands to get the Paint out and walk him to the trailer while they unload Warrior and take him over to the big corral.

Once Warrior's settled and the Paint's loaded, Sam asks, "How much do ya want?"

The cowboy reaches his hand out and says, "Mister, you're unbelievable. I can't take your money. You got the raw end of the deal as it is now. My conscience won't allow me to ask for any more. Besides, you already gave me some great advice."

"I did?" Sam wrinkles his brow. "Mind telling me what that is?"

"Don't mind at all," the cowboy says as they shake hands. "Let's just say I'll be checking out that service next Sunday morning."

Sam shakes his hand and slaps him on the back. "Just go with an open mind, young fella."

"Thanks, Mister," he replies, and climbs in the truck and heads out.

✧ ✧ ✧

The sun filters through the curtains on this late afternoon as Anna reads on the couch. Clyde and Conrad are playing checkers on the coffee table, when the phone rings. Conrad gets up and walks into the kitchen where the phone hangs on the wall. He picks up the earpiece and says, "Evening, this is Conrad."

"I have a person-to-person call for a Mr. Clyde Lewis," the operator responds. "Is he there?"

"Yes, he is," Conrad replies into the mouthpiece. "Hold on and I'll get him."

"Clyde, the phone's for you," Conrad hollers out the doorway.

"For me?" Clyde asks as he gets up from the floor. "Maybe it's Harold! Sure hope everything's okay."

As Conrad hands him the ear piece, Clyde says, "Hello, this is Clyde."

"Go ahead, sir," the operator instructs.

"Hey, Half-Pint, how ya doin'?" Harold asks.

"Harold, it's great to hear from ya!" Clyde answers. "Where ya callin' from?"

"We're at Mr. and Mrs. G's. They're having a big barbeque."

"That sounds like fun. When ya comin' to get me?"

"That's the reason I called. I figure I'll leave in the morning and get to your place around suppertime. Do you think we could stay with the Beckers for a night or two?"

"That sounds great! Look forward to hearing all about the weekend," Clyde says, before asking, "Did ya see my family?"

"I'll tell you all about it when I get there, but is it okay for us to stay?"

"I suppose so," Clyde replies. "Let me ask."

"Okay, I'll hold on."

Clyde lets the earpiece hang from the wall as he walks into the parlor. It sure doesn't take Anna long to respond, "You two can stay for as long as you like."

"Whoa there, maybe not as long as you like," Conrad says with a chuckle. "But sure, a couple days would be fine."

Clyde picks up the earpiece again and confirms the plans. Harold lets out a whoop and says goodbye. Clyde hangs up and goes back into the parlor to listen to "The Adventures of the Thin Man" that is just getting ready to start.

✳ ✳ ✳

True to his word, Harold arrives in town right after supper. He walks into the café as they're busy cleaning up as the last customers are finishing their meals. Anna gives him a hug and points him toward the back where Clyde is working. He comes through the double swinging doors and Clyde looks up with a grin.

"Well, how can I help?" Harold asks.

"You can come over here and start drying some of these pots. Oh, by the way, it's great to see ya!" Clyde says as Harold jumps right in.

Over the next couple of days, the guys talk about what they're going to do after the last rodeo of the season. Harold shares about the offer Sam made them, and, just as he thought, Clyde has no interest in it at all. The next option is going back to the ranch in Texas and seeing if they can work through the winter. That would be quite a drive for a "maybe," and besides, Harold has something else on his mind, Audra. Their last option is following Myron and Audra to their place, but Clyde's not too keen about that idea either. He finally agrees, on one condition; no more dairies. After further conversation, they reach an agreement.

The next day they pack up, say their goodbyes, and head out to the last rodeo. As they drive, Clyde recaps the year; from working the dairies, to the Texas ranch, to riding the rodeo circuit.

"It's been a pretty successful year," Harold concludes, "even with all the stuff that's going on in the world."

Clyde nods in agreement, while thinking, *Yeah, but you forgot one thing; Audra. You met Audra and I think you're getting pretty serious about her, too. I wonder how long it'll be before they. . . can't think that way; things will probably stay the same. Harold really enjoys riding. I'm sure he won't give it up for a girl. But what am I going to do if he does? I'll cross that bridge when I come to it.*

They ride in the last rodeo, and, after a couple days drive, pull into their new town. It's not much of one, but it's where they will call home for the next few months. Before long, and with the help of Myron, they find a couple of odd jobs. He treats them like they're his own sons. It's not much, but enough to get by on. They'll have to save enough to carry them for the first few rides next year.

Chapter 13
A WHOLE NEW YEAR

The off-season is short, and before long, they're all back on the circuit. Their first year was just a small taste of what riding the circuit's like, and by midway through the season, the glamour has worn off. It's taken its toll on the guys, from the mental stress to the physical hurts and pains, especially Clyde. He still enjoys the adrenaline rush, but the rides keep getting harder.

The year has flown by and they've done quite well financially. One or both of them always seem to finish in the top three. In a short period of time, Clyde's earned the reputation of being one of the top riders.

Clyde, Harold, and Audra have turned into quite a team. They do everything together and Myron comes along for the ride most of the time. Not having a family to call his own, Clyde adopted Audra as one of his sisters. This often brings them to his mind; how he wishes he could have this kind of relationship with them! *That'll never happen,* he thinks.

As the season winds down, he realizes that one of the last stops will be in familiar territory, his hometown. Last year he decided to skip it and is considering doing that again, but he hasn't discussed it with Harold yet. He figures that's a few weeks away, so he doesn't have to think about it right now. Besides, he's excited because their next stop is where the Beckers live. Hopefully, he'll get to see them again and maybe Beth will be visiting. During this past year she's come to his mind numerous times and no matter how hard he tries, he can't seem to forget her.

They drive into town and head for the diner. On their way, Harold notices that the bank's reopened and points it out. Clyde laughs when he sees new paint on the old jailhouse where he spent some time. It's almost closing time when they stop in front of the café and see Anna through the big front window, busy at work cleaning a table.

When they walk in, she doesn't even look up as she says, "Take a seat; I'll be with you in a minute."

"Can we have our old table in the corner?" Clyde asks.

She pauses for a second, attempting to recall the voice, then finally looks up and turns around with a big smile. "Clyde, it's great to see you!" she squeals. "Hey Connie, look who just walked through the door," she hollers in to the kitchen.

Holding a plate full of food, Conrad pokes his head out the swinging doors. "Welcome back! We've been expecting you. Take a seat; I'll be right out."

The place is almost empty as Anna escorts them to their table and sits down next to Clyde. She puts her arm around him and gives him a peck on the cheek. "We've missed you and sure do enjoy the updates you send, just real short and to the point."

Clyde lets out a hoot. "I don't take much time to write only two letters when I do, if you can call them that; that's you two and my mom."

"You write your mom?" Anna asks. "That's being a good son, after what she did." *I may have crossed a line with that comment,* she thinks when she sees Clyde's expression change. "I shouldn't have said that. Sorry, Clyde."

Conrad walks up and shakes Harold's hand, gives Audra a howdy nod, and then looks at Anna and asks, "What did you do this time? You're always saying things that get your in trouble."

"Oh, that's fine," Clyde assures them. "Make no never mind about it. I don't think my mom wanted to do what she did; it was just the times that forced her to. Anyway, I can't believe it's been a year already! How have you guys been?"

"Just the same: work, sleep, eat," Conrad says.

Anna walks to the front door and locks it. "It's time to wrap it up for the day. You guys hungry? It's on the house tonight; got to celebrate."

"Yeah," Conrad joins in. "I think I got enough of our special left for all of you."

"What's the special?" Clyde asks.

"My specialty: liver and onions; it don't get no better than that!"

They look at each other, and Harold says, "Sounds good to us. Bring it on."

Tired from the long day, Conrad scoots his chair back and ambles toward the kitchen. Anna grabs some place settings and brings them to the table as Conrad brings out the food. The plates are heaping with a big piece of liver, sautéed onions, an ample mound of mashed potatoes, and a large corn on the cob. Clyde can't wait to sink his teeth in.

When they finish up, Clyde tells Harold and Audra, "You guys go on and check into the motel. I'm going to stay and help clean up."

"Now, Clyde," Conrad says, "you go along with them. You don't need to help."

"I know I don't, but I want to spend some time with you guys," Clyde explains. "That's if you'll have me. Besides, I've seen enough of them to last me a lifetime."

Everyone laughs as Anna interjects, "Connie, you let the boy be! We'd love to have you. It'll be like old times."

"Okay then, we'll see you at the room," Harold says as Anna escorts them to the door. Clyde waves and then clears the table.

Connie and Anna make short order of cleaning the front as Clyde mops the floors. Then all three attack the kitchen, which always takes longer. Clyde tries to build up the courage to ask about Beth the whole time.

Finally, he takes a deep breath and blurts out, "Heard from Beth lately?"

Anna's head snaps up and she looks toward Conrad. "Yeah, we heard from her. What, Connie, about three or four months ago?"

"Let me think. Yeah, about that," Connie answers without raising his head.

Seeing how they responded, Clyde contemplates not questioning any further, but decides to go ahead. "Is she okay?"

"Oh, sure, she's fine," Anna hesitantly says in a chipper voice.

"That's good," Clyde replies. "Is she still on the island?"

"Not exactly; she moved."

"Oh?" Clyde says, thinking she may be close. "Mind if I ask where she's living?"

"I'm not too sure right now," Anna softly answers. "Like I said, it's been a few months."

Clyde stops what he's doing, puts his palms up about shoulder height, and looks questioningly at Conrad.

"Just tell him, will you?" Conrad blurts out.

"Tell me what? Is she okay? Does she need some help?"

Anna stops drying the pots and looks at Conrad, who nods his head and mouths, "Tell him."

"She's fine, Clyde. The reason we don't know where she is, well, she married a soldier and they move around a lot. The family was against it, so when she did it anyway, they wouldn't let her live at home."

"Oh, I'm so sorry," Clyde says as he sits on a barstool and tries to conceal his hurt. "I know you two thought the world of her." He thinks, *I really thought she was the girl for me.*

Seeing the hurt look on Clyde's face, Anna quickly changes the subject. "So Clyde, are you riding this weekend?"

Confused, he replies, "Yes ma'am, I am." *Why else would I be here?* he thinks.

"Connie and I have talked about it and we're going to close the cafe during the rodeo hours, opening before it starts for breakfast, and again for dinner each day when it's over. We'll stay open late to accommodate the riders," Anna shares. "You about done? We need to get this young man back to his place so he's on top of it tomorrow."

"You two head on out," Conrad hollers back. "I'll just put this stuff away and be right there,"

"Okay, we'll wait for you at the car."

✿ ✿ ✿

Clyde slides out of the backseat and says his goodnights. He checks in and gets a room key, knowing that Harold's probably already asleep. He unlocks the door as quietly as he can, and tip-toes to the bathroom to get ready for bed. As he slips under the covers of his twin bed, Harold asks, "Half-Pint, can we talk for a minute?"

"Sure," Clyde says as he sits up. "What do ya want to talk about?"

"Well," he begins as he rolls over and clicks on the lamp, "ya know you're my only family, right?"

"You bet, we're family," Clyde agrees. "In fact, you're the only family I got."

Noticing Harold's hesitation, Clyde says, "Go ahead, come right out and say it. We're family, after all."

"I want you to know we'll always be family," Harold assures him. "Nothing's going to change that, but I want ya to be the first to know."

Not sure what's coming next, Clyde furrows his brow. "Know what?"

Harold leans over on his elbow and clears his throat. "I'm going to ask Audra to marry me!"

"WHAT?!" Clyde squeals. "You're kidding, right?"

Smiling from ear to ear, Harold answers, "No, I'm not, and I wanted you to be the first to know."

"When?" Clyde enthusiastically inquires. "When are you going to ask her?"

"When we get back home to ride," Harold responds. "I have it all planned out. You're going home with us, aren't you? I want you to be there."

"I hadn't made up my mind yet, but I wouldn't miss this for anything," Clyde says. "So it'll be us three on the road together?"

"Uh, not exactly, Half-Pint," Harold haltingly replies.

"What does that mean?"

"Mr. G offered me a job on his place and I'm going to accept it. I'll be staying there working for him."

"Oh, okay. That sounds good. You know, I'm tired. We better get some shut eye," Clyde says as he starts to slide under the covers. "By the way, I don't think I said 'congratulations'. She's a great babe."

Harold reaches over and clicks off the light. "Thanks, Half-Pint. Goodnight."

Clyde rolls over. "Night, Harold."

Harold lies there thinking, *I know he's disappointed. We'll talk about it later when we have more time.*

✵ ✵ ✵

Friday and Saturday rides go off without a hitch. Both Clyde and Harold are in the top five of their events going into Sunday. Clyde's still thinking about Beth being married and has mixed feelings about Harold and Audra getting hitched.

It's Sunday morning and Clyde wakes to the reality that in a few days, he'll be back at the old homestead. He's the first one out of bed and decides to soak his aching body in a tub of hot water. As he sits in the small tub, he begins to contemplate what kind of reception he'll get. The more he thinks, the less he wants to go. *Darn you, Harold! Why'd you have to pick that place to ask her? It sure would be easier on me if you'd done it somewhere else.* He closes his eyes when it dawns on him: *I only have a few more rodeos to go until I have to find something else to do.* Panic sets in. *That's right, Harold won't be with me anymore. I wonder what that's going to be like. Maybe after the last rodeo I'll go back to where we were last year. Everyone was so friendly there. What am I going to do without Harold? Wait a minute! I don't have any transportation. I'll have to ride the rails like so many other guys do. But what if . . . and what if . . .*

A rap on the door stops his train of thought. "You going to soak in there all day?" Harold asks. "A guy could wear a hole in the floor out here dancing, you know."

"Getting right out," Clyde laughs. "You can come on in if ya want."

Clyde quickly towels off and heads into the other room to get dressed.

✠ ✠ ✠

Sam is making his way down to check on the bulls when Harold comes running up. "Mr. G, you got a minute? I've got something I need to ask ya!"

"Sure! I always have time for you, my friend," Sam warmly greets him.

"Well, like I said, I got something to ask ya."

"Okay. Go ahead, shoot."

"Remember when ya offered me that job?"

"Yeah. What about it?" Sam asks.

"Well, if it's still open, I'd like to take it!"

"That's not funny, Harold. Don't kid around," Sam responds. *This can't be happening right now. I just got done praying and told The Man upstairs that if He was really the Messiah that He'd provide someone I could trust to step up and help. Not quite sure what to think about all this.*

"I'm not, really. I want the job!" Harold exclaims.

"This got anything to do with the little filly you've been seeing?" Sam suggests.

"Sure does, but please don't tell her. I'm going to ask her to marry me when we get to town."

"I wouldn't dream of ruining the surprise. But to answer your question; you bet I have a job for you! In fact, you're just the guy I've been looking for," Sam says as he extends his hand to seal the deal. "I have a lot of ideas about growth, and we can grow together. You do right by me and I will always do right by you. Deal?

Harold clasps his hand and says, "Deal."

"Welcome aboard, Mr. Foreman," Sam congratulates him. "Oh . . . what about Clyde? Is he coming, too?"

"Nope, not right now. He doesn't want to settle in town. Ya know, the family and all."

"Sure wish they'd get that fixed," Sam laments.

"Me, too!" Harold agrees.

✻ ✻ ✻

The rodeo's less than a week away and Dorris can't wait any longer to tell the girls. Since she and Jim have been seeing each other regularly, she recruits his help. The first thing she has to do is tell him, so one evening, through tears, she shares with him the story behind Clyde leaving. While shocked, Jim agrees to help her put her words together and she rehearses them over and over.

It's been a while since the family has been together, so she decides to prepare a meal for them, thinking, *News always seems to be better accepted when food is involved.* Since she's already shared Clyde's story with Maggie, she invites her, too, for additional moral support.

Sara and Rachel are in the kitchen helping Mom when Martin and Ruthie arrive, and Jim and Maggie aren't too far behind. The girls finish setting the table and they all sit down to eat. Conversation flows as the food is passed around. The three girls, not able to get together often, catch up with the latest happenings.

As Dorris listens to the easy flow of conversation, she can't help but try to talk herself out of bringing Clyde up. Knowing what she has to do once supper's over, she doesn't have much of an appetite. Everyone is having a good time, and, by the looks of their plates, they're about full. Jim is the first one to push away from the table. Dorris glances over and notices that Martin has placed his napkin on his plate, so she nods her head at Jim.

He stands up and asks, "Martin, would you mind taking a short walk with me? I have a couple of questions I'd like to ask ya about my car."

"Sure Jim, I wouldn't mind at all," Martin replies, a little bewildered. He stands up and gives Ruthie a peck on the forehead, and follows Jim outside.

As the door closes, the girls stand up to clear the table. Before they can pile the plates, Mom tells them, "Let the dishes go for a few minutes. We have something we need to talk about as a family. Let's go into the main room."

Sara and Rachel move to the davenport and Maggie wiggles in between them. The girls glance at each other as if to say, "What's happening?"

Ruthie sits in the chair Mom usually sits in and Mom stands by the fireplace. "Girls, you've probably heard the rumors about Clyde coming to town for the rodeo." They each nod in agreement.

"Well," Mom hesitates and looks at Maggie, who nods her head and mouths, "Go ahead."

"I need to share something with you. It's something I should have told you a long time ago." Sara glances at Ruthie, who looks as if she's going to say something, but Mom quickly continues. "You remember when we were struggling to eat and were unable to pay rent? Things were pretty bad and I needed to make some tough choices."

"I don't understand what ya mean, Mom. What's this got to do with Clyde?" Sara quickly responds.

"Please, don't interrupt me. Let me tell you the whole story."

Ruthie sits back in the chair and folds her arms as Mom continues, "With Ruthie taking the job at the WD, and with Sara doing what you did to Jonathan, I felt like our family was falling apart. We didn't have enough food, and I didn't know what else to do."

"Mom! What in the world are you talking about?" Ruthie pleads.

"This is hard enough. Please, let me take my time."

"I'm sorry, Mom," Ruthie apologizes, "but I'm confused. What are you getting at?"

"Okay, here it goes! Since Clyde left I've allowed all of you to think that he ran away, but that's not the truth. I asked him to leave."

"What?!" All three girls ask in unison.

"Mom, you wouldn't do that!" proclaims Sara. "It doesn't make any sense! You're just making this up so we'll be nice to Clyde."

"No, Sara, it's the truth. I asked him to leave."

Ruthie hasn't moved; it's like she's in shock. Rachel begins to cry and Maggie holds her to comfort her.

Finally, Ruthie looks at Mom. "How could you do this? Why in the world would you deceive us like this for all these years? We've just about disowned him for what we thought he'd done."

Maggie decides to jump in before it gets too far out of hand. "Listen, girls, your mom did what she thought was best for all of you." Dorris can no longer contain it and begins weeping uncontrollably. Maggie continues, "Now's not the time to allow this to divide you. Clyde is coming to town and it can be a great opportunity for the family to heal. You have a decision to make: you can let this tear your family apart, or you can allow it to bring you together. It's your choice."

Then through her tears, Dorris tries to explain, "I have lived with this for so many years and it's been so painful. I didn't want to tell you for fear you'd leave and never talk to me again. I simply did what I thought needed to be done for the best of the family. Clyde's done very well for himself and I'd love to have the family together again when he comes home. And one more thing."

"What else, Mom? I don't know how much more I can take," Sara replies.

"All these years Clyde's been sending us money to help out. He's really been a good son and brother. He loves us very much."

With that, they all begin to cry. Sara whimpers, "I can't believe how I treated him at Ruthie's wedding! The horrible things I said! He'll never forgive me." Through her sobs, Mom cries out, "God, forgive us!"

Chapter 14
WELCOME HOME

As they roll into town, Clyde thinks, *The place just doesn't look the same. It's changed quite a bit and sure is growing.* He's not sure if it's due to the rodeo coming to town or just normal goings-on, but there are people all over the place.

Harold's arranged for him and Clyde to stay at the Goldberg's, while Audra and her dad will be in town at the WD, where Al's given them a complimentary room. Tomorrow night's a big one for Harold, and he's spookier than a wild horse. He's arranged with Myron that after Audra rides into the arena carrying the U.S. flag, he'll ride out on a horse to meet her and ask her to marry him. He can hardly wait.

They make their way through town and head south about a mile to the Goldberg's. As they pull through the gate, Clyde is amazed. The place is beautiful; to the left sits a huge ranch house, then south about a hundred yards is another good-sized house. The bunkhouse is across from that and looks like new.

He scans his surroundings, and then declares, "Boy, has this place changed!"

Harold's also stunned. "Wow! I can't believe this place. It's been totally redone." They pull up by the bunkhouse and take a quick survey. The ranch house is western style with a porch that wraps all the way around it. The upstairs windows are almost as large as those downstairs. The second house is about half the size, single story with a full-sized porch. Clyde nudges Harold as he points to a road that leads east about fifty yards. Off the road is the huge red barn with a riding corral between the barn and bunkhouse.

Harold is almost speechless. "What a great place."

They see someone waving as they head toward the main house, it's Sam. He reaches out and says, "Howdy! Welcome to our ranch."

Still taken aback, Harold replies, "Thanks, Sam. This sure is beautiful!"

"Yeah!" Clyde chimes in, still looking around.

Harold pulls his bag from the back of the truck. "Any particular bunk we should take?"

"What?" Sam returns. "Oh no, you're not in the bunkhouse."

"We're not? Where do ya want us to bed down?" Harold inquires.

"The house over there," Sam says as he points to the house on the other side of the road.

"Over there?" Harold points.

"Yep, that's right. We had that built for our foreman and his family, and you are my foreman, right? And you are getting married, aren't you?"

"Well, yes sir, as long as she says 'yes'. I just thought . . ."

"I can't have my foreman living in the bunkhouse, can I? Besides, you need a place to bring that little filly of yours."

"Yes sir, but I'm not getting married for a while."

"That's okay, enjoy it," he says with a wink. "It won't be quiet for long," he chuckles.

Clyde begins laughing while Harold is expressionless. "Okay. Well, thanks Sam," he stammers.

Sam turns his attention to Clyde. "Sure we can't convince you to stay on with us? I'd love to have ya."

"Thanks, but I think it's best that I get this ride over with and head out of town. Besides, one day I'm going to ride in The Garden."

"Okay, but just remember, if ya ever need work, give us a call. You always have a spot here."

"Thanks a bunch. I won't forget that."

They walk over to the house and Sam opens the front door. "I'll let you get settled. I have some chores I need to get done, so relax. You have a few busy days ahead of you."

As Sam walks off the porch, Harold steps through the front door. This is something he's only dreamed of.

Clyde wastes little time putting his bag down and taking a self-guided tour. The first place he walks into is the large sitting room, then down the hallway that leads to the back of the house and two bedrooms. When he opens the bedroom door, he thinks. *It doesn't get any better than this.* He goes into the room that is his for the weekend, sees a full-size bed, and flops down to take a nap.

Harold walks in and asks, "What cha think, Half-Pint?"

"Sure beats motel rooms," Clyde chuckles. "Look at the size of this bed!"

"It's all yours, my friend," Harold grins. "Enjoy. How about if we head back into town? I'd love to get ahold of some chicken fried steak."

"Makes my mouth water just hearing you say it," Clyde answers. "Besides, you've got that cute little filly waiting for you."

They climb into the truck and head back to town. On their way Clyde thinks, *I wonder how people are going to greet me. Sure hope I don't see any of the family, but I will sometime this week.* They pull in front of the WD and walk into the bar where Audra and Myron have just finished supper and join them.

The evening goes smoothly. Clyde hasn't been noticed and he's thankful for that. Soon after dinner Audra, Harold and Myron decide to call it an evening. Clyde decides to stay around. Every once in a while, someone recognizes him and says hi.

Al's still not feeling well. He's had a bunch of tests taken, but with few results, and he keeps losing weight. Over this past year, he's learned to live with it. Pastor Red explains it as being a thorn in his side. The closer the rodeo gets, the more Al's seen around the WD. He always enjoys the rodeo and doesn't want to miss it. When he moseys into the tavern, Clyde hardly recognizes him as he walks up and hollers at the bartender to bring Clyde another drink on the house. He pulls up a chair and starts making small talk. It's not long before the conversation turns to Whiskey.

"As you float from town to town, have ya ever run into that Jonathan fella?" Al asks.

Taken aback by the question, Clyde asks, "Why do ya ask?"

"I have some unfinished business with him," Al chuckles, "and I was just wondering if you'd seen him."

"I think that business ya have is over," Clyde says with a smirk.

"Why? What cha mean by that?"

"Well, a while back I ran into old Jonathan. He was robbing a bank," Clyde begins.

"What? A bank-robber? Was he that one that we heard about?" Al inquires.

"Probably," Clyde suggests before proceeding to tell the rest of the story.

Hanging on his every word, Al leans back as Clyde fills him in on the details. As the story unfolds, Al shakes his head in amazement. By the time Clyde finishes, Al has a big smile and says, "Well, young man, it looks like God beat me to it! It couldn't have happened to a nicer guy. He got exactly what he deserved. Sorry for what you had to go through, though." Al stands up and shakes Clyde's hand. "Young man, you just made my day. So much so, your drinks are on me the rest of the evening." Clyde puts his fingers to his forehead and flips them as a thank you gesture. Al walks up to the bartender thinking *I sure am glad Pastor Red wasn't around to hear me say that. God, forgive me for feeling that way.* He tells the bartender, "Whatever that young man wants, it's on me tonight. But make sure he gets some supper."

"I think he already ate, Boss."

"Well, he's a growing boy. Give him something else," Al demands as he leaves the WD.

The rest of the evening Clyde sits alone. Right around midnight Harold comes looking for him, spots him off in the corner, and walks over. "Come on, Half-Pint, time to head back to the ranch." By this time, Clyde's pretty subdued. He's had one thing on his mind all evening. *Later this weekend I'll be heading out on my own, for the very first time. I have so many unanswered questions. Oh well, it'll work out.*

Harold pulls up a chair. "Half-Pint, I need to tell you something."

With his head on the table, Clyde looks up. "Go ahead."

"I want you to know," Harold says, "if ya ever need me, just call."

Clyde reaches out his hand. "Thanks, Harold, your friendship means a lot. In fact, I was sittin' here thinkin' how much I'm gonna miss ya."

Harold pulls Clyde to his feet and they head to the truck. "I've got something else to share."

"Okay, what's that?" Clyde asks.

"I'm giving you the truck."

Stopping in his tracks, Clyde says, "What? Ya can't do that!"

"Listen, Half-Pint, Sam told me as foreman he provides a vehicle and Audra already has hers, so you take this. It ain't much to look at, but it'll get ya where ya need to go."

"I can't do that," Clyde reiterates.

"You can and will, so don't argue. Things have worked out just right for me and I want them to work out for you, too."

As they slide in, Clyde takes a moment to think about it. "Okay, if ya insist. Thanks, ya'll never know how much I've learned from ya. It's pretty scary moving on without ya, though."

"You'll be fine. You just keep ridin' the way you do and you'll end up at The Garden one day," Harold says as he hits the starter button on the floor and drives down the road.

"Ya really think I'll be ridin' in the big city at The Garden?" Clyde says.

"There's no doubt in my mind. You're that good," Harold states before he voices some observations. "But I've got a couple of issues we need to discuss."

"Like what?" Clyde asks.

"Well, first of all, now that I have a steady income, I want ya to have the money we've earned together."

"No, Harold, I can't take the truck and the money. I can't leave ya with nothing!"

"You're not. You're my little brother, and I want to take care of ya. There won't be two of us anymore; you're on your own. You'll need it and there's enough to keep ya going for a while, that's if you take care of it. Think of it this way; it's like the money you sent home, only I'm giving it to you in person."

Clyde hesitantly accepts. "Thanks, Harold. What was the other thing you wanted to say?"

Trying to choose his words carefully, Harold peers out the windshield. "You're going to be fine, if ya don't drink it all away."

"What? Are you talking about tonight?" Clyde asks. "I was just there because there wasn't no place else to be. Harold, ya know I don't make this a habit. Besides, not everyone will serve me."

"Just beware! The money's not going to come as easy with just you."

"I promise," Clyde reassures Harold. "We've had a lot of fun together and I am going to miss you, but can I ask one thing?" Clyde pauses as Harold stops in front of the house.

"What's that, Half-Pint?"

Clyde cocks his head, then adds, "Well, maybe two."

"Go ahead, shoot."

"Please don't call me Half-Pint anymore. And if I make it to The Garden, will you and Audra come?"

Harold reaches over and ruffles Clyde's hair. "Sure, I won't call you that anymore. But I want you to know, you'll always be my Half-Pint. As far as The Garden goes, we wouldn't miss it for the world. You can count us in," Harold says with a grin.

Harold looks out through the windshield into the starlit sky and ponders the beauty of the Lord's creation. Then he tells Clyde, "Look at that clear sky and all the stars out tonight. Just think, Half . . ." he chuckles and continues. "Clyde, this time tomorrow, I'll be an engaged man."

Opening the door, Clyde slides out and looks over the hood as Harold steps from the truck. "Aren't you forgetting one thing?"

"What's that?' Harold asks.

"She hasn't said 'yes' yet!" Clyde says with a grin and chuckle.

Harold waits for Clyde to walk around the front of the truck, and gets him in a headlock and says, "Okay, 'Half-Pint'! I gotcha right where I want ya."

They're both laughing so hard that Harold has a hard time holding Clyde still as he tries to wrestle loose. Harold finally loses his balance and they both tumble to the ground and lie side by side in the pebble driveway, hitting each other with their hats.

✫ ✫ ✫

The sun rises over the eastern plain and catches Harold out on a morning walk. In anticipation of today's events, he didn't sleep well. The rodeo doesn't begin until early afternoon and he's already jumpier than a bull frog. When he walks into the house, Clyde is fixing breakfast. "Come on! Sit down and relax. Here, have some coffee." Harold takes a seat, but he doesn't eat much. As he sips his coffee, he thinks, *What if she says no, or what if I fall off the horse riding into the arena?* Already in panic mode, Harold shares his thoughts with Clyde, who's no help. He throws out more ideas of things that can go wrong, and, by the time they're ready to leave for the arena, Harold is a basket case.

He tosses Clyde the keys. "I'm a mess. Here, you drive. Besides, it's yours."

Clyde plucks the keys out of the air and opens the driver's side door. He's never driven his very own vehicle before.

They make their way to the back gate of the arena and Clyde parks. Harold jumps from the truck and tells Clyde, "I'll meet you behind the chutes. I have to find Myron." Clyde has a short hike to the stock pens where, like always, he stares down the bull he's going to ride. Suddenly, the introductory music begins and he knows it's only moments before Harold will ride into the arena.

✫ ✫ ✫

Audra takes her place in the front of the rider's line-up, inside the gate leading into the arena, on her beautiful Appaloosa. She's had him since she began riding in the rodeo. He has mottled skin, striped hooves, and eyes with a white sclera; all characteristics of an Appaloosa. He rides in comfort, shipped by train from one rodeo to the next.

The gate's about to open when the gatekeeper, who knows what's about to happen, sees Harold mosey up and waits a few extra minutes before he opens it.

Harold strides up to Audra, places his hand on the saddle horn, and says, "Smile nice and pretty for the crowd."

She puts her hand on his and leans over and gives him a peck on the cheek. The public address announcer belts out, "Ladies and gentleman, boys and girls, we want to welcome you to this year's county rodeo. Now sit back and enjoy the wonderful evening of entertainment we have planned for you. Please welcome the ceremonial riders into the arena." The gate swings open and Audra leads the way, waving the American flag as the crowd stands up and begins to applaud.

Once Audra starts her ride, Harold hurries over and mounts his waiting horse as one of the riders hands him a bullhorn. He waits for Audra to come to a stop in front of the grandstands, when the announcer declares, "Ladies and gentlemen, please rise for the playing of our national anthem."

Harold slowly makes his way up behind the riders as the song plays. When it finishes, Audra notices that no one is moving like they normally do and turns to see Harold riding toward her. Panicking, she thinks, *What's wrong? Did something happen to Dad?* Her stomach takes a leap and begins to churn. She quickly glances toward the announcer's booth and sees him standing there with a big grin. He puts his hand to his lips and blows her a kiss. Now she's really confused.

Harold rides up beside her, dismounts from his horse, and holds the bullhorn up to his lips. "Audra, you are the one I want to spend the rest of my life with. Will you marry me?" he announces for all to hear.

She immediately looks up to Dad, who nods in approval. Another rider comes alongside of her and takes the flag. Tears well up in her eyes and she begins to shake, choking back the tears as he walks toward her with ring in hand. She gets down from her horse, grabs the bullhorn and says, "I'll think about it." Then she weeps and falls into his arms.

✳ ✳ ✳

When he hears the music, Clyde runs over and jumps upon the back of the chutes. He watches Harold propose and thinks, *I sure am happy for him, but I can't waste any more of my time. If I don't ride well, I don't get paid. In fact, it costs me my entry fee.* After Harold gives her the ring, Clyde goes back to prepare for the night's ride.

✵ ✵ ✵

It's early afternoon when the family and Jim settle into their seats and the announcer declares the rodeo open. As they stand up and wait for the national anthem to end, Mom looks around for Clyde. When she looks toward the chutes, she sees someone that looks like him, but at this distance she can't tell for sure. She tries to focus more to determine if it's him or not, but her attention is diverted when someone from the arena speaks from a bullhorn. She watches Harold propose to the cute little lady riding an Appaloosa, and by the time she remembers to look back to the chutes, he's gone. She has a long wait to see her son until he rides later tonight.

The girls move around to get in the right seats, as Rachel wants to sit between Ruthie and Martin. They're excited about watching their brother ride, and as the horses come into the arena, Rachel jumps up and screams. She loves horses and has been riding CH since Mr. Goldberg brought him to the ranch.

It's been a while since they've even seen Clyde and now that they know the truth they're looking forward to sitting down and catching up on the years they lost. During the proposal, Ruthie reaches around Rachel and grabs Martin's hand, and they exchange smiles.

The rodeo finally gets underway and Jim buys Rachel almost anything she wants; a hot dog and cotton candy, just to name a couple.

As the early evening is ushered in, the bull-riding event is only minutes away and the family's excited about watching Clyde ride. Preparation of the grounds for the bull-riding begins. They roll out the clown barrel and soon after, two clowns come running out, dressed in red, white, and blue costumes with tufts of hair sticking out from under their Stetsons. While they're funny looking and do a great job entertaining, their main purpose is to protect the riders. If the truth is known, they're probably the real athletes out there. They have to be agile, quick on their feet, and fearless.

The first wave of bulls are led into the chutes, as it's about ready to begin. The girls can tell Mom's getting more nervous by the minute. Jim is on one end and Dorris is on the other when she leans over and says, "Maybe he won't ride, at least I hope not."

"Now, Dorris," Jim says before taking a swig of his drink. "Relax, he's going to be fine." He always has something to drink. Though he tries to keep it a secret, everyone knows it's spiked with some kind of alcohol.

Mom scoots back on the bench and puts her hands over her mouth. "I think I see him," she whispers to Ruthie. "Isn't that him in chute three? Ruthie, look. He's getting on top of that big ugly bull. Oh my, that thing's big! He shouldn't be doing this; he's going to get hurt."

"Mom," Ruthie says, "he's been doing this for some time now. Just calm down."

"Stay calm, huh," Mom replies. "That's easy for you to say. Wait until you have children and you'll know what I mean."

"You may be right," Ruthie agrees. Before she can finish, the gate opens and the rides begin.

Chapter 15

A DAY TO REMEMBER

After his ride on the bareback, it's finally time for the bull-riding and Harold looks around back for Clyde. He spots him jumping upon the back of a chute and peering into the stands.

"What cha lookin' at?" Harold asks, already knowing what the answer is.

"Just lookin' at the crowd," Clyde calmly replies.

"Did ya find them?"

"Who?" Clyde asks, as if Harold didn't know.

"Oh, come on. We've been together too long to play this game. You know who I mean."

"Yeah, they're up there," Clyde says, smirking as he climbs down the chute railing.

Harold pats him on the back. "You just relax and enjoy the ride."

Clyde nudges Harold with his elbow. "Thanks, big guy."

The second wave of bulls is escorted into the chutes. Harold walks up behind Clyde, gives him a shove, and says, "Go get 'em, Half-Pint." Clyde gives him a funny look. Harold smiles as he replies, "I had to say it one last time."

Clyde returns the grin. "I've thought about it and you can call me that anytime ya want. I'm sure going to miss ya, but I'm happy for you and Audra."

Then something happens that's never happened before; Audra walks up behind the chutes and says, "Clyde, I'm so excited for you. You must be thrilled to be able to ride in front of your friends and family."

He nods as he climbs over the chute and straddles the bull. *That's the first time she's come back here.* He thinks, *Guys say it's bad luck for women to be behind the chutes. Sure hope that ain't true.* Once again he glances in the stands and clearly sees the family watching. Mom looks worried as she sits back on the bench with both hands over her mouth.

The bull jerks, bringing Clyde back to the task at hand. Then the announcer says, "Next, coming out of chute number three, is our very own Clyde Lewis! Let's give him a warm welcome." The crowd's applause is louder than Clyde has ever heard before. He settles down on the back of the bull; wraps his right hand, places his left hand on top of his hat, and moves it down even with his eyebrows. After scooting up to the bull's hump, he glances at the gatekeeper and nods his head. As if the bull knows when the gate's going to swing open, he follows it with a giant leap to his right. His front legs touch the ground and his rear end swings to the left. Clyde's right on him in perfect rhythm, so much so that he decides to spur him, which is something that's rarely done. Usually, all the rider wants to do is hang on, but this is a special night. The more you spur, the more points you get. So each time the bull bucks, Clyde scrapes the spurs against him. With time about up, the bull takes an unexpected turn to the right and starts to spin. *He's never done this before,* Clyde thinks. *I just need to hold on for another second . . . come on, buzzer!*

Even though he tries to hold on for all he's worth by digging his right foot into the bull's side, he's so far to the left that he can't pull himself back up. He knows what will happen next; he's seen it hundreds of times before, and there's nothing he can do. As the bull's back legs land, Clyde falls off right under the bull's belly. The bull's rear legs go back up and then head right toward Clyde's midsection. He sees it coming and everything seems to slow down; he quickly puts his arms up to protect his face as the bull's left rear leg glances off his rib cage and his right leg nearly stomps the top of Clyde's head. He's thankful it's only a glancing blow, but still feels as though someone has beaten him with a lead pipe. He lies there gasping for air, with a burning sensation running through his upper body. He finished the ride, but what now as he lies there in pain? The clowns run over, distract the bull and lure him from the arena before attending to Clyde.

✻ ✻ ✻

The family jumps to their feet as the gate opens, and Rachel shouts at the top of her lungs. Dorris covers her mouth as Sara leaps up on the bench and hollers and hoots as loudly as she can.

When Clyde slips to the side, Mom hollers, "No!" She grabs Ruthie's hand as she hears the buzzer and sees Clyde fall under the spinning bull. It's only a split second before she sees her only son lying under a 2,000 pound bull, and a thousand thoughts run through her head. She gasps as Clyde doubles up when the bull stomps him. A hush comes over the crowd as the bull takes another kick towards Clyde, just missing him. The clowns rush in, and the bull turns his attention to them. The first clown runs in front of the bull and barely gets out of the way. He takes a short charge toward him before he sees the second clown who leaps into the middle of the barrel, far away from Clyde, who's still on the ground. The bull makes a charge at the barrel, and, just before he knocks it over, the clown ducks down inside. The gateman opens the exit gate and the bull smoothly gallops out. Both clowns run over as Clyde lies motionless. The girls embrace each other, waiting for some movement.

✻ ✻ ✻

Clyde lies in the middle of the arena, unable to move. He can see the bull in his peripheral vision and prays that he doesn't return. Finally, the clowns run over and start asking him questions that he can't get the air to answer. He takes a few short breaths as he gasps for air, but that first deep breath sends pains throughout his chest. Before he tries to sit up, he lets out a loud groan.

Harold and Audra run out to see if they can help. By the time they arrive, the clowns have Clyde on his feet, and the crowd is giving him a standing ovation. He's not too sure if it's because of the ride or simply because he survived. With Harold on one side and Audra on the other, they head for the doctor's tent to get Clyde examined. He lifts his arm to acknowledge the crowd as they leave the arena.

Mom sits down on the bench, drops her chin to her chest, and lets out a big sigh. The girls embrace and Sara says, "I thought we lost our brother before we even had a chance to talk to him!"

Mom looks toward the heavens and says to herself, "I am so sorry girls for the years I cost you with your brother." She still has a hard time with this and looks down as tears drop on her skirt.

Ruthie notices her sitting with her head down and sees the spots form on her dress. She passes in front of everyone, sits down next to her, and gives her a hug. "Mom, we love you," she reassures her. "Thank you for telling us. You only did what you thought you needed to. That's behind us now; let's look forward. Just think of it this way; we can be a family again." During the evening closing ceremony, the family heads to the doctor's tent to see Clyde.

✶ ✶ ✶

Clyde sits down on the table as the doctor walks in. He helps him take his shirt off and slowly pokes and rubs his hands across Clyde's ribs. Every once in a while, he cringes or twitches in obvious pain. Finally, the doctor turns and says, "It's hard to say without X-rays, but I'm pretty sure you've got a couple of cracked ribs and a few more that are bruised. There won't be any riding for a while."

Clyde jerks his head up. "Doc, I've gotta ride or I can't finish in the money."

"Young man, if you ride, you're in danger of getting hurt worse," he warns.

Clyde pauses a moment before asking, "What's the worst thing that can happen?"

"I'm going to level with you. If you have another fall like that, a rib could puncture your lung, and you could die. This is something that you shouldn't take lightly."

"Thanks for telling me, Doc," Clyde replies. "Now I have a question for you."

"Yeah, what's that?"

"If I decide to ride, are you gonna stop me?" Clyde asks.

"That's not my place, young man. I'm just advising you."

Clyde lets out a sigh of relief, then flinches in pain. "Thanks, Doc!"

Clyde turns to Harold and asks, "Mind if I head back to the place? I need to get some rest!"

"Sure, but tell me one thing first," Harold requests.

"Yeah, what's that?" Clyde grunts as he cautiously steps down from the table.

"You're not gonna ride, are you?"

"Harold, you know I have to. I'd do it even if we were still a team, but I really have to now," Clyde reasons.

"Go ahead and take the truck. I'll catch a ride with Sam or Audra."

"Thanks!" Clyde says and takes off to Sam's place. He decides to stop by the WD on his way to pick up some pain-killer.

After talking to the doctor, Harold knows he has to convince Clyde not to ride. On his way out, he bumps into the family. "Evening there, folks! Are ya looking for Clyde?"

"Yes, we are. Do you know where we can find him?" Mom asks.

"He wasn't feeling too well after his ride, so he headed back to the Goldberg's," Harold responds.

"Then he's okay?" Sara inquires.

"Not exactly; he's got a couple of cracked ribs, along with some bruised ones."

Mom hangs her head and walks away.

Ruthie shakes Harold's hand. "Thank you, Mr. Harold. I guess we'll just have to wait until tomorrow to see him."

Confused by the sudden concern they have for Clyde, Harold answers, "Yeah, I guess ya will," and heads to the back of the arena to wait for Audra to finish up.

✳ ✳ ✳

The air is filled with the aroma of bacon and eggs as Clyde lies in bed in the twilight of sleep. He tries to move to his side, but the pain stops him. It takes a few minutes to gather himself enough to stand erect and gingerly walk down the hall into the kitchen where Harold is cooking breakfast.

"Mornin', partner," Harold greets him as he flips the bacon. "How ya feelin'?"

"Really sore," Clyde grunts as he places one hand on the table to steady himself while he eases himself into the chair. "I could hardly move to get out of bed."

Harold sets a plate of food down in front of him. "Well, I guess you won't be ridin' today."

Clyde gingerly picks up his fork. "Oh yeah, I will! As the day goes by, I'll loosen up."

Harold pauses. "Come on, Clyde, you're in no condition to walk, let alone ride. You heard what the doctor said; you could really get hurt!"

Before he takes a bite, Clyde counters, "I know, but I've got to ride through the pain."

Harold tries to reason with him. "Why don't you just stay here and work with us? You only have one rodeo left, then what are you going to do?"

"I haven't reached my goal yet! If I stay on here, I may not go back to riding, and then I'll never ride at The Garden! One day I will, ya know." Clyde says with an air of confidence.

"I believe ya will, I really do; but if ya hurt yourself any more, you won't be good enough to be a rodeo clown. Clyde, you have to be wise with the choices you make, and I'm just afraid this is a bad one."

Clyde spends the rest of the morning trying to loosen up. Harold runs to the local drug store to get aspirin, in addition to what Doc gave him. With each passing hour, it gets closer to the start of the rodeo. Harold is committed to helping Audra and her dad before he his ride, so he tells Clyde, "You stay here, and I'll come back to get you right after I'm done riding."

"Can I trust you?" Clyde inquires.

"I'd never do anything like that to ya; we're family. Oh yeah, I almost forgot to tell you. Your family was looking for you last night.

"What? Who?"

"Your mom asked for you, but the whole family was there."

"Wonder what they wanted? They probably wanted to tell me to leave town as soon as the rodeo's over."

"I don't know, but they seem concerned," Harold contradicts as he grabs his hat. He opens the front door and stops. "I almost forgot. I never asked: Will you be my best man? "

As the pills begin to kick in, Clyde slurs, "Wow, I never thought of that! You bet I will!"

Harold smiles as he adjusts his Stetson. "That's great! Now you stay here and get yourself ready for the ride of your life."

✻ ✻ ✻

The family is waiting at the gate as Harold pulls up. Recognizing the truck, they wave him over. "Where's Clyde?" Dorris asks. "Did he decide not to ride today?"

"Oh no, he's riding; just relaxing for now. And let me tell you, he needs all the time he can get."

"How's he going to get here?" Sara asks.

"I'll go pick him up later, after my ride."

"I'll go," Sara eagerly volunteers.

"I'll go, too." Rachel adds. "I haven't been out there for a few days."

"I don't know if that's a good idea," Harold responds, trying to be diplomatic. "He told me you lit into him the last time you saw him. He really doesn't need to be upset before he rides; it could cost him financially, as well as cause serious injury."

"I think I can help, not hurt the situation," Sara retorts.

Harold hesitantly agrees, "Okay, but if anything comes of this, it's all on you."

"That's fine with me. When should I leave?"

"Right after I ride."

"You can count on me," Sara confirms.

✻ ✻ ✻

The wrapping the doctor did the night before loosened up, so Clyde's in the bathroom unwrapping himself when someone knocks at the door. Gazing in the mirror, he can see the discoloration already beginning. With every movement, pain shoots through his chest cavity. He thinks, *How am I going to ride today? Come on, be a man; it's only for eight seconds. I can do that!* There's a second knock and he wonders, *Who can that be? I know it's not Harold; he'd just walk in. He must have sent Audra to pick me up.* He steps from the bathroom and hollers, "The door's unlocked; come on in. I'm in the bathroom."

He hears the door open and then footsteps coming down the hall. Standing in front of the mirror with his shirt off, he sees a reflection of someone peeking in the door. He can't believe it! *What's she doing here?* Without turning, he asks, "What do you want?"

"Harold sent me. I'm here to pick ya up," Sara informs him.

"Well, that wasn't too smart. I ain't going nowhere with you," Clyde retorts as he attempts to wrap his ribs.

She opens the door wider and steps into the small bathroom. She gets a glimpse of Clyde's rib cage and can see small lumps. "Oh, my God, Clyde! You can't ride tonight, not looking like that! Look at those bruises coming out. Clyde, please don't do this!"

Clyde grabs his shirt and covers his ribs. "What's the big deal? I already know how you feel about me. I'm ridin' and there's nothin' you can say or do to stop me! And I'll say it again: I ain't goin' nowhere with you."

"You ain't got a choice," Sara chuckles. "If you want to ride, I'm the only way there. Besides, we need to talk. Just give me a minute to explain, and then if you want me to, I'll leave. Deal?"

Clyde sighs. "Okay, but make it quick. It's a long walk to the arena. I'll give you more time than you gave me. Go ahead, I'm all ears," he agrees sarcastically.

"I'm so sorry for what happened at Ruthie's wedding; I was so rude."

"You can say that again," Clyde mutters.

She hesitates, wanting to respond, but decides to not acknowledge it. "Just the other night Mom sat all of us down and told us the truth about why you left." She stops to take a deep breath. "All I want is my little brother back." Fighting back tears, she swallows hard. "Our family has been robbed of so much already, I just want to . . ." She's unable to finish before she totally loses her composure. Clyde stands there for a moment in shock, and then reaches out and grabs her by the shoulders and pulls her to himself. He has thought about this moment for so long that it's hard to believe it's here. It literally hurts, but he doesn't want to let go and begins to cry. When he's finally able to speak, he says, "Thank you! I've been waiting for this for so long, but I have to get going or I'll miss my ride."

"Clyde, please don't ride tonight!" she pleads.

"Sorry, sis, I have to. But if ya don't mind, you can help me wrap up these ribs. The Doc told me how to, but I need some help." He gives her instructions and it only takes a couple of minutes. He grabs a clean shirt off the bed and they scurry out the door. The car's parked by the corral across from the house, and, as they reach it, Clyde sees movement out of his peripheral vision. Sara walks around the back of the car and leans against the top rail of the corral fence.

Curious, Clyde joins her. A horse gaits into the corral, followed by a rider who runs in and places her hands on its hind quarters and leaps upon it. Then she gently kicks its sides as it takes off at a gallop.

The rider begins to do tricks on the back of the horse. Clyde's awestruck watching this young lady ride. Dressed in black Levis with two-tone cowboy boots, her white blouse is embroidered on the upper chest and back. Her Stetson is secured with a string that comes under her chin. She stands in the stirrups and waves her left hand in the air. Then, in one smooth motion, she moves to one side of the saddle with the horse at full gallop. Next, she grabs the saddle horn and leans her body to the left. Next, she, drags her foot on the ground and springs herself from one side to the other.

Clyde watches and whispers to Sara, "They both look familiar."

"They should," Sara grins.

Clyde gives her a funny look and then decides to watch the show. As he looks back, the rider turns upside down on the left side. All they can see are her legs in the air. Then she grabs the reins and pulls up until she stands on the saddle, while guiding the horse over toward Clyde. On the other side of the fence, in front of Clyde, is one of the barrels that's used in barrel racing. Just before reaching them, she pulls back on the reins, bringing the horse to a stop as she steps off the saddle onto the barrel. Standing akimbo, she says, "Hey, Cowboy!"

Clyde takes a closer look and asks, "Rachel? Is that you?"

"Hello, big brother."

"Where did you learn to ride like that?" Clyde asks.

"I taught myself," Rachel replies. The horse walks up to the fence and puts his head over the top rail next to Clyde.

He takes a closer look, and asks Rachel, "Who's the horse?"

It's "CH."

"CH? That's a funny name for a horse," Clyde points out.

"CH stands for Clyde's Horse," Sara jumps in. "Don't you recognize him?"

Clyde takes a closer look. "It's Warrior!" He grabs him around the neck, rubs his hand between his eyes, and looks at Rachel. "You sure have grown up, young lady," he states.

Her lip begins to tremble and she cries, "Welcome home, Clyde." She steps onto the top rail and leaps into his arms, forgetting all about his ribs. They fall to the ground laughing and crying together. Sara looks at her watch and exclaims, "Clyde, you're going to be late! We have to get going!"

They quickly remove the tack from Warrior, hang it over the fence, and then scurry off to the car. "This is one great day," Clyde sighs.

Chapter 16
REUNITED

At the rodeo, the family settles in their seats, saving extra spaces for Rachel and Sara.

Once Harold finishes his ride, he heads around back to help with the stock and whatever else is needed. When he realizes the bull-riding event is next, he scans the area for Clyde, but he's nowhere to be found. Even though he's riding next to last, he still needs to check in. Harold's mind races; *I wonder if Sara went to get him. If she did, how upset will he be when he gets here?* He spots the family in the bleachers about six rows up, except for Sara and Rachel; he hopes they're on their way back. Harold helps guide the first group of bulls into the chutes. The event is moments away from starting, and if Clyde doesn't check in before it begins, he'll be disqualified. Harold walks over to the sign-in table, where he spots Clyde signing in. Then, like he always does, Clyde makes his way to the stock pens. Harold decides to leave him alone until he comes up to the chutes.

After a bit, Clyde approaches the chutes sporting a big grin, like the cat who ate the canary. "Everything okay?" Harold asks.

Clyde looks into the stands and says, "It couldn't be any better."

"That's wonderful, but you need to get your head together for this ride. What you're doing here is dangerous," Harold reiterates. "You need your mind on this moment right now."

Listening to Harold as he slowly climbs the chute, Clyde realizes he's right. He doesn't ride until the third wave so. Without thinking, he takes a couple of deep breaths like he normally does. But this time it sends pain shooting throughout his upper body; it hurts just to breathe. None of the riders are having a particularly good evening; the bulls are winning hands down. In fact, by the time it gets to Clyde, only one rider—the first one of the evening—has ridden through the buzzer. Clyde quickly calculates the score he needs and realizes that this event is his to lose. If he can ride this bull until the buzzer, the only rider who can beat him is the last one. The first rider to finish his ride tonight is in last place and has too big of a hill to climb, so if Clyde can somehow stay on and get a good score, he may not have to ride tomorrow, and that sounds good to him. He thinks back to what others have said about injuries: *Things like this always get worse the second day.* Using this as a motivator, he gathers his thoughts and focuses until he doesn't hear the crowd anymore.

He watches the guy just before him prepare for his ride, and then settles down on his bull. It doesn't take that cowboy long to find the ground, either. Clyde glances over as the last rider limps from the arena, and then finishes his wrap with his right elbow tight against his ribs. He can already feel the pressure. He never realized how much he tucks that elbow against his body. Once comfortable, at least as comfortable as he can get, he slowly scoots up over his hand, bringing sharp pains shooting through his chest cavity. The pain is so excruciating that he becomes light-headed. It's almost too much to take. He blinks, trying to focus, and then slowly moves his head from side to side. *Take short breaths,* he thinks. *Focus, . . . get this over with. After all, it's only eight seconds.*

✵ ✵ ✵

Sara and Rachel hurry to their seats just in time to see the bull riding commence. Mom starts to ask all sorts of questions and Sara calmly says, "He's in a lot of pain. Let's just watch what happens."

Not getting the answers she wants from Sara, Mom turns her attention to Rachel, but gets the same response. "Mom, not now, please," Rachel insists. "Let's watch Clyde. It's only eight seconds."

Mom turns her attention to the chutes and whispers a prayer.

✲ ✲ ✲

Grimacing, Clyde nods. The gateman notices his expression and hesitates. Clyde nods his head again and this time the gateman tugs on the rope. As the gate jerks open, the bull releases, and it seems as if everything else does, too. From the first buck, Clyde screams in pain. He grips the rope as tightly as he can, while his other hand flaps in the air. With every buck and turn, pain shoots throughout his upper body, and he can feel pops in his rib area. He tries to hold his breath, because with each new breath comes another round of pain. Still screaming at the top of his lungs, the pain's too much to bear. He thinks, *Enough is enough, I can't do this anymore. But how do I get off without it hurting even worse? That's going to be impossible,* so he decides to just let go. As he does, the horn sounds. He's done it, he's finished the ride! After the last buck, he tumbles off to the right side of the bull and attempts to land on his feet but stumbles and falls. The pain is unimaginable. He attempts to get to his feet but only makes it to his knees. Bending over to breathe, what was intermittent pain is now constant. He thinks, *How dumb am I? I'll never do this again!*

Then he hears it; the cheer of the crowd. Still on one knee, he looks up toward the bleachers to find the family. They're standing up, applauding his ride. Then he notices that the rest of the crowd is standing, too. He picks up his Stetson and waves it at the crowd.

Harold walks up and pats him gently on the back. "I don't know how you did that, but unless the guy behind you rides like a crazy man, you won't need to ride tomorrow."

"Good," Clyde grunts, "because I don't think I can. Mind giving me a hand?" he asks.

Harold reaches down and gently helps him to his feet.

✲ ✲ ✲

Still worried, Mom watches Clyde stand up and put the Stetson back on. She focuses on the hat because it has a familiar look to it. Then she recognizes it. Seeing her son wear her Elmer's hat brings a thousand thoughts to mind and a new freedom to her heart. She sits down on the wooden bench as a tear rolls down her cheek, sweeping away years of heartache and anguish with it.

Hunched over, Clyde walks ever so gingerly toward the chutes, with Harold alongside. They stand together to watch the last rider, who makes the horn, but is disqualified because his free hand touched the bull.

No one's quite sure whether it's his ride or his guts the judges admire, but Clyde leads the event and probably won't have to ride tomorrow. Harold and Audra escort him to the medical tent where they spend the next few hours getting Clyde doctored up.

Once the events are over, the family makes its way to the back area and waits outside the medical tent. As they wait, Sara finally shares what happened when she and Rachel went to pick up Clyde. At times, Mom interrupts, but Sara, still upset over this whole thing, ignores her questions and continues her story.

Visibly upset, Mom is about to say something when Jim asks, "Dorris, would you mind taking a walk with me? I want to see if I can find something to eat. There should be a booth open over at the carnival."

She hesitates before answering, "I don't want to miss Clyde, Jim. You go ahead."

"Mom, go ahead," Ruthie insists. "I have a feeling it's going to be a while. Besides, we won't go anywhere when he does come out."

"Okay," she reluctantly agrees. Jim grabs her by the hand and they walk toward the carnival.

When they're out of earshot, Ruthie lets Sara have it. "Sara, what do you think you're doing? Mom was asking you questions and you just ignored her."

Indignant that Ruthie would take Mom's side, she fires back, "What do you mean by that? Mom hid the truth from us! Let's call a spade a spade; she lied. I'm so upset about that and you should be too, but all you want to do is holler at me! Just leave me alone. If you want to go on as if nothing's happened, that's fine for you. But don't try to tell me what to do."

Watching Ruthie's expression change, Martin can see this is about to get ugly and tries to calm things down. "Listen, ladies, over the past 24 hours, you've both been on an emotional roller coaster. Please slow down and take a couple of minutes to think about this. You have your brother back, and you're going to be able to spend time with him! Don't allow anger and bitterness to ruin the wonderful blessing you've been given."

That takes the wind out of their sails; neither knows what to say. Finally, Sara responds, "Thank you, Martin, that's what I needed to hear." With a chuckle, she continues, "Not really what I wanted to hear, but you're right. There have already been too many mistakes made." She looks at Ruthie. "You're right, I shouldn't have done that to Mom. I'll deal with it later."

Shocked that Sara gave up so easily, Ruthie apologizes. "I'm sorry, too. Tell you what, let's enjoy this time."

"That sounds good to me," Sara concludes.

☆ ☆ ☆

"What are you hungry for?" Dorris asks as they walk toward the carnival.

"I'm not really hungry," Jim confesses. "I saw how Sara was ignoring you, how upset you were getting, so I thought a nice walk would help."

"Jim Bodine, you lied to me!" Dorris proclaims.

"Hold on a minute," he says as he walks up to a booth. "Can I have some cotton candy, please?"

"You sure can," the vendor answers. "Hold on one second."

As he waits for the cotton candy, he tells Dorris, "No, I didn't. I said I wanted to find some food. See, I found some."

Dorris shakes her head as she laughs. "Why would you do that?"

"Do what?" Jim asks.

"Want to take me away from the conversation."

He pays the vendor and as they walk away sharing the cotton candy, he explains, "I could tell you were upset and needed a break." She stops in her tracks and is about to say something when he continues, "Now let me finish, please. The girls, well Sara at least, are upset with you right now. They probably feel deceived. Think about it from Sara's perspective; all this time she thought her brother had run out on the family. Then when she sees him for the first time in quite a while, she tells him off. Now she finds out he didn't leave after all. Don't you think you'd be pretty embarrassed and upset?"

"Yeah, I suppose you're right, but . . ."

"Dorris, there can't be any *buts* right now," Jim interrupts. "You have your son back, don't lose your daughter over it. You're a family again. Isn't that all you ever wanted?"

With that said, the tears begin to flow. She nods as she takes her handkerchief from her pocket and wipes her eyes. "Yes Jim, it is. You're right; I'll take care of this later. Thank you."

"You're welcome. Now we better get back. Clyde is probably done."

They walk toward the tent and when they're about a hundred yards away, they can see silhouettes standing out front. "There's my boy," Dorris declares. She picks up her pace, thinking, *With every card and with every gift, I have longed for this day. I can't wait to hold my son again.* Jim lags behind, not wanting to get in the way of this reunion.

✲ ✲ ✲

The doctor gives his instructions as the nurse finishes wrapping Clyde's ribs. He got off lucky this time. The cracking he heard while riding was the ribs moving around; he was lucky one didn't break loose and puncture a lung. The doctor never dreamt that Clyde would be riding tonight, so this time he's much more demanding. As they leave, he asks Harold, "Do you care for this young man?"

"He's like a brother to me," Harold responds.

"If he means that much to you and he even thinks about riding tomorrow, you'd better hogtie him to the bedpost or something. I'm afraid you can't be that lucky two days in a row."

"Okay, Doc," Harold agrees, "I'll do something far worse than that."

"I don't think either one of you have to worry about that," Clyde groans. "I can guarantee I won't be riding tomorrow. Night, Doc, and thanks."

"Goodnight, young man, and take those pills because I can guarantee you one thing; you're going to need them."

They make their way from the tent and he sees the family standing outside, waiting. The first one Clyde sees is Ruthie. He tears up as he walks over and gives her a gentle hug. "It's so good to see you again. Sorry I didn't stay around at the wedding."

"That's okay," she says, sniffling. He looks over her shoulder and spots Martin standing behind her. He extends his hand; Martin takes it and gently shakes it.

"You've got yourself one fine woman. Make sure you take care of her," Clyde warns, "or I may come lookin' for ya." The group laughs, knowing how Martin feels about Ruthie.

Clyde softly asks, "Where's Mom?"

"She and Jim took a little walk," Sara says as she walks over and hugs him. "They'll be right back."

Rachel spots them in the distance. "There they are," she says.

Clyde has thought about this day for so long, when he would be able to give his mom a hug and peck on the cheek. As she gets closer, he can tell she's spotted him as well and quickens her pace. He's still hunched over a little and begins to make his way toward her. As she gets closer, he can tell she's forgotten about his ribs, so he slowly puts both hands up. He takes a couple of steps back and hollers, "Easy, Mom! I'm hurting, but I so want a hug."

Dorris stops. "I'm so glad you said something! I'd forgotten all about that," she acknowledges as she walks over and gently puts her arms around him. She lets out a big sigh, and starts to cry on his shoulder. While she weeps, she tries to talk, going a mile a minute, and no one can understand anything she's saying.

Finally, Harold speaks up. "Audra and I have to get going. Clyde, I'll see you back at the ranch. Audra can give me a ride, and you can take the truck."

Arm in arm with Mom, with the girls wrapped around them in a circle, Clyde thanks Harold as he walks off. At the same time, Jim says, "It's getting late, I best be moving along myself. I'll see you all later. Have a wonderful evening."

"Thank you for coming with us. I'll talk to you in a few days," Dorris shouts as Jim walks away. He waves his arm, acknowledging that he heard her.

To give the family some time to themselves, Martin says, "I just remembered I need to check on my dad and, make sure he's okay. See you at home, Ruthie!" Still in the group hug, Ruthie wrinkles her nose and mouths, "Thank you."

There's little talking going on, so Clyde breaks the silence. "Can we go somewhere to sit down and talk? My ribs are killing me."

"Let's go home," Dorris answers.

"That sounds great. I'll follow you," Clyde agrees.

"Clyde, can I ride with you, please?" Rachel implores.

"It's okay with me, if it's all right with Mom."

"I'll go, too!" Sara quickly adds.

"We can fit three in the cab," Clyde offers.

"Beat ya home," Rachel challenges, taking off on a dead run.

"Sara's taught her one thing," Ruthie tells Mom.

"Yeah, what's that?" Mom asks.

"How to be competitive," Ruthie answers with a laugh. Mom nods in agreement. They make their way to the outer parking lot and head for home.

✵ ✵ ✵

It's early morning before the visiting begins to wind down and the only reason for that is because everyone is about to fall asleep. Clyde took one of the pills Doc gave him, and it didn't take long to take effect. Slurring his words like a drunk makes for a lot of laughter, something that hasn't been there for quite some time. Half asleep, Clyde gingerly walks out to the truck and heads back to the Goldberg's.

✵ ✵ ✵

It's not long before the sun peeks through Clyde's bedroom window, and he tries to roll over. He feels a pop and lets out a yell. Harold comes running, flings open the bedroom door, and sees Clyde doubled up on the bed.

"What's wrong, Half-Pint?"

Clyde looks up and says, "Remember the doc said that one rib would have to reset itself?"

"Yeah?"

Wincing in pain, Clyde whispers, "I think it just did."

Harold lets out a hoot, then explains, "Sorry, it ain't funny, but your scream sounded like a cow getting branded."

"Oh, go ahead and laugh, and enjoy it. I ain't always going to be around to laugh at." With that, they both pause at the realization that in a couple of days, Clyde's words will come true.

To break the silence, Clyde says, "Hey, get out of here so I can get ready to go. I have to collect my well-deserved earnings."

Making light of the situation, Harold adds as he turns to go, "Ah, well-deserved, my foot! All you did was ride two bulls for a total of sixteen seconds."

Clyde looks up and begins to chuckle. "Ouch! Please don't make me laugh; it hurts."

✵ ✵ ✵

It's early Sunday morning at the ranch and Al's not feeling well, so he sends one of his workers over to get Doc.

Red is putting the final touches on his sermon when someone knocks on his door. He swivels his chair and says, "Enter."

The door opens a crack, and Doc pokes his head in. "Do you have a couple of minutes?"

"Sure, come on in. You're here early for the service, though," Red jokes, as Doc doesn't normally attend.

"I'm sure the service is going to be great, but I'll miss it," Doc says.

"Sorry to hear that, but you must have come by for something," Red states.

"I'm sorry for disturbing you, but I just thought you would want to know."

"Know what?"

"I just got the results back on Al's final tests, and it's what I was afraid of."

"You mean . . ." Red asks.

"Yeah, it's what I had told you."

"Have you told him yet?" Red asks.

"No, I waited; figured you'd want to be there when I tell him."

Red takes a deep breath. "Yeah, I definitely want to be there."

Another knock comes at the door. Red quietly says, "Enter."

A worker from the ranch peeks in. "Pastor, I'm looking for Doc. Someone told me they spotted him heading this way. Have you seen him?"

From the blind spot behind the door, Doc says, "I'm here. What do you need?"

"Oh, hey Doc, Boss ain't feeling so well. He asked if I'd fetch ya."

Doc stands up and says, "Tell him I'll be right out."

"Okay, thanks Doc," the worker says and shuts the door as he leaves.

✵ ✵ ✵

Harold and Clyde make their way to the truck. Clyde is walking gingerly, favoring his ribs, and makes a quick stop at the corral to groom Warrior, when Sam makes his way over. Harold walks around the back of the truck to shake Sam's hand as he walks up. Clyde picks up a brush and brushes Warrior's mane.

"I hear Rachel surprised you yesterday," Sam says.

"She sure did," Clyde confirms. "That girl can really ride."

"Here's a little history for you. That young lady has been on Warrior almost every day since I got him," Sam explains. "She's taken care of him like he was her own. Her name for him is CH."

"Yeah, that's what she said," Clyde smiles.

"Well, I want you to know that he's yours. I'm keeping him for you, and Rachel is taking care of him until you can take him."

"I don't know what to say, Mr. G. Thanks!"

"Your pop and Walter would want it that way. With them both gone, I wanted you to have something to remember them by," Sam explains.

"This sure has been one great weekend; I'm reunited with the family, it looks like I'll win the bull-riding event, and I'm partnered up with the horse my dad gave me and I trained. You know I'd cry right now, but it would hurt too much," he says with a chuckle.

"Yeah, don't forget, you had a little help breaking that horse," Harold reminds him.

Clyde smiles. "I'm so grateful to both of you. Thank you so much. I don't know how I can ever repay you."

Harold winks at Sam. "I want to go to New York, so you can repay us by riding at The Garden."

"You've got yourself a deal!" Clyde grins.

Chapter 17

GOOD NEWS, BAD NEWS

As Doc moves toward the door, he looks back at Red. "Do you want me to wait for you?"

"You better not, he may really be hurting," Red points out. "But do you think you can wait to tell him until I get there?"

"I can do that. What time are you usually done?" Doc asks.

"Usually around noon, but I'll move it along faster today. How about if I meet you at the ranch a little after twelve?" Red proposes as they walk out of the office toward the sanctuary. The early arrivals greet them as they walk down the aisle toward the back of the church.

When they reach the double doors, Claire approaches them. "Hope your sermon's good this morning, Pastor. I haven't gotten much out of the last few."

Red smiles as Doc rolls his eyes. "Now, Claire, you'd get a lot more out of my sermons if you stayed awake."

"Pastor, how you can say such a thing!" Claire protests. "You know I'm not sleeping; just resting my eyes."

Chuckling, Red tells Doc, "See you in bit."

Doc nods and thinks, *How does he take someone telling him they're not getting anything out of his teaching? I'm glad I didn't choose that profession!*

✲ ✲ ✲

It's early afternoon and the arena is packed for this last day of the rodeo. The opening ceremonies go off without a hitch, and Audra rides back behind the chutes, where she's greeted by Harold.

"That's the last time you'll be doing that," he remarks as he helps her from her horse.

She pretends to fall and Harold catches her. "Nice catch! I guess it'll be worth it," she teases.

Harold pulls her close and gives her a kiss on the cheek as her hat falls and hangs by the fabric cord under her neck. It's too much for Clyde, who slowly heads toward the grandstands to see if he can find the family. He slowly climbs the steps while surveying the crowd.

"Clyde! Up here!" a familiar voice hollers. Looking up a few rows, he spots Sara and Rachel waving their arms. He pauses every few steps and takes a short breath as he makes his way toward them. When he finally reaches the top, the crowd around the family recognizes him and begins to applaud. He tips his hat and tries to sit down, but soon realizes that puts too much pressure on his ribs, so he excuses himself and heads back to the staging area as the calf-roping begins.

✵ ✵ ✵

Once the church service is over, Red quickly closes up and heads to Al's. While it's not all that far from town, to Red it seems like it takes forever. As he drives, all kinds of different scenarios run through his head and he prays, *Lord, I don't know what to think right now, but I know You're there with me and Al. Please give me the right words to say as Al and I talk. Lord, give him peace when he hears that he is going to be home with you soon. In Jesus' name, Amen.* He wraps up his prayer as he pulls onto the gravel road that leads to the ranch house. Off in the distance, he notices two figures standing on the porch. Once he's close enough, he sees Doc talking to Al's housekeeper. As he pulls up, they each acknowledge him with a wave. He shuts off the engine, gets out, and makes his way to the porch just as the housekeeper steps back inside.

Doc places his hand on Red's shoulder and says, "You ready for this?"

"I guess so," Red responds. "But don't you think you should tell me before we see him?"

"Thanks for reminding me," Doc pauses, and then looks toward the ground and back up again. "I almost forgot; Al has cancer. I think it's in his lungs and probably other organs, too."

"Are you sure?" Red responds, shocked. "Is that what the tests showed?"

"These tests aren't always conclusive," Doc continues, "but I've checked with a couple of my colleagues, and that's our best guess."

"How much time do you think he has?" Red asks.

"From what I know about this and the way he's acting and feeling, I don't think he has much time left."

"What do you mean by 'much time'?" Red asks, trying to pinpoint the time frame. "You mean a year or two?"

"Oh my, no! It could be a matter of days, weeks at the most."

"What? Days or weeks? Are you sure, Doc?"

"Red, when was the last time you saw him?"

"Let me think." He purses his lips. "Just over a week, now. Why?"

"I saw him a couple days ago, and he looks totally different now; so when you see him, don't be shocked," Doc warns as he opens the front door and they head upstairs.

When Doc opens the door to Al's room, they see him struggling to sit up in bed. By the expression on his face, Red can tell he's in a lot of pain. *Doc was right,* he thinks, *he does look really bad. His face has gotten so thin; nothing like the Italian I first met. He's so pale; maybe I just didn't notice it before. How could this happen so quickly?*

Hearing the door creak, Al looks over, gives them half a grin, and weakly says, "Red, what are you doing here? Aren't you supposed to be preaching or something?"

"Oh, it doesn't take long to put them to sleep nowadays," Red chuckles. "When they were all asleep, I thought I'd sneak out here and preach to you. I heard you needed some rest, too."

Al laughs, but then begins to cough. It takes a minute for him to catch his breath. "I remember the last time you two were here together. Not my best of days," Al smiles as he maneuvers himself, trying to get comfortable.

Doc clears his throat. "Al, I've got something to tell you and thought it would be best for Red to hear it at the same time."

Al looks at the ceiling and closes his eyes. "Doc, for you to ask Red to be here, it has to be bad news. So let me save you some time." He turns to Red, "You've taught me that my days on this planet are numbered." Then he turns back to Doc. "And what you're trying to say is that number is about up." Doc looks down at his unpolished black shoes as Al continues, "I've had a great life and have made peace with The Man upstairs. So Doc, it's okay. Really. But I do have a question for you."

"What's that? Doc asks.

"We're all going to die, right?" Al inquires.

"That's what I hear," Doc responds with half a grin.

"Then, if we're all going to do it, we should be ready to meet The Man upstairs, right?"

"Sure, I suppose so, if that's what you believe. I'm not quite sure where you're going with this, Al."

He rolls to his side to face Doc and Red and asks, "Are you ready, Doc?"

Surprised by the question, he responds, "Still don't know what you mean, Al. I'm not the one who's sick."

"You're right there," Al grins, "but I'm ready. In fact, I'm looking forward to it! No more pain, no more sorrow, no more Benny." This brings a chuckle from Red as Al continues, "I'm really tired now, got to get some rest. Red, do me a favor."

"Sure, my friend, whatever you want."

"I can tell by the look on Doc's face that he's not sure what I meant. I'd love to explain it to him, but I don't have the energy. Would you do that for me?"

"I'd love to," Red responds. "Now you get some rest. I'll be here; just ring the bell if you need anything."

"Okay," Al whispers as he closes his eyes and drifts off into a medicated sleep.

Red goes to the door and just before he closes it, looks back at Al and prays to himself: *Lord, my friend is in Your hands. Thank You for allowing me the privilege of knowing him. Please take him home and don't allow him to suffer more than he has already, in Jesus name.*

They head downstairs and take a seat in the parlor. Before Red can say anything, Doc says, "You know, Red, I've heard all that religious stuff most of my life, so what you're going to say I've probably already heard."

"You probably have, but I did promise my friend," Red counters.

"Okay, I'll give you that. I'm all ears," Doc answers.

As Red begins to explain the difference between having a religion and a relationship with God, he can tell Doc is more interested than what he thought he'd be. He explains how Jesus came and died as the payment for our sins, that it wasn't about any religion, but how he could have a personal relationship with the Creator of this world.

When he finishes, Doc admits, "I've never heard it explained quite that way before. I always thought that you had to follow a certain religion, and then the question is, which one? What you said makes a lot of sense to me now, and I would love to hear more about it when we have time. But now we need to figure out what's happening with Al. Do you plan on staying out here until the time comes?" he politely asks.

"Probably," Red responds. "I see what you mean about how weak he is."

"And it's only going to get worse. He has really gone downhill over the last few days; it won't be long."

☆ ☆ ☆

Clyde enjoys being behind the chutes and listening to all the conversations. He's never really paid much attention to them before, since he's always focused on preparing himself mentally for his ride. As he gingerly leans against the chute railing, he sees Harold and Audra walking toward him. Not wanting to move much because of the pain, he nods his head as they approach.

"You feeling better?" Audra asks as she ever so gently gives him a hug.

"I guess it's better. Still hard to move and breathing can be a struggle at times, but other than that, I guess I'm fine," he says with a slight laugh.

"That doesn't sound good! Sounded like you wanted to say, 'I'm okay, it only hurts when I breathe'," Harold tosses in with a chuckle.

Clyde nods his head in agreement as the announcer bellows, "It's now time for the bull-riding event, our final event of the day and the rodeo."

As Audra excuses herself to get ready for the closing ceremonies, Clyde and Harold move to the platform just below the announcer's booth, which is in front of some of the VIP's and all the way over to the other side where Sam and his wife are sitting. Sam stands up and offers his seat to Clyde, who at first declines, but then accepts the invitation when the pain becomes more intense. These seats are different than the bleachers; they have a soft comfortable back with a lower back-support, which helps Clyde sit more upright. As he settles in his seat, the first bull leaves the chute. Clyde watches one rider after another until finally the last ride of the weekend is about to take place. He's the only cowboy who can beat him now, and he'll need to have a perfect ride. It doesn't take long for Clyde to relax; the bull leaps from the chute, and the rider can't hold on. He flies off the backside and slams against the gate. As the bull takes another buck, its back hoof kicks the cowboy's mouth, slamming his head against the chute, and he's knocked out cold. A hush comes over the crowd as the clowns quickly disperse the bull from the arena and others run to the cowboy's aid. He's unconscious, lying on his side, with blood flowing profusely from his mouth. The doctor runs over with a hand gurney, and they carry him off. Silence fills the arena as the announcer barks out the winner of the bull-riding. "Ladies and gentleman, the winner of this year's bull-riding event is our very own Clyde Lewis! Congratulations, Clyde!"

After what just took place, the crowd's not sure how to respond, and neither is Clyde. Finally, a few begin to applaud, and then others join in. Sam and Harold encourage Clyde to stand up and acknowledge the crowd. It takes a bit for him to finally get upright and wave his hat. Embarrassed, Clyde's not sure how to gracefully bow out. He gets bailed out when the arena gates open and riders enter to begin the closing ceremonies. Once they're all in and lined up facing the grandstands, the front-row riders take off their hats and bow as their horses bend on their front knees. Then a lone horse and rider enter from the far end at a slow trot. The announcer bellows, "Ladies and Gentleman, we have one more local treat for you. Would you please welcome into the arena Rachel Lewis, riding Warrior." The crowd applauds as Rachel trots by and then goes into her routine. Clyde can't believe it's his little sister doing her trick-riding in front of this large crowd, doing the same thing she did for him yesterday. Harold puts his arm around him and says, "Welcome home, my friend, welcome home."

"Did you know about this?" Clyde asks.

"Sam told me this morning when I got here. He said he wanted you to know how much your family is loved."

Clyde slowly sits down and fights back tears. Rachel finishes her ride in front of the grandstands.

The family members make their way to the arena floor and start hugging Rachel as Harold, Sam, and Clyde walk up. Clyde walks over and gives Rachel a gentle hug as Mom stands back, watches, and begins to tear up.

Sam interrupts the family reunion by saying, "I want everyone to come out to our place for our annual after-the-rodeo barbeque."

They accept his invitation and head out for an evening of eating, drinking, and visiting. All evening Sam and Harold try to convince Clyde to stay around and work until the next season begins. While tempted to do so, he thinks, *The longer I stay, the harder it will be to leave later. I can't get caught up in all of this.*

✵ ✵ ✵

True to his word, Red hasn't left Al's side since he found out about how short of a time he has left. He called Al's family in Chicago and informed them of his condition, and Benny is on his way. It's only takes a few days for Doc's prophecy to be fulfilled.

The medication makes Al drift in and out of sleep. Then, one afternoon while Red's reading the Bible to him, Al whispers, "Remember those two regrets I shared about my life?"

Red puts down the bible and leans over to hear. "Yeah, I remember. Why?"

"Naming you as executor took care of one, but I couldn't do the other."

"Which one?"

All Al can get out is, "Warrior."

Red beams. "I forgot to tell you. We prayed for God to take care of that and He did. Sam ran across the cowpoke who had him and bought him back. Rachel's been riding him, and she's pretty good. So see, God honored your request."

With half a grin and a sparkle in his eye, Al says, "Good. I'm really tired, going to rest a bit."

"Go ahead, I'll read to you."

"Thanks, and take care of Maggie," Al whispers.

"I will, my friend, I will," Red replies. While sitting next to him, Red alternately reads and prays. Sometime within the next hour or so, Al slips off into eternity. Red covers him up and goes downstairs with tears streaming down his face to make the appropriate calls.

✵ ✵ ✵

Clyde spends the next couple of days getting reacquainted with the family. With his ribs still hurting, he decides to forgo the last rodeo of the season and stay around town a while longer. He's enjoying this time with Mom, but he's not quite sure about Jim's intentions. While it's hard to remember Mom being with his dad, he's uncomfortable seeing her with another man. Even though they're just friends, Jim does seem to be coming around more frequently.

One evening as they're sitting around having dinner, Clyde announces that he's leaving the next morning. "I got a telegram from a friend who has a job opening until the rodeo season kicks back up, and I've decided to take it."

Even though they would never admit it, they all knew this day would come. You could hear a pin drop in the silence. No one knows what to say, so Ruthie takes the opportunity to make an announcement of her own. "Clyde, I wish you weren't leaving. We lost you once and don't look forward to losing you again, but there's another reason why I hate to see you go."

He raises his brow. "Yeah, and what would that be?"

"You're going to miss the birth of your little niece or nephew," Ruthie says with a grin.

Mom jumps up and shouts, "You mean I'm going to be a grandma?"

"Yes, Mom, you're going to be a grandma."

"Hot diggity dog," Sara joins in. "Auntie Sara has a pretty good ring to it, don't it!"

Clyde sits back, glad the focus is off of him, and thinks, *Life is full of changes and surprises. It's all about learning how to accept them as they come and then moving forward.*

Maggie gets up and gives Ruthie a hug and congratulations just as someone knocks on the door. With the celebration going on, Martin's not sure if they heard it, so he steps over and opens the door.

"Martin, is Maggie here?" Doc asks.

"Sure Doc, come on in," Martin replies as he steps aside. "Maggie, Doc's here to see you."

"Evening, Maggie. Sorry to disturb your get-together, but I thought you'd want to know that Al passed on today."

Maggie sits down at the table and begins to cry. "I'm so sorry to hear that. I knew he was ill and wanted to go see him, but I didn't think I could handle going back in the house."

Dorris moves around the table and places her hands on Maggie's shoulders. "It's okay, Maggie. That would've been hard for any of us."

Standing next to Maggie, Ruthie asks, "Was he alone when he passed?"

"No, Red was with him, reading the Bible," Doc acknowledges.

"Oh, good. We had our differences, but he sure did change over the last few years," Ruthie notes.

"Yeah, a lot of people say that," Doc agrees. "Well, I best be on my way. Sorry for interrupting your gathering; just thought you'd want to know."

Maggie stands up to walk him to the door. "I'm glad you did. Thank you, Doc."

"You're welcome. Goodnight now."

"Goodnight."

Chapter 18

AL GETS THE FINAL SAY

The sun's peeking over the horizon as Clyde says his goodbyes to Harold and heads to town to gas up and say goodbye to the family. As he pulls in front of the house, he can smell breakfast cooking. Opening the door, he sees Mom cooking his favorite; homemade biscuits and gravy. It doesn't take him long to find a seat at the table, and, with his mouth watering, he waits for Mom to say grace before they dig in.

With his first bite, Rachel begins to cry and Clyde asks, "What's wrong?"

"I don't want you to leave," she says as she wipes her tears with her blue-checkered apron. Then Mom begins to sniffle, and Sara struggles to hold back her emotions.

"Oh, I'll be back. It's only for a short time; you'll see," Clyde assures them as he takes another bite.

After a few helpings, he stands up and heads to the coat rack to get his hat as the ladies follow closely behind. He gives each of them a hug and a kiss on the cheek.

Mom holds him a little longer than the other two and tenderly says, "Please take care of yourself and come home soon."

"All of you are always with me," Clyde quietly assures her. "This has been a great time and I look forward to coming back." He turns and walks to the truck. As he pulls away, the ladies stand on the porch waving until he's out of sight.

He can't help but think he may be doing the wrong thing. These last few days have been some of the best of his life. Mom, Ruthie,

Martin, Sara, Rachel, and then Harold and Audra, are the most significant people in his life, and now he's leaving them for the unknown. It doesn't make much sense, but it's what he believes he has to do.

✦ ✦ ✦

Clyde pulls up to the pumps as Martin looks out from the shop. They greet each other and Clyde tells him to fill it up. Martin puts the hose in the top of the tank, and then asks, "Where're you headed?"

"East; that rodeo buddy of mine is just across the Oklahoma Texas border."

Martin thinks for a second before responding, "Ruthie doesn't understand why you don't stay around here, and, quite frankly, this doesn't make much sense to me, either."

"I know it don't look too smart," Clyde reasons, "but the way I figure it; if I don't leave now, I may never leave. I've got some things to do and places to see. Besides that, I love ridin' the bulls, and I'm afraid I'll get too comfortable here and not get back to ridin'."

Martin still doesn't agree and can tell he's not getting anywhere. "Well, I don't know nothing about riding, but my pop told me that if you came by this morning, I should tell you that it's on the house."

"Now, you can't go doing that. I've got the money," Clyde assures him.

"Nope, your money don't work here. It's a thank you from us for making us proud," Martin tells him.

"Okay, if you insist," Clyde says, giving in. "But I want you to know that I'm looking forward to meeting that there nephew or niece when they arrive."

"We'll keep you updated. Now you be safe," Martin says as he shakes his hand and walks back to the garage area.

Clyde carefully slides into the truck, his ribs still hurting, and makes his way out of town.

✦ ✦ ✦

A couple of days pass before Benny arrives to claim Al's body. The family's decided to take him home to Chicago for the burial, so Benny made all the arrangements.

Maggie and Dorris are at the kitchen table having a cup of coffee and Dorris can tell there's something on her mind. "Is everything okay, Maggie?"

"I don't know," Maggie thoughtfully responds as she places both hands around her cup. "Did you hear that Benny came by the house yesterday?"

"No, I didn't. What did he want?" Dorris inquires.

Maggie takes a deep breath and begins, "He told me to start packing my bags. Now that Al's gone, he'll need the house for more important matters."

"What?" Dorris exclaims. "Who does he think he is, Mr. Big Shot, coming into your place and telling you to leave?"

"That's what I thought at first, too. But you know, it is legally Al's home. We never did do any paperwork," she acknowledges and begins to cry.

"But Maggie, Al said he'd take care of you. Remember?"

"That's what he said, but he's not around anymore. I can't believe this; I lost the ranch and now I'm going to lose my place to live. I don't have any money or a job or anything. I don't know what to do," Maggie despairs as she puts her head down.

"He's not going to get away with this!" Dorris threatens. She reaches over and grabs Maggie's hands. "Everything is going to be fine. If things get bad, you can always move in with us; we'd love to have you. But let's take it one day at a time."

As she finishes, someone knocks at the door. Maggie scoots her chair back from the table and wipes her eyes with her apron as she gets up. She stops for a moment at the door, trying to regain her composure. When she opens it, to her surprise there stands Claire.

"Morning, Maggie," Claire greets her. "Sorry for just dropping by like this, but I tried to call. Your phone must be off the hook."

Maggie glances over and sees the receiver hanging from the cord. "It sure is. I'm sorry, what can I do for you, Claire?"

"Pastor Red wanted me to contact you. He's going to read Al's Will this afternoon in his office and would like you to be there."

"Why would he want me there? Who else is going to be there?" Maggie asks.

"I don't know why he wants you there; I'm just delivering the message. As far as I know, he's invited Benny, the sheriff, and the Lewis family. But I haven't been able to raise anyone over there, either."

"Oh, Dorris is here," Maggie says as she steps aside and opens the door a little wider.

"Hello, Dorris, it's good to see you," Claire greets her.

Dorris tries to clarify what she heard. "Did you say I'm supposed to be there, too?"

"Yes, you and the girls."

"What time?" Dorris asks.

"At two o'clock sharp. Well, got to run. You two have a nice day," Claire says as she turns and goes.

Maggie slowly closes the door. "Dorris, why would Red want us there for that? Oh, this can't be good."

"I don't know. You may be right, but what bothers me is that he asked the sheriff to be there. What is Red up to?" Dorris questions.

✵ ✵ ✵

Red sits quietly behind his small oak desk reading the Scriptures while he waits for the others to arrive. He glances up at the wall where the hands on his oak Mauthe clock with the Roman numerals point to 1:53 p.m. He closes his Bible and begins to pray, *Lord, give me the strength to read his Will and help me to stay calm. Prepare the hearts of those who hear. In Jesus name, Amen.*

As he finishes, the office door swings open and in steps Benny. "Looks like I found the right door," he declares and turns to his bodyguard. "You stay right there. I'll be out in a minute; this isn't going to take long."

Standing in front of Red, in his double-breasted brown pinstriped suit, he doesn't even greet him. He takes off his wide-brimmed brown Fedora and places it on the desk in front of him. "Okay, let's get this over with. I got things to do. So, where is it?"

Shaking his head in disgust, Red asks, "Where's what?"

"You know, *The Will!* It can't be that much to read. My little fratello didn't own much; just that little old shack, and I took care of that."

Opening the top drawer of his desk to pull out The Will, Red looks up and asks, "What do you mean by that?"

Benny takes a seat, crosses his legs, and snickers, "Went by there the other day and told the old lady that she'd better pack-up and get ready to move."

"You didn't have any right to do that!" Red says as he stands to his feet.

"Slow down there, Pastor. You don't want to do anything like that. I figured it's my property and I can do what I want with it, and she needs to get out."

"You don't know that, either," Red suggests.

Benny uncrosses his legs and sits on the edge of his chair. "Oh, no? Let me tell you something, Parson. Everything Al owned is the family's; he bought it with family money. That's just the way it is. Now, get on with the reading."

Red rolls back in his oak and leather schoolhouse desk chair. "I can't read it until everyone is here."

"What?" Benny demands. "What do you mean 'everyone'?"

"I've invited a few others to witness the reading. They should be along any time now."

Before Benny can say anything else, Maggie quietly knocks and opens the door. "I hope I'm not interrupting," she says.

"Oh no, come right on in," Red replies. He's a little shocked when she enters. Maggie always dresses very conservatively, but today she's wearing a fancy grayish-blue dress with two pockets on the top and gold buttons down the front. Then, one after another, the Lewises enter behind her.

"Sorry we're late, but the gentleman outside wouldn't let us in. At least not until the sheriff showed up," Maggie explains. With Benny sitting in the first of three chairs, Maggie makes her way over to the farthest one from him and takes her seat. This means Dorris must decide to either sit next to Benny or stand. It doesn't take long for her to decide to stand toward the back of the small office.

When Benny hears that the sheriff's there, he quickly turns his head and spots him standing right behind him. Noticeably uncomfortable, he asks, "What's he doing here?"

He no more has that out of his mouth when the sheriff stretches out his hand, offering it to Benny. "Just here to keep the peace," he calmly replies.

Benny ignores the gesture and folds his arms across his chest. "I don't know what they're all doing here, but let's get this over with."

Red chuckles and thinks, *This guy sure likes to tell people what to do. I'm glad the sheriff's here.* "Okay," Red begins, "Before I read The Will, I want to thank all of you for coming. Everyone knows everyone, correct?" They all nod in agreement. "Good, then let's get started."

"It's about time," Benny mutters under his breath.

Red ignores him and begins to read:

> *"I, Albert Napoli, of the Township of Monte Vista, County of Rio Grande, and State of Colorado, being of sound and disposing mind and memory, do hereby make, publish, and declare this to be my Last Will and Testament, hereby revoking all Wills and Codicils previously made by me.*
>
> *I declare that I have never been married as of the date of this Will. I further declare*

that I have no children born to or adopted by me.

I direct that all of my legally enforceable debts, funeral expenses, and estate administration expenses be paid as soon after my death as may be practicable, except that any debt or expense secured by a mortgage, pledge, or similar encumbrance on property owned by me at my death need not be paid by my estate, but such property may pass subject to such mortgage, pledge, or similar encumbrance."

Benny starts to squirm in his chair. "Okay, okay, let's get to the main part."

"Sorry, Benny, but I checked with the judge and all of this must be read to make this legally binding, so just be patient."

The sheriff walks up behind him and pats him on the back. "Easy, it'll only take a minute."

Benny glares at him before turning his attention back to Red.

Red continues:

"To the individuals listed below, I give and bequeath the following:

To my brother Benny Napoli of Chicago, if he survives me, I leave my portion of the Western Drake located at 110 'A' Street and all related equipment."

Benny scoots up to the edge of his chair and furrows his brow, but doesn't say anything.

> *"To my wonderful friend, Maggie Livingston, of Monte Vista, Colorado, if she survives me, I leave the house at 213 5th Street and all related equipment, if owned by me at the time of my death."*

Maggie sits back in her chair, and asks, "Pastor, you sure you read that right?"

Benny stands up. "You better read that again," he sneers, "because Al couldn't give something away that wasn't his."

Red puts down The Will and declares, "Benny, I've checked all this out and had the judge to go over it with me. Everything written and recorded in this Will is legal and binding, so please sit down and be quiet."

Red picks up The Will and resumes reading:

> *"To the Lewis family; Dorris, Ruthie, Sara, Clyde, and Rachel, I have set up an estate in your name, and in that estate I place the two acres of the Circle A ranch, located 1.2 miles south of the town of Monte Vista, Colorado, if any of them survives me, if owned by me at the time of my death. These two acres shall include the two acres as you enter the ranch and include all buildings on the site of the two acres. The rest of the property shall be placed in the hands of*

Benny Napoli for the disposal of or whatever
he sees fit."

The girls look at each other and Dorris begins to cry. Rachel shouts, "Hot diggity-dog, now I can be around CH all the time!"

This really chaps Benny's hide and he jumps to his feet. "That property's part of our corporation, and he didn't have the right to give anything away." The sheriff reaches over, takes Benny by the shoulders and gently sits him back down.

Red continues:

"To my closest friend, Pastor Patrick Duffy,
better known as Red, of Monte Vista,
Colorado, if he survives me, my remaining
pieces of property for the use of the church,
however he sees fit. To Maggie Livingston,
who is listed above, I leave the sum of
my cash after all expenses are paid by my
executor."

Red continues through the rest of The Will. He concludes by reading Al's signature and that of the witness, Sheriff Dan Drummer.

When Red sets the papers down on his desk, Benny goes into another rant. Knowing this was likely to happen and feeling pretty safe with the sheriff there, he calmly sits back and listens to everything Benny has to say. Once he's done, Red says, "You have thirty days to clear out your belongings from the ranch house."

"I don't want any of that junk," Benny retorts. "I'll wrap up my business here and leave."

The sheriff bends over and says, "Il paffuto piccolo fratello non era così muto era?"

Benny's shocked by the sheriff's flawless Italian. All this time he had no idea the sheriff understood when he spoke Italian. He picks up his hat and storms out of the office, slamming the door behind him.

Red looks at Dan and asks, "What did you say to him?"

"I don't know why he got so mad." Dan smiles. "I just told him, 'Your chubby little brother wasn't so dumb, was he?'"

✿ ✿ ✿

Once on the road, Clyde heads toward the Texas Panhandle, where Monte has a job waiting for him on a ranch. He's excited about traveling solo at first, but after a few days of being alone, he can tell this isn't going to be easy. On the third day, he pulls into a service station in Amarillo, Texas and says, "Fill it up, please, and can you tell me how far Wellington is?"

The attendant pulls the hose from the pump, removes the cap, and answers, "You mean the Wellington that's in Collingsworth County?"

"Is there more than one?" Clyde asks.

"Well," the middle-aged attendant says as he places his index finger and thumb on either side of his face and moves them together so it purses his lips, "I've heard it said, mind you now, I ain't never been there, but I hear there's a Wellington up there in Kansas somewhere."

Clyde raises an eyebrow. "I guess it would be the one in that county you said before. What was it? Cottonsworth County?"

"No, no, Collingsworth," the attendant corrects Clyde. "I reckon you've got about 100 miles or so to go yet. Just head east on Route 66, then take, I think it's highway 83, south. You got kin folk down there?"

"Nope, just a friend. Going to work on a ranch," Clyde responds with a grin.

"Wow, not many of them left down that way. They've mostly turned to planting cotton," the attendant informs him as he hangs the hose back up on the pump.

"I was close, then, with the Cottonsworth name, uh?" Clyde chuckles.

"Yes, sir, I guess you was," the attendant agrees as Clyde pays him for the fuel.

"Thanks for the info! Have a nice day," Clyde says.

"You too, young man, and be safe."

Clyde hops back in the truck and heads east on highway 66.

As the sun drops below the horizon, he pulls into Wellington. It's a cute little place with a lot more buildings than he thought there'd be. The ranch is on the south side of town, so he gets to take a quick survey of the place. He drives down the nicely paved road past a large three-story building that the sign out front identifies as the county courthouse. On his way into town, he noticed a lot of cotton gins, a large creamery, and an ice plant. As he approaches the center of town, the paved roads give way to red brick streets. While they're pretty, they sure make the ride a little rougher, especially in his old truck. He quickly makes his way to the south side of town and follows the instructions Monte sent him.

About a mile out of town he sees a sign that reads: "Fourmen's Ranch," so he turns down a short dirt road. As he comes to a stop, he spots Monte walking toward the barn. They greet one another and Monte shows him where he'll be staying for the next few months. *Maybe I should have stayed home;* Clyde thinks. *This is going to be a lot rougher than I thought.*

☆ ☆ ☆

Benny leaves town shortly after the reading of The Will, leaving some men behind to watch over the rest of the property. They stay at the WD with instructions from Benny not to cause any problems and to pack up and head back home in thirty days. The townsfolk stay as far away from the WD as possible, so Benny decides to close its doors.

Almost the whole town shows up for Al's memorial service, even though Benny had already left town with the body. After a short message, Red allows for a time of sharing. He's surprised with the number of people who want to participate. He finally has to cut it off or they could be there all day, it appears. It amazes Red to hear the impact that Al had on so many, especially the testimonies from the last few years of his life. After the service, is over they all head to the ranch house for a gathering that Maggie's arranged. She can't believe how well Al has taken care of her. As long as she's careful, she'll never have to worry about anything anymore.

Dorris and the girls feel bad about receiving the home. They think, *This was Maggie's and it just doesn't seem right that we should be moving in,* but Maggie's excited for them.

"It would've been yours, anyway, when I'm gone. So enjoy it," she assures them.

Chapter 19
THE BEST MAN

The days have been long and the work has been hard, but Clyde has enjoyed every working moment on the ranch. He's only a week away from being back on the rodeo circuit. He can't believe how time has flown by, and now he gets to do what he believes he was made for. While he misses Harold, he's stayed in contact with him through letters and the occasional phone conversation. The wedding date's been set, and while he's excited for him, he can't believe that they scheduled it right in the middle of the riding calendar; but he maps out his plans to make sure he's there for it. A few other guys from the ranch are heading back on the circuit, too, so they decide to buddy up and head north together.

The first few weeks are tough on everyone. While the bulls seem to be in mid-season form, it takes the riders longer to get in the groove, and Clyde's no exception; he's pretty rusty. Over the next few months his travels take him throughout the mid-west; from Colorado to Missouri and from Texas to Montana. The first few rodeos are like old times, with the exception of Harold not being there. After the second rodeo, guys partner up, but no one wants to be around him, so he travels alone. He thought it would be hard, but never imagined it would be like this.

From one town and lonely motel room to another, Clyde begins to isolate himself from the others, even choosing to avoid Sam Goldberg. Every once in a while, he'll pick up a hitchhiker and give him a ride. While loneliness is the worst of it, physically his body is taking a beating; the bumps and bruises pile on top of each other.

This leads to more poor rides, and it's been a while since he's finished in the money. This translates into a lot of nights sleeping in the truck. He thinks, *It sure was easier when there were two of us making money. I don't know what happened to all the money I had. Between what I saved and what Harold gave me, I thought I'd be good for almost the whole season. Oh well, must have miscalculated.* One thing he didn't heed was Harold's warning about spending too much money on extras. Since the first rodeo, he's spent his spare time in places where little good takes place. In places like that, there's always plenty of "friends" at first, but once the finances dwindle, so do the friends.

Harold's wedding is quickly approaching and Clyde's almost out of money. He thinks, *If I don't finish in the top three in this rodeo, I won't have enough to make it home. I can't let Harold down like that; after all, I am his best man.* So, with more determination than ever, he rides hard over the weekend, and, on the final day, pulls the top score to finish second overall. He's the first in line to pick up his winnings, and then he jumps in the truck and heads home. If he figured it right, he has enough money to get home, but he's not sure how'll he'll get back.

✫ ✫ ✫

The sun shines through the back window, causing Clyde to open his eyes. He places his hands behind his head and reflects on some of his childhood memories as he watches the sky turn a brilliant pink. The fluffy white clouds seem close enough to leap from one to another. Then, as always, it quickly fades, motivating him to sit up and start the truck. He folds his small blanket and sets it next to him. Then he drives to the small town about thirty miles from home to clean up and grab some grub. He wastes little time before he gets back on the road.

It's mid-morning when he pulls into town and decides to head straight to the Goldberg's. He can't wait to see Warrior and maybe take a short ride. As he pulls down the drive, Harold's walking toward the corral. When he spots him, he gives Clyde his all too familiar big old grin, waves, and lets out a hoot. This excites Clyde and he smiles and waves back. When the truck comes to a stop, Harold swings the door open and gives Clyde a tug, practically pulling him from the vehicle.

"Hey, Cowboy, it's great to see ya!" Harold hollers.

"Thanks, old man," he jokes back as he steps from the truck. "Great to see ya, too!"

"Let's head to the house," Harold suggests. "We have a lot of catching up to do."

One of the first questions out of Harold's mouth is, "Have you been avoiding Mr. G?"

Looking down, Clyde was hoping this wouldn't come up. "Well, not really avoiding him, but not seeking him out, either."

"He told me you're having a rough time," Harold says, "nothing like last year. Is everything okay?"

Trying to carefully choose his words, he hesitates before answering, "Yeah, everything's okay. It's just been harder than I thought, but I'm doing okay, I guess." He quickly changes the subject. "I still have those dreams of riding at The Garden, and one day I will."

"That's what I want to hear. And I look forward to being there with ya, too."

Clyde knows the possibility of that happening is growing smaller by the day, but he says it anyway to make Harold feel good.

"Okay, enough about me," Clyde insists. "Tell me about the wedding plans." As Harold shares, Clyde notices that Audra's been busy at work decorating the house. The main room's totally different from the last time he was here.

As they talk, Clyde thinks, *It's sure nice to be back with Harold.*

He tunes back in just in time to hear Harold explain, "Friday night we'll all get together to go over the wedding and then grab some grub. On Saturday we'll get to the church early. Everything starts at 11 and the ceremony won't be very long. Okay, enough talk about that. Let me give you a tour of the place."

As they walk, Clyde's mind drifts to his family. He finally asks, "Would you want to run over to my mom's place with me?"

Harold places his hand on Clyde's shoulder. "I'm so sorry. I've been so wrapped up in my plans that I never thought about you wanting to see your family. Ya know, I've got some errands to run. Why don't you head that way, and, if I need ya, I'll stop by; that sound okay?"

"Sure does. Thanks!" Clyde says with a smile.

"I have one more question. When are ya leaving to go back?"

"Sunday," Clyde quickly answers.

"Well, enjoy every minute you're here. You want me to drop ya off at your mom's?"

"Nah, I'll take the truck. That way I can leave when I want to," Clyde explains as they walk out the door.

"Oh, that's right, I almost forgot. You do know that your mom and the girls moved?"

"What? No, I didn't. Where to?" Clyde inquires as he wrinkles his forehead.

"Did you know that Al passed on?"

"Last I heard he wasn't doing too well, but I didn't know he had died. What's that got to do with my mom?"

"In his Will, he gave Maggie almost all he had, but because of what your family has gone through, he left the ranch house and a small piece of the property to your family."

Shocked, Clyde shakes his head. "What? You mean Mom and the girls are living in Maggie's old place?"

"Yep, exactly."

"Now if that doesn't bring everything full circle!" Clyde concludes as he slides into the driver's seat. *How strange is that? Years ago Maggie and Walter wanted us to move in with them, but Mom said no. Now she's living there, anyway. Sometimes you just can't stop things from happening.* As he starts the truck, he sees Sam walking toward him, so he rolls down his window and extends his right hand.

"Good to see you, Clyde! Welcome home!" Sam greets him. "How are things?"

Clyde gives him the condensed version of what's been happening, and, once again, Sam offers him a job. "You know we can always use another good hand around here. In fact, we're looking to expand, and I think you're the right guy to help us do that."

"Thanks, Mr. G," Clyde says, "but right now I want to ride' em not raise' em." He doesn't know why, but he always seems to say the things that he thinks people want to hear. If the truth be known, since he's broke, he won't be riding much longer. He may have to look for some steady income, but to take this job would be as if he has given up and he doesn't want the town people talking about him that way.

"Just remember, when you decide to hang 'em up, give me a shout," Mr. G offers.

"Thanks, Mr. G, I will. I best be going; I want to see the family and haven't been there yet."

"I'll let you go, but one last thing. Please call me, 'Sam'."

"Okay, Mr. . . . I mean Sam, I'll talk at ya later."

Clyde puts the truck in gear and drives toward Mom's. As he drives through town, he waves at those who recognize him. Pulling up to the gate sure is different than the last time he was here. He snickers to himself and thinks, *The last time I was here, I was sneaking around on my belly.* As he gets closer to the house, he sees Jim standing on the front porch. Then he notices him, turns and hollers into the house. In a few seconds, he sees his mom step out and wave.

He parks out front and takes a moment to reflect on how great it is to be here with the family. As Dorris and Jim wait for him on the porch, he takes his time, wanting to savor the moment. He's run this moment through his mind time after time, and it's just like he imagined; well, except for Jim being there.

He steps up on the porch and gives Mom a long bear hug, not wanting to let go. Then he extends his hand to Jim. Mom pulls up a chair for him and sits down in the white porch swing, held by two chains that are firmly attached to the top of the porch. Before either one says anything, Jim asks, "Can I get you some tea or coffee?"

"Tea would be great," Clyde answers. "Thanks."

Jim turns to Dorris and says, "I'll get it, if you don't mind. You stay here and talk with your boy. Can I get you something?"

"Tea, please. Thank you so much, Jim."

Clyde thinks, *He seems really nice and seems to care about her. Just volunteering to get the drinks is pretty impressive.* As they sit on the porch, Mom starts to tear up. "It's so good to have you here. You're going to stay with us, aren't you?"

"No, I'm going to stay with Harold. That way, if he needs help, I'll be there for him. He was always there for me." After saying it, he thinks *Oh no, I hope she's not offended by what I just said.*

Oblivious, Dorris says, "That's okay, but next time, you have to stay with us. We have plenty of room now."

"I'd like that," Clyde replies as Jim returns with the drinks.

He hands each of them their tea and sits down in the swing next to Dorris. He thinks, *I'm so happy for her. Just look at that smile! This is something I know she has desired for a long time. What a great son, such a wonderful young man, that Clyde. He could be really bitter, but he doesn't seem to be holding any grudges or anything.* Jim pushes the swing ever so gently with his foot, when the phone suddenly rings. He stops the swing and asks, "Would you like me to get that?"

"If you would, and please take a message," she requests.

"Will do! Be right back," he says as he hops up from the swing and dashes inside. From the porch, Dorris and Clyde can hear Jim's conversation and can tell that it's one of the girls. Dorris chuckles to herself, as Jim has a habit of speaking louder on the phone than he needs to. *I should have just answered it myself,* she thinks as she glances at Clyde and shrugs her shoulders, as if to say, 'What can you do?'

Jim ends the short conversation with. "I'm sure that will be fine. Okay, we'll see you in a bit." He hangs up and walks back out to the porch.

"Who was it?" Dorris asks.

"Ruthie; she said she was going to stop by, if it was okay. I told her it'd be fine."

"That's great!" Clyde adds. "I can't wait to see her."

"She's quite pregnant, you know," Dorris reminds him.

"That's right! She must be ready to pop that kid out any time now," Clyde chuckles.

"Clyde Lewis, that's no way to talk! Don't say that to her. She's excited about this baby."

"Sorry, Mom," Clyde respectfully says, "didn't mean anything by it. Guess I've been around the cowboys too long."

"If that's the way they talk, they should have their mouths washed out with soap," Dorris cautions Clyde.

✲ ✲ ✲

After finishing his errands, Harold has to stop by the church to meet Audra. He ends up having some extra time and contemplates driving by Dorris's to see Clyde, but he decides to let him have this time alone with his family and drives straight over to the church. When he pulls up, Audra and Red are already standing outside, so they have a quick meeting and decide to get something to eat. Since the diner's within walking distance, they stroll there hand in hand. As Harold opens the door, the chimes welcome them in, and they take a seat next to a window. As people walk by, they tap on the window and wave. This wedding is a big event for the town and everyone is looking forward to it.

When they walk back to get their vehicles, they notice Myron, Audra's dad, talking with Red outside the church. When they're close, Myron excuses himself, grabs Harold by the arm, and takes him off to the side, leaving Audra with Red.

Myron puts his hand on Harold's shoulder and says, "Now son, do you have the honeymoon taken care of?"

"Sure do. It's all done." Harold assures him. "I'll tell you where if you promise not to tell anyone."

Chuckling, Myron asks, "Who would I tell?"

Harold cocks his head, closes one eye, and gives him a funny look. He knows Myron loves to play practical jokes, so he wouldn't put anything past him. In spite of all that, he decides to tell him. "We're going on the Rio Grande Scenic Railroad. We'll be gone for a couple of days enjoying the wonderful mountains and seeing new areas."

"Now listen here," Myron says as he deepens his voice, "I've put some cash away for when Audra gets married, and I want you two to have it, but don't tell her. If she knew it was from me, she wouldn't take it."

Harold glances her way as she talks with Red. "What makes you think I'll take it?"

"I'm not sure that you will, but as a dad, you want your little girl taken care of. I know you'll do whatever you can for her."

Harold places his hand on Myron's shoulder. "Sir, I will do everything in my power to take care of that little girl of yours."

"I know you will, son, or I wouldn't be letting you marry her," he says. They both chuckle and walk back toward Audra.

✼ ✼ ✼

When Ruthie arrives, Clyde can't believe how large she is. She waddles to the porch and up the three small steps. He stands up and hugs her, then reaches over to offer her his chair so she can sit down. He leans against the hand railing that goes around the porch before he decides to boost himself up on it. As he steadies himself on the railing, he notices Sara and Rachel off in the distance. Once Rachel sees him, she takes off on a dead run, and he slides down the railing and meets her at the foot of the steps. She leaps into his arms as he spins her around. When Sara walks up, she slaps him on the shoulder before giving him a hug. Once the family's all here, Jim feels it's time for him to leave.

He stands up and announces, "I need to get going. Thank you, Dorris, for the coffee."

"You don't have to run off." Dorris assures him.

"I have some things to get done before dark," he insists, "but thank you for the invite. Goodbye, ya'll."

After his exit to a chorus of goodbyes, Sara suggests, "How about we go inside so Mom can play some songs on the piano, and we can all sing along. We haven't done that for a long time."

Clyde stares off into space thinking, *It has been a long time since we've done that. I remember Dad leading the family in song and then playing checkers. Boy, those sure were the good old days!*

"Clyde," Dorris says, "Clyde, you okay? Did you hear what Sara said?"

He comes out of it with a smile. "Yeah, I heard her, Mom, and that sure does sound like fun." He extends his hand and helps Mom to her feet, while the two girls help Ruthie up. As they walk into the parlor, Mom sits down at the piano and asks for requests as she warms up by playing a medley of tunes.

"You're first, Clyde. What would you like to sing?" Sara asks.

He contemplates for a few seconds before suggesting, "I haven't sang this one in a long time; how about 'Red River Valley'?"

Mom stops playing and notes, "That was your dad's favorite."

Clyde walks over and sits next to her on the piano bench. "I know. I didn't want to leave Dad out of this. It's our first gathering around the piano for a long time, and I thought he should be part of it."

Dorris caresses Clyde's cheek and tears up while she finds middle 'C' and then begins to play the music that is so dear to her heart. The girls gather around behind them and heartily join in, "From this valley they say you are going, we will miss your bright eyes and sweet smile . . ." Clyde stands up as they continue, joining arm in arm with his sisters. They sing as loud as they can, with tears rolling down their cheeks. Rachel gets caught up in the emotion of the others and begins to cry, too. They sing a few more songs before Clyde brings his visit to a close.

Chapter 20
ANOTHER DAY, ANOTHER DOLLAR

The next few days are wonderful for Clyde; being able to spend time with the family, watch Rachel ride Warrior, and get some riding of his own in, too. The outside world seems to have faded away. He's forgotten all about his problems, like where the money's coming from for him to leave, and what's going to happen if he doesn't place over the next few rodeos. Why, he's never been happier! Well, except for when he hears that buzzer go off, and he's still on the back of a bull.

Early Saturday morning Clyde heads down the staircase and finds Harold pacing in the living room. "Everything okay?" Clyde asks.

"Yep, just nervous. You know, them darn butterflies. It reminds me of just before I get up on a bull or a wild horse."

"Oh, yeah?" Clyde teases, "I won't tell Audra you compared marrying her to riding a bull or a wild horse."

"You better not! You know what I mean, don't ya?" Harold pleads.

"Take it easy, there. I know what ya mean, I was just tuggin' yer rope."

Harold takes a deep breath. "Sorry, Half-Pint, I'm a little on edge."

"Shoot, no problem! Let's have a quick drink to calm your nerves," Clyde suggests.

"It's a little early, don't ya think?" Harold rebuts.

"Nah, not for occasions like this," Clyde assures him.

They walk into the kitchen and Harold pulls out a bottle as Clyde grabs the glasses. Harold pours them half-full, and says, "Bottoms up."

"Wait a second," Clyde says. "I want to make a toast. To the best friend anyone could have and his bride-to-be. May you have a long, healthy life together."

With that, they tip their glasses, and, in one gulp, it's gone. Before they head upstairs to get ready, Harold puts the bottle away while Clyde cleans the glasses. They don't want Audra coming home to a dirty kitchen.

Harold's the first one ready and nervously waits for Clyde, who has to pack up because he's staying at Mom's.

They arrive at the church right on schedule. The closer it gets to the ceremony, the more nervous they both become. To their relief, it starts right on time. Red and Harold walk in the side door to the front of the sanctuary. Then the back doors swing open and Ethel Mae, Audra's long time rodeo friend and Maid of Honor, is escorted down the aisle by Clyde. They take their positions in front, and the wedding march begins. Audra and her dad slowly walk down the aisle to meet Harold at the front, where Myron shakes his hand and gives Audra a peck on the cheek as a tear runs down his own. Shaking, Harold takes Audra's hand and leads her to the altar. Clyde watches Harold take his vows and listens as Pastor Red explains about marriage. Clyde thinks, *Poor Harold's as nervous a wild horse in a corral.* Though nervous, he repeats all the right things, and, before long, Pastor Red proclaims, "Ladies and gentlemen, I would like to introduce to you, for the first time, Mr. and Mrs. Harold Ritter. Clyde thinks, *I can't believe it, they're really hitched! This is going to change so many things between Harold and me; they'll never be the same.*

The reception afterwards is uneventful and Clyde realizes it's time for him to move on. He decides against staying the night at Mom's, but still has to figure out how to get some much- needed cash.

The happy couple is getting ready to leave when Harold finds Clyde and takes him aside. "Heard you're short on cash. Myron gave us some money and Audra and I have decided we want to share it with you."

Shocked, Clyde asks, "How do you know that?"

"Let's just say a little birdie told me," he hedges. Harold sticks out his hand, with some bills rolled up in it. "Just don't do anything stupid, okay? Get yourself back on the circuit and ride like you've never ridden before."

Not one to take charity, Clyde resists at first. Harold finally grabs his hand and shoves the roll in it. Not knowing what to say, Clyde finally blurts out, "Thank you so much! I will! You guys will be proud of me."

"Half-Pint, we already are," Harold assures him as he ruffles Clyde's hair.

A few seconds pass and Audra walks up. She gives Clyde a peck on the cheek and a hug. "Go get 'em, Cowboy!" she says. Speechless, Clyde smiles and hugs her back. The happy couple says their goodbyes and heads out. Once they're gone, Clyde finds the family and tells them his change of plans. They're all disappointed, but say their goodbyes as they help clean up the place. With a heavy heart, Clyde walks to the truck and Mom follows closely behind. Before opening the door, he gives her a hug and a peck on the cheek. "Thanks, Mom, I'm going to miss you guys, but I'll see you when the rodeo comes to town."

Mom gives him a long squeeze. "Clyde, I heard you needed some cash. Maggie is helping us out since Al left her his money, so I want to help you. It's not much, but for all those years you sent us money, it's the least I can do."

"But . . ."

"No buts, take it. Just go and make us proud."

"Thanks, Mom. I will," Clyde assures her as he climbs in the truck while thinking, *That's two people who said that tonight. I have to pull myself up by my bootstraps and get back on track.* He glances in his rear view mirror and sees the reflection of Mom standing there waving and wiping her eyes with her handkerchief.

✼ ✼ ✼

While they're sad that Clyde has left, the family quickly resumes their everyday lives.

It's around three in the morning when Ruthie wakes Martin up. "Honey, you need to get up!" she urgently requests.

Martin shakes his head and blinks in confusion. "Did I oversleep again? Dad is going to be so mad!" he mumbles as he jumps out of bed and pulls on his pants without looking outside to see the evening moon. "What are you doing?" he asks Ruthie, who's packing her bag. "Where are you going?"

She looks up with a smile says, "It's time."

"What?" Martin asks, "You mean now? Right now?"

Then a labor pain hits and she quickly takes a seat and hollers, "Yes! Right now!"

Martin grabs his shirt and throws it on without snapping it, reaches for Ruthie's bag, and runs to the car with Ruthie close behind. She loves this wonderful man, and she's never seen him this nervous before. He opens her door as he fumbles with his shirt snaps. Ruthie slides in and he hustles to the other side. He'd normally be frustrated that he can't snap his shirt, but at this point he doesn't really care.

She lets out a little giggle. "Did you know your shirt is inside out?" she observes as he starts the car. Just then Ruthie has another contraction.

Martin throws the car in reverse and backs down the driveway; then he heads out on the road for the twenty-minute drive to the hospital in Del Norte.

✲ ✲ ✲

The road is long and each town seems the same. Clyde catches up with the rodeo and is determined to change his luck, but after the first few days and rides, he can tell nothing's changed. He thinks, *What's wrong with me? I've never had this problem before; riding has been so easy. I had a week off and got refocused at home with everyone behind me like they are. Why, I'm just going to let them down. Well, next week will be different.*

But it's not. His first ride barely gets out of the chute before he finds himself on the ground. He thinks, *No day money again and finances are about out. I guess I shouldn't have been out with the boys again last night. If I don't win any money this weekend, I'll have to look for other work and give up on my dream. I won't even be able to ride back home. Boy, have I messed things up!*

With his luck still the same, he decides to head to the local tavern to forget about his problems for a while. Just outside stands a tall young man in his early twenties, well over 6 feet tall and as thin as a board. Clyde's seen plenty of guys like him before who stand on their soap boxes and holler about God and this Jesus fella. As Clyde and his buddies approach the tavern door, the young man with dark wavy hair, a long forehead and protruding nose, looks straight into Clyde's eyes and asks, "Want to hear about God's love?"

"I believe in God," Clyde smirks, "and that's good enough for me."

"So, you know where you're going when you die?" the young fella counters.

Clyde tries to ignore him, but the young preacher won't let him. "Hey, you with the big Stetson, did ya hear me?"

Clyde stops before he walks in. "Oh yeah, I heard ya," Clyde replies.

This young man with a tanned complexion, steel gray eyes, and clothes big enough to fit a 300 pound guy replies, "Could I please just have a minute of your time?"

"Not right now. I have someone to meet," Clyde says.

The preacher falls for it, like so many others have. "Who would that be?" he sheepishly asks.

"Jack, Jack Daniels." His buddies laugh as Clyde starts to head in and then turns and says, "We can talk if you're still here when I come out." He knows that won't be for quite some time, and when he finally does come out, he probably won't be in any condition to talk.

"Okay, see ya when ya get done," the preacher agrees.

Once Clyde gets into the tavern, he quickly forgets about the guy outside and drowns his sorrows with his friends, who leave when he stops buying their drinks. About out of money, he says his goodbyes to the bartender and heads out the door thinking, *What am I going to do now? There's not enough money to head to the next rodeo. Oh well, I'll worry about that tomorrow.*

It's cooled off since he entered the tavern and Clyde can feel the gentle night air blowing as he opens the front door and steps out onto the sidewalk. The sky's clear and the crescent moon hangs over the top of the buildings across the street. He turns to his right and can't believe his eyes. There sits the young preacher on one of the old wooden chairs against the building.

"What are you still doin' here?" Clyde demands.

The young man jumps to his feet. "I told you I'd wait for ya! Always want to be a man of my word."

Clyde has a hard time standing and leans against a support pole. "Why would you wait out here for me?"

"Because I've got a message for ya!" the young man insists.

"Sure you do! I suppose you're going to say it's a message from God. Okay, I'll bite; tell me what the message is."

The young man positions himself by his chair, grabs another and says, "Have a seat and I'll tell ya."

Though he doesn't want to take a seat or listen, Clyde's impressed with the young man. To have the integrity to do what he said he would and stay out here for this long, Clyde doesn't want to be rude and just walk away, so he steadies himself with the chair before straddling it, cowboy style. "My name's Clyde, what's yours?" Clyde asks as he extends his hand.

Grasping Clyde's hand, the preacher responds, "Ulysses Grant Shoemaker, but everyone calls me Skinny."

"Okay, Skinny, what have ya got to say? Does this here message have anything to do with a job?"

"Well, Clyde, you may need something more important than a job!" Skinny replies.

Clyde sits back and pulls back on the chair, raising two legs off the ground. "You may be right, but right now eatin' and livin' are on the top of my list."

Skinny leans forward. "What do you need a job for? I thought you were riding in the rodeo."

Clyde puts the chair back down. "You see, a funny thing happened; I didn't make any money, and now I'm almost broke. I need to make some cash to get back to ridin'.'"

"I may be able to help," Skinny says. "I work up at the coal mine, riding shotgun for the drivers. You can check with them in the morning. They're always looking for drivers. Just go to the office at the bottom of the hill, ask for the foreman and tell him I sent ya."

"Gee, thanks! You mean ya ain't gonna preach at me?"

"Nah, not this time. I want to help in any way I can." Skinny gets up from his chair and heads toward the motel. As he goes, he turns and asks, "Got a place to stay?"

"I've got my trusty old truck. Been using that for some time now."

"If ya like, you can bunk up on the floor in my room."

"No thanks, my soft seats sound better than a hard floor."

"Okay, I'll see ya later," Skinny says as he walks away.

As Clyde stumbles toward his truck he thinks, *He's a pretty nice guy.*

✵ ✵ ✵

Just before sunrise Clyde hears a tap on his window. He begins to stir when another tap causes him to sit up and open his eyes. The first thing he sees is the glitter of a badge on the front of a shirt. He flashes back to the last episode he had with the law, and his stomach begins to churn. He rolls down his window and asks, "What can I do for you, officer?'

"You can't sleep here, young fella. You've got to move on."

"Sorry, officer, I'm waiting for the office at the coal mine to open. I'm looking for a job and hear they're hiring."

"That's fine, but ya can't loiter around here, so please move on. There are some public showers at the edge of town and a café just down the street where you can grab a cup of coffee. Tell them I sent ya. It's on me."

"Thank you, officer," Clyde replies as he cranks up the truck and drives to the end of town. He showers, has that cup of coffee, and heads to the coal mine.

The office is a small one-room building with a back door that leads to an outhouse behind it. As Clyde walks in, the guy behind the desk looks up. "Kin I help ya?" he inquires.

The door slams shut behind Clyde and as the guy stands up from behind his desk, Clyde notices a gap in the fella's front teeth under his bushy mustache. "I hope so," Clyde replies. "I'm looking for a job!"

He steps out from behind the desk and asks, "Is your name Clyde?" as he extends his hand.

"How'd ya know?" Clyde asks, shaking his hand.

He chuckles, "Skinny came by the office early this morning and said you were coming by."

"Really?" Clyde can't believe it. *I barely know this guy,* he thinks, *and he remembers my name and even tells his boss about me. What a great guy!* "Well, sir, like I said, I'm looking for a job. I really need one and heard you may need a driver."

The foreman offers Clyde a chair. "What have you been doing for work?"

Clyde takes a seat and crosses his legs. "I've been ridin' the rodeo."

The foreman sits back down at his desk and leans forward, "What event?"

"Bull-riding."

"I was there last weekend. Did ya ride?"

"I'll put it this way," Clyde chuckles, "not for long."

The foreman sits back and laughs. "Why ya stopping?"

Clyde thinks, *I don't want to tell him I don't have the money for it. What should I say?* So he says, "I just got tired of all the travel," he bluffs. "I'm looking to have a more steady income. Ya know, stay in one spot for a while."

"Let me tell ya something," the foreman explains. "Driving up and down this hill isn't all that easy! When that there road gets a little damp, it gets pretty slippery. You driven much?"

Once again, Clyde chooses his words carefully. "Oh yeah, been drivin' for some time now."

"Ever driven a big truck?" the foreman inquires.

Without hesitation, Clyde responds, "Oh yeah, know how to shift an all like it's second nature." He knows that's not quite the truth. He's driven trucks before, but nothing like these coal trucks. He thinks, *As long as I get the job, I'll figure out the rest later.*

The foreman leans back. "Well, since Skinny recommended ya," he leans forward and extends his hand, "you're hired. My name's Stan. Oh, I almost forgot. Skinny asked to ride shotgun with ya."

Clyde shakes his hand and asks, "What do those guys do?"

"They're there to assist the drivers in any way they can. They're an important part of the ride; we don't let anyone drive without one. There's one more thing I want you to understand before you agree to come to work."

"What's that?" Clyde hesitantly asks.

"This is a dangerous job. We've lost numerous trucks over the side, so we always have new drivers walk over and look down at the pile of metal that the mountain's claimed."

Not even thinking about what Stan just said, Clyde boasts, "I don't think I need to do that. I've been riding bulls for a living, so just hand me a set of keys and let's get to work."

Stan can't believe the confidence of this young man, but plans to be very cautious with him. "I'll tell ya what. Let's plan on ya starting tomorrow. You need to get yourself settled somewhere. Besides, Skinny's riding shotgun with someone else today. Don't know how much cash you got, but go to the local boarding house and tell them Stan sent ya and they'll put ya up. They'll send me the bill, and I'll take it from your first check."

Clyde reluctantly agrees and walks out to his truck. When he reaches for his door, he thinks, *Since I'm already here, maybe I should take a look at the trucks, just so I know what I've gotten myself into.* He makes his way toward the bottom of the mountain where numerous trucks are parked and can hear the engines of the other trucks running up and down the hill.

Stan sits in his office thinking, *I sure hope I didn't make a mistake in hiring that young fella. I wonder why he wasn't even interested in looking at the trucks.* Not hearing Clyde's vehicle start, he walks to the window just in time to see him make his way over and climb up on a big truck. He thinks, *Okay, now I feel better. Thatta boy, take a look inside and have a seat. That's the truck you'll be driving, so make yourself comfortable.*

✲ ✲ ✲

He looks around before he grabs the rail and pulls himself up onto the running board. As he opens the door and takes a seat, he observes some pretty strange-looking features. It has a long nose that houses the big diesel engine, and a cab with only enough room for two. The top's removable for ventilation when it's hot. The cab's cut off right behind the seats with a flat back window so they can watch the huge trailer they're towing. It has duel axles with duel wheels on each axle. It's connected to the truck with a single large pin and air lines for the brake system. Clyde thinks, *It doesn't look that hard to drive. After all, how fast can ya go?*

As he climbs out, he looks up the hill at the road leading to the coal mine. It's one lane; so when one truck is up loading, another is down unloading and a third is making a trip up or down. There isn't enough room for going two directions at the same time. The mountain's lined with broken shale on one side and a 1,000-foot drop at the highest point on the other. If you go over, it really will be over. He glances to his left and notices several coal trucks and trailers littering the bottom of the gorge.

Clyde takes his time heading back to town and thinks, *I forgot to ask what the job pays. Oh well, no matter; I need a job.* He finds the boarding house and, just like Stan said, they welcome him with open arms, just in time for lunch.

Chapter 21
ANOTHER TWIST IN LIFE

By the time they arrive at the hospital, Ruthie's contractions are close to a minute apart, but they seem to be lasting longer. Martin runs in for help, and it's not long before a nurse comes out and helps transfer Ruthie from the car to a wheelchair. Then she wheels her into the birthing room. As Martin paces in the waiting room, he remembers that he forgot to call Doc and Dorris, so he scurries over to the pay phone in the corner.

In a deep sleep, Dorris hears a ring off in the distance and begins to wake up. When she realizes it's the phone ringing downstairs, she leaps from her bed, grabs her robe, and rushes toward the staircase thinking, *Who in the world can be calling at this hour?* As she passes the girls' rooms, they poke their heads out and Sara hollers, "Hurry, Mom, it must be Ruthie!"

She steps up her pace and grabs the phone from the wall. "Hello Ruthie, is that you?"

Surprised at her greeting, Martin replies, "No ma'am, it's Martin. I'm calling to let you know that Ruthie's in labor. We're already at the hospital, and Doc is on his way."

Excited, Dorris says, "I'll call Jim and see if he can bring me over. See you in a little while!" She hangs up and immediately calls Jim. By this time, both girls are standing next to her talking as she tries to explain to Jim what she needs. She finally has to cover the mouthpiece and tell them to be quiet. Jim agrees to take her and heads right over. She runs upstairs to get herself presentable as the girls petition to go, too.

Dorris finally stops them. "You're not going with us. We don't know how long it's going to be, and I want you here taking care of things. Now, no more; I've made my decision, understand?"

Not liking it, but realizing that when Mom makes up her mind there's no changing it, they both agree and give her a hug and kiss before going back to bed. Since Jim's not too far away, it's only a couple minutes before he arrives and they're on their way.

When they pull up in front, Dorris leaps from the car. Jim finds a place to park while Dorris hurries in. The receptionist directs her to the waiting room where she finds Martin still pacing. She gives him a hug and asks, "Have you heard anything yet?"

"No, ma'am, and that's what worries me. It's been a long time now, and no one has said anything. Do you think she's all right?"

When Jim comes in, he and Dorris sit down near Martin. "These things take a while," Dorris informs him. "Nature has a way of making you wait. I'm sure she's fine. I was in labor for almost ten hours with my first one."

"What? You mean I may have to wait ten hours to hear anything? I don't know if I can make it that long," Martin responds, almost in a panic.

"Now, now, take it easy. I don't rightly know," Dorris offers, "but it could be."

Suddenly, the door to the waiting room opens and the receptionist steps in. "I wanted to let you know that the doctor has arrived and everything is coming along nicely. We'll try to keep you updated the best we can. Would any of you like coffee, or a roll or something?"

The first to speak, Dorris replies, "That would be nice. Three coffees, please, and do you have doughnuts?"

"We sure do!" the receptionist replies. "Three coffees with donuts, coming right up." She looks at Martin and places her hand on his shoulder. "Just sit down and relax. Everything is going to be fine. She's in good hands," she assures him.

✲ ✲ ✲

Up before the sun, Clyde's filled with excitement about his new job. The boarding house has breakfast ready when he comes downstairs. *I could get used to this,* Clyde thinks. *Nothing beats homemade biscuits and gravy, with an added plus, bacon.* He takes a seat and savors each bite. He hasn't worked a full day for a few months now, so this is going to be different, but he's never shied away from work. Once he's finished with breakfast, he makes his way to the mine. As the sun begins to light up the sky, he pulls up to the base of the mountain. To his surprise, Skinny's already standing next to the truck waiting for him.

Before Clyde can get out, Skinny walks over to his truck and opens his door for him. "Mornin', neighbor! I guess we'll be ridin' together for a while."

Clyde grabs his horseshoe off the seat and slides out of the truck. "Yeah, I guess so. We'll make the best of it, I'm sure."

"Lookin' forward to it!" Skinny notices Clyde putting the horseshoe in his back pocket but decides against asking about it.

"Where do we start?" Clyde inquires.

Skinny pats him on the back. "That's what I like, a man who's ready to get busy. We need to check in at the office and get the keys."

"Okay, let's get a move on," Clyde says as he picks up the pace to the office. They sign in and grab the keys for the truck. As they climb aboard, Clyde thinks, *This is sure different than the ones I've seen before.* He puts the key in the ignition and pushes the starter button on the floor. Then he pauses for a moment as he tries to read the instructions on the dashboard without being obvious.

Noticing his hesitation, Skinny can tell it's all new to him. "Ever driven a truck with a split-shift transmission before?" he asks.

Not knowing what to say, he thinks, *If I say no, he'll probably tell Stan. Then he'll know I lied to him. What can I say?* "It's been quite a while. I just have to refresh myself, it won't take me long," he lies. Clyde's right about one thing, though. It never takes him long to catch on to anything. He only has to be shown once how to do something, and he perfects it after that. It's a gift from God.

Suspicious, Skinny asks, "When was the last time you drove one of these beasts?"

Clyde realizes he's caught and won't be able to hide it once he gets going, so he decides to make a joke out of it. "Let's see, umm, let me think for a moment. I think it was way back." He puts his elbow on the steering wheel and rubs his chin. "Well, maybe back before I was born." He lets out a hoot and glances over at Skinny, who gives him a funny look.

"You tellin' me you've never driven one of these before?" he confirms.

Realizing Skinny either didn't get the joke or didn't think it was funny, Clyde fumbles around for his words. "Well, not exactly, but I guess you're right. I am a fast learner, though."

Skinny breaks into laughter. "Oh my, I'm riding with a rook."

"A what?" Clyde asks, bewildered.

"A rookie, a beginner, you know," Skinny says, chuckling. "Okay, at least I know. We need to get this thing rolling or the boss is going to wonder what's taking us so long. He wants these things rolling all the time. He's a hard man, but honest and fair. Ya ready?"

"Sure, let's get a move on," Clyde agrees.

"Okay, see that switch on the side of the gear shift?" Skinny asks.

"Yeah, what about it?" Clyde says.

"You start out with the switch down, that's called low range." He continues to read the instructions off the dash and explain the process, finishing up with, "You just reverse the order when you downshift. Got it?"

"That sounds easy enough. Let's get to work," Clyde says. Just before he puts the truck in gear, he reaches into his back pocket, pulls out the horseshoe, and sets in on the seat between them. He looks over at Skinny. "It's a long story," he offers. "I'll tell you later." Then he puts the truck in gear and heads up the hill.

True to form, it doesn't take him long to get the hang of it. Skinny's quite impressed, and, by the end of the day, Clyde's driving like he's done it all his life. There really isn't much to it; they don't go very fast up or down the mountain, so most of the time is spent in the lower gears.

✲ ✲ ✲

Time seems to creep by after the three finish their coffee and munch on the doughnuts. Jim found himself a corner to nap in and Martin is back to pacing around the room. It's close to six in the morning when the doctor walks in and announces, "Martin, you're the proud father of a six-pound, eight-ounce baby boy. Congratulations!"

Martin runs up and hugs him. "How's Ruthie doing?" he asks.

"She's fine, a little tired. She had a pretty hard time, but she's enjoying that wonderful baby boy."

Dorris gives Martin a hug as Jim wakes up and they tell him the news. She asks the doctor, "Can we go in and see them?"

"The nurse will come get you when you can see the baby through the nursery window. You can see Ruthie anytime you'd like, just don't stay long. She needs her rest, and it looks like you folks do, too."

"Thank you, Doc, we appreciate it," Martin says as he sits down.

The doctor walks out, and, a couple of minutes later, the nurse enters the waiting room.

"Would you like to see that baby boy?" she asks.

"Oh boy, would I!" Martin eagerly replies, jumping to his feet. "But can I see my wife first?" She escorts them in to see Ruthie. Taking the doctor's advice, they don't stay long. On their way out, Martin follows the nurse to see the newest member of the family. As they stand in the hallway and peer in the big nursery window, the nurse brings the baby up for them to see. He's screaming his lungs out, so much so his little cheeks are red. Dorris taps on the window and blows kisses before she and Jim say goodbye to Martin and head back home.

✲ ✲ ✲

The trip up and down the mountain is pretty monotonous, and Clyde's glad Skinny's along for the ride. The first day is spent getting to know each other; with ten hours together in a truck, there's really not much more to do. Clyde does a lot of listening, while Skinny does most of the talking. He does like to talk and ask tons of questions. Most of their conversations lead back to talking about God. Clyde can't believe that someone could have so much to say about God. He's pretty uncomfortable about it at first, but as the day progresses, he realizes that's just the way Skinny is. Clyde thinks, *When I talk to people, I always talk about a topic I'm comfortable with, and that's all he's doing. I just wish he was comfortable with another topic. Oh well, got to take the bad with the good.*

As they wrap up their day, Clyde notices that Skinny isn't wearing a jacket, and it gets pretty cold at times. Climbing down from the truck, Clyde shouts, "Aren't you cold?"

"I'm all right," Skinny assures him.

"Don't ya have a jacket?"

Skinny chuckles. "I did, but the last guy I rode shotgun with didn't, and, he got pretty cold, so I let 'im have mine. I'll go to the church closet store and get another one when I get the time and money."

Clyde gets to his truck and says, "You don't need to do that. I've got an extra one you can use. It used to be my pop's. It'll be a little big, but it's nice and warm. It's a cowboy's trench coat. I'll bring it for ya tomorrow; it's back at my place."

Shaking his head, Skinny says, "I can't take that, Clyde. It was your pop's."

"I ain't givin' it to ya or anything; you can use it 'til you get your own."

"Okay," Skinny says. "Thanks a ton."

"No problem! See ya tomorrow."

"Yeah, see ya tomorrow."

☆ ☆ ☆

The sun's just above the horizon as they begin the twenty minute or so ride home. Having a hard time staying awake, Jim contorts his face while Dorris, excited about her first grandbaby, talks a mile a minute. About five miles from town, Jim, always a careful driver, sees a horse on the side of the road, unattended. He starts to slow down, but it's too late; the car spooks it.

As it gallops across the road, Dorris sees it and screams. It runs right into their path. Jim slams on his brakes and the car starts to slide sideways, bringing the passenger side around and hitting the horse in its midsection. The impact shatters the headlamp and crushes the front fender. Then the hindquarter of the horse flips onto the hood and slides up, shattering the front window. Dorris throws her hands up to protect her face as shattered glass sprays throughout the inside of the car. The force of the impact slams her head against the doorpost, knocking her unconscious. The car comes to a stop and Jim's chest hits the steering wheel, knocking the breath out of him. While trying to catch his breath, he looks over at Dorris and sees blood on her face. He attempts to move toward her, but becomes lightheaded and feels something warm running into his eyes as he loses consciousness.

✳ ✳ ✳

A car rounds the corner and its occupants see another car in the middle of the road with a horse lying next to it. There's steam spewing from under the crushed hood, and the front end looks destroyed. The driver pulls over to the shoulder of the road and notices Jim making his way out of the car. He staggers a few steps, and leans against the car.

The driver sprints over to help steady him. "Jim, are you okay?" the driver asks. He hears a faint moaning from inside the car. "Is Dorris with you?"

Finding it difficult to breathe, Jim nods his head in confirmation. As Dorris starts to regain consciousness and her moans become louder, Jim steadies himself with the hood as he stubbles around to Dorris's side of the car and recognizes Sam Goldberg. "Sam, please help me with Dorris. I think she's really hurt," Jim pleads.

Sam moves in to help as Dorris begins to cry in pain. "Dorris, it's Sam Goldberg! Jim and I are going to get you out. Please try to relax."

She tries to move as Sam asks, "Can you scoot this way so we can get you out through the driver's door?"

"I think so," she says as she feels around.

"Be careful," Sam warns her. "There's glass all over. Don't try to wipe it off, or you'll cut your hands. I can see some pretty sharp pieces. Listen, Dorris, move slowly to your left, across the seat."

Dorris wipes her eyes and says, "Sam, something's wrong."

"What's that?" he inquires.

"Can you see my eyes?" she asks.

"Yeah, why?"

"Are they open?" she questions.

"Sure they are. Why?"

"They feel like they are, but I can't see," she replies, concerned. "My eyes are open, but I can't see anything!"

The men position themselves around the driver's door and reach in. "Dorris, take my hand," Sam requests. "I'll help you out. Do you hurt anywhere else?"

"Just my head and ribs, but I think I can get out," she says as she gropes around trying to locate Sam's hand. She finds his hand and grabs hold as he gently pulls her from the wreck. Jim's still having a hard time breathing, so he leans against the car. By this time, another car has stopped and the occupants help to get them to Sam's car. They lay Dorris down on the back seat and Jim sits up front.

"I'll take you to the hospital in Del Norte," Sam says as he puts the car in gear and speeds off.

"That's where we just came from," Jim says.

"What were you doing there?" Sam probes.

"Ruthie had the baby early this morning," Jim answers in a shallow voice, struggling to catch his breath between words.

"Oh, my! Okay, just don't talk anymore. You doing okay back there, Dorris?"

"I'm okay, I guess. I just wish my vision would come back."

"Oh, it's probably only temporary," Sam tries to assure her. "You'll be seeing and holding that grandbaby in no time."

They pull through the parking lot toward the front door of the hospital and Sam sees Doc walking to his car. He pulls up in front, jumps from his car, and hollers, "Doc, over here!" as he waves him over.

"Sam, what in the world are you doing here?" Doc asks as he walks over.

"Jim and Dorris got into a wreck, and I brought them here," Sam explains as the two make their way to the car. Doc opens the hospital door and hollers for assistance, and the hospital crew comes running. They wheel both new patients into the examination rooms for Doc to take a look at.

He examines Jim first, while the nurses take care of cleaning Dorris up. The glass did a pretty good job on her hands and arms. He determines that Jim is in pretty good shape with a few bumps and bruises, along with a couple of cracked ribs from the steering wheel. He instructs the nurses to wrap his ribs tightly and give him some pain medication.

Dorris is sitting in a chair when Doc walks in and the first thing he notices is the laceration on the side of her head. He looks it over and determines that she'll need a few stitches. He praises the nurses for doing a good job of cleaning the wounds on her hands and arms. The last thing he examines are her eyes, "Can you see anything yet?" he asks.

"Well, it's not totally black anymore, it's more like gray. I can't make out anything. At times I can see a figure, I think, but I'm not too sure." He looks into her eyes and notices small particles of matter, so he asks the nurses to flush them out before he reexamines her.

The flushing makes little difference, so he decides to wrap them and see what happens. "If things don't change in the next couple of days," he says, "I'll call a friend of mine and ask him to take a look."

"Thank you so much for everything, Doc, but you just take care of that grandbaby," Dorris says with a grin.

"I will certainly do that. He's doing fine, and so is Momma."

Sam pulls the car up to the door and an orderly helps them into the car for the drive home. The girls come running out to greet them as they pull up the driveway. Mom had asked Martin to call the girls and fill them in on what happened. They lead her into the parlor and help her sit down on the couch. What a roller coaster of feelings for the family; excitement for Ruthie and Martin, and now concern for Mom.

Sam and Jim head back to town. "It's all my fault, Sam. What if she's blind for the rest of her life?" Jim asks.

Sam tries to comfort him. "Jim, it was an accident. There was nothing you could have done to prevent it. It's just one of those things that happens in life."

"But she might not ever get to see that grandbaby again," Jim counters.

"Let's take it one day at a time," Sam suggests. "You don't control tomorrow; only God has a hand in that. You need to trust that He knows what's best."

"I suppose you're right," Jim acknowledges as they pull up in front of his place. "Thanks for the lift. I'll talk to you later." He cautiously gets out of the car and waves goodbye. As he takes a step toward the front door, he thinks, *I need something to relax me. The good book says something about using a little wine for your stomach and ailments. If a little is good, maybe a lot will be better.* Jim twists the Scriptures around to justify what he wants to do, when he really doesn't know what they say.

Chapter 22
BAD NEWS A COMING

Since that first day, Clyde and Skinny have become pretty close friends. Skinny loves Dad's coat, and Clyde enjoys seeing him wear it. Since meeting Skinny, Clyde doesn't frequent the taverns the way he used to and is surprised with the extra money he has. He hasn't quite figured out why.

Day after day, they're together; yet, they still don't know a lot about each other. Clyde finally brings it up. "Hey, Skinny, we've talked about a whole lot of stuff, but I still don't know much about your family. How about sharing?"

"It's funny you asked that," Skinny replies. "That old horseshoe has been bothering me since the first day you set it on the seat between us. I'll share with you if you tell me all about the horseshoe."

"Well, now," Clyde answers, "that's a long story, but I'd love to share it with you. You first."

"Just to give you fair warning," Skinny chuckles, "mine is a pretty boring story."

"Go ahead! Can't be any more boring than what you've been telling me all this time," Clyde teases with a grin.

"Ouch! That bad, huh? Oh well, here goes nothing."

Skinny tells him that he left home to ease his parent's financial burden. His dad is a circuit pastor for numerous churches in Texas and Oklahoma. He loves preaching, but doesn't want the constraints of being in one church. Mom's a simple lady and loves to make the kids' clothes. He tells Clyde numerous stories he remembers about his brother and sister. He's thankful to his parents for raising him in the things of God and teaching him how to live with minimal means. He finishes up with a little about himself. "I believe God has called me to different areas, doing odds and ends jobs to provide for myself. It's what the scriptures call being a 'tentmaker'."

Clyde doesn't understand what that means, but decides not to interrupt. He thinks, *Skinny knows what he's talking about, and that's good enough for me.*

"I've been on the road for the past three years sharing God's love," Skinny continues, "and it's taken me all around. My shopping sprees are at secondhand stores, and that's always a challenge when looking for my clothes. There's not many out there with arms as long as mine. The only clothes I can find that fit my arms are extra-large, which are specifically cut for large, heavy men. I can hardly ever find a pair of pants that are long enough."

"Yeah, I know," Clyde laughs, "I can tell when you need to do laundry; you have different colored socks on. You know how to stop that, don't ya?"

"Can't say that I do," Skinny replies.

"Wear cowboy boots; then they can't see your socks." Clyde laughs out loud just picturing Skinny in a pair of cowboy boots with his pants tucked inside.

Skinny laughs at the thought of it, too. "Okay, I've told you my story, now how about that horseshoe?"

Clyde smiles. "Okay, but like I said, it's going to take a while."

"Go ahead, partner. We've got all day together in this truck," Skinny replies as he makes himself comfortable in his seat.

✠ ✠ ✠

Doc gets more and more concerned about Dorris's sight, or rather the lack of it. It's been a while and nothing's changed. He finally calls his specialist friend who agrees to take a couple days off and come to town to see if he can help.

Late one morning, Dr. Atkinson calls the family and they make an appointment to bring Dorris to the office that afternoon. Before she arrives, the two doctors sit down in Doc's office and discuss the case. Dr. Milstad is an eye specialist and has studied cases such as Dorris's, but he has never actually worked on one, so he's eager to examine her. They go over the three possible outcomes, none of which are very good. Milstad puts it this way: "The first possible cause is *vitreous hemorrhage*, but it's the least likely one. Usually, if people have this, their sight comes back on its own. The second is *retinal detachment*. This usually affects just one eye, but in rare cases, it can affect both. The third, *optic nerve damage*, is what I think we're looking at. Any severe head injury can cause increased pressure in the head, which can, in turn, puts pressure on the nerves, cutting off their blood circulation and causing blindness. If I had to guess, it would be number three, but I'll wait to draw my conclusion."

They hear the front door open as the nurse greets the family and leads them to the examination room. "Make yourself comfortable," she says, "the doctors will be with you in a moment."

The doctors wait a couple of minutes before they walk in and Doc Atkinson introduces Dr. Milstad to the family. He begins his examination immediately by asking a lot of questions, trying to write down every detail that he can. He completes his thirty minute exam, stopping only to jot down notes for later.

Once he's done, he excuses himself, along with Doc Atkinson. The family remains in the room, talking about things that happened throughout their day. After what seems like hours, the doctors finally return and Dr. Milstad sits down on the little stool. "Mrs. Lewis," he begins, "we've discussed your case, and my professional opinion is that you have what we call *optical nerve damage*. The results of my tests all lead me to that conclusion."

"Good," Sara concludes, "at least we know what it is now. So what do we do to fix it?"

Dorris sits with perfect posture, her hands on her knees. The doctor leans over and takes Dorris's hands in his. "Mrs. Lewis, at this time, there is nothing we can do. Research is being done and there could be a breakthrough at any time, but currently there is no treatment for it."

Sara and Rachel both gasp. "Momma," Rachel protests. "your eyes are too pretty to go dark this way." Then she covers her eyes and breaks into tears.

Dorris stands up, reaches for Rachel and pulls her to her bosom. She takes a deep breath before she speaks. "Thank you, Doctor, for coming all this way. These are the cards I've been dealt, and now it's time to learn how to live with it."

"But, Mom," Sara protests as she begins to cry, "what are you going to do now?"

"I don't know, but we'll figure something out." She stands up, bids the doctors a good day, and the girls lead her out.

"That is one strong woman," Dr. Milstad states. "I've only had to tell a few people that they'd be blind for the rest of their lives, and none ever responded that way."

"Stronger than you will ever know," Doc Atkinson confides. "She's been through a lot. I'm buying dinner, and I'll tell you her story then. It'll break your heart."

"Sounds good to me, I'm starving!" Dr. Milstad says as he grabs his hat and coat.

✭ ✭ ✭

The rodeo circuit is winding down and Sam's been looking for Clyde so he can tell him about his mom, but up to this point he's been unsuccessful. The last rodeo before they head back home he runs across some of the cowboys Clyde used to hang out with and asks, "Any of you cowboys seen Clyde Lewis?"

They look at each other and go around the circle shrugging their shoulders. Confused, Sam asks, "I thought you guys were his buddies! You don't know where he is?"

"His buddy?" one of them laughs. "You must be joshing. Just because we went drinking with him didn't make us buddies. He was good for a few rounds." They all laugh and Sam knows he's not going to get any help from this group. "One more question: Can you tell me the last time you saw him?"

One of the guys who Sam noticed didn't laugh answers, "Sure. The last time I saw him was in a tavern a while back. We left before he did, but come to think of it, I haven't seen him since."

"Can you remember when that was?" Sam asks.

"Not really. It's been a long time, though."

"Thanks for your help. I really do appreciate it," Sam says as he walks away thinking, *What am I going to do now? I need to find him so he knows what's happened to his mom.*

A few weeks pass and Sam's still asking around. Finally, he runs into a cowboy who remembers Clyde talking about finding a job and thought it was at a coal mine. Sam starts to call the mines around the towns they've passed through, and, after a few, he connects with the right one. "Hello, my name is Sam Goldberg. Do you have a Clyde Lewis working for you?"

"Why do you ask?" demands the voice on the other end.

"I need to get a message to him about his mother."

"Okay, I'll give him the message at quitting time. Go ahead," Stan says.

"Tell him his mother was hurt in an automobile accident. She's alive, but she is blind."

"You want me to give him that kind of news?"

"You said you would."

"Yeah, I did, but this ain't going to be easy. What was your name again?"

"Sam, Sam Goldberg, and thank you very much."

"You're welcome, goodbye."

✵ ✵ ✵

During their time together, Skinny's taught Clyde numerous hymns which they sing as loudly as they can throughout the day. They've sung them so much that Clyde knows them by heart. Even on the days he doesn't work, he finds himself humming or singing them to himself. Skinny knows so many that every once in a while, he'll slip in a new one just to keep things interesting.

Another thing Skinny likes to do is ask questions about the lyrics. Then he uses his responses to further inquire about Clyde's relationship with God. When Clyde gets to the point where he can't answer anymore, Skinny shares God's plan of salvation. Clyde listens each time he tells about how much God loves us and how He sent His Son to suffer and shed His blood for our sins. It's not a new message to him, but Skinny just has a way of saying it that's different. The last part of the story always excites Clyde. Skinny tells how the Romans crucified and buried Jesus in a tomb, and how He got even with them when God raised Him from the grave. Skinny always finishes with the song, "Low in the Grave He Lay." Clyde loves singing the refrain to the hymn; "Up from the grave He arose, with a mighty triumph o'er His foes." The same question always comes up and Clyde continues to give the same answer. "Yeah, I know there's a God and I'm a nice guy an' all."

At times, the conversation gets to the point where Clyde doesn't think there is an answer. That's when Skinny turns to his trusty old Bible and reads a passage that deals with what they're discussing. There are times when he doesn't have it with him and he'll quote it right off the top of his head. Clyde thinks, *It's amazing how he can just blurt out an answer from the Bible to almost anything I can ask.* This helps keep the job from wearing on them. It's pretty demanding; they frequently work for days on end, and long days at that.

Clyde tells Skinny all about Harold, how he met Audra and they got married. This turns into quite a conversation: Skinny brings out his Bible and reads about how sacred marriage is. Clyde had never thought of it being spiritual; he always thought it was just something two people did. That's what Clyde is enjoying so; Skinny always brings in the spiritual side of life. Clyde never knew how much the Bible talks about everyday life.

It's finally time to call it a day. They park the truck and head to the office. When they open the door, the foreman looks up from his desk. The secretary knows what's coming and decides to take a walk outside. With a chuckle, the foreman asks, "Calling it a day already?"

Clyde grunts as he throws the keys on the secretary's desk. He's heading out the back door when Stan hollers, "Hey Clyde, hold up there! I got a message for you."

"For me?" he asks, surprised.

"Yeah, from some guy name Goldbond, Holdberg . . . oh, I don't remember. I wrote the message down and it's here on my desk somewhere."

"From Sam Goldberg?" Clyde asks.

"Yeah, that's the name. Oh, here it is. I'll read it to you. Probably can't read my writing, anyway," Stan says. "Tell him his mother was hurt in an automobile accident. She's alive, but she is blind."

"What? Read that again," Clyde requests as he moves closer. Stan looks down and proceeds to reread the message. "I have to go home right now," Clyde states.

"Clyde, we're shorthanded," Stan protests. "We have to work all weekend to get caught up and you're asking me to let you take off. I'm not sure I can do that!"

"No disrespect, sir, but it don't matter what you say. I've been here for some time now and done all you've asked and more. I'm not askin', I'm lettin' you know that I'll be gone for a few days and be back on Monday," Clyde says.

The foreman cracks a little smile. "You get worked up rather quickly, don't ya?

"Only if I have ta," Clyde shoots back.

"Clyde, it's your mom; you need to go. Take Skinny with you, you'll need some company. Oh, one more thing."

"Yeah, what's that?"

"I appreciate both of you fellas. You never complain about anything and always work hard, so I'm going to pay you for the days you're gone as long as you're back by Monday."

You could have knocked Clyde over with a feather. "Really? We appreciate it! We'll see you bright and early Monday morning. Come on, Skinny, before he changes his mind." They both let out a hoot and head to Clyde's truck. As they approach it, Clyde's thoughts are on the seriousness of the situation. When Skinny glances over and sees the concern on his face, he reaches over and touches Clyde's shoulder. "Your mom's going to be okay," he assures him.

"I hope so," Clyde says, "I hope so."

✡ ✡ ✡

They drive all night and, when they pull into town early Friday morning, banners are strung across Main Street welcoming the rodeo to town. It never entered Clyde's mind that this was rodeo weekend. "They really go all out for this, don't they!" Skinny observes.

"You ain't seen nothin' yet, my friend. Do you mind if we head out to the homestead?"

"Not at all, that's what we came for!" Skinny replies.

As they get to the far end of town, Clyde spots Harold's truck about the same time Harold spots him. They pull over to the side of the road and Clyde introduces Harold to Skinny. They talk for a few minutes and Harold asks, "You riding this weekend? I know they need more riders."

"Nah, came here to see my mom," Clyde hesitantly responds.

"It only takes a few seconds, ya know," Harold counters.

"Yeah," Clyde chuckles, "some fewer than others."

"Think about it. I can still get you signed up."

"Thanks, Harold, but I don't think so. Not this time."

They make their way out to the ranch house and Skinny is pretty impressed with the place. Clyde gives him a short synopsis of how they got the property and Skinny sums it up. "God sure is watching over your family."

Without saying anything, Clyde thinks, *Yeah, He sure is. My mom's blind. God really is looking out for us!*

When they stop in front of the house, Rachel's the first one out and jumps into Clyde's arms. Then Sara leads Mom out onto the front porch. Mom, always smiling, stands at the rail waving. With Rachel in his arms, they walk up to the porch and Clyde introduces Skinny to the family.

"I knew you'd be home," Rachel says. "Can't pass up ridin' in our rodeo."

"Come on inside and I'll get you all something to drink," Mom suggests.

"Oh, I can get it, Mom. You don't need to be waiting on us," Clyde replies.

Sara shakes her head and moves her hands to signal Clyde to be quiet, but it's too late. Mom says, "Listen up; I might be blind, but my legs and arms still work, so you two sit your little rears in the parlor, and I'll bring you something to drink." Clyde and Skinny stifle their laughter as Sara mouths almost every word Mom says. She must have heard it before.

Rachel can't let the rodeo go. "So, do you know what bulls you're riding yet?"

Clyde looks at her and repeats, "Rachel, I'm not riding this weekend. I came home to see how Mom's doing, and we have to be back early Monday morning for work."

"What?! You ain't ridin'? What's wrong with you? You're the best rider this side of the Mississippi, and if the truth be known, probably in the whole country!" Rachel declares.

"Rachel, I've decided to move on to other things. I can't explain it any better than that."

She walks away muttering, "That don't make no sense to me! What a waste, to give up so soon on your dreams!"

Clyde shrugs his shoulders and looks at Skinny and Sara as Mom walks in with the iced tea. He can't believe how well Mom gets around without being able to see. Sara explains that as long as everything is in the same place, she does a great job, but if someone moves something or leaves something laying out, then she can fall and hurt herself.

Mom sits down and says, "Clyde, you come here and let me get a good look at you."

Confused, Clyde asks, "What? I thought you . . ."

Before he can finish, Mom says, "Just be quiet and come here." Clyde stands up, walks over and kneels down. Mom feels his face with her hands and says, "You're a mighty fine-looking young man, Clyde Lewis. I'm proud to have you as my son. Now what's this nonsense about you not riding this weekend? You love to do it, and you're so good at it! I hope it's not because of me."

"No, Mom, it's not because of you. It's a long story; I'll tell you sometime, but not now. I just want to be here with you."

"Okay," Mom says, "and I'm glad you're staying here with us, but we want to go to the rodeo this weekend. So, if you want to be with us, you'll both have to go. And if you go, you might as well ride! It only takes a few seconds, ya know."

Clyde thinks, *That's the second time someone told me that today!*

After they finish their tea, Mom takes them upstairs and shows them their room so they can catch a few winks before the rodeo tonight.

☆ ☆ ☆

When they enter the rodeo grounds, the girls help Mom to their designated seats that Sam made special arrangements for. Harold grabs Clyde on the way and says, "We need one more rider! I have all your equipment here. Come on, make it a surprise for your mom."

Skinny, knowing Clyde's desire to ride, gives him a nod and follows the rest of the family while Clyde makes his way to the back of the chutes to get ready for what he loves best.

He ends up riding all of his bulls and taking third overall, earning some much-needed traveling money. The weekend flies by, and it's soon time for Clyde and Skinny to head back to work. With tearful goodbyes behind them and a long drive ahead, they grab a thermos of coffee and hit the road. It doesn't take long before the conversation leads to bull-riding.

"It sure was nice meeting your family," Skinny says. "Thanks for taking me!"

"You're welcome," Clyde replies. "Next to Harold, you're the best friend I've ever had. I hope we can be friends for a long time."

"I'm sure we will be," Skinny hesitantly says.

"Why'd you say it that way?" Clyde asks.

"Well, Clyde, I ain't much into the rodeo scene. You know I've already told ya that I believe my calling is telling people about Jesus."

"Yeah? What's that got to do with us being friends?"

"I saw you ride this weekend and you're very good. I have a passion to preach, and you have a passion to ride."

"I don't know, Skinny. I love the ridin', but I'm not quite sure I can deal with all the other stuff that comes with it. Since I've been with you, my mind is sharper, and I feel a lot better."

"I don't know about all the other stuff," Skinny points out, "but when you're on the back of a bull, I can tell you're having the time of your life. Don't let other things get in the way of what you were made for. God has a plan for all of us, and I think you've found yours." Skinny pulls his coat over his shoulders. "Wake me when you need me to drive," he concludes.

Chapter 23
THE LAST RIDE

They make it back early Monday morning and get a few hours of shuteye before they head to the mine. Clyde's pretty sore from riding all weekend but knows he can't miss any work. It's not long before they're back to the everyday grind. Each day seems to run into the next. So many days straight and countless hours of hauling coal from the mines; it never seems to stop. There are times when Clyde is so sleepy that they come seconds away from tragedy. From Clyde's perspective, their friendship is closer than with any brother he could ever have. It's hard to imagine, but in such a short period of time, they have developed a friendship that's deeper than the one he has with Harold. Having faced life and death with someone, it's inexplicable the type of bond you develop with that person; and this describes their friendship, being willing to lay down your life for the other. Over these past months, the mountain has claimed numerous trucks but as luck would have it, hasn't taken any drivers or riders over with them. Once a driver loses a truck, he's pretty much done; he never wants to go back up the mountain.

It's the last day before a well-deserved few days off, and they're looking forward to this day being over. The weather is beginning to turn chilly and they've worked ten days straight. The boss wants to get in as many loads as he can before the bad weather sets in. It's toward dusk and the other trucks have already finished up. The boys, with the boss's encouragement, decide to take one more trip up the mountain.

On their way up, Clyde tells Skinny, "Road's getting a little muddy. I'm gonna have to be real careful on the way down."

"We've done it before, it'll be all right," Skinny assures him. "Let me pray for a safe trip down."

Earlier in the day, they took off the top of the cab to help disperse some of the steam that builds up. But now, with the weather turning cold, they put their coats on to keep warm. As they ease away from the mine, Clyde's fighting the truck to keep the speed down and avoid sliding. After lowering the gears, he tries to stay off the brakes, but it's a lot harder than he thought it'd be. The added weight of the coal pushes the trailer closer to the edge. Unable to slow it enough with just the gears, he has to tap the brakes, and that's all it takes for the trailer to begin a slide. At first it moves toward the mountainside, which is a relief for Clyde, but only for a few seconds. Without warning, the trailer taps the mountain and starts to head toward the cliff, while Clyde does all he can to keep the truck going straight. He slams the gear box into the lowest gear in an effort to keep the trailer from going any closer to the edge, but it doesn't work; the trailer continues to slide slowly.

"Drive her out, Clyde," Skinny yells, "drive her out!"

The trailer begins to pull the truck toward the edge, and Clyde thinks they may have to bail out, but Skinny has other thoughts. He hops from his seat and Clyde hollers, "Where you goin'?"

"Gonna pull the pin and dump the trailer! You just keep drivin'." Skinny carefully goes over the back and stands on the small trailer tongue. Balancing himself, he bends down and unscrews the brake line from the truck and tugs on the lock pin. "Drive her out!" he yells again.

Fighting it with all he has, Clyde taps the accelerator and the truck's rear wheels begin to slide over the edge. Clyde looks over his shoulder just as Skinny pulls the trailer pin. With the trailer disconnected, he starts to get the truck under control. Skinny grabs the back of the cab and shouts, "Yahoo!"

Before Clyde can look back, one of the air hoses hooks Skinny's coat and the full weight of the trailer going over the cliff pulls Skinny along with it. The last thing Clyde sees is Skinny waving his arms and repeating, "Drive her out!" before he disappears over the side. Clyde bounces off the cliff's face, knocking out a headlight and denting a fender. Then he slowly heads to the bottom of the mountain, screaming at the top of his lungs words that are not fit to tell. His emotions have gotten the best of him. As he nears the bottom, he has a hard time focusing through his tears. He brings the truck to a screeching halt and collapses over the steering wheel.

Stan and the secretary come running to the truck. "Where's the trailer? Where's Ulysses. . . Skinny . . . oh, whoever?" he hollers.

Without looking up, Clyde stutters through a cracking voice, "Went over with the trailer." The foreman hollers at the secretary to call for an ambulance and then races to the side of the mountain. Clyde remains in the cab, unable to move. He knows there's no reason to head over with Stan; no one could have survived that fall. A couple of minutes pass and an ambulance whizzes by.

Clyde picks up the horseshoe from the seat, grips it in his hand, and hammers it on the steel dashboard, blaming God, yet thankful for Skinny's faithfulness. It's hard for him to believe what just happened. He thinks, *Why, God? Why would You allow that to happen to someone who loved You so much? You make no sense to me! His life was about telling people about You and now he's gone.*

Clyde sits there for the longest time, until he finally sees the ambulance pull out and Stan makes his way back over to Clyde.

"Let's go in the office and have a little drink," Stan suggests. He opens the truck door while Clyde turns to get out. When he steps out, he falls to the ground, unable to make his legs work. By this time, some of the town's people have made their way out to the yard and a couple of them help Clyde to his feet and assist him to the office.

Stan pours himself and Clyde drinks and asks, "What happened up there?" They sit down at a table, and, playing with his glass, Clyde explains the last ride, beginning with the slippery ride up. As he continues, Stan pours himself another drink. Clyde's emotions are like a roller coaster; at times he can speak normally, but most of the time, his voice is weak and cracking. Throughout, he keeps repeating, "I can't believe Skinny's gone," after each time another wave of emotions overtakes him.

Finally, he looks at Stan and pulls the truck keys from his pocket. "I'm done," he says, "I can't drive up that mountain anymore. I'll clean out my locker."

"Take a few days and think about it. You can stay on if ya want. You're one of my best drivers." Stan tries to encourage him, knowing that few ever drive back up that mountain.

"Thanks, but I can't. It wouldn't be fair for the next guy riding shotgun."

Clyde scoots back from the table and steadies himself as he stands. He reaches out to shake Stan's hand and slowly heads toward the locker room. When he walks into this old building, he smells the familiar moisture in the air. He picks up an old paper bag from the garbage, walks over to his locker, and dumps everything in it. To the right is Skinny's locker with nothing in it except his old Bible. He can just see Skinny sitting there reading from it. He reaches in and pulls it out. Then he sits down on the bench, holding it with both hands. He turns it over, then back again before noticing a piece of paper sticking out of it. With his hands shaking, he slowly pulls it out and opens it. There are two scripture references written on it; the first is Psalm 23:4 and the second is Psalm 116:15. He slowly scans the Bible looking for Psalms, and about halfway through, he runs across it. When he finds Psalm 23:4 he reads:

> Yea, though I walk through the valley of the shadow of
> death, I will fear no evil: for thou art with me; thy rod
> and thy staff they comfort me.

Clyde thinks, *I wonder why Skinny would write that down.* Now he can't wait to look up the next verse. He turns the pages to the right and locates Psalm 116:15:

> Precious in the sight of the LORD is the death of his
> saints.

This confuses him even more. *What does that mean? Skinny was truly a saint, but why would that be precious to Him?* Clyde ponders this. When he reaches over to put the Bible back, another note falls out. This one reads:

> *Dear Mom and Dad,*
> *I've made friends with a great guy. I ride shotgun for him. No Dad, he doesn't know the Lord yet, but we have a great time singing hymns and he's always open to me sharing with him. He's the best friend I've ever had, and I pray for him all the time. I know God has me here just for him. In fact, the week I met him was going to be my last week here, but I wholeheartedly believe God wanted me to stay just for him.*

(Clyde's hand begins to tremble as he attempts to get a grip on his emotions.) He continues to read:

> *Please pray for him. His name is Clyde Lewis, and you'd really like him. Got to go. We have a long day today.*
>
>

Your son,
Ulysses (that's for you, Mom)

Clyde thinks, *Skinny would still be alive if I hadn't come along.* He puts Skinny's Bible under his arm and heads out the door.

Stan catches up with him as he nears his truck. "Clyde," he says. "I just spoke with the office, and they'll have your check here by Friday."

Clyde climbs in his truck and says, "Thanks, but I don't know if I'll still be around."

He pulls out of the mine parking lot and heads to town, his head still spinning from what just took place. It's not long before he pulls up in front of the boarding house, walks in, and heads straight to his room. He sits on the edge of his bed with his mind racing about what he should do next. After a few minutes, he decides to get some fresh air with one destination in mind: *Get me to the tavern.*

He approaches the bar with his shoulders drooping, takes a seat, and asks for a drink. As others walk in, he becomes very self-conscious, thinking that they're all looking at him. When someone whispers, he thinks they're talking about him. He picks up his beer and walks to the farthest corner table, trying to hide from everything and everybody. *Is this what Skinny would want you to do?* Keeps running through his mind. And every time, the answer is the same. *No! But what should I do? This is the only thing I kno. . ., the only way to get peace.* Every once in a while, the cocktail waitress asks him if he's all right, and he assures her that he is.

Like in most small towns, news travels fast. By the time it gets around town, the story has been embellished, and it's much bigger than the original. As Clyde sits in the corner listening to people talk about their days and the rumors they've heard, few of them notice him sitting there. He has no one to talk to; no Harold, no Skinny, just himself, all alone again. The alcohol begins to kick in, and his mind becomes clouded. That little voice inside his head continues to tell him he needs to leave, but where will he go? He puts his head on the table and the next thing he knows, he's waking up in the backroom of the tavern. He sits up on a small army cot and tries to clear the cobwebs from his mind. The bartender walks in and Clyde asks him, "How did I get here?"

"You fell asleep with your head on the table," he explains. "When you came to, you started to leave, but some guy from out of town made a comment about the accident, not realizing who he was talking to. You didn't hesitate; you cold-conked him, and that's when a little brawl began. I grabbed you and brought you back here to sleep it off. Thought you'd already had a tough day."

"Thank you. I didn't break anything, did I? If I did, I want to pay for it," Clyde assures him.

"No, you're fine. Some other folks broke some stuff, but they paid me for it."

"What time is it?"

Looking at his wrist, the bartender answers, "Right around 8:30."

"In the," Clyde shouts, then tones it down when his head begins to throb, "morning?" he whispers.

"Yeah, can't believe you slept through all the racket," the bartender chuckles.

"Thanks for everything. Do I owe you anything?" Clyde asks.

"Not a dime, young man. You just take care of yourself. Oh, I almost forgot. This horseshoe was on the table. Is it yours?"

"Yeah, that's my lucky horseshoe. Sure didn't work yesterday, did it? Oh, never mind. Thanks, I'll take care. You have a nice day," Clyde says as he heads out the backdoor. He knows he can't stay around here, and there's only one other thing he knows he can do, ride bulls. Everyone's so polite and sympathetic as he walks around town. He's grateful that Skinny helped him save some money. The bank is about to open, so he waits outside to close his account.

Once he finishes there, it's off to the boarding house to pack up, which doesn't take long. He packs Skinny's Bible in the steamer with his other important items. Before leaving, he thanks the elderly couple for their hospitality and offers to pay them a couple of weeks extra for leaving so suddenly, but they explain that Stan had called and said he'd take care of it.

He gets into the truck and heads to the coal mine one last time. As he pulls up next to the office, he can't look at the mountain that took his best friend's life. When he walks into the office, Stan's standing by the counter. He puts his hand on Clyde's shoulder and asks, "Have you had a change of heart?"

"No, sir! I just stopped by to give you the address to mail my last check, and who to make it out to. Address it to Dorris Lewis."

"You headed home?"

"Nope, going to do what I should have been doing all along. If I had, Skinny would still be alive today."

"Ya don't know that, Clyde," Stan insists.

"Yeah, I do, and you can't say anything to convince me otherwise. Just make sure my check gets to my mom, please."

"There are two checks. The company gave us bonuses for all our hard work."

"Well, give that one to Skinny's parents to help with the funeral. I need to hit the road. Please make sure they get the money."

"I will, and good luck to ya. It's been a pleasure getting to know ya."

"Thanks," Clyde says as he walks out.

✳ ✳ ✳

The next few weeks are a blur. He picks up odd jobs where he can to fill in until the circuit starts up again. When it finally does, it's hard to find out just where the next rodeo's going to be. With all the traveling, he reverts back to his old self, hanging out in the taverns when he can. He's more careful now with his money and doesn't drink as much, but he still does a lot of hanging around. He goes from town to town and woman to woman, trying to forget what happened at the mine.

Now back in the saddle, or should I say on the backs of bulls, he's more determined than ever to be successful. As time flies by, he hopes each rodeo will help him get back on track. He hasn't been at his best, but he's doing well enough to survive. The long ride to the next rodeo gets him thinking. *When I was riding with Harold, I wasn't drinking and was doing quite well. Now that I'm drinking, I'm not doing very good. That settles it. I'm going back to living like when I was with Harold: I won't drink until the rodeo's over.* It works! He ends up winning the weekend rodeo, and, once it's over, he heads to the tavern.

There's a cute little dame that follows him around. She's so impressed with him being a bull-rider that she begins to put her hooks in. She follows him to the next town, and, before you know it, they're standing in front of the justice of the peace getting married. She's excited about all the traveling and the thrill of her man being one of the top bull-riders. That quickly wears off, though, and after a few rodeos without placing, she starts to see a side of this profession that she doesn't much care for. As the season winds down, she starts to nag him about finding a real job and settling down. He tells her, "I am who you married and ya ain't gonna change me." With little money left and the next rodeo about to begin, Clyde wakes up one morning to an empty bed. He calls out her name, but there's no answer. When he goes into the bathroom, he finds this note:

> *Clyde,*
> *You just don't get it. This ain't no life for*
> *me, and you don't want to make me happy.*
> *So I got on the early bus out of here. Good*
> *luck to ya.*
> *Mabel*
> *P.S. I needed the money.*

Clyde can't believe it. *She took all the money! Now what am I going to do? I'll have to place, I guess,* he chuckles to himself. He moseys up to the motel office and explains what happened. The older couple behind the counter feels sorry for him and tells him to stay in the room and forget about paying. "Why would you do that for me?" Clyde asks.

The wife looks at her husband and says, "Because it's already been paid for." With that, her soft voice breaks into a song, one Clyde hasn't heard for some time now:

> *And when before the throne I stand in Him complete,*
> *Jesus died my soul to save,*
> *My lips shall still repeat.*
> *Jesus paid it all,*
> *All to Him I owe;*
> *Sin had left a crimson stain-*
> *He washed it white as snow.*

The song brings back memories of driving up and down that old mountain with Skinny.

The lady looks up and asks, "You ever hear that song before?'

"Oh yeah, my friend and I used to sing it all the time," Clyde softly replies.

"Are you a Christian?"

"No ma'am, but my friend was. Not sure it's right for me."

"Where's your friend now?" she enthusiastically asks.

"I'm sure he's in heaven," Clyde confides as he hangs his head. "Ya see, he died a while back."

"I'm so sorry," she says, "Any time you'd like to talk about it, let us know."

Clyde thinks, *Her husband isn't saying much; just standing there letting the little lady do all the talking. It seems a little strange, but hey, to each his own.* Clyde thanks them for the generous gift and tells them, "I'll come back and pay what I can from my winnings this week."

They smile and wave as Clyde walks out.

That weekend he goes on to win the bull-riding event. Something happened listening to that old hymn he and Skinny used to sing. In fact, it was really weird. Sunday morning as he walks past the tent services, he slips into the back and listens to the preacher. He thinks, *Skinny was a lot better than this guy!* He quickly exits when the service is over, but things are different. The old desire to ride is back, but we'll see how long it lasts this time.

Chapter 24
TO THE RESCUE

It's been a long season and the results have been like a roller coaster, up and down. Clyde partnered up with a bareback rider by the name of Monte, and at first, things rolled along pretty well. But as time went by, Monte seemed to be riding less and spending more. For a number of rodeos now, he's come up with numerous reasons why he can't ride. A while back, he got on the back of one nasty horse and it took him for a ride that would have scared a religious man into cursing. By the time the ride was over, he was pretty beat up and lucky to be alive. The horse missed trampling his head by inches, and all he could do was lie there and watch. Since then he's had one excuse after another. Clyde thinks he's too scared to ride again. That's also why they've been spending so much time in the taverns. When Clyde avoided those places he always had extra money to do things with, but not for the last month or so.

It's Sunday evening; Clyde's thankful the rodeo is over and that he finished in the money. Monte didn't ride again, so what little Clyde won will have to hold them over. It's been raining the last couple of days, and it's raining cats and dogs as they walk into the tavern. Clyde warns Monte to take it easy tonight because they don't have much to blow, but he ignores Clyde's request and saunters up to the bartender. "We're going to be here most of the night. How about opening a tab for me and my partner?" he asks.

The bartender obliges and the rest of the evening goes off without a hitch until Monte gets ready to leave. Clyde's been passing the time like most nights, off in the corner alone. Since Mabel walked out, he hasn't had any desire to look again, and, like most nights, Monte spends it buying drinks for others and ignoring Clyde.

When Monte finally gets up to leave, the bartender hollers, "Hey, don't forget to pay your tab!"

"Oh, that," Monte hollers back over the packed crowd. "See that guy in the corner over there?" He points to Clyde. "He's the one carrying the money, he'll pay you," he adds before walking out.

Hearing Monte, Clyde bellows, "Hey, I don't have that much money. Get back in here!"

The bartender walks up to Clyde. "Here's the bill; pay up," he demands.

Clyde picks up the paper, looks at the total and thinks, *What am I going to do? I don't have that much money!* Clyde smiles at the bartender standing in front of him. "Sir, I don't have that much money on me, but if you'll give me a minute, I'll run to my room and get it for ya." Clyde knows that's not the truth, but he's trying anything he can think of to avoid what he figures is coming.

The bartender shakes his head. "Son, I'm not letting you out of my sight," he declares and then motions to two big guys. One positions himself behind Clyde and the other stands right in front of him. The bartender moves to the side. "Now, son, if ya know what's good for ya, you'll pay up."

"Like I said," Clyde repeats, "I don't have that much money on me."

The big guy behind him grabs his shoulders and holds him down while the other one bends over and gets nose to nose with spit flying as he speaks. They rough him up, empty his pockets, and discover he's short about half the money. Disgusted, the bartender mutters, "Throw the bum out." They each grab an arm, with Clyde kicking and screaming, and head to the front door. When they throw him out, he lands on the dirt sidewalk in the middle of a huge mud puddle. Doused, he sits there a moment trying to gain his composure when Monte and a couple of cowboys walk up.

"Clyde, you need to take better care of yourself," he taunts. They burst out laughing as Monte bends over and picks up the truck keys on the ground next to Clyde.

As he turns to walk away, Clyde protests, "Hey, those are my keys!"

Laughing, Monte says, "I know that, but you don't need them. I'm taking the truck. Find your own way to the next rodeo."

✵ ✵ ✵

Meanwhile, inside the tavern the bartender wipes the counter while everyone else watches what's going on outside.

An older guy walks up and startles him. "Evenin', partner!" he says.

"You scared the crap out of me! Where'd you come from?" he demands.

"I was over yonder," he answers and points to the back of the room. "I saw you throw the young fella out. How much does he owe ya?" the stranger asks.

"I don't rightly think that's any of your business, unless you're going to pay the bill," the bartender sarcastically replies.

The stranger shakes his head. "I reckon that's the reason I asked, partner. But if you're gonna be that way, I'll move on," he explains as he turns to go.

"Whoa, slow down a bit! Did you say you were going to pay the tab? Why would you do that? You know that kid?'

The stranger stops. "Can't say that I do," he admits, "just thought I'd help out." The group at the window catches their attention as they guffaw at Clyde sitting in the puddle.

"If you're still interested, here's what's left on his tab," the bartender says as he slides the paper over.

The stranger reaches into his pocket, pulls out some cash, and lays it on the bar. "Keep the change," he says, then leaves.

One of the guys at the window hollers, "Hey, you gotta see this! Hurry!"

The stranger approaches Clyde and offers him his hand, but Clyde points down the street and says, "Hey, that guy's taking my truck!"

He helps Clyde to his feet and says, "Wait here, I'll be right back." He takes off toward the truck and when he gets about halfway, he yells, "Hold up there, cowboy! I got something to ask you."

☆ ☆ ☆

The bartender scampers over to the big picture window. "Hey, that guy was just in here! How'd he get out there so fast? Anyone see him leave?"

"Nope, he didn't walk by me," one of the guys says. "I never even saw him. Where'd he come from?"

"He was just in here and paid that young fella's bar tab," the bartender says, lifting his hand to show the cash.

"Why would he do some fool thing like that?" one of the fellas at the window asks.

"Don't rightly know, but I'm sure glad he did," the bartender replies. "Has anyone seen him before?"

They all shake their heads before someone marvels, "I don't even recall seeing him in here tonight, and I've been here most of the evening. Hey, look! What's that old man doing now? He's walking over toward that truck." The guy rubs his hands together and says, "This could be interesting!"

Clyde glances around as people gather to see what's going on. He glances at the tavern and sees people in the window laughing and pointing at the stranger walking to the truck. He looks again toward his truck just as the old man reaches the door.

Monte slides behind the steering wheel and hears someone shout. Before he closes the door, he looks over and sees this old cowboy-looking fella walking toward him. As he approaches, Monte squints to try to distinguish who's hollering at him. He thinks, *What in the world does he want? I ain't never seen him before.* With a worn old Stetson on his head and cowboy boots that don't look like they've been polished in a coon's age, the stranger saunters up. He's not much to look at; with all his wrinkles and scars you can tell he's seen better days.

When the old man gets closer, Monte asks, "What can I do for ya, Old-Timer?"

"Is this here truck yours?" the stranger asks.

Monte can't believe the gall of this old man! "What business is that of yours?" he demands.

The Old-Timer leans against the stout door and explains, "Well, I read in the good book that it ain't right to steal."

Taken aback by the old man's audacity, Monte says, "Well now, ain't that real nice! You can quote the good book! What else can you do, Old-Timer?"

With that, the Old-Timer places one hand on Monte's shoulder and leans in and whispers in his ear.

Clyde and the rest of the group watch him lean against the truck door, and bend over and say something to Monte. Clyde knows Monte has a short fuse and waits for him to react. He's really surprised that he's even listening at all. As the old man stands up, Monte puts his hands over his ears, jumps out of the truck, and sets off on a dead run with his hat in his hand. Even from a distance, Clyde can see the expression on Monte's face. He looks like he's seen a ghost or something.

With Clyde's keys dangling in his hand, the stranger ambles back to him. The others, who by this time have stepped out of the tavern, can't wait to ask what he said. The old man extends his hand and says, "They call me Crunchy, young fella, and I hear your name is Clyde. Oh, before I forget, here are your keys."

"How'd ya do that?" Clyde asks as he grasps Crunchy's hand.

"Do what, young fella?"

"I ain't never seen anyone look so scared in all my life. What did ya tell him to make him run like that?"

"I'm not quite sure what got 'im all shook up. Didn't really say anything except that it wasn't kind to take other people's property."

✳ ✳ ✳

With his knees pumping like a cylinder, Monte runs down the block and around the corner, not stopping until he's out of breath. He bends over and places his hands on his knees, his hat hanging between his legs. Huffing and puffing as he tries to catch his breath, he thinks, *I can't believe what just happened! There's something strange about that old man. I wonder who he is? When he leaned in and touched my shoulder, he 'bout crushed it. Then those eyes; they were like magnets. I couldn't take my eyes off them! They drew me in and then, just as fast, they changed.* He closes his eyes and pounds the side of his head as if attempting to knock the thoughts out. Dropping his hat, he stands up and places both hands on top of his head, interlocking his fingers. He tilts his head back and thinks, *His eyes were like blazing fireballs! That was so strange. At first his words were so soft and gentle, but after I spoke his voice changed. It was like thunder! It scared me so bad. I've never had anything like that happen to me before, and I sure don't want it to happen again! I'm saying "adios" to this town. Don't ever want to see Clyde or that old man again!*

He sticks out his thumb as the first car passes. When it stops, he jumps in.

"Where you headed?" the driver asks.

"To the next town. Are you going that far?"

"Sure am! Be glad to have the company." They take off as Monte introduces himself.

✳ ✳ ✳

Clyde takes his keys and the crowd heads back into the tavern. "Thanks, I owe ya one," he tells Crunchy.

"Ah, think nothin' of it," Crunchy says. "Ya got a place to lay your head?"

"I got my trusty truck. We've been spending a lot of time together lately," Clyde confesses as he wipes off his hat with his sleeve.

"I got an offer for ya, then," Crunchy proposes.

"What's that?"

"Well, I just got into town and checked into my room. I asked 'em for one bed, but they said all they had was a room with two, so if ya'd like to occupy the other one, I'd consider it a privilege," Crunchy explains.

Clyde thinks, *That sure sounds nice, but I don't know. I've never ever seen this guy before! Can I trust him? He did get my truck back for me. Oh, what the hay. I ain't got nothin' left for him to take, anyway. Besides, he's footing the bill!* "Okay, I'll take you up on that. Thanks a lot! Don't know how I'll ever repay ya."

"No need to worry about that. I'll enjoy the company."

They make their way to the room and as soon as Clyde's head hits the pillow, it's lights out.

Early the next morning, Clyde wakes to Crunchy walking into the room holding two cups of coffee. "Got some coffee for ya, just the way you like it; nice and black," he says.

He sits up and reaches for the coffee. "How'd ya know I like it black?"

"You're a cowboy, ain't ya?" Crunchy teases.

"I appreciate the room and the coffee," Clyde chuckles.

"What are you going to do now?" Crunchy asks.

"Not really sure. Probably head out and find some work."

"How are ya gonna do that without any money?" Crunchy inquires.

"Good question," Clyde snickers, "never thought of that. But I don't know if the rodeo life is for me anymore."

Crunchy sits on the edge of his bed, sipping his coffee. "Why do you say that?" he asks.

Setting his coffee down on the night stand, Clyde says, "It just seems like I always hook up with the wrong people and get myself in trouble."

"If ya care to listen, I got some advice for ya."

Not knowing what to expect, Clyde adjusts his pillow. "Go ahead, I'm all ears," he says.

"I've seen ya ride. You're talented; one of the best I've seen, but you let outside activities influence you too much. One thing you need to understand is that bad company corrupts good morals. It also takes your eyes off the goal ahead," Crunchy warns him.

Clyde listens intently. He hasn't quite figured this old fella out yet, but each time he speaks he hangs on his every word. Clyde remembers hearing the statement about bad company before, but he just can't place where. "Yeah, I know you're right, but I just don't know how to."

Crunchy lies back on his bed, "Your dream is to ride at The Garden and you're good enough to do it, but ya never will unless ya get your head screwed on straight. I'm offering you my services; I'll help you get to The Garden, but you have to do everything I tell you . . . and you need to trust me."

Clyde's pretty skeptical. "Oh, yeah? And what's that going to cost me?"

"Nothing," Crunchy says. "Not a thing. Well, that's not totally true."

"Yeah, that's what I figured. I knew it. What's the catch?"

"You have to work harder than you've ever done before."

"That's it?" Clyde asks. "There has to be more to it. You want part of my winnings?"

"Not a penny. In fact, you don't have a dime to your name, so I guess I'll have to fund us for a while," Crunchy reminds him.

"But the season's almost over, so how is this going to work?"

"I'm going to get you ready! You're right, the season is about over here, but we're going west to prepare," Crunchy informs him.

Clyde sits on the edge of his bed, "You mean California?"

"Yep, California."

"I've heard they got some big rodeos out there."

"Bigger than you can imagine," Crunchy agrees.

"Okay, now let me get this straight," Clyde clarifies. "I'm out of money, so you're going to pay for us to go all the way to California, and then you're going to help me get ready to ride. And you're doing all this for nothing?"

"Oh, and don't forget about The Garden," Crunchy laughs. "It sounds too good to be true, huh?"

"You can say that again! Why would you do something like that?"

"Let me put it this way; it's what I do. Just enjoy it! Besides, I can't wait to hear all about your life. I bet you got some stories to tell," Crunchy says.

Clyde falls back on the bed, "Oh boy, do I! You won't believe some of them." After saying that, Clyde thinks, *Somehow, old fella, I think you already know. Don't know how you would, but I wouldn't put it past you.* "It's a deal. So what do I do with my truck?"

"You drive it," Crunchy says, laughing.

"What about your vehicle?" Clyde asks.

"My vehicle? I don't have one. I don't even drive. That's your part of the deal; we use your truck and you drive."

Clyde nods his head. "Okay. When do we get started?"

"In a few days we'll hit the road for California."

Clyde jumps up from the bed and exclaims, "I could use some biscuits and gravy! How about you, partner?"

"Would love some, partner."

☆ ☆ ☆

Dorris has grown used to her blindness and the family is thankful for the house Al left them. Maggie comes over almost daily to keep Dorris company and help keep the place up. Dorris spends a lot of time playing the piano and really enjoys it. Almost every time someone comes by, she sits down and plays for them. While she's adjusted, the girls have a hard time leaving her by herself, and Jim has a real hard time dealing with the whole accident. He doesn't drop by as much as he used to. Before the accident, he was considering asking Dorris to marry him, but now he's not so sure.

With his car newly repaired, Jim pulls into Buck's place for fuel and steps out. Martin saunters out of the back room and asks, "What can I do for you, Jim?"

"Fill it up, please. Could you check the tire pressure, too?"

"Sure can!" Martin replies before asking, "Do you mind if I ask you a question?"

Jim hesitates before saying, "No, not at all. Go ahead."

"I don't want to be butting in and all," Martin states and pauses for a moment, "but I guess I am, in a way. Ruthie and I are just curious if you have any intentions toward Mom, I mean Dorris?"

Jim takes a step back as Martin bends over to check the tire pressure. "I, um, don't quite know what you mean by that," he stammers.

Standing up and moving to the other side of the car, Martin replies, "You and Dorris were spending a lot of time together before the accident, and I thought you might be getting ready to pop the question. Since then, you rarely go over to see her. I told Ruthie I'd ask you if I saw you."

Jim leans against the fender. "I don't know. That's a tough question. I was going to ask her, but I don't think I can deal with her being blind."

"You're joshing me, aren't you?" Martin demands as he pulls the gas hose from the car.

"Why would you ask that?" Jim questions, wrinkling his brow. "I have some real concerns."

Martin's face turns red. "Do you hear what you're saying? She was good enough to ask when she could see, but now that she can't, your feelings for her have changed. I can't believe that! It may be a good thing you didn't ask her. I don't think I'd want someone like you for a father-in-law."

"That's pretty harsh," Jim rebuts as he gets back in the car.

"Just the way I feel, Jim. Have a nice day," Martin says as he heads back inside.

Jim sits in the car thinking, *That young man's right. Just because something happens to someone shouldn't change the love you have for them. Maybe I didn't love her the way I thought I did. Good thing I didn't ask her before the wreck!*

Chapter 25

CALIFORNIA HERE WE COME

They hit the road bound for California, stay in motels each night, and stop at nice diners when they get hungry. Whatever Clyde mentions he'd like to have, Crunchy seems to be right there with it. Clyde wonders where he gets all his money. He's surely never been able to afford all this!

Along the way people seem to know Crunchy. From motel owners to waitresses, they say "hi." It's pretty rare when they stop in a town and someone doesn't. Every once in a while, he'll help out around one of the motels. "We've got to do all we can to help folks," he says.

While hesitant to at first, Clyde joins in figuring it's probably helping to pay for their room. *The closest I've been to someone this generous was Skinny,* Clyde thinks. *I mean, he literally gave the jacket off his back.* This takes him back to that awful day. *I can't believe he's gone. If I hadn't stayed, he'd be alive. If I hadn't given him dad's coat maybe he'd . . . oh, I have to stop! I can't go back and change it. I remember Skinny telling me something about some guy in the Bible saying, "Forgetting what is behind, I have to move forward," or something like that. I have to move forward, and boy, it sure was lucky running into Crunchy.*

After a few days of traveling, they roll into Southern California where the weather is beautiful. Crunchy notices that Clyde's face lights up and says, "I see that grin. What cha thinkin' there, boy?"

Clyde takes a deep breath and sighs. "I remember Maggie telling us that she and Walter were headed to California when they found the place in Colorado. I never thought I'd ever be here! Guess I always wanted to go the other way."

Crunchy reaches over and puts his hand on Clyde's shoulder. "I told you, son, you'll get to New York. You just need to be patient. Think of it this way; you're starting the year on one coast and you'll finish it on the other."

Clyde lets out a hoot. "That's right! Uh, there's one problem."

"Yeah? What's that?" Crunchy asks.

"Where're we staying while we're here? You got some place for us, or do we just find a room?"

"Oh no, no motel. Just follow my directions and I'll show you our place for the next few months. Oh, by the way, you start work day after tomorrow."

"What? I got a job? Doesn't look like there's too many ranches around this place," Clyde chuckles.

"Nope, not a ranch. I thought ya needed a more rounded life, so you're working down on the docks."

His smile quickly fades. "The docks? I don't like working on those cattle-loading docks."

"Cattle-loading docks? No, these are where the big ships come in."

"By the ocean? You mean I get to see the ocean?" His excitement, however, quickly tails off. "Wait a minute! I don't understand! You said you were going to help me get to The Garden. I'm on the other side of the country, and now I'm working at the docks. How is that going to work?"

When they turn a corner, Crunchy tells him to pull into a circular drive. "Clyde, I also told you to trust me, didn't I? And you agreed. Don't go second-guessing me now."

"Ah, okay, I did agree and I am a man of my word. But I have one question."

"What's that?"

"What are we doing in front of this house? We stopping to see someone?" Before Crunchy can answer, Clyde adds, "And what in the world are those things?" as he points to the trees that line the driveway. "They look like someone stripped them down to nothing," Clyde observes.

Chuckling, Crunchy answers, "To answer your first question, this is where we're staying for the next few months. The second answer is, those are palm trees. They're all over the place down here."

Looking at the yard and then at the house, Clyde asks, "How did you pull this off?"

"It belongs to a friend of mine. He'll be gone for a while and said we could stay here."

"I've seen some pretty ranch homes before, but nothing like this one. You sure this is the right place?" Clyde asks as they get out.

"Yeah, he's a down-to-earth kind of guy, a cowpoke just like us," Crunchy assures him.

"Like us?" Clyde returns. "How can you say that? Look at this place! You say he's a cowpoke? Did he ride in the rodeos?"

"Don't think he ever rode the way you do, but he's been involved in a few. Some folks call him 'the singing cowboy'," Crunchy explains as he pushes the doorbell button. A few seconds later a middle-aged lady opens the door. "Hello, Señor Crunchy. The mister said you'd be here today. He tell me to tell you to make yourself comfortable and enjoy. This the young man you talking about to Señor?"

"Yes, Maria, it is. This is Clyde, and it's good to be back."

Clyde removes his hat. "It's a pleasure meeting you, ma'am."

She nods her head. "Polite young man, too. You sure do know how to pick 'em!"

"Now, Maria, you know I don't do that. That's left up to someone a lot wiser than I."

Clyde stands there thinking, *What's that all about? He was the one who found me. I wasn't even looking! A lot about this whole thing doesn't make much sense to me, but I'm here in California. If this don't bust your britches, nothing will,* he chuckles to himself.

☆ ☆ ☆

It's late Friday afternoon and Dorris is in the parlor playing the piano while the girls are outside. Rachel's riding Warrior and Sara's feeding the other animals as a car pulls down the drive. She hollers over at Sara, "Hey, look who's here!" and waves as the car comes to a stop in front of the house. Sara walks out the side barn door and waves as she heads down the road a piece to the old house where they lived when Dad was alive.

Rachel lets go of Warrior and climbs the fence. "Haven't seen you for a while," she jokes.

"Yeah, sure Rachel, you are so funny. I was just here last night," he says.

Rachel turns and shouts, "Hey, Sara! Where are you going?"

"Down to the old homestead," she shouts. "I'll be back in a jiff. You two go on in. Mom will be happy to see him." *He sure is spending a lot of time here lately,* she thinks.

Rachel leads him up the steps and into the house as Sara makes her way to the old house. She steps up on the porch and gently kicks open the front door. Cobwebs have taken over the place, and the door slowly creaks on its hinges. She looks above the door and can still see the shadow from where the old horseshoe once hung. She wants to reach up and slap it, but with all the spiders, she thinks better of it. She comes here every once in a while just to revisit those great memories of growing up and being a family. So many pictures flash through her head as she looks around. It's funny how she can hear certain conversations going on as if everyone was still there. She doesn't stay long, never does. Walking back out she hears the loft doors swinging in the wind on the old barn across the way. It reminds her of the time she saved Clyde from falling out of the loft. Then she recalls that it was the same storm that took the life of her dad, and her smile quickly turns to a frown. Not wanting to remember any more, she takes off running to the house. Everyone's in the parlor when she gets there and Rachel's already served the tea and started to prepare dinner. She hurries into the kitchen to help Rachel.

✳ ✳ ✳

It's Clyde's first day on the job, and Crunchy rides along so he doesn't get lost. He introduces him to the foreman and watches as Clyde heads off to his workstation. Crunchy says his goodbyes and catches a bus back to the house. He's not worried about him finding his way back. Clyde has a pretty good sense of direction once he's gone somewhere.

The soft ocean breeze brushes against Clyde's face as he thinks, *I can't believe I'm this close to the ocean!* On his break, he wanders to the edge of the dock and looks out at the ships that are coming and going. He sits down Indian style and stares out over the ocean. *I can't believe it, water as far as you can see. I wonder what kind of fish are out there. I betcha there's some whoppers. I'd love to get in a boat and go fishing.* Then, like he does a lot, his thoughts change direction. *Dad, you would have enjoyed this. Never thought of it before, but I wonder if you ever saw the ocean? It sure is pretty. I love ya, Dad.*

✵ ✵ ✵

The next few months fly by. On Clyde's days off, he and Crunchy drive out to a place where they're able to ride horses. He loves it out at the ranch and hates to leave. All that's missing are the bulls.

Things have gone really well for Clyde. He's put his trust totally in Crunchy, who's living up to his end of the deal. There's one thing Clyde doesn't quite understand, though. Crunchy takes his paycheck and gives him spending money, but he's not sure what he does with the rest of it. One evening as they're sitting around the house, Crunchy says, "Better get to bed early. We have a big day tomorrow."

Bewildered, Clyde asks, "What do you mean? I don't have any plans, and I don't have to work."

Smiling, Crunchy responds, "I've made arrangements to take you deep-sea fishing tomorrow. You've said for the past month how'd you love to do it, so tomorrow morning about four, we're heading out to catch a boat for a day of fishing."

"Really?" Clyde exclaims. "You really did that? Hot diggity dog! It's going to be a great day."

Before he knows it, they're in the truck and headed to the boat. He's got butterflies just like before he rides and can't wait to step on that big ship. As they pull up to the docks, he observes that these boats are a lot smaller than the ones he works around. "Where's the ship we're takin' fishing?" he asks.

"Right there," Crunchy says as he points to the boat right in front of them.

"That one?!" Clyde exclaims as he points to the dock. "Don't you think that's a little small to be out on all that water?"

Laughing, Crunchy answers, "They go out every day! The captain's a friend of mine. We'll be fine."

"Okay, then let's get this show on the road!" Clyde says as he jumps from the truck.

The boat leaves the dock with Clyde, Crunchy, and about ten others on board. Clyde stands in the back, enjoying the smooth ride out of the small bay. It's his first time on a boat, and he's having a great time looking around and watching the sea gulls. He spots a funny looking bird and asks Crunchy "What is that?"

"Oh, that," he says, pointing. "It's a pelican."

"It sure is funny looking!" Clyde laughs.

As land looks smaller and smaller, he feels the sway of the boat become more and more intense. The waves rock it back and forth as they head out to the captain's favorite fishing spot. At first, Clyde enjoys the up and down motion, but eventually his stomach gets a little queasy. Now he understands why Crunchy keeps asking him if he's all right. It doesn't take long for his breakfast to hit the water. Afraid he may fall in, too, he hangs onto the railing with all his might as he empties his insides. He's not alone; a few more riders are right alongside. Seeing others in the same boat doesn't make it easier, so he moves to the other side and grabs a pole.

The captain reaches the first spot and stops the boat for the fishing to begin. Clyde thinks, *Okay, I made it this far, now I want to fish. This is a huge pole, nothing like the one Dad and I used when we went fishing! Let me get the line in the water.* After carefully listening to instructions, he finally gets the line out and is fishing; well, at least between 'the feeding of the fish'. Before long, he hooks one and starts to reel it in. With the boat swaying with the waves and turning the handle on the reel, it's hard to keep his footing. Finally, he brings it aboard and is thrilled to have landed his first deep-sea fish. The day goes by quickly and they finally head in.

Crunchy tells Clyde as he leans over the railing, "I bet this will be your last fishing trip!"

"Why do you say that?" Clyde remarks.

"You were seasick more than you fished!" Crunchy declares.

"Oh, that? That was nothing; been sicker for a lot longer. You ever rode a bull with busted up ribs?"

"Can't say that I have," Crunchy admits.

"Well I have, and this ain't nothing compared to that. I had the time of my life today and look at the fish I caught! Nope, I'll do this any time you want to set it up. Crunchy, I was out on the ocean! Life don't get much better than this, except for being on the back of a bull," Clyde declares.

"Clyde Lewis, you are something special," Crunchy chuckles. "We better be gettin' on back home."

✳ ✳ ✳

They finish their tea and Sara announces that dinner is ready when there's a knock on the door. Rachel sprints over to answer it, but before she gets there, Ruthie swings it open for Martin, who's carrying little Mervin. They walk in the parlor and Mom, having heard their voices, is grinning from ear to ear. "Bring that little one to Grandma and put him here on my lap," she directs as she pats her thighs.

Ruthie uncovers Mervin and sets him on her lap. "Be careful, he just got done with dinner," she warns.

Giggling, Mom replies, "Oh, that doesn't matter. He's my boy!" she coos as she finds and caresses his chubby cheek and gives it a little squeeze. "I'm so glad you came by! We were just getting ready to eat and have our Friday night sing-a-long and play games. Would you like to join us?"

"We'd love to!" Ruthie says as she glances up at Martin and receives his approving nod. They make their way into the dining area for dinner, and pitch in and help clean up afterwards.

"Betcha I'm going to beat ya at checkers," Martin challenges Rachel.

Rachel grabs the checkerboard and heads to the parlor. "You don't have a chance! I hate to be the one to tell you, but you're not very good at this."

"You've told me that before," Martin laughs.

They settle in the parlor and start playing games. Charlie, who's grown into a fine young man, is seated next to Sara on the davenport. When someone else knocks, Sara gets up to answer it, saying as she goes, "What is this? Grand Central Station?" When she opens it, Maggie steps in and greets her.

"Good evening, Sara. I thought I'd drop by and see how your mom's doing." She takes her coat off and hangs it on the rack to the right of the door.

"I'm so glad you did," Sara replies as they walk into the parlor where everyone greets her.

The games continue for about an hour, then Mom hands Ruthie the baby and moves to the piano bench. As they put away the games, she starts to play songs the family's been singing for years before moving on to the newer ones she's been listening to over the radio. Toward the end of the singing, Jim stands up and walks over to the piano bench and sits down next to Dorris.

"Jim, is that you?"

"Yes, Dorris, it is. I'm here because I need to ask you something," he begins.

"You could've asked me from your seat, you didn't have to come over here. But since you did, what's your request?" she asks as she stops playing.

Jim motions for everyone to sit down, then turns his attention back to Dorris. "It's not a song request, but I do have something important to ask you," he says, reaching for her hand.

"What's that, Jim?" she asks, waiting for his answer.

"We've been through a lot together," he says, then clears his throat, "and I was wondering if you'd consider going through the rest of our lives together."

"What? Are you asking me to marry you?" she exclaims. "Is everyone still in the room?"

"Yes, Mom," Ruthie answers, "we're all here. Now answer him, will you?"

"Jim, I'm not sure, with all that's happened over these years. My Elmer was a wonderful man . . ."

"Dorris," Jim injects, "I will never be Elmer and I won't try to replace him, but we need each other. I need a strong woman like you and you need someone who is going to be around to help. So please, don't say no."

"I wasn't going to say no, I just want you to know right where I stand. Yes, Jim, I will marry you," she says.

Sara leaps to her feet. "Yahoo! We're having another shindig!"

"What a minute," Mom shouts. "No big party, it's just going to be the family. Right, Jim?"

"Any way you want it, Sweetie, any way you want it," he replies.

A few months down the road, Dorris is true to her word and they exchange vows and rings with just the family and Maggie present. Well, all except for Clyde, that is. They received a card from him the week before telling them of his trip to California, so they knew he couldn't make it.

✳ ✳ ✳

It's that time of year again for the rodeo season. While Clyde's upstairs packing, Crunchy's downstairs talking on the phone, making arrangements for this year's west coast circuit. When Clyde comes downstairs, he picks up Crunchy's bags by the door and takes them to the truck. The truck looks like a million bucks. During this past week, Crunchy made arrangements to have it all spit-shined and worked on. The mechanic, one of Crunchy's friends, naturally, went through the whole thing from stem to stern. You can really tell; it runs so smoothly and the brakes have never been better. It feels like driving a new truck.

They say their goodbyes to Maria and pull out of the driveway. Their first stop is the bank where Crunchy says he has some unfinished business to attend to. They pull into the parking lot and Crunchy, with his no-hurry attitude, ambles into the bank. He returns with a small briefcase and sets it down on the seat. He looks over at Clyde and says, "Open it."

Clyde reaches over, clicks the locks and lifts the top. "What did you do? Rob the bank?"

"No," Crunchy grins. "Remember the money I took from your paychecks?"

"Yeah, what about it?"

"That's what you saved. It's all yours."

This is more money than Clyde's ever seen at one time. "What do you mean it's . . . all mine?"

"I told you I'd take care of you and help you get to The Garden, right?"

"Yeah?" Clyde hesitates.

"This was step one. In order for us to get there, we need money, so you worked and this is the money that's getting us through to The Garden."

"I saved all this? It sure looks like a lot!" Clyde exclaims.

"Well, to tell you the truth, a lot of it is what you saved, but I have other resources that I threw into the kitty so we can be sure to have enough," Crunchy adds.

"Okay, where do we go from here?" Clyde asks.

"Our first few stops are small rodeos around Southern California, just to get you warmed up to riding a bit," Crunchy explains. "Then we'll make our way up the state. We'll ride in a place called Clovis, then over to Salinas, and after a few smaller ones, we'll end up in San Francisco at the Cow Palace."

"San Francisco!" Clyde shouts. "I've heard about it, with all the hills and everything, but I can't believe I'm really going to ride there!"

"Believe it! That's the last one before we head east to The Garden."

Slapping and rubbing his hands together, Clyde says, "Let's get this pony on the road! We got places to go and bulls to ride!"

Chapter 26

THE INVITATION

Over the next few weeks, Clyde heeds everything Crunchy tells him. *He's gotten me this far* he thinks, *might as well do all I can and see what happens.* It doesn't take long to reap the benefits; he finishes the first few rodeos in the top three. He understands they're small ones and the competition isn't top notch, mostly local riders, but it is getting him back in the groove.

Each week Clyde wins enough to replenish what they spend. One evening, while sitting in their room, Clyde asks Crunchy, "Why'd you help me?"

Taken aback, Crunchy replies, "Now that's a good question. Why do you think I did?"

"I don't know; I guess ya felt sorry for me," Clyde ventures.

"That may be part of it, but like I told ya before, I saw something in ya that I ain't seen with many riders: God-given talent. Clyde, I know we haven't talked much about God, but He's given you a special gift. When He does that, ya don't want to waste it," Crunchy advises him.

Embarrassed, Clyde drops his chin to his chest. "We've been together for a while now and I've shared my life's story with ya. How can you say that God has blessed me? I think it's the opposite! I think He's cursed me! Look at how you found me! That was a blessing from God?!"

"Listen here, young man," Crunchy admonishes him, "don't go blaming God for decisions you made. That really chaps my hide when I hear people blame God for bad things but take all the credit when things go right. You can't have it both ways, Clyde. I imagine there's been a lot of friends and family praying for you. God does things His way. Just look what He's doing now! You've gotten away from the bad influences in your life, and now you're headed down the right track."

"But that's because of you. You were the one who picked me up from the mud and got me headed in the right direction. I can't believe all this God stuff, especially since Skinny died. Don't see no good in that! I'm just thankful you came along."

"Well, I have one thing to say about that, and I don't want you answering it. Just think on it," Crunchy requests.

"Yeah, okay. What's that?"

"How do you know God didn't send me along to watch after you?" Crunchy rises from his bed and walks outside to enjoy the evening sky.

Not knowing what to say, Clyde stares at Crunchy as he walks out. He sits expressionless, thinking, *Whoa, where did that come from? How do I know God didn't send him? Is he telling me that God sent him to watch after me? He did just kind of appear. I don't recall ever seeing him before at any of the rodeos. Nah, why would God do that? You know, God, if You really are there, You gave me my dad and then took him from me. Then You gave me Harold and he got married. Then came Skinny and You took him from me, too. Now I have Crunchy. When are You takin' him? What am I doing thinking like this? It don't matter any, who. What matters is here and now. You can't convince me that there is someone or something up there looking out after me. I think I'll go out and join Crunchy star gazing. He seems to like that.*

Early the next morning, Crunchy packs up and tells Clyde, "Okay, it's time to get a move on up the state. We can't gain any more from riding in these locals."

"Where're we headed?" Clyde asks.

"To a place called the San Joaquin Valley. It's north of here 'bout 200 miles," Crunchy says. "We'll be going through some mountains on what they call the Ridge Route. It'll test this here truck pretty good."

Crunchy loves to give Clyde history lessons about each place they visit. It's amazing how much this man knows about so many things. So, knowing it's coming, Clyde asks, "What kind of rodeo is it?"

Sure enough, the question triggers another history lesson. So, as they drive, he listens to Crunchy explain about this place called *Clovis*. "Let me tell you about it," he begins. "First of all, it's right next to a town named *Fresno*. Ever hear of that?"

"Can't say that I have," Clyde responds as they make the climb up the mountainous pass.

"It's the bigger town of the two," Crunchy explains, "but Clovis puts on a top notch rodeo. From what I understand, it's been around since 1914. It's a great little town, and you're going to really enjoy visiting."

Clyde's curiosity piqued, he asks, "So it's like the ones we've been riding in?"

"No, not really. It's a bigger event. They have a parade and everything. The grandstands are wooden, but the arena is topnotch. They've made some nice improvements over the years. It didn't used to attract national riders, but now more and more are seeing how well it's organized. They're even getting better stock to ride," Crunchy explains.

"That sounds good. I need to ride some better bulls," Clyde agrees.

"That's why we're here. It's a step up, getting us ready for Salinas and then the Cow Palace," Crunchy reassures Clyde.

The truck labors around the turns and up and down the road through the mountains. "You sure this thing's going to make it?" Clyde asks.

"Mechanic gave his okay, but it's pretty tough on it," Crunchy admits.

They finally get to the top of the hill, and, as they go down the other side, they get their first glimpse of the valley. It extends north as far as the eye can see, flanked by the coast range to the west and the Sierra Nevada Mountains to the east.

A few hours later, they drive into Clovis where banners span the streets and crowds mingle amongst the food booths and concessionaires hawking their wares. People are everywhere and Clyde has to make frequent stops to allow them to cross in front of him. As they approach downtown, Clyde reads "Clovis, Gateway to the Sierras," on a sign hanging over the street. Once he stops, he notices the snowcapped Sierra Nevada's in the distance. While it's nothing new for him to see these mountains, it is different seeing them from the other side.

He follows Crunchy's directions to their home for the rest of the week. A sign out front reads Hotel Lillie Francis. While Clyde parks and grabs the bags, Crunchy goes in to register. As Clyde enters through the hotel's front doors, he notices a framed article on the wall describing the short history of the place. According to the article, it used to be named The Hoblitt Hotel until it was sold in the 1920s. The new owners renamed it after their daughters, Lillie and Francis. Clyde chuckles thinking, *What if they named a hotel after me and Crunchy? It'd be The Hotel Crunchy Clyde.* The town's a great place to visit, even though he doesn't wander far from the room over the next couple days. When he does, he notices how friendly the people are. In an attempt to get all the rest he needs to heal some bumps and bruises, he lets Crunchy do most of the exploring.

Saturday morning, with the rodeo just hours away, they walk down Clovis Avenue to a downtown café just as the parade begins. It's a lot larger than any Clyde's seen before. The car carrying the Grand Marshall passes with a sign that reads Grand Marshall Frank Drury. *He must be someone important,* Clyde thinks. *I wonder how someone gets to be a Grand Marshall. Maybe someday they'll have a parade in my hometown and I can be the Grand Marshall.* He chuckles loud enough to attract Crunchy's attention.

"What was that about?" Crunchy inquires.

"Just doing some silly thinking, that's all; nothing too big," Clyde answers.

"Oh, okay. How's the body feeling?" he asks.

"Feeling really good. I'm ready to ride!"

"Good, I want you to stay sharp. It's nice that the rodeos out here are spaced out a bit to give ya plenty of time to heal up," Crunchy says.

"It sure is," Clyde agrees.

That evening Clyde makes his ride, and the next day, too. He scores well and places second overall. Since they don't have to be at the next rodeo for a few weeks, Crunchy decides to stay around the area and do some sightseeing. Some locals share about a national park that's just up the road a bit, so early the next morning they decide to head up and see it. It's even more amazing than what people described. Clyde can't believe the size of the trees, especially the one called the *Tunnel Tree*. The plaque at the base reads 227 feet tall and 90 feet in circumference. There's a hole in it big enough to drive a vehicle through that was cut out back in the late 1800s.

Clyde can't believe all the sights as they drive through the park; waterfalls, valleys, and meadows, all in one place. The beautiful waterfalls are huge, with thousands of gallons of water pouring over them. *I sure wish the family could see this,* he thinks. *Mom would love it.* Then it dawns on him; *That's right, she can't see it, anyway.*

He must have changed facial expressions, because Crunchy asks, "Everything okay? You went from a smile to a concerned look quicker than an eagle swoops down on a field mouse."

"I was just thinking about my family," Clyde replies, "and how they'd love this place. Then I remembered that Mom can't see any more."

Crunchy places his hand on his shoulder. "Ya know, your ma may not be able to see much, but she's still going to enjoy life. She's a strong woman."

Clyde shakes his head in disbelief. "How do you know? You've never even met my mom! Crunchy, sometimes I don't think you're human."

Crunchy slaps his leg and lets out a hoot. "What? You think I'm one of them space creatures or something? I figured that out from what you've told me about her. You've shared a lot about her, you know, and I hope to meet her one day." He pauses and then asks, "You really think I'm from another world?"

"Naw, I don't really think that," Clyde laughs, "but sometimes . . . oh, never mind. It don't matter no how."

It's dark by the time they make their way back to Clovis. Early the next morning, they head west to their next stop in Salinas. This rodeo's been around for 30 years. Cancelled during the war, this year it resumes, thanks to the efforts of the downtown merchants who raised some $7000 to help kick it off. They're glad to have the increased traffic.

Crunchy explains that he wants Clyde to ride in this one so he doesn't lose momentum for going to the Cow Palace. He goes along with what Crunchy recommends and prepares himself, like he always does before each ride; he goes off by himself and focuses on the task at hand, visualizing each ride over and over in his head.

Tonight, though, he's having a hard time concentrating. Before the bull-riding started, they introduced a new event called *Wild Cow Milking*, one of the funniest things he's ever seen. He watches as the cows are led into the chutes with a rope around their necks. Three cowpokes stand outside each chute and work as a team. The chutes open and the cows take off. Clyde watches one of them grab the rope and get dragged around the arena. Another guy attempts to grab the cow's head, while the third guy tries to help the guy with the rope slow the cow down. Once they finally get it stopped, one of them lets go of the rope and starts to milk it. When they get enough milk in the cup, they hurry back to the chutes, completing the race. It's hilarious to watch. Clyde's never seen this before, and he busts up laughing as he watches these guys being dragged all over the arena. When it's over, he knows he has to get his mind back to the task at hand but is having a difficult time doing so.

Crunchy notices and walks up. "You okay?" he asks.

"Yeah, that was the funniest thing I've ever seen!" he exclaims.

Crunchy rests his hand on Clyde's shoulder. "It was funny," he agrees, then changes his tone. "Listen, Clyde, you need to forget about that and move on. This is your night! Keep in mind what we discussed about riding this bull."

Clyde takes to heart what Crunchy says, takes a deep breath, and focuses on the task at hand. Once again he visualizes the ride; he can just see the bull take a hard left and begin his spin. After the horn sounds, he sees himself standing up, waving his Stetson in the air. The ride goes pretty much the way he envisioned it, and, by the end of the evening, he's on top of the leaderboard. He's on a roll now and can't believe how easy this seems. After his early struggles, he's back to his old self. The rest of the weekend is pretty much the same and they leave town with change jiggling in their pockets, which is always a good thing.

Next stop: the Cow Palace. It's only a few hours north, on the south side of San Francisco, where they spend the next few days exploring Lombard Street, Fisherman's Wharf, Nob Hill, and Golden Gate Park. One of the main attractions Clyde can't get over is the Golden Gate Bridge. He wonders how something like this could be built over water.

After all the sightseeing he could possibly do, Clyde's ready for the riding to begin. With more butterflies than normal, he walks into the arena before anyone is there. "How many people do you think can fit in here?" he asks Crunchy.

Crunchy purses his lips and closes one eye. "If I remember right, when the place fills up it, holds right around 11,000." Upon hearing that, the butterflies in Clyde's stomach flutter all the more. He looks over and sees the first persons of the crowd file in. Crunchy slaps him on the back. "You okay there, partner? You look like you saw a ghost or something."

The butterflies get the best of him. Holding his stomach, he shakes his head and runs out behind the chutes, where he bends over and loses his biscuits. *I've never ridden in front of this many people before*, he thinks. *I don't know if I can do this.* He starts to stand up when he feels another cramp in his stomach and quickly bends over again.

Crunchy walks up behind him and gently places his hand on Clyde's back. "Those cotton pickin' ol' butterflies won't leave you alone, huh? It's okay; you'll be fine. I've known a lot of riders that this happens to. Just take a few deep breaths and you'll be fine."

Heeding Crunchy's advice, he inhales a couple of times, which seems to settle the butterflies. Still bent over, he says, "Crunchy, I don't think I can do this."

Crunchy softly pats his back. "Sure you can, son. It's all about mentally preparing yourself for the moment, and that's what I'm here for. Besides, this ain't nothin'. The Garden seats more than this and if you can't ride here, you sure can't ride at The Garden."

Clyde thinks, *What?! More than this? Well, I might as well get used to it, because I am riding at The Garden.* Clyde stands up and wraps his arm around Crunchy's head. "Okay then, let's get this done," he agrees.

After the horses and riders fill the arena it's time for the grand parade . The crowd's been standing up applauding since they started filing in. *I sure wish Audra was here for this,* Clyde thinks. *She would enjoy herself.*

After what feels like an eternity, the events begin, and Clyde tries to relax behind the chutes, patiently awaiting the bull-riding. Like Salinas, just before his event, they introduce Wild Horse Racing. Clyde thinks, *This must be unique to west coast events, because I've never seen it before.* Curious, he climbs one of the chutes as the horses are led in to watch.

Ten teams of three men walk over and take their positions in front of the chutes. Clyde notices that they're differentiated by the color of the ribbons tied to their arms. The goal is to catch, saddle, and ride a wild horse, who's only wearing a halter with the team's corresponding colored ribbon. The horses are simultaneously released into the arena. Chaos ensues as the men try to catch their designated horses, saddle, and then ride them. It's a hoot to watch, and Clyde does just that for a couple of minutes, until he decides it's time to get himself ready for his own ride.

He's the third one to come out of the chutes and stays on for the full eight seconds, but the bull isn't very good, which reflects in his score, leaving him in the middle of the pack. On their way back to their room, Clyde grumbles about his score. He flops down on his small bed as Crunchy sits on the edge, knowing he has to get Clyde's mind off of the score.

"You carry that old steamer around, but you've never shown me what's inside," he remarks.

Excited to be asked, Clyde leaps to his feet, grabs it from under the bathroom counter, and brings it over. The first thing he pulls out, after carefully unsnapping the top, is Skinny's Bible. "This belonged to that friend I was telling you about," he explains as he hands it to Crunchy. He gently flips through the pages as Clyde reaches in and pulls out the buckle.

Crunchy immediately puts the Bible back in the steamer and takes the buckle from Clyde. He turns it over and gives it a close examination. "Where'd you get this?" he asks.

"It was my dad's," Clyde responds, wrinkling his brow. "Why? Is there something wrong with it?"

"No, nothing's wrong. I've only seen a couple of these, and they're pretty rare."

"Rare? Why's that?" Clyde asks.

"There's not many floating around. They only hand out a few each year," Crunchy explains.

Now Clyde is really confused. "I don't understand. What are you talking about?"

"Clyde, buckles like this are only handed out for those who win at The Garden."

"What?!" Clyde exclaims. "You mean my dad rode at The Garden? Oh, I can't believe that."

"All I'm saying is, if this was your dad's, then there's only one place he could have gotten it; The Garden." He turns it over and MSG is engraved in small letters on the back.

Clyde is in disbelief. He never noticed the letters before and asks, "Do those letters stand for Madison Square Garden?"

"Yep," Crunchy replies as he hands the buckle back to Clyde.

If my dad rode at The Garden, he thinks, *then I want to do it, too.* Now he's more motivated than ever.

The rest of the weekend goes well. While he doesn't finish in the top five, he moves up far enough to earn some money.

As they gather their things to leave, Crunchy says, "Well, I guess it's about time to head east."

"How far?" Clyde asks. "We haven't heard anything about ridin' at The Garden."

"We're going to New York City," Crunchy declares. Clyde's about to ask him what makes him think that, when a gentleman steps up next to him and introduces himself.

"Greetings! My name is Scott Esposito," he says, extending his hand.

Clyde returns the solid handshake. "Do I know you?" he asks.

"I don't think so, but I know you. I've been watching you these past few months, and I'd like to extend an invitation to New York City. Son, how would you like to ride at The Garden?"

Clyde's seen this guy before, but never knew who he was. To have an invitation to ride at The Garden is a dream come true. "I'd love to," he says, shaking the gentleman's hand again.

"That's wonderful! I'll submit your name. Congratulations!" he concludes and walks away.

"Thanks!" Clyde says as his insides jump like Mexican jumping beans. He waits for the guy to get far enough away before he yells "Yahoo!" Then it hits him. How did Crunchy know what was going to happen? And the guy acted like Crunchy wasn't even there! "That guy didn't say anything to you," he points out to Crunchy.

"He wasn't here to see me," he responds. "They don't even know I exist. Those kinds of people know what they want and they go after it. They're all business. Here's a warning :Be careful of them; they'll chew ya up and spit ya out. Seen 'em do it before. Just be on your guard."

"But how'd ya know? You said we were going to New York City before he even came up and extended the invitation."

"Let's just say I had a gut feeling about it. We'd better get a move on. It takes a while to go from one side of this wonderful country to the other, especially when one guy does all the driving," he chuckles as he places his hand on Clyde's shoulder and they walk to the truck.

They discuss which route they'll take as they head back to the room for one last night in San Francisco. Crunchy always seems to have what they need and pulls out a road map of the United States. It's a little tattered and yellow, but they can make out most of the main roads.

"Can we go through my hometown on the way and see the family?" Clyde asks.

"Not too sure we'll be able to do that; don't have much time to waste. We got the weather to think about, too. Don't want to get stuck in some snow storm. It ain't quite winter yet, but this time of the year ya never know what the wind may blow in," he reminds him. After saying that, Crunchy remembers that it was one of those freak storms that took Clyde's dad's life. Now he doesn't know what to say.

Clyde thinks, *Yeah, he's right, but I sure would love to see the family and maybe spend Christmas with them. Oh well, we're headed to Madison Square Garden. Can't get much better than that!* While he heard what Crunchy said, it never registered about his dad.

Crunchy hesitates before he continues. "I think we should head south. That way, we will avoid a lot of the bad weather."

"Okay, sounds good to me! How long do you think it'll take us to get there?"

"A lot depends on the weather," Crunchy says while rubbing his chin. "With my best calculations, I'd say around ten days, give or take a couple."

Clyde cocks his head. "You really don't know, do ya?"

"Well, to be perfectly honest with ya, nope. But I do know one thing."

"Yeah? What's that?" Clyde asks.

"If we don't get a move on, we'll never get there. Let's get up before the crack of dawn and hit the road," Crunchy suggests.

"Sounds good. I always love driving during that time of the day. Ain't nothin' better than seeing the sun rise over the mountains. Night, Crunchy."

"Night, Half-Pint," Crunchy says.

Clyde thinks, *Ain't no one called me that since Harold. How'd he know what to call me? Oh, I must've mentioned it. Sure don't remember it, though. It don't matter. Got to get some shuteye. We got a lot of driving to do tomorrow and in the days to follow.*

Chapter 27

THE GARDEN

The guys are on the road for a couple of hours before the sun peeks over the mountains. They're headed to Route 66, which they'll follow into Oklahoma. Instead of heading north where there could be bad weather, they'll stay south until they reach the east coast, and then they'll head north to New York City.

The days seem to drag on, and while Clyde's traveled quite a bit, this trip is taking longer than he thought it would. With each passing day, he gets more excited about seeing the big city.

The morning of their anticipated arrival, Clyde is squirming in his seat like a worm on a hot sidewalk, and Crunchy takes note. "What's wrong with you this morning? You got ants in your pants?" he teases.

Wrinkling his nose, Clyde replies, "Don't know what you mean."

"You're wiggling," Crunchy explains.

"Oh, that. I just can't wait to see that city you've been talkin' about," Clyde responds.

"Ya don't have long to wait," Crunchy promises. "Ya may be able to see it a little bit as we go around this next bend."

Sure enough, as Clyde makes the next turn, he can see the silhouette of the New York City skyline just ahead. His first thought is, *The buildings don't look that big,* but the closer they get, he realizes how massive the buildings are. He comes to a sign that reads *Holland Tunnel.* Staying in the right lane, he enters the darkness of the tunnel, reaches over and flips on the headlamps, and steps on the floor button to turn on the high beams.

"Wow, I can't believe this tunnel! How did they ever do this? We're traveling under water; look, it's seeping through! You sure this is safe?"

Laughing, Crunchy reassures Clyde, "It's been around since 1927, and it took around seven years to build. They called the guys who worked on it *sandhogs*. When we come out the other side, let's go to the hotel and park this thing. You won't want to drive around in this town. Our room is within walking distance of The Garden."

"That sounds good to me! I don't really like driving in this traffic," Clyde agrees. "Just tell me where to go."

He follows Crunchy's awkward directions through town and finally pulls into the hotel parking lot. They register and unload the truck before they head to their room. The tall buildings fascinate Clyde. He thinks, *This is the Big Apple, home of Madison Square Garden. I'm in New York City!* Just being here is huge for Clyde. He's heard all about this place and even read about it a little, but seeing it is unbelievable.

After they settle into their room, they decide to take a stroll around town. The first place Clyde wants to see is The Garden. He checks the front door and it's locked, but a security officer walks up and asks, "Can I help you gentlemen?"

"Maybe," Clyde says. "I was wondering if we could just look around inside. I'm a bull-rider, and I've never been here before."

"I'm not supposed to do that, but if you make it quick, I'll let you in."

"Thank you so much. We'll only be a few minutes," Crunchy assures him.

They walk into the lobby and Clyde notices framed articles on the wall detailing the history of The Garden. As Crunchy walks into the arena area, Clyde walks over to read one of the articles;

The first two Gardens were located at the northeast corner of Madison Square (Madison Avenue and 26th Street) from *which the arena derived its name. The first Garden was built in 1879. It was primarily built for a velodrome, an oval bicycle racing track with banked curves, then one of the biggest sports in the country. It closed in 1890. The second Garden, finished in 1890 on the same location, was designed by Stanford White. The new structure was 200 feet by 485 feet of Moorish architecture with a minaret-like tower soaring 32 stories over Madison Square Park and was the city's second tallest building. The Garden's main hall, which was the largest in the world, measured 200 by 350 feet with permanent seating for 8,000 people and floor space for thousands more. Where you now stand at 50th St. and 8th Avenue is the third Garden built. Erected in 1925 at a cost of $4.75 million; built by boxing promoter Tex Rickard and dubbed "The House That Tex Built."*

Clyde thinks, *Wow, what a great place!* He opens the double doors leading into the arena and senses someone coming up behind him. Thinking it's probably the security guard, he doesn't want to turn around; he just hopes he doesn't follow.

As the doors are about to close, a voice says, "Trying to avoid me, Cowboy?" Clyde recognizes the voice and stops. Sure enough, he guesses right. It's Audra and Harold.

"What are you doing here?" he asks.

"I told you if you made it, we'd come," Harold replies.

"It's so good to see you guys!" Clyde says as he hugs Audra and shakes Harold's hand. "How'd ya get here?"

"We came on the same train as the bulls. Sam found out you were ridin' and he knew what we agreed on. So instead of him coming, he sent Audra and me to watch out for the bulls. I guess you can say we're your enemy this week," Harold says, chuckling.

"It's so good to see you," Audra says, "and he might be, but I'm not your enemy this week." After more small talk, they say their goodbyes and head off in different directions.

Sam's Brahma bull ranch has gotten quite a reputation. The top promoters ask him to supply as many bulls as he can for their events. He usually accompanies the stock to the rodeos, but this time he allowed Harold to take this one. He told him to take Audra along for the honeymoon they never had and arranged for them to arrive a couple of days early. They've taken a carriage ride through Central Park and toured the Empire State building. It's hard to believe how people could build something so large; 102 stories high with 1860 steps leading to the top and 6,500 windows overlooking the city. And to think it only took one year and 45 days from start to finish! New York is a unique city with the sophistication of an eastern town, along with boroughs, a waterfront, and just a short drive from rural areas. Sam's also arranged for them to attend a musical called "Oklahoma." The employees of their hotel have told them how great the western musical is. Harold leaves early to feed the bulls, so as not to miss the beginning of the show.

✻ ✻ ✻

It's late afternoon when Clyde and Crunchy take a walk from their room back to The Garden. This time, as they go through the participants' entrance, Clyde can feel butterflies in the pit of his stomach. He heads straight to the corrals where the livestock are held and sees Harold there getting them ready for feeding.

Not wanting to spook the bulls, Clyde slowly walks up and whispers, "What cha up to?"

Harold looks up, and says, "Feeding the bulls so Audra and I can head over to the show."

"Show? What show?"

Harold gives him the short version, a man's version, of Sam's provision for a late honeymoon.

"Hey, I'll finish up for ya," Clyde offers. "Go ahead, head on out."

"That's okay, don't want to impose on ya." Harold responds.

"Impose? Man, we're friends, and I want to help ya any way I can. Go, enjoy your time with your misses. I got ya covered here."

"Okay," Harold says as he tosses the hay to the ground, "if you insist. Have a great evening."

"You, too," Clyde says as Harold heads to the door.

After he finishes feeding, he sits down on a hay bale and opens the packet he got when he registered. This is different from most other places; a five day rodeo with bull-riding the last three days. The first two days all riders ride one bull a night. The cowboys call these the "Go-rounds." Each rider's points will be totaled and the top twenty riders will ride the last night in the event known as the "Short-go." When all three rounds are complete, the cowboy with the most points wins.

Clyde will be the fifth man to ride on the first night, but he still has a few days to think about it, since the bull-riding is Friday and Saturday, with the finals on Sunday afternoon. Also in the packet is a program that reads: *22nd Annual World Championship Rodeo Contestants, NYC, 1947. Program 25 cents.*

He's thankful that the next few days go slowly as it gives them more time to explore the city. By the time Friday arrives, Clyde is raring to go. He makes his way to the side door, where a guard directs him to the rider's area behind the chutes. He can't believe how many people there are in the arena. He's never seen so many in one building! When they cheer, it's almost deafening.

The first few riders have a tough time staying on through the horn. As Clyde gets ready to go, Crunchy stands on the back of the chute and reminds him to focus on the bull, not the crowd. The stock here is the best that can be assembled, and if Clyde doesn't concentrate on the task at hand, it will be one of the shortest rides he's ever had. He takes a deep breath as he climbs the chute and slowly lowers his small frame, all 125 pounds, onto the back of the bull. Then he hears the public address announcer.

"Now in gate number 4, out of Colorado, Clyde Lewis!" The crowd lets out a deafening cheer. This sends a shot of adrenalin through Clyde as he meticulously wraps his hand, then scoots up on top of it. With his left hand, he pulls his Stetson down to his eyebrows, glances at the gatekeeper, and nods his head as he says, "Open the gate!"

As it swings open, Clyde's eyes focus on the huge hump on this bull's back. He jumps out and Clyde is in perfect rhythm with him from the beginning. He can't believe how easy this ride is! The horn sounds and he jumps off to the roar of the crowd. He's the first of the day to complete a ride, but he knows the scores aren't going to be very high. The bull was really a pansy, not much to him. True to his thoughts, the scores aren't very high, and the crowd shows its displeasure by booing as the scores are displayed. By the end of the evening, Clyde finds himself in tenth place, far off the lead with a ton of points to make up.

✳ ✳ ✳

The next day they leave their hotel early and head to The Garden so Clyde can get a closer look at the bull he's drawn for that evening. As they enter through the participant's gate, Harold's walking out. Crunchy excuses himself and heads to the arena.

"Hey, Cowboy, where ya headed in such a hurry?" Harold asks Clyde.

"Got to take a look at this bull for tonight," Clyde says.

"Which one?"

"Whirlwind"

"That's one of ours!" Harold exclaims. "Want some info?"

"Sure! Anything I can get helps."

"Okay, he's a spinner. Once he leaves the chute, he'll turn to the left and spin and spin. He may try to stop and go the other way, but most times, he'll just keep on spinning. Spur him all you can. He'll be a big point ride if you can stay on."

"Thanks, Harold," Clyde says, almost apologetically.

"No problem. Good luck!"

"I got all the luck I need," he says as he pulls the old horseshoe out of his back pocket.

"You still got that old thing?" Harold asks, bewildered.

"You bet! I can't wait to hang it above a door. Well, got to run and get focused for this ride."

"It's still early," Harold points out.

"I know, but this time tomorrow will be the finals. I'm preparing myself and my body for that ride."

"Okay, I'll catch up with ya later!"

"See ya."

Clyde walks to the stock pens to look for Whirlwind. When he finds him, he looks him in the eye and starts to talk. Right on cue, when Clyde stops to take a breath, the bull snorts as if he's talking back. This makes Clyde smile, and he thinks, *So you want to talk back, huh? You don't have a chance tonight. I'm ridin' ya, no matter what ya say.* As he straightens up, the bull takes a few steps back and kicks, as if to say, "Bring it on!"

With thirty-two guys still in the competition, Clyde won't ride until late in the rotation. The order is determined by points awarded from their first ride. If they have an incomplete ride, their names are placed in a cowboy's hat and drawn. To keep busy, Clyde decides to help his fellow riders prepare for their rides. He climbs on the chute and encourages each rider who goes out of chute three. Tonight's different from last night. It seems like everyone is riding to the horn.

Things are running pretty smoothly until a couple of guys before Clyde. A rider settles in but is still wrapping his hand when the gatekeeper thinks he sees him nod and opens the gate. He doesn't even make it out of the chute. As the bull turns to leave, he throws him into the air and the cowboy comes down on top of the gate, bouncing off, and snapping his right arm as he hits the ground. Once on the ground, the bull turns on him and kicks him in the side, slamming him against the chute. The rider is lucky the bull didn't turn his head, or he would have been gored.

The bull turns to charge again, but is distracted when a clown steps between him and the rider. The clown takes a leap, and the combination of his momentum and the force of the bull flings him over the bull and onto his back. The bull stops and stands there until the other clowns step in and herd him from the arena. The fallen clown struggles to his knees and then slowly rises to his feet, while the rider lies on the ground. The medical staff runs into the arena to attend to the two. They gently place the rider on a stretcher, being especially careful with his broken arm. It's scary because he's not moving.

Having watched all this from the chute, Crunchy grabs Clyde by the chaps and takes him to the back to go over his ride. He needs to help him take his mind off of what just happened.

The hatch door leading into the chutes opens and the next group of bulls is ushered in. Whirlwind isn't taking kindly to these cramped spaces, but Clyde climbs to the top of the chute and straddles him. He goes through his regular routine, and when he's comfortable, he nods. Just like last night, things just seem to fall into place; he gets into a great rhythm. Whirlwind does everything Harold said he would and when the horn sounds, Clyde thinks, *That can't be the horn for the ride to end; I just got started.* As he dismounts, he comes down and rolls his ankle, but catches himself before he falls.

Realizing he just made it to the finals, he throws both hands in the air and makes his way to the riders' area, where Crunchy is there to greet him. He gives him a hug, the first Clyde can remember getting from him.

Then Audra grabs him and hugs him, while he sticks his hand out for Harold to shake. "Congratulations, Half-Pint! That was a great ride! The only thing left to see is where you place for the finals."

After the rest of the riders finish up and the points are totaled, they announce that Clyde's in third place, eight points off the lead. It's going to take a great ride tomorrow afternoon to win the championship.

✳ ✳ ✳

The next morning Clyde's up early. It's different today, and he can't explain it; there's no nervousness or butterflies. While Crunchy's gone for his walk in Central park, there's a knock at the door. Dressed, but lying on his bed, he doesn't want to get up. "Come on in," he hollers, "its unlocked!"

The door flings open and Audra and Harold walk in. "What are you two up to this early in the morning?" Clyde asks.

"We thought we'd take you to breakfast. Where's Crunchy?" Audra asks.

"He's on his morning walk. It's funny you asked, because I was just getting ready to go grab some grub myself. Let me leave Crunchy a note. Where're we going?"

"Just down the block. Tell him to join us!" Harold suggests as Clyde writes the note.

They settle in at one of the window booths at the corner café. Before they order, Crunchy joins them. They sit around the table enjoying each other's company for the next hour or so. Topics range from the rodeo to how to handle life's issues. Clyde shares about Skinny and doesn't notice how quickly time slips away.

Harold glances at his watch and says, "Hey, it's getting late! I almost forgot about it being an afternoon session. We'd better head to The Garden."

"Just hearing you say that gives me goose bumps," Clyde confesses. Crunchy goes up to the register and pays the bill, much to Audra and Harold's disapproval.

The walk to The Garden is a quick one. The rodeo's already begun and they're within an hour of the bull-riding event. Clyde says his goodbyes as he ducks into the riders' area. Harold and Audra head toward the livestock pens, while Crunchy lingers behind the chutes.

Off by himself, thinking about and envisioning his next ride, Clyde reaches the chutes just as bareback riding is wrapping up. He still can't believe it; something peculiar is taking place. He's still not nervous; no butterflies or mind racing. He's as cool as a cucumber.

The time has come for the bull-riding to start. The top twenty riders have one more shot at winning, or at least moving up to place. The guys at the bottom have the biggest hill to climb because of the point system. The bulls are moved from the back, and the first group is guided into the chutes. The first five riders take their places behind the chutes and prepare for their rides.

During breakfast Harold shared with Clyde that the promoters wanted the best bulls saved for the finals, so these are the best of the best today. As the rides begin, you can see the difference in the quality of the bulls. Out of the first five, only two riders stay on until the horn sounds. The top rider has a total of 210 points for his three rides.

The second group of bulls is led into the chutes. As the first rider of the group is preparing for his ride, his leg slips between the chute and the bull just as the bull moves to the right, smashing it against the chute. After a few minutes, he decides he's unable to ride, so the gate is opened and the bull is let out, disqualifying him. The riders don't do as well this round, as none of them make it to the horn. Clyde thinks, *These bulls are nasty.*

Now it gets interesting. The top ten riders are the only ones left, and there's only a seventy-one point spread from the top rider to the tenth. From what Clyde's seen, any of these riders can take home the grand prize. But first, they have to stay on until the horn blows.

Out of the next group, all five riders stay on. Of these, number six was the best. He actually had a great ride, for a point score of eighty-five, giving him a total of 247. This raises the bar to the next level. It's going to be tough for the last five riders. To keep their spots, they'll have to score at least eighty-two on their rides.

Clyde's getting ready to step up on the chute when he hears a soft voice behind him. It's a familiar voice, but he can't put a face to it. "Hey, Cowboy, where's the lucky horseshoe?"

He turns around and reaches into his pocket. "Right here!" he exclaims. He can't believe his eyes! Who's standing there is, the waitress who helped him get out of jail. "Beth! What are you doing here?"

"Just thought I'd stop by and say hi."

Standing on the top rail of the chute, Crunchy hollers, "Come on, Clyde! You need to get up here and get ready!"

"Stay here," he tells Beth. "I'll be right back."

"Take your time, cowboy. Win this thing, will you?"

Clyde's adrenalin is really pumping now. As he sits down on the back of this 2,000 pound beast, Crunchy turns Clyde's head and looks directly into his eyes. "Keep your mind focused right here," he pleads. "Remember, all you need is the next eight seconds."

Clyde smiles and says, "All 125 pounds of me! Crunchy, this thing doesn't even know I'm on his back." He wraps his hand and then settles in for the ride of his life.

Crunchy slaps him on the back. "You're going to win this, Cowboy," he declares.

With a grin and a wink, Clyde pulls his Stetson down, nods his head, and the chute gate swings open.

Chapter 28
IT'S A SMALL WORLD

The bull leaps from the gate, bucks left, right, and then into a small spin. It's funny how much the mind can process in eight seconds. *This is one of the better bulls I've ridden,* he thinks. Totally relaxed, he can't recall ever having a ride like this before. About halfway through, he starts to spur, which was his plan from the beginning, knowing that if he doesn't, he probably won't score enough points to win.

When the horn sounds, Clyde releases the rope and bails to his right. He lands on his side and immediately jumps up to a huge roar from the crowd. He tips his Stetson and stands in the middle of the arena awaiting his score. It seems to take forever, but when the crowd lets out another huge roar, he can tell he's taken the lead. Forming a fist, he throws his arms in the air and walks to the chutes. He's congratulated by cowboy after cowboy as he looks for Crunchy. His adrenalin is running full force from the noise of the crowd as he gets behind the chutes to watch the last two riders. They'll need almost perfect rides to catch him.

Crunchy reaches out his hand as he walks up to Clyde, who grabs it and gives him a big old bear hug. Then he notices Beth in the crowd behind Crunchy, grinning from ear to ear.

"Nice ride, Cowboy!" she yells.

Crunchy lets go and says, "Go ahead, I got some business to attend to."

Clyde meanders over and when he's within reaching distance, she throws her arms around his neck and gives him a hug. "Thanks!" he replies. "Do you want to watch the last two riders with me?"

"That sounds nice," she confesses.

They step up on the chutes just as the gatekeeper releases the next rider. He does a nice job, but only scores a seventy-seven, finishing eight points behind Clyde. The last rider is released from the gate, and the bull is pretty nasty. He's struggles to hang on, but somehow manages to finish the ride. Clyde thinks, *It'll be close, but I don't think it was good enough to beat me.* It takes a couple of minutes, but they finally post the scores and the public address announcer declares, "The winner of this year's Madison Square Garden bull-riding event is Clyde Lewis of Colorado!"

He walks out into the arena to a standing ovation. The other event,-winners are introduced and given belt buckles. The prize money will be available tomorrow when they check in at the office. As he stands in the middle of the arena, he sees Harold and Audra and motions for them to join him. Then he scans the place for Crunchy, but he's nowhere to be found.

As the closing ceremony wraps up and the horses parade by, the announcer thanks everyone for coming and the crowd begins to disperse. Clyde, still looking for Crunchy, looks toward the chutes and notices Beth still standing there. He waves her over and introduces her to Audra and Harold.

Then it dawns on him. "What are you doing here?" he asks.

She chuckles. "I live on Long Island and my dad's the mayor of the town. He gets tickets every year, so we decided to come into the city for the last two days. When I heard your name announced last night, I wasn't sure if it was you or not. Then I saw you from a distance and knew it was. I just had to come see you."

"That's great, I'm glad you did! I'm starved; you guys want to go to dinner?"

"I have a better idea," Beth suggests. "My family, along with some others from New York, is putting on a party in the executive suite of our hotel, and they wanted me to invite you, along with whomever you want."

Clyde slaps Harold on the shoulder. "You guys up to it? Or are you like those old married folks now?"

Harold glances at Audra and says, "Might as well. We don't have to get the livestock ready until morning, so let's celebrate tonight."

"I need to go back to my room and clean up," Clyde says. "Has anyone seen Crunchy?"

"Nope, we haven't. We need to get ready, too," Harold adds.

"That's great! My driver's outside," she explains. "He'll take you wherever you need to go and wait to bring you to the party. I'll ride back with my family."

"Your driver?" Clyde inquires.

"Yeah, when we're in New York, we have drivers available to us. So let's go!"

As they walk out the contestants' entrance, Clyde turns around and takes one last look. As he gazes at the empty arena, he thinks, *I always wanted to do this. I'll never forget this moment. That was for you, Dad.* Someone bumps him, bringing him back to the moment. "Crunchy, where have you been?" Clyde asks.

"I had to take care of some unfinished business."

"Oh, okay. Well we got a ride back to the hotel, so come on!" Clyde says as he pushes him out the door to the waiting car.

As the driver opens the door and they climb in, Harold says, "Wow, Clyde, this thing is even bigger than that tank we had!"

"Yeah," Clyde laughs, "but ours was more comfortable."

They both laugh before Harold asks, "Who is this girl?"

Clyde shrugs. "I told you all I know."

It's easy for the driver as they're all staying at the same hotel. They hurry to their rooms to freshen up and Crunchy tells Clyde, "I'm a little tired. I'm going to stay in tonight. You go and enjoy yourself; you've earned it."

Clyde doesn't want to leave him, but he does want to see Beth again. "Are you sure? Come on, you were the one who got us here."

"No, I didn't do anything; you did it all by yourself. Now run on ahead and have a good time," Crunchy insists.

By the time he gets down to the lobby, Harold and Audra are waiting. They climb in the car and are taken to a fancy hotel in downtown New York where they're welcomed at the door and directed to the top floor. When they exit the elevator, they walk into a large room with windows all around, giving them a beautiful view of the New York City skyline. They stop for a moment to take in the sight before Clyde spots Beth in an adjoining room. When he waves at her, she acknowledges him with a wave in return. Then she takes the arms of an older couple and directs them toward the group. When they get close, she introduces them as her parents, Fred and Ida Becker. They welcome them and congratulate Clyde on winning his event.

Fred turns to the crowd, claps to get their attention and introduces Clyde as the bull-riding champion. The people applaud, and, one by one, make their way by to congratulate him. Fred tells them, "Please enjoy yourselves! If there's anything you'd like, just ask."

"Thanks!" they reply in unison.

Beth takes Clyde by arm and gives them all a tour of the place. As she does, Clyde thinks, *This is hard to believe. Here I am in a large suite of some fancy hotel in downtown New York; just some young country guy from Colorado. What am I doing here?* With Beth by his side, they spend the next few hours in one conversation after another. Finally, it's time to head back to their hotel and they make their rounds saying goodbye.

Beth tells her parents, "I'm riding back to their hotel with them. That is, if you don't mind."

Before Dad has a chance to answer, Mom says, "You go right ahead. We'll see you when you get back."

They all climb in the car, and Beth tells the driver to go through Times Square so they can see the lights. They drive all around town and stop to take a walk at Battery Park. When they finally pull up to the hotel, Harold thanks Beth for the great evening and the tour of the city.

"Hope to see you again!" Audra says as she gets out.

Beth wishes them a good evening while Clyde stays in the car. As they sit there together, Beth asks, "Will you meet me tomorrow morning down by the docks? We have a donut shop there, and I have some things I need to tell you. Can you meet me?"

"What time?"

"How about between 8 and 9 o'clock."

"Sounds great! See you in the morning," Clyde says as he reaches over and gives her a hug.

When he gets to his room, Crunchy's already asleep, so he tries to be as quiet as he can.

✧ ✧ ✧

Morning comes early. Clyde wakes up and sees that Crunchy is already up and gone. He wants to stay in bed because he's sore from the three days of riding, but he promised Beth he'd meet her at the donut shop. He hates being late for anything, so he literally rolls from his bed to get ready. He thinks, *I sure wish Crunchy would come back before I leave. He could come with me.* When he walks into the bathroom he finds a note:

> *I've got plans for today. You take care of*
> *whatever you've got planned this morning.*
> *Hope to see you later.*
>
> *Crunchy*

Clyde thinks, *How did he know I had plans this morning? Oh, I've given up trying to figure him out. I wonder what he has planned for us next; can't wait to hear. I better get a move on.*

It's quite a bit further than he thought to the donut shop, but it sure does feel good to stretch out his muscles in the long walk. The closer he gets, the smell of the ocean is almost intoxicating. When he rounds the final corner, the gentle ocean breeze blows against his face. The docks where he worked this past year are nothing compared to these. There are ships docked all around, passenger and supply ships from around the world. But the best thing about this harbor is that it's the main one the soldiers use on their return from fighting in Europe. He always wonders what would have happened if he had gone off to fight in the war. Somehow, it passed him by. He was fighting to survive his very existence and didn't really keep up with the events of the world. But he's sure thankful the war is over and our young men are coming home.

The donut shop is busy and the only seat available is at the counter, next to an older couple with what looks like their young daughter. He takes a seat next to them and greets them with a tip of his Stetson as he removes it and places it on his knee. The waitress brings him a cup of coffee and he notices the daughter whisper to her mother, who then turns her head and looks straight at him with a grin, making him uncomfortable.

She finally asks, "Excuse me, young man, this may sound a little strange, but are you a cowboy?"

Clyde nods his head. "Yes, Ma'am, I am."

"Did you ride in the rodeo at The Garden?" she asks.

"Yes, Ma'am," Clyde politely answers.

With that, the young girl says, "See, Momma, I told you so. Didn't you win the bull-riding contest?"

Clyde finds it hard to believe that someone would recognize him from the rodeo. "As a matter of fact I did, young lady," he replies.

"WOW! We were there last night, right in the front row. We watched you ride! You're really good."

"Thank ya so much," he says as he turns red. "Ya'll from around these parts?"

"No, we're here to pick up our son," the dad replies as he jumps in on the conversation. "He's coming home from Europe."

"Oh, my!" Clyde responds, leaning over the counter just enough to see their daughter a few stools down. "Young lady, all I did was ride a bull. That brother of yours did something far more important. He's the real hero; I salute him for his courage."

"Yeah, I'm proud of him, too, just as I was my other brother."

"You should be proud of both of them," Clyde agrees.

"I am," she responds, then looks at her dad. "Can I go across the street and watch for Robert E's boat? It should be here any time."

"Okay," he hesitates, "but just across the street where we can see you. Take your donut with you."

"Thanks, Papa," she replies as she spins the stool and heads toward the door.

Clyde's furrows his brow as his mind scans through his memory banks. He looks at the older gentleman and asks, "Did your daughter say your son's name is Robert E?"

"Yep, that's it. I know it's an odd one, but it's kind of a family thing," he replies.

"Wow, if that don't beat all. I had a good friend who had a brother with the same name," Clyde recalls.

"Does your friend ride in the rodeos with you?" the older gentleman asks.

Clyde peers down into his cup of coffee. "Oh no, he was a friend a while back."

"When was the last time you saw him?" the older gentleman asks.

"Well, I don't like remembering that day, but the last time I saw him was the day he died," Clyde recalls, dropping his chin to his chest.

Curious, the wife asks, "Your friend died?"

"Yeah, it was a tragic accident."

"What was his name?" she inquires, leaning over the counter.

"I called him Skinny, but his real name was. . ."

Before Clyde can finish, the husband says, "Ulysses?"

Clyde raises his head and looks at both of them. "Yeah! How'd you know that?"

With tears running down her cheeks, the wife says, "He died in a coal mine accident?"

"Yeah!" Clyde exclaims.

"That was our son," Mrs. Shoemaker adds as tears well up in the old man's eyes, too.

Clyde is dumbfounded. *With all the people in this city,* he thinks, *what are the odds that two people can meet in a small place like this with so much in common?* "I can't believe this!" he says.

"We do, young man," she declares. "We've been asking God to help us understand what happened, and this is His answer for us. We praise God for this meeting!"

As she speaks, Clyde remembers that he has something for them and says, "Don't move! I'll be right back." He quickly spins his seat, grabs his hat, and runs to the door.

"Please don't leave!" she shouts.

"I'll be right back. Don't go nowhere."

She looks at her husband, shrugs her shoulders, and picks up her cup to take another sip of coffee. On a dead run with his hat in hand, it doesn't take him long to get back to his room. He scurries up the stairs, flings open the door, and heads for the steamer. When he opens it to get the Bible, he's surprised because it's not there. He thinks back to the last time he saw it and looks around the room. There on Crunchy's pillow is the Bible with a note:

> *Clyde - was hoping to see you again before I left, but things just didn't work out that way. Here is Skinny's Bible I think you'll need it. You are a great young man and a great student. Don't ever let people tell you that you can't do something. Your life will have its ups and downs, but a little advice, keep looking up. Your friend Skinny had it all correct. May God richly bless your life.*
>
> *Crunchy*

Clyde reads the note over again and then puts it in the steamer. With tears, he heads back to the donut shop thinking, *Crunchy sure was some kind of a guy. I wish he hadn't left. I have to hurry back to Skinny's parents.*

He rushes back into the donut shop and sits down at the counter next to Mr. Shoemaker. With his hands shaking, he hands him Skinny's Bible.

"I didn't have an address to mail it to you. I'm so sorry I took it," Clyde says, his voice cracking.

He turns to Skinny's mom and says, "I have something for you, too. If we can move to a booth, I'd like to share it with you." Clyde looks around and waves the waitress over. "Excuse me, could we move over to that booth?" he asks as he points toward the back. "And could you wrangle up four or five donuts and some more coffee, please."

"Sure," the waitress agrees, "but how about this booth in the corner? It's away from everyone."

"That would be great," Clyde says.

They pick up their cups and move to the booth. Just like the waitress said, the booth is off all by itself in the corner of the room. As they sit down, the waitress refills their cups and sets down a plate with an assortment of donuts. "Is there anything else I can get you?" she asks.

"Oh, I almost forgot," Clyde adds. "If you see Beth come in, could you steer her back this way?"

"Oh, that's easy. She should be in any time now. If you need anything else, just let me know."

"Thank you," Clyde answers.

As they sip their coffee, Clyde takes out the note he found in the Bible and hands it to Skinny's mom. Then he sheepishly says, "When I found the Bible, I was only thinking of myself and how I wanted to keep it, in memory of your son."

She slowly unfolds the wrinkled and yellowed note. With her husband looking over her shoulder, she begins to read. It doesn't take long for the tears to flow.

> *Dear Mom and Dad,*
> *Have made friends with a great guy, I*
> *ride shotgun for him. No Dad, he doesn't*

*know the Lord yet, but we have a great time
singing hymns, and he's always open to me
sharing with him. He's the best friend I've
ever had, and I pray for him all the time.
I know God has me here just for him. In
fact, the week I met him was going to be my
last week here, but I wholeheartedly believe
God wants me to stay just for him. Please
pray for him. His name is Clyde Lewis; you
would really like him. Got to go, we have a
long day today.*

Your son,
Ulysses (that's for you Mom)

Clyde continues, "A few weeks after I left town, I realized they would have sent all of his belongings to you: all except the Bible. Then I remembered the note, and I didn't know what to do next. I'm sorry for being so selfish."

By now, both parents have tears flowing down their cheeks. They sit there reading the note over and over. Mrs. Shoemaker finally looks up from the note and asks, "When did he write this?"

Taking a deep breath, Clyde says, "Well, I'm not quite sure, but I think it was the morning he passed away." With that, she breaks down sobbing. Mr. Shoemaker puts his arm around her as she turns and buries her face in his shoulder. With tears in his eyes, he asks Clyde, "Can you please tell us what happened that day? We've always wondered."

He takes another deep breath and with his voice cracking, admits, "It's always fresh on my mind, but it's really hard to tell." Before he begins, he sees Beth walk through the front door and sees the waitress point her to the back table. As she walks up, Clyde slides from the booth and introduces her to the Shoemakers. He asks if it's all right if she joins them and both nod. They sit back down and Clyde tells the story of Skinny's last day. Beth reaches in her purse and pulls out facial tissues for everyone.

As Clyde ends the story, everyone's in tears. The Shoemakers' daughter comes running through the door hollering, "Dad, Mom, Robert E's boat just docked! Hurry, we don't want to miss him!"

With that, they slide from the booth and the Shoemakers each give Clyde a hug and thank him for helping them put their questions to rest. As they get up to leave, Mr. Shoemaker reaches his hand out with the Bible in it and says, "Here, put it to good use," before heading to the door.

Clyde stands there with Bible in hand wondering if there really is a God, and if there is, what does He have in store for him next?

☆ ☆ ☆

Grandma has repositioned herself to look into the eyes of her man. Sitting there next to him and holding his hand, she doesn't want it to ever end. She looks into his turquoise blue eyes and, with tears rolling down her cheeks, says, "So that's how your mom and dad met?"

"Yep, and like they say, 'It's all history after that'."

"Thank you for sharing. I truly love you."

He scoots to the edge of the couch, trying to stand, when she asks, "You need some help?"

He turns toward her and strokes her cheek with the back of his fingers. "Always willing to help, aren't you? I love you so much. No, I want to do this by myself."

Bewildered, she asks, "What do you mean?"

As he slowly stands, he reaches over to the end table and grabs the old horseshoe. He looks down at his bride and asks, "Do you know where the hammer is?"

"Sure, it's in the drawer where it always is. Why?"

"Got something that needs to be done," he says as he makes his way to the drawer and grabs the hammer. With hammer in hand, he heads toward the front door and grabs his Stetson as he walks by the coat rack and places it on his head, adjusting it with his forefinger.

Mom already has an idea of what's happening and asks, "Where are you going, you old coot?"

"Got to put something back where it belongs," he says and smiles as he opens the door.

"You wait a second. I can't let you have all the fun," she states as she makes her way toward the door. "You got nails?"

"Sure do, right here," he assures her, opening the palm of his hand. "Come on, let's have some fun."

Mom walks up and takes the hammer. "I get to put the first nail in," she declares.

As they make their way down the short road to the old house, he looks at her and says, "You may be too short in the britches to do that." They both laugh.

Once they hang the horseshoe, they walk by the old truck that now has weeds growing up all around it. As he walks by, he takes his hand and runs it across the old hood. "Sure brings back good memories, doesn't it?"

All Mom can do is shake her head. *That hat, the horseshoe and the truck sure have a history behind them. I pray it never dies,* she thinks.

This would be the last trip he would make to the old house. You see, over the next few weeks the family would gather again, but for a different reason. Grandpa would be called to his heavenly home. While it was a sad time, it was also a time of rejoicing. How can it be a time of rejoicing? Read on to see.

Epilogue

I believe a man leaves a legacy; whether good or bad, it's up to him. My dad and mom, while not the perfect couple or parents, left behind their own legacies. My children, Lord willing, will learn from my mistakes and grow from counsel.

These books began as a simple recording of some of the stories I recall my dad and his friends passing along. While elaborated on, with a lot created from my imagination, the main story-line is that of my family.

I want to thank our Lord for inspiring me to write and for what He has done, not only in my life, but for each one who calls Him theirs, also. As I wrote these books, I tried to portray the different ways that people view God; from the deeply religious to those who have little or no faith. I want everyone to know that I am a man of faith; not of empty faith, but faith in the God of Abraham, Isaac, and Jacob. The Bible is not merely a book of simple religious stories, but a recording of historical facts in both the Old and New Testaments. It's a record of the history and life of Jesus Christ, inspired by the God of the universe.

The following are some of the characters in the books. While not all are listed here, the main ones are. Hopefully, by reading these bios, you may learn a little more about my family.

The Lewis family – I got the name from a family I dearly love and respect.

Elmer Lewis – The grandfather I never got to know. The storm took his life before I was a twinkle in my father's eye. The story of his life is what I gleaned from members of the family, plus elaboration. His name was Elmer, and he died of pneumonia shortly after being caught in a snowstorm.

Dorris Lewis – My grandmother, or Nannie, to me. She was a wonderful person and loved deeply by my dad (Clyde). The story of her life is pretty much as written, and her name was actually spelled *Dorris.* I loved singing along as she played the piano. She was blind the whole time I knew her and played the piano by ear. I will share a short story: When I was about nine, she decided to give me piano lessons. Our first lesson she sat down with me and showed me where middle C was, then said, "Let's play something." She picked "Little Brown Jug" and started to hum it, then said, "Okay, start playing." My attempt wasn't very good. So she quickly concluded I wasn't a pianist.

Jim- The only grandfather I knew. I remember sitting in his pickup and him letting me shift the truck. He passed on my senior year in high school.

Clyde Lewis – My dad; what can I say? While not the perfect dad, I loved him until he passed in 1990. He was a man of many trades from setting bowling pins, to riding in the rodeos, to working as an electrical engineer, with many jobs in-between. He stopped riding bulls when one bucked him off and kicked him in the mouth, knocking out a lot of his teeth. For six weeks, he could only sip through a straw. He enjoyed life and I can't remember him ever complaining about anything. I am proud to be his son. His real name was Don. Oh, and yes, he actually left home at ten, not eleven.

Harold and Audra – This was my dad's best friend, Chet Lewis and his wife, Lillian. While Chet and Dad were as close as brothers and traveled the rodeo circuit together, Chet and Lillian didn't meet the way our characters did. The whole story about Harold and Audra was made up, but knowing how they loved each other made it easy to write. While Chet is gone now, I still get to see Lillian every now and then.

Ruthie, Sara, Rachel – My dad's three sisters. I didn't get to know them very well, so most of what I wrote about them was pretty much made up. Don't hold any of this against them! What I do remember is that they were great ladies and all very hard workers. Their real names are Marietta, Lucille and Ethel Mae.

Walter and Maggie Livingston – They were totally fabricated, a family dedicated to the Lord.

Al & Benny – More made-up characters. I used different businesses and the like, but most of their story line was created by me and my friend, Gary Stiff.

Elizabeth (Beth) – My mother, Barbara, what a wonderful woman. She loved her three sons very much and would do whatever she needed to provide for not just our needs, but also a lot of our desires, too. While a lot of her story was fictitious, they did meet when Dad was riding bulls and her cousin was the mayor of a town on Long Island, where she was from. I am thankful that God blessed me with such a great mom.

Skinny and Crunchy – While you always wish there were more people like these two, they were totally made up. I guess I put into these two characters some things I would like to see in myself or look for in others; someone who is totally giving of themselves, a characteristic that is hard to find.

Jonathan (Whiskey) – While my dad did have a friend with this nickname, this character bears no resemblance to his friend. I think I got this character from my dark side. Don't judge me by that, because we all have that side. Yes, even you do! Some of the storylines I picked up through my life experiences.

Sacred and Warrior – Totally made up. While my grandpa had his favorite horse, the storyline was one that came from my imagination.

www.ingramcontent.com/pod-product-compliance
Lightning Source LLC
Chambersburg PA
CBHW070543260626
47161CB00002B/489